"Don't you want to teach?"

The vague feeling of discontent she'd been ignoring welled up inside her. "I certainly enjoy it. However, to be honest, it isn't really what I want to do."

He frowned. "Then what *do* you want to do?"

I want to have a family with a husband and children of my own.

"Helen?" Quinn's use of her Christian name for the first time drew her full attention. "I need to talk to you. I know this probably isn't the right time, but I can't hold it in."

"This sounds serious. Go ahead and tell me."

"My eldest nephew and niece are always going on about you and I've noticed that you seem to care a whole lot about them, too. That's true, isn't it?"

"It certainly is."

"Well, I'm doing my best for them, but anyone can tell that isn't good enough." He waved away her protests. "Now, that's just the plain truth and you know it. The fact is that they need a mother." She stared at him, wondering where this conversation was going before he spoke again. "I was wondering if you'd be willing to marry me—for the children's sake."

Noelle Marchand
and
Jan Drexler

The Texan's
Inherited Family
&
A Home for His Family

LOVE INSPIRED
INSPIRATIONAL ROMANCE

LOVE INSPIRED®
INSPIRATIONAL ROMANCE

ISBN-13: 978-1-335-50317-6

The Texan's Inherited Family and A Home for His Family

Copyright © 2022 by Harlequin Books S.A.

The Texan's Inherited Family
First published in 2015. This edition published in 2022.
Copyright © 2015 by Noelle Marchand

A Home for His Family
First published in 2015. This edition published in 2022.
Copyright © 2015 by Jan Drexler

This edition published by arrangement with Harlequin Books S.A.

For questions and comments about the quality of this book, please contact us
at CustomerService@Harlequin.com.

Love Inspired
22 Adelaide St. West, 41st Floor
Toronto, Ontario M5H 4E3, Canada
www.LoveInspired.com

Printed in U.S.A.

CONTENTS

Noelle Marchand is a native Houstonian living out her childhood dream of being a writer. She graduated summa cum laude from Houston Baptist University in 2012, earning a bachelor's degree in mass communications and speech communications. She loves exploring new books and new cities. When she's not scribbling out her latest manuscript, you may find her pursuing one of her other passions— music, dance, history and classic movies.

Books by Noelle Marchand

Love Inspired Historical

Bachelor List Matches

The Texan's Inherited Family
The Texan's Courtship Lessons
The Texan's Engagement Agreement

Unlawfully Wedded Bride
The Runaway Bride
A Texas-Made Match

Visit the Author Profile page
at LoveInspired.com for more titles.

THE TEXAN'S
INHERITED FAMILY

Noelle Marchand

Instead of shame and dishonor,
you will enjoy a double share of honor. You will
possess a double portion of prosperity in your land,
and everlasting joy will be yours.
—*Isaiah 61:7*

This story is dedicated to my faithful friend Elizabeth Tisdale. Thank you for always listening, appreciating my love for Disney movies and encouraging me to have fun. Here's to all of the adventures we've had and all that are sure to come.

Chapter One

October 1888
Peppin, Texas

Quinn Tucker was not a smart man.

If he was, he would have realized he needed to get married as soon he'd found out he was going to be a foster father to a group of orphans. Three whole weeks had passed since then. Three weeks in which he'd struggled to be both father and mother to four children he hadn't even known existed until they'd been dropped on his doorstep by a stranger named Jeffery Richardson. The man had said the children had belonged to his brother, Wade, who along with Quinn's father, had gone off to seek a fortune for their poverty-stricken family. Quinn had been eight years old at the time, so he'd been left behind to be raised by and eventually take care of his ailing grandmother. Nana had died when he was fourteen. Quinn had been on his own. Until now....

Now, he was afraid to be on his own long enough to visit the outhouse for fear that one of the children would get hurt or wander off in his absence. Not that he regretted taking in his own kin. He didn't. Each of them had become real special to him during the short time that they'd lived with him. It was just that their entrance into his life had changed everything faster than he'd imagined possible.

He was still trying to get his bearings, which must have been why it had taken him seeing his friends Lawson Williams and Ellie O'Brien exchange vows yesterday for him to realize that he needed a wife. After all, a wife was supposed to be a helpmeet and he needed help—desperately. There was only so much bathing, washing, mending, braiding, baking and cooking a man could handle on his own with a farm to run.

Maybe he ought to ask Ellie for some advice on finding a wife. The town's newest bride was also its most successful matchmaker. Even as busy as he'd been lately, Quinn hadn't been able to escape hearing all the ruckus she'd caused over the past two months by gradually compiling a list of the town's most eligible bachelors and the ladies Ellie saw as their matches. Her intent had merely been to find her own match through the process of elimination. However, it seemed everyone had been hankering to get a peek at what had been deemed the "Bachelor List" to find out who their match was.

Quinn needed to know if he had one, but he wasn't sure what qualified a man to be considered "eligible." If it was looks, education or riches, he didn't have a chance. Women never seemed to get silly or swoony over him—at least not that he'd ever noticed.

Of course, that didn't mean one hadn't captured his attention.

Helen McKenna, the town's schoolmarm, caught him watching her from across the crowd of folks who'd gathered for a good old-fashioned shivaree at the ranch where the newlyweds lived. Her mahogany eyes seemed to sparkle in the lantern light as she tilted her head inquisitively and stared right back at him. A blush spread just below her high cheekbones, making him wonder just how long he'd been staring. He sent her a nod as if that's all he'd been trying to do in the first place, then glanced away.

He'd noticed her in church the first Sunday after she'd arrived in town, but hadn't met her until he'd enrolled his eldest nephew and niece in school. That first meeting had confirmed everything he'd feared about the schoolmarm. She was beautiful, refined, intelligent and far too good for him. Every time he looked at her, Nana's warnings rang in his ears. *Chasing after more than you deserve will only get you hurt or dead.*

Hadn't his pa and his brother proven her right? No need for Quinn to follow their example. He'd best stay far away from Miss McKenna—not that he actually had a chance with her, anyway.

Staying away from her tonight would have been a sight easier if she hadn't hung back to talk to him. The rest of the group followed Sheriff Sean O'Brien, who was the bride's brother and Quinn's closest neighbor, toward the cabin where the newlyweds lived. Quinn's grip tightened on the neck of his banjo in his left hand as Helen's generous smile set his heart thumping in his chest. Not wanting her to stumble in the dark, uneven field they traipsed across, he dared to place a cautionary hand near the small of her back. She angled closer to his side and chanced a whisper.

"I wasn't expecting to see you tonight. Who's with the children?"

"The groom's parents were kind enough to insist on watching them for me," he whispered back. "You can't get much better than the town doctor and Mrs. Lettie Williams for temporary caregivers. They even brought us supper."

Her lips tipped upward in a brief smile. "What about Reece? How is his black eye?"

"All right, I suppose, but it's turning an awful shade of green." Reece was Quinn's oldest nephew at nine years old and was the self-designated protector of the siblings. He hadn't taken kindly to one of the other schoolboys picking on his younger sister Clara. The seven-year-old was a true sweetheart and destined to be a heartbreaker with her rich brown curls and big blue eyes. "I'm not sure what to do. I don't want to encourage him to fight, but I don't want Clara to be bullied, either."

She nodded with understanding and concern written across her face in a frown. "I've already spoken to the other student's father about it. Hopefully, the teasing will stop. As for Reece, I'm sure he'll settle in soon."

"I hope so. He's been through a lot with his father and stepmother dying in that boating accident on their honeymoon only two years after his mother died in childbirth. Then he traveled thousands of miles to live with an uncle he'd never even met."

"It couldn't have been an easy transition for you, either." The empathy in her tone wrapped around him like a warm blanket.

"I manage well enough." At least, that's what he kept telling himself. Helen started to respond but someone shushed them, so she just nodded. He counted about twelve or thirteen people creeping along beside her to where a cozy cabin for two sat at the edge of the woods.

Even the katydids stopped singing. A snicker sounded above the soft rustle of grass but was quickly drowned out by more shushes.

Sean lit the lantern he held and gave a single nod. A cacophony of sound shattered the stillness. Quinn's lightning-fast fingers picked an out-of-tune melody on his banjo. On his right, Helen banged an old frying pan with a mangled metal spoon while her good friend Isabelle Bradley rang the bell that usually sat on the Bradley Boardinghouse's front desk. On his left side, his best friend, Rhett Granger, played a jumbled assortment of chords on his harmonica before settling in on a single warbling note. Beside Rhett, Chris Johansen's fiddle screeched. Other folks added to the discordance by banging more pots and pans, whooping, hollering and whistling.

A cheer went up when the door opened a few seconds later. Lawson appeared, looking startled and drowsy but with a wide grin on his face. Ellie followed him out, laughing even as she covered her ears. In true shivaree fashion, the husband and wife were each made to sit in wheelbarrows. The ride ended on the banks of the farm's creek where the couple was finally allowed to stand. The noise and the music died down so that Sean's wife, Lorelei, could speak.

"Lawson and Ellie, this shivaree is to show you that your marriage has the full blessing of your family, friends and community." Lorelei gestured toward the creek. "As you take the plunge into married life, we take it with you."

Ellie eyed the creek then tilted her head and stared at her friends with calculating mischief. "Does that mean if we jump in, everyone else has to, as well?"

Quinn grinned at Ellie's exuberance. It was a pretty balmy night for mid-October. Of course, that didn't mean the creek would be anything but frigid.

Sean nodded. "That's the deal. Afterward, women will change in the cabin. Men will change in the barn."

Lawson gave a slow grin and winked. "Well, in that case…"

Ellie didn't seem the least bit surprised when Lawson lifted her into his arms and barreled into the creek with what could only be described as a war cry. Pandemonium broke out as folks tossed their noisemakers on the ground and men started picking up whichever woman was handy to follow their leader into battle. Quinn spotted Helen backing away from the melee as he set his banjo in the cushioned wheelbarrow with the other instruments. He cut off Helen's escape, swept her off her feet and plunged into the creek.

Rushing water muted the sound of Helen's shriek and the rest of the hollering until Quinn resurfaced, gasping from the cold. Helen pushed away from him and immediately headed to the creek bank. A wave of water rushed over Quinn's head. He soon found himself embroiled in a water fight with Rhett and Chris. Once they'd had all they could stand of the cold, they staggered to the creek bank to follow the rest of the party in the rush toward warmth and dry clothes.

Quinn didn't make it very far along the path before he realized he hadn't seen Helen head for the trees. She was probably on the path ahead of him, but even with only three weeks of experience in the role, the parent in him already knew not to leave the creek without making sure she wasn't straggling behind the group. Quinn doubled back to the creek bank. Sure enough, she was staring at the ground as she walked back and forth along the bank of the creek. "Miss McKenna, what are you doing?"

"I'm looking for something."

"Well, you aren't going to find it in the dark."

She sighed. "You're probably right."

"You should change before you catch cold. You must be freezing."

"I certainly am." Her gaze swept the creek bank one last time before she joined him at the edge of the woods. "Thanks to you."

His caught her elbow to escort her onto the path. "Aw, I just gave you a little help getting in the creek, that's all. You would have jumped in eventually."

"Yes, but not quite so enthusiastically." Her smile flashed in the darkness before she gave him a stern look she must have perfected on her students. "Is there a particular reason why you seemed to take such sheer pleasure in throwing me into that creek?"

He couldn't help but chuckle. "Maybe I don't like schoolteachers."

"What did they ever do to you?"

"Plenty." He tugged her onward, hoping his grim tone would put an end to her question. It seemed to have the opposite effect.

She stopped and looked up at him. "Now I'm intrigued."

The last thing he wanted was to delve into that, so he angled a grin her way as he helped her around a fallen branch. "Truthfully, I hoped you would come out looking as messy as the rest of us. Of course, you didn't. Look at you…prim, proper and perfect as usual. Not a hair out of place. How'd you manage that?"

"Is that what you think I am?" She didn't seem to re-alize that she was leaning into him to share what little warmth their bodies produced. Or maybe she was just too cold to care. "Prim, proper and perfect?"

A rush of heat tinged his face. It was too late to take back his words, so he just shrugged. "It sure doesn't seem like you're the type to ever let down your hair."

They reached the edge of the woods, but she didn't rush toward the cabin. Instead, she lingered with a hand on her hip. "I jumped in the creek, didn't I?"

"I thought you said I threw you." He winked as she seemed to scramble for a defense. "I guess I was just wondering what you'd look like a little mussed up, is all."

"Is that so?" She lifted her chin along with her brow. "Well, I've been wondering what *you'd* look like with a haircut and a shave."

He ran a hand over his thick beard. "That'll happen the day you let down your hair and enjoy yourself."

"Deal." She released his arm and started fiddling with the fancy knot of hair on the back of her head.

Alarm prompted him to take a few cautious steps back. "What do you think you're doing?"

"Letting down my hair."

"That isn't what I meant."

"No, but it's what you said, so you can't go back on our deal." She shook her head until her hair tumbled from its style then slipped her hand into her thick dark hair and teased it into disarray. "Is that mussed enough for you?"

He stared at the dark waves of hair that framed her face and slid past her shoulders to stop at her waist. The only other woman he'd seen with her hair down had been his grandmother. She hadn't looked anything like Helen. The schoolmarm seemed to capture the sparkle of starlight in her mahogany eyes while the glow from the cabin caressed her delicate features and stained her hair with a subtle dusting of gold. His hand reached out of its own accord to slide through the thick locks that were slick and heavy from their recent soaking.

The sound of her breath catching in her throat brought him up short. Suddenly realizing just what he was doing and to whom, he extracted his hand from her hair and restored the distance he hadn't realized he'd covered. "I'm sorry, ma'am. I had no right to do that. Guess I just wasn't thinking."

She deftly twirled her hair and pinned it into a simple style. "You get that haircut and shave and we'll call it even."

"You must think I need them awful bad to go through all this."

Her expression turned innocent, though her eyes were full of mischief. "Well, you do remind me a bit of a bear."

"A bear, huh?" He glanced toward the cabin as the door opened and Lawson walked out with a bundle of clothes in his hand. Quinn urged Helen into the clearing. "You'd better go on inside before you catch a chill."

She complied, greeting the bridegroom as she passed him. Lawson lifted a skeptical brow as he met up with Quinn and they walked across the field toward the barn. "Did you two get lost back there or something?"

Quinn shrugged. "I caught her dawdling by the creek, so I rounded her up and brought her in."

"Well, don't let her hear you describe her that way."

"What way?"

Lawson's eyes started twinkling. "Like a cow."

"I guess it did sound kind of bad." Quinn grimaced as Lawson laughed and clasped him on the shoulder. How was he ever going to find a wife at this rate? Lollygagging with a woman he didn't have a chance with then talking about her like she was a heifer. It wasn't a good start. He needed more than just an expert on love like Ellie. He needed divine intervention.

Being the last one into the tack room gave Quinn a moment alone to do what needed to be done. He bowed his head to whisper a prayer. "Lord, I might not be much and I may not deserve the finer things in life that other folks have, but I'm not asking for me. I'm asking for my children… All right, and maybe a little for me, too. Please send me a mother for them. Someone to be a helpmeet. That's all I ask, Lord."

"Quinn, everyone else has gone ahead," Rhett called through the door. "I'm going to head to the cabin. You'd better get your banjo out the wheelbarrow and come on."

"I'm coming." Quinn finished dressing, then left the tack room. Rhett waited at the barn door jumping up and down to get warm while looking longingly across the field toward the cabin. Quinn found his banjo resting right where he'd placed it. Whoever had been in charge of gathering the noisemakers from the creek bank hadn't been particularly careful in their treatment of his instrument. It had all manner of things piled on top of and around it. He pulled the instrument out only to find a stray piece of paper entwined in its string.

"Quinn, hurry up, will you? Lawson said Ellie was making some hot cider."

"Aw, stop your caterwauling. I've said I'm coming."

Quinn tucked the folded paper into his pocket before joining Rhett. They ribbed each other all the way to the cabin, but Quinn's gaze kept rising to the starry sky that stretched above him. He could only hope that God had heard the pleadings of his heart and see fit to answer.

Fast.

Helen couldn't believe she'd lost the Bachelor List. That thought, along with the chill in the air, sent her snuggling farther into her covers the next morning. Amy, the oldest of the three Bradley girls at the boardinghouse where Helen lived, had begged off from the shivaree with a headache then entrusted Helen with a secret note for Ellie. Helen hadn't had any idea that note was actually the Bachelor List until she'd told Ellie about losing it at the creek. Hopefully, the matchmaker would have more success finding the list in the daytime than Helen had last night. She didn't understand why Amy hadn't just given it to Ellie herself later. Well, it was just one more thing that hadn't made sense about last night—like her sudden attraction to Quinn Tucker.

"Attraction" was the only explanation for why she'd lingered in the woods with him despite her drenched condition. But why would she feel that way? She'd been telling the truth when she'd said he reminded her of a bear. Just like the one she'd seen at the circus when she was a child; Quinn was big, hairy, arresting and more than a little intimidating. She couldn't help but wonder how he ate without getting things lost in that unruly-looking mustache and beard. His hair was also overly long. However, there was always that indescribable something about a man with hair that nearly reached

his shoulders that made her want to chase after him…
with a pair of scissors.

Raised in Austin's high society, she was used to polished gentlemen who were always perfectly groomed.
But she'd learned her lesson about the cold hearts that
could be hidden by gentlemanly exteriors.

As for Quinn, she couldn't stop thinking about the
gentle, almost awed way he'd reached out to touch her
hair. She ought to be outraged by his audacity, but then
she'd have to be equally shocked by her own behavior.
After all, she was the one who'd taken her hair down in
front of a man who was practically a stranger. She ought
to be ashamed of herself, but she wasn't. He'd made her
feel comfortable, accepted and precious. It was unnerving. More than unnerving—it was dangerous!

It was dangerous because she might actually start
believing what he'd said about her. Prim and proper she
could handle since that was what every good schoolmarm should be, but she knew all too well that she was
not perfect. Never perfect—especially not as a woman.
Any doubts she'd had about that had been cleared away
six months ago when she'd made the mistake of telling
her fiancé, Thomas Coyle, that a riding accident she'd
had at sixteen had left her unable to have children. Sub-
sequently, their engagement had ended before the engagement dinner was over.

Helen had quickly studied to become a teacher then
moved to Peppin in order to forget her humiliation. If
only it was as easy to forget the dreams she'd cherished
since she was just a child. Back then, she'd often been
found playing house in her mother's dresses with at least
one baby doll clutched in each arm. She'd thought being
a teacher would be close enough to the fulfillment of

that dream to keep her satisfied. Instead, it only fed the longing for the one thing she knew she'd never be able to have—children of her own.

No, Quinn wouldn't have called her perfect if he'd known the truth. Or, perhaps he wouldn't care that she'd never have children. He did have four of his own. She saw the two eldest every school day. She knew a teacher wasn't supposed to have favorites and she didn't let it show in the schoolroom, but the Tucker children's plight had paved their way straight into her heart.

She tossed the thoughts away along with her covers and dressed for the day. What was wrong with her? She knew better than to let herself think things like that. Hadn't she learned anything from her fiancé's rejection? Yet, she could almost hear the comforting tones of her mother's voice in the aftermath of that disaster. *I promise you, my darling, if Thomas loved you—truly loved you—it wouldn't have mattered to him that you can't have children.* As pretty as those words were, Helen wasn't entirely sure she believed them.

She grabbed her teaching materials then hurried out of her room. A quick glance at the grandfather clock in the main hallway told her that she'd better hurry if she planned to get that cantankerous schoolhouse stove going before class started. She popped into the kitchen only long enough to glean a muffin from a rather tired-looking Mrs. Bradley, before heading out the front door.

A whirlwind of yellow-and-brown oak leaves swirled around her as she hurried down Main Street toward the schoolhouse—their chaos an apt visualization of her nervousness, which increased the closer she got to the schoolhouse. There had been a few minor disturbances early in the school term while she had been adjusting to teaching and the students had been adjusting to her. The president of the school board, Mr. Etheridge, had warned her that another incident of any kind would warrant a discussion of her fitness for the teaching position with the rest of the school board. Sending the man's son home on Friday with a black eye and bloody nose courtesy of Reece Tucker couldn't have helped matters.

Helen took a deep breath to calm herself down. Surely Mr. Etheridge must have understood from her note that she'd managed to de-escalate the situation quickly. If nothing else, he had to appreciate the fact that she'd kept the boys from hurting each other further and had even gotten them to apologize.

Feeling a bit more confident, Helen unlocked the schoolroom door and got the fire in the stove going just as students began arriving. A few called jaunty hellos, but most just silently stored their dinner pails in the coatroom then rushed out to play until she was ready to call them in. She had the school bell in hand to do exactly that when Violet, the youngest of Mr. Bradley's three daughters, met her at the schoolhouse door. "Helen, why didn't you stay for breakfast? You missed all the excitement!"

She ought to remind Violet to refer to her as Miss McKenna during school hours, but technically the bell hadn't rung yet, so Helen allowed herself to be drawn in by the fifteen-year-old's exuberance. "What excitement? What's happened?"

"Amy eloped last night!"

"Eloped?" Her mouth fell open. "I don't believe it. How? With whom? Why?"

"With Silas Smithson, of all people! I don't think you've met him. He left town over a year ago. He stayed at the boardinghouse while he was here, which is how he and Amy became sweethearts. He tricked us all into thinking that he worked with the railroad when he was actually an undercover Ranger. I guess Papa's pride was hurt by Silas's deception, because he forbade us to have anything to do with him once the truth came out. That didn't stop Amy from corresponding with him in secret all this time. At least, that's what she said in the letter she left us."

Helen shook her head. "No wonder Amy asked me to give Ellie the Bachelor List. She wasn't planning to be around long enough to do it herself."

"*You* have the Bachelor List?" Excitement lit the girl's blue eyes. She caught Helen's arm. "What is it like? Where is it? Did you find out who your match is?"

"I *had* the Bachelor List. It was nothing grand—just a folded-up piece of paper. I didn't find my match because I didn't know the paper was the list until Ellie figured out what it must have been. By that point, I'd already lost it at the shivaree."

"You lost it? Oh, Helen. That's tragic."

Helen sighed. "It certainly is, and I feel horrible about it. Hopefully, Ellie will find it today. Meanwhile, I need to ring the school bell or we're going to start the day late."

"But I have so much more to tell you! This elopement is the most exciting thing that's happened to me."

"You'll have to tell me the rest at dinner. Now, hurry and put your things in the coatroom. I need to ring the bell."

Violet gave a dramatic sigh as she opened the cloakroom door then shut it immediately. She glanced back at Helen with wide eyes. "There's a man in there!"

Before Helen could do more than frown, Quinn Tucker emerged, hands raised as though he was a victim of a holdup. "I'm sorry, ladies. There just didn't seem to be a good time to interrupt."

Helen held back a laugh at the guilty expression on his face and crossed her arms. "Yes, well, there generally never is when you're eavesdropping. What were you doing in there, anyway?"

"I was bringing Clara and Reece the dinner I ordered for them at the café." He slipped his hands into his pockets then glanced at Violet. "I won't tell anyone what I overheard."

"Oh, half the town has probably heard the story by now and the other half will know soon enough. Tell whoever you want. I don't mind." Violet gave them a quick smile before disappearing into the coatroom.

Quinn opened the schoolhouse door for Helen then gave her the same crooked grin Reece often used when he knew he was in trouble. "Does that square me with you, Miss McKenna?"

"I suppose it does." She glanced up at him when they reached the grass. "Of course, I'm still waiting for you to keep your half of the deal we made last night."

"I got suckered into that deal and you know it." He narrowed his eyes at the innocent smile she gave him and lifted a brow before setting his hat on his head. "Good day, Miss McKenna."

"Good day, Mr. Tucker." She rang the school bell as she watched him stride toward Main Street and wondered what it was about him that she found so attractive. In Austin, she'd preferred gentlemen with a certain level of suavity, affluence and ambition; but those very qualities were the ones that had left her ringless at her engagement dinner. Quinn seemed to be a different sort of man—honest, unassuming, devoted and a bit desperate in his attempts to be a good uncle. Perhaps that was what she found attractive.

A small hand tugged at her skirt. She dropped her gaze to find Reece's sparring partner standing before her with a greenish-yellow ring around his left eye. She knelt down. "How are you, Jake?"

He shrugged. "Aw, I'm fine, ma'am. Pa told me to be sure to give you this."

She took the envelope he handed her then thanked him and sent him into the schoolroom with the rest of the children. She tore open the letter, which was so brief it was almost a waste of good paper. She was to dismiss the children thirty minutes early so that an emergency meeting of the school board could convene at the schoolhouse that afternoon.

She pulled in a calming breath. No need to panic. Despite all of her hopes to the contrary, she'd seen this coming. Perhaps it didn't have to be a bad thing. After all, this meant her job performance would be reviewed by *all* the members of the school board—not just Mr. Etheridge. The two other members had seemed nice and welcoming when she'd met them at the beginning of the term. But what if Mr. Etheridge was able to convince them that she was inept at her job?

She could always return home. Her parents had made sure she knew their door was always open to her, but she didn't want to leave Peppin. In this town, she was known for what she did and who she was. In Austin, people knew her for what her family did and who they were in society. She'd received this teaching position based on her own merit, not on the influence of her family. She meant to make the most of this opportunity and that did not mean getting fired only five weeks into the semester. If Mr. Etheridge thought it would be easy to get rid of her, he had another think coming. She might not be able to be a wife and mother, but she had no intention of letting her replacement dream slip through her fingers without a fight.

Chapter Two

❦

Please. Please. Please. Quinn's pleading matched the hurried rhythm of his steps as he left the schoolhouse behind. What were the chances that God had seen fit to answer Quinn's prayer for a wife only seconds after he'd spoken it? That could very well be the case if the paper that had gotten caught up in his banjo strings was the same one he'd overheard Helen saying she'd lost—the Bachelor List.

If Ellie had included him on the list, surely she would have matched him with someone who would be a good mother and wouldn't mind hitching up with the likes of him. Why, he might not have to do any courting at all if he showed the woman they'd been matched on the list. The children could have a mother by the end of the week if this panned out.

He waited until he could duck into the alleyway beside Maddie's Café then pulled the list from his pocket, grateful that his lack of time to do laundry meant he had on the same pants he'd worn the night before. He unfolded the paper and pressed it against the side of the building to smooth it out. It certainly appeared to be a list of some kind. He ran his finger down the column of script, looking for the circle with the line through the side of it that would signify the beginning of his name. There it was. Q-u-i-n-n. Quinn. The only word he knew how to read and write.

"Thank You, God! I'm on the list."

He threw a kiss heavenward to thank his grandmother for giving him the skills to figure out that much. However, as usual, it wasn't enough. He knew from all the talk he'd heard about the list that the name of the woman he was supposed to marry should be right next to his. That looked to be true, but whose name started with a letter that looked as if he was staring straight at a beefy Longhorn bull?

Folding the paper back in his pocket, he blew out a sigh and pounded the side of his fist on the wall. He was going to have to ask for help. There was no way around it this time.

Two years. He'd been in this town for two years and no one knew that he was illiterate. Never once had he needed to set aside his pride and admit defeat until now. What else could he do? The children needed a mother. *He* needed them to have a mother.

He knew just who to go to for help, even if it would be a bit humbling. He walked into Maddie's Café and waved his thanks to the proprietress for keeping an eye on the two youngest children while he'd taken the elder two their dinners. Maddie offered him a distracted smile as she went about filling orders. Quinn realized it probably hadn't been a good idea to leave them with her since they were quietly drawing on *the table* with their colored chalk rather than the slates they'd been given. He wiped the evidence away with his sleeve the best he could before removing the chalk from their hands, which started Olivia wailing.

Quinn placed the eighteen-month-old on his hip then grabbed the hand of four-year-old Trent and hurried outside. The only blond in the family, Trent's brown eyes stayed as solemn as he'd been silent since soon after his parents' deaths. The boy's little legs chugged along as he frowned up at Quinn, who took that as a sign to slow down. Olivia stopped wailing long enough to push away from him and stare at a passing lady. The little girl reached out for the stranger. The woman saw her and smiled. It was a heartwarming moment until the girl's hand latched on to the fake red bird on the lady's hat. There was a struggle and when the woman finally managed to get away, she was missing the ornament. Quinn gently wrestled it from his niece's hand and offered it to its owner. "I'm sorry, ma'am."

The woman shook her head as she backed away. "She can keep it."

"Sorry!" Quinn called again then stared into Olivia's blue eyes as he gave the bird back to her. "The last thing I need is for you to start running off women."

The girl hugged the fake feathered ornament to her chest. Looking at him very intently, she said, "Doggie."

"No. That's a birdie."

"Doggie."

"Sugar, you can talk real good for your age, but most of what you say just isn't right. Maybe I ought to get Miss McKenna to have a talk with you." He reached down to grab Trent's hand again but came up empty. He glanced down. There was no trace of the boy. Panic rose in his throat. "Trent!"

Something landed on his boot—a little hand, which

was attached to a pudgy arm. That was all he could see because the rest of Trent's body was underneath the raised wooden sidewalk. Quinn knelt down to haul the boy out of there. "What are you doing? How did you even fit under there? Now you're covered in dirt."

The boy didn't respond. He never did. Instead, he just frowned even harder and lifted a bright red feather that obviously belonged to the bird's tail. The sight melted Quinn's heart and it was all he could do to remain firm, when he wanted nothing more than to hug the boy close. "Thank you for picking that up for your sister, but you must not do that again. Do you understand?"

He waited for Trent to nod before wiping the dirt from the boy's face and combing the mussed blond hair into place. "That's good because you scared me. I thought I'd lost you. Hold on to my hand and don't let go. We need to cross the street. Are you ready?"

With Trent dutifully clutching his hand and Olivia on his hip, Quinn made it across the street into the blacksmith's shop. Rhett Granger glanced up from whatever he was pounding on at the iron. "Be right with you, Quinn."

Quinn put Olivia on the counter and set Trent beside her, caging them in with his arms and body. Olivia was too busy playing with her ill-gotten gains to care, but Trent immediately started wriggling. "Hold still, son. This will only take a minute."

Rhett tucked his work gloves in the pocket of the leather apron he was wearing. He approached the counter with smiles for the children, who completely ignored him. "How can I help y'all?"

"Rhett, you're one of the most trustworthy men I know and a real good friend."

His friend's amber eyes lit with surprise. "Thanks, Quinn. I could say the same about you, but you didn't just come in here to shower me with praise, did you? Not that I mind if you did…"

"No, and I don't have the time or the patience to beat around the bush, so I'm going to come out with it." Quinn reluctantly allowed Trent to slide to the floor since the boy was trying to climb down his body, anyway.

"That's always a good policy."

Quinn looked around to make sure they were alone then leaned forward. He kept his voice low. "I have the Bachelor List."

"*You* have it?"

"Yeah, and I'm willing to give it you if you will just read it to me."

Rhett stiffened. "I've already been told who my match is. Since that woman ran away with someone else last night, I'm not particularly interested in the list."

"Amy? Your match was Amy? I didn't know. You didn't tell me. I mean, I knew you were sweet on her, but…" Quinn shook his head, searching his friend's face to see how hard the news of Amy's elopement had hit him. "I'm real sorry. How are you holding up?"

Rhett shrugged. "I don't know. To tell the truth, I didn't know her that well since our conversations mostly consisted of me tripping over my tongue like an idiot while she looked at me in confusion. Other than that, all we ever exchanged were a few looks and smiles. I guess my heart might not have been quite as involved as I thought it was."

"But you're disappointed."

"Yeah." Rhett sighed. "I'd hoped she was the one—especially since we were paired on that list."

"Well, this might not be much of a comfort, but I'm sure there's someone else out there. Perhaps someone you'll be able to talk to without being nervous around."

Rhett lifted a skeptical eyebrow. "I'm not sure how likely that is since my brain seems to abandon me anytime a relationship turns romantic. I'll tell you one thing, though. If there is another woman out there for me, I won't find her with the Bachelor List. You'd be wise to give it back to Ellie and find a woman on your own."

Quinn grimaced. "I hate to point this out, but Ellie has gotten every other match she's ever made right, so I'll take the chance. Please read it to me."

"Rub that in harder, why don't you?" Rhett narrowed his eyes and leaned against the counter. "If you're so interested, why don't you just read it yourself?"

"I would if I *could*." He stared Rhett in the eye and waited for confusion to turn to enlightenment then pity. The pity never came—only compassion—which was almost as bad, except it didn't leave quite as awful a taste in Quinn's mouth.

"I'll read it for you. Have you got it on you?"

"Yeah." Quinn laid the list on the counter between them and pointed to the only word he recognized. "My name is right there. I know that much, but whose is next to it?"

Rhett glanced down at the spot Quinn indicated before folding up the list and handing it back as if he couldn't get rid of it fast enough. "Ellie put you with Helen McKenna."

The words reached his brain then fell flat as the pancakes he'd tried to make that morning. "Come again?"

"The schoolmarm. Helen McKenna."

"That isn't funny." Quinn tried to give the list to Rhett again. "Read it right."

Rhett held his hands up and refused to take it. "I'm telling you, Quinn, it says Helen McKenna. I wouldn't joke about this."

Quinn closed his eyes and lowered his head in defeat as the hope that had flared in him burned out like a faulty matchstick. What had Ellie been thinking? Helen McKenna was far too good for him. She'd been nice to him—friendly, even—but she'd never consider him as a marriage prospect. He had nothing to offer a woman like her.

A tiny forehead braced against his. He opened his eyes to see Olivia blinking up at him from inches away, her big eyes nearly crossing in the effort. He kissed her tiny nose then straightened to his full height. He may not be Helen's first choice in a man. However, judging by the way Reece and Clara talked about her nonstop, she'd probably be the children's first choice in a mother. That was enough for him. "She might not love me, but I dare her not to fall in love with my kids. She'll marry me, if only because of that."

Rhett looked dubious. "Are you sure that's best for them? For you to marry a woman you don't love?"

"A mother is what's best for them. She'll be a good one. Ellie must have thought the same thing. Otherwise, she wouldn't have matched us up." He put the paper back into his pocket. "I'll need this as proof. I promise I'll give it back to you as soon as possible."

"Don't bother. I have no use for it. Besides, I've had

enough woman trouble to last me a good while." Rhett gave him a nod of silent encouragement. "I'll be praying for you, man."

"Thanks. I'll need it." He scooped Olivia back onto his hip, reached down for Trent's hand…and came up empty. He pulled in a deep breath. "Trent!"

A head poked out from beneath a bench in the waiting room. Quinn strode over and held out his hand. "We just talked about this, son. You are not allowed to crawl under anything that puts you out of sight without letting me know first. That includes benches."

Quinn opened the door with his shoulder then stood outside trying to figure out what to do next. He should probably get the haircut and shave that Helen seemed so particular about. He'd need to find someone to watch the children for an hour or so to get that done. Maybe the doctor's wife? He hated to impose on her again so soon, but she had said she'd be happy to help if he needed someone to watch the children again.

He frowned as he rubbed a hand over his thick beard. He could hardly expect a schoolmarm to accept the proposal of an illiterate man who reminded her of a bear. While he couldn't do anything for his lack of book learning, he *could* get rid of some of his wildness.

He shook his head. Helen McKenna. He might as well be reaching for the moon. He might not deserve her, but his children did and that's exactly who they were going to get.

Mr. Etheridge reminded Helen of a thundercloud with his snapping gray eyes, prematurely silver hair and commanding voice that filled the schoolhouse with a confidence that dared anyone to disagree with him.

"Miss McKenna, you have demonstrated a concerning inability to maintain proper discipline during school hours. The school board overlooked the troubling pranks that took place at the beginning of the school term, but now our students are brawling in the schoolyard."

A frown etched across the face of Mr. Johansen, whose youngest son was in the fifth grade. "I heard there has been fighting."

Mr. Etheridge's pacing steps in front of her desk seemed intended to slowly, deliberately sever any connection between her and the two other members of the school board. "My son, Jake, finds himself in constant need to defend himself from the aggressions of his fellow student Reece Tucker, who is treated with blatant partiality. While my Jake was sent home from school on Friday with a black eye and bloody nose, Reece was allowed to stay at school for the remainder of the day."

Nathan Rutledge's gaze locked on Helen's. The final member of the three-person school board was Ellie's brother-in-law and the father of a little boy in the same class as Reece Tucker. "Is it true that you only sent Jake Etheridge home, Miss McKenna?"

Helen forced herself to adopt a more pleasant look as she straightened her back and lifted her chin. "Yes, but—"

"You see?" Mr. Etheridge turned to face the other members. "I think it is quite obvious that Miss McKenna lets favoritism get in the way of good discipline. Despite her high recommendations, her inexperience is detrimental to the welfare of our students."

The indignant flush rising in her cheeks from Mr. Etheridge's interruptions and the urge to defend herself faded into confusion. "High recommendations?"

Mr. Johansen nodded, though he didn't take his gaze from Mr. Etheridge. "He means the letter from the governor."

Her hands tightened into fists. "The governor recommended me for this position?"

"Yes," Nathan agreed. "It was the deciding factor that led us to choose you over the local candidate—Mr. Etheridge's daughter."

Everything suddenly became clear. No wonder she'd been placed at a school so quickly after taking the teaching exam despite having no former experience. She'd thought it was a sign from God that she'd made the right decision in giving up on the impossible to focus on the attainable. Instead, it was simply a sign that her loving, overprotective parents had asked a favor from the governor, who had been a friend of the family for years.

"My daughter was unable to find another position and would be willing to replace Miss McKenna should the need arise."

She stared at Mr. Etheridge, finally able to understand the reason for his attitude toward her. No doubt he saw her as the interloping city girl who'd stolen the position that rightfully belonged to his daughter. Maybe that's exactly who she was. Maybe she'd stolen some other girl's dream. She had no right to do that just because she wasn't woman enough achieve her own. She shook the thoughts away and forced herself to focus on the situation at hand. Nathan Rutledge was watching her with concern. "Is there anything you would like to say in your defense, Miss McKenna?"

She swallowed and tried to remember the charges Mr. Etheridge had laid against her. "I think any teacher would have been subjected to the same pranks I was at the beginning of the semester. They were harmless and I put an end to them as soon as I could. I can't deny that Reece and Jake have been fighting. Jake seems to have a bit of an unrequited crush on Reece's sister Clara and often teases her to the point where Reece feels compelled to defend her."

"That isn't true." Mr. Etheridge interjected.

"I'm afraid it is, Mr. Etheridge." Turning back to the other members of the school board, she continued, "I didn't send Reece home on Friday because I thought he lived too far out of town to walk home alone in his condition. If that's showing favoritism and poor discipline, then I suppose I'm guilty."

Mr. Johansen gave a weary sigh. "Will you please step outside so that the board may talk privately?"

She nodded and stepped down from the platform. The rustle of her skirts was the only sound that filled the room until she stepped outside and closed the double doors behind her. Only then did she hear the muffled sound of men's voice rise inside. She stared at the schoolhouse door. That had not gone at all the way she'd planned. She'd practically given up. What was wrong with her?

"Miss McKenna?"

Startled, she spun toward the deep voice. A steadying hand stilled her forward momentum in time to keep her from tumbling down the schoolhouse steps. Words of gratefulness stalled on her lips as she glanced up to the stranger who'd lunged up the stairs to catch her. Her gaze slid from the chiseled angles of his jaw to the thick golden-brown curls of his close-cropped hair before settling on his vibrant blue eyes. Everything else went blurry as a strange weakness filled her knees. He steadied her once more. She shook her head, blinked and refocused. "Mr. Tucker?"

He didn't release his hold on her arm but stepped closer, his brow lowered in concern. "I'm real sorry, Miss McKenna. I sure didn't mean to scare you like that. You didn't hurt yourself, did you?"

"I'm fine." She eased back slightly as she allowed her gaze to trace his features again. "You look…nice."

A sheepish grin flashed across his lips, carving a shallow set of dimples into his cheeks. "Thank you. My own kin didn't recognize me when they saw me like this, so I reckon you were right and I was overdue for a shave and a haircut. I picked up some new duds, too, but that isn't important right now. What's going on in there?"

"In where?"

He pointed to the sign hanging from the doorknob that read Private Meeting. "In the schoolhouse."

Land sakes! How could she have forgotten about that? A sinking sensation filled her stomach so she sank along with it to sit on the top step. She rested her chin in her hand with a heavy sigh. "It's possible that I might be getting fired."

"Fired?" Quinn frowned at the door then sat one step below her. "Why would they want to fire you?"

"Apparently there are several reasons."

"But you're a great teacher."

She gave a short laugh. "You still say that after your nephew went home with a black eye last week?"

His eyes narrowed. "Is that what this is about? I'll go tell them it wasn't your fault."

He moved to stand but she placed a stilling hand on

his shoulder then lowered her gaze to avoid his questioning look. "No. Don't. Perhaps it's for the best."

"The best?" He stared at her then shook his head. "Why? Don't you want to teach?"

She shrugged as the vague feeling of discontent she'd been ignoring welled up inside of her. "I certainly enjoy it. However, to be honest, it isn't really what I want to do."

He frowned. "Then what *do* you want to do?"

I want to have a family with a husband and children of my own. She sighed and leaned back against the stair railing thinking about how foolish she'd been. Of course, teaching school wasn't anything like having children of her own. She'd been reminded of that at the end of each day when the students all rushed out the door, leaving her behind.

"Helen?" Quinn's use of her Christian name for the first time drew her full attention. "Do you mind if I call you that?"

Surprised, she offered a quizzical smile. "I suppose you might as well. Many of the other students' parents do."

"I need to talk to you. I know this probably isn't the right time, but I can't hold it in much longer."

"This sounds serious." She crossed her arms on top of her knees and nodded. "Go ahead and tell me. We may have a few moments before they call me back in."

He sent a speculative look toward the door. "My eldest nephew and niece are always going on about you and I've noticed that you seem to care a whole lot about them, too. That's true, isn't it?"

"It certainly is."

"Well, I'm doing my best for them but anyone can

tell that isn't good enough." He waved away her protests. "Now, that's just the plain truth and you know it. The fact is that they need a mother."

She stared at him, wondering where this conversation was going as he unfolded a piece of paper she hadn't realized he was holding. He handed it to her. She didn't bother to look at it. She couldn't have if she'd tried for his gaze held hers captive with its intensity. "I prayed for a helpmeet and God sent me the Bachelor List. It says you're my match. I was wondering if you'd be willing to marry me—for the children's sake."

Her gaze finally dropped to the paper unseeingly as she tried to make sense of what he'd just said. "Will you repeat that please?"

His hand covered hers. "You're my match. My nieces and nephews need you. I need you. Will you please marry me?"

The schoolhouse door opened startling them both as Mr. Eldridge stepped outside. "We have reached a decision, Miss McKenna. Please, come in."

Quinn helped her stand murmuring, "I'll wait here."

She gave him a brief nod then stepped inside. The grim faces of the school board members spelled out her not-so-surprising fate. She glanced down at the paper she held. Her attention caught on the sight of her name printed as clear as day next to the name of the man who was waiting for an answer to his proposal.

"Miss McKenna," Mr. Etheridge began in a cadence that seemed unnaturally slow juxtaposed by her racing thoughts. "On behalf of the school board and the citizens of Peppin—"

Quinn was offering her exactly what she'd always

wanted. Well, not exactly—but the closest she was likely to get to the marriage and children she longed for.

"—I would like to thank you for the kindness, energy and time you have devoted to the children of this community."

Quinn hadn't mentioned love in his proposal. Of course, she could hardly expect him to since they barely knew each other. Who was to say that it wouldn't turn into love eventually? Her parents had an arranged marriage and they'd grown to love each other deeply.

"I would also like to apologize for any behavior on our part that would make you doubt our gratefulness—specifically my own."

Most important, there were the Tucker children to consider—children to whom she could give so much love and care. She and Quinn wouldn't be able to have children of their own, but she'd learned her lesson and would keep that bit of information to herself. What could it hurt? With four little ones of his own already, he might not have time to notice.

"We would be happy to have you stay with us through the rest of the school year per our original agreement."

Quinn wanted her. Quinn *needed* her. She had a chance with him—with *them*—that she might not have ever again. She wouldn't walk away from that. She *couldn't*.

Her gaze snapped up from the Bachelor List as Mr. Etheridge's words finally registered in her brain. "You want me to stay?"

"The school board has concluded that I might have been a bit hasty and overprotective as the matters concerned my own children." The poor man looked as if he'd swallowed a marble. "We will honor our original agreement with you concerning the position."

"That's wonderful!" Her smile was returned by the other members of the board then she bit her lip. "You did say that your daughter is willing to start immediately, though. Didn't you, Mr. Etheridge?"

"Well, yes, I did."

"In that case…" She took a deep breath then couldn't stop the smile that spread across her face or the way her chin rose with pride. "I resign."

Chapter Three

Quinn paced in front of the schoolhouse steps waiting for Helen to return. He felt nervous and even a little light-headed. Of course, that might be from the haircut and shave he'd just had but it was uncomfortable nonetheless. He rubbed his hand over his clean-shaven jaw as he remembered the shocked look on Helen's pretty face at his clumsy proposal. He'd done the best he could. That didn't mean it would be good enough. It certainly didn't mean she'd agree to marry him. Why hadn't she just outright told him no and put him out of his misery?

He stopped pacing long enough to stare at the schoolhouse door then across the schoolyard to where his children were playing with the Rutledge boy. Reece's eyes had been as wide as plates when he'd seen Quinn with his new haircut. Clara had turned downright shy. Olivia had started crying. Even now, Trent kept sending him suspicious looks. Helen couldn't refuse him after he'd alienated his children just to please her. Besides, there wasn't any other woman in town he'd have a chance with. Not that he personally had a chance with Helen, but the children did.

Please. Please. Please, he prayed again. *I know I don't deserve her, but she isn't for me. She's for them.*

He jumped when the schoolhouse door opened. Helen was nowhere in sight as the members of the school board clomped down the steps. A grin flashed across Mr. Etheridge's face and he reached out to pump Quinn's hand up and down. "May I be the first to congratulate you? What a wonderful surprise!"

Quinn could only respond with a confused grunt.

Mr. Johansen winked. "She's waiting for you inside."

Nathan Rutledge clapped him on the back. "I wish you and Helen all the happiness in the world."

"Me and Helen——" Quinn stopped breathing. His heartbeat pounded in his ears. He stammered some sort of reply though what it was he'd never know. The men left him at the bottom of the stairs staring up at the schoolhouse door. Could it be possible? It certainly seemed likely. What else could they have meant?

He grabbed hold of the banister and took a tentative step up, then surged up the rest of the stairs into the schoolroom. Helen stood at the front of the room cleaning the day's lessons from the blackboard. His noisy entrance caused her to turn and meet his gaze with a smile. Quinn swallowed, cleared his throat and jerked his thumb toward the door. "They said— I mean, they told me…congratulations. Does that mean that you're saying yes? That you're going to marry me?"

Her mahogany eyes sparkled. "I suppose it does."

"You mean it? For real, now?" He strode forward until he stopped at the edge of the teacher's platform. "You aren't joking, are you?"

Her voice turned gentle as she met him there. "Quinn, I'd never joke about something like that."

"You're going to marry me." It wasn't a question this time. It was a statement even if his tone did hold a hint of disbelief. Trying those words on for size, he found that he liked the way they fit in a terrifying sort of way. He stepped back a little just in case a bolt of lightning struck him in holy retaliation for daring to marry a woman so far above him in every respect. He wouldn't want it to hit Helen by mistake.

"Yes, I am." She stepped down from the platform and lifted her face to stare up at him. "Well, isn't there anything you'd like to say or do about it?"

His attention honed in on her lips which offered a smile far more tempting than anything she could have intended. He'd never kissed a woman before and today wasn't the day to start him. He'd already pushed the Almighty far enough in asking for what he had no right to claim. Besides, she wasn't for him. She was for the children. That's what he'd promised God and he'd be smart to remember that if he wanted to have any chance of actually marrying her. Realizing he was leaning toward her, he pulled himself back. He took her hand to pump it up and down in a fair impression of what Mr. Etheridge had done earlier. "I'm real glad about it, Helen. Real glad."

A hint of confusion marred her brow as she glanced down at their hands before she pulled hers free with a funny little frown. "Good. I have to finish out this week of school, but we can be married anytime after that."

He watched her gather papers and books from her desk. "I reckon I'd better talk to the preacher about performing the ceremony."

"And the judge. We'll need to start the paperwork for the marriage license right away."

He held back a groan. The marriage license. He'd completely forgotten about that part of the process. Anxiety rose in his gut. "Do we have to do that? I mean, wouldn't it be all right if we just let the preacher hitch us up?"

She set the stack she'd gathered on her hip and cocked her head at him. "Not if you want it to be legal."

"Of course, I do." He ran his fingers through his close-cropped hair, hating that he'd made himself look foolish. "Guess I'll talk to Judge Hendricks tomorrow then."

"We can go together."

"Great!" Even to his own ears, his reply was a little too enthusiastic to sound genuine. He couldn't help it. With her along, he wouldn't be able to ask for help with the reading and writing even if he had a mind to humble himself enough before the judge to do so. She'd be right there watching, expecting him to know something when he didn't know much of anything.

"I'm sure it won't be too laborious and, after all, it must be done."

Looking into her intelligent eyes, he couldn't help wondering if he was making a mistake. They had to be the most mismatched pair in town. However, they *were* a pair and they were going to stay that way as long as he could help it so he took the load from his intended's hands and followed her outside. He stashed her things on the seat of the wagon he'd parked nearby. "I'll drive you to the boardinghouse after we tell the children."

"Oh, it isn't far. There's no need—" Her eyes widened. "You mean we're going to tell them right now?"

"Sure we are. You don't want them to hear it from someone else, do you?"

"No. I just..." She glanced over at the children, smoothing her hair as if she could make herself look more perfect than she already did in her cranberry colored gown.

Somehow her nervousness set him at ease—mostly because it meant he wasn't the only one feeling that way. His shoulders relaxed, his breath came a bit easier and he felt more like himself than he had all afternoon. Catching her hand in his, he smiled. "I'm sure they'll be as pleased as I am."

She sighed when he tugged her forward. "I certainly hope so."

He stopped at the fenced-in lawn that was shaded by a large oak tree. His nieces and nephews were the only ones left in the school yard, but they didn't seem to mind a bit for they were completely involved in playing kick the can. Quinn waited, not wanting to interrupt as Reece held Trent back and Clara helped Olivia take a turn at kicking. A squeal erupted from Olivia once her little foot set the can spinning a short distance and Quinn couldn't help but grin at the sight. "Good job, Olivia! Y'all come on over here now. Miss McKenna and I have something important to tell you."

Helen stepped a bit closer to his side as the children approached. Trent arrived first, huffing and puffing from all his misplaced exertion. Clara came next with her sister in tow. Finally, Reece joined them with apprehension dogging each slow step. "I didn't do it, Miss McKenna. Honest."

Quinn glanced over at Helen for explanation. She shrugged in confusion before turning back to the children. "You didn't do what, Reece?"

"I don't know, but I've been trying hard to be good so if something's messed up, it wasn't me."

Amusement warmed Helen's voice. "Reece, you aren't in trouble. Your uncle has an announcement to make, that's all."

Clara tilted her head, her wide blue eyes ripe with curiosity. "What kind of announcement?"

"Miss McKenna and I are going to be married."

Clara gasped. Reece frowned. Trent's brow furrowed. Olivia stuck her thumb in her mouth and leaned into her sister's side. The three eldest exchanged glances then their expressions settled into varying degrees of confusion, fear and sadness. Their reaction stunned him. They must not have understood him correctly. Quinn tried again. This time he used more enthusiasm. "That means she is going to be your aunt! Isn't that exciting?"

Reece crossed his arms. "Does that mean she won't be our teacher anymore? I like having her as my teacher."

Helen placed a gentle hand on the boy's shoulder. "Oh, but being an aunt is so much better than being a teacher."

Clara looked nothing if not doubtful. "Why?"

"Because, I am going to live with y'all so that I can love you, and laugh with you and help take care of you." Helen caught Clara's free hand. "Don't you see? Having an aunt is kind of like having a Ma—just like having an uncle is kind of like having a Pa. I want to be that for you more than anything in the world."

Longing filled the children's eyes for an instant before Reece shook his head. "I still think you'd better stay our teacher."

"Me, too. Besides, Uncle Quinn takes care of us really well. He doesn't need help." Clara looked to him for confirmation. "Isn't that right, Uncle Quinn?"

"No, it isn't right, Clara." He frowned at them out of confusion and concern more than displeasure. "I don't understand. I thought you would be pleased. You *should* be pleased. I am. I want what's best for you and that's Miss McKenna, which is why I'm going to marry her."

Trent bowed his head as his shoulders shook in silent sobs. Before Quinn could blink, Helen was on her knees in the grass with his youngest nephew cradled in her arms. She looked up at Quinn with a myriad of emotions darkening the usual spark in her eyes. "Oh, Quinn, maybe we shouldn't—"

"Yes, we should." He sat in the grass beside her then gave a gentle tug to first Reece then Clara to compel them to do the same. His arm tightened around Olivia as she scrambled into his lap. He split his focus between Clara and Reece. "Do either of you know why Trent is crying?"

Clara scooted a little closer into their huddle. "He just a little upset seeing how y'all are going to die and all."

"What?" he and Helen exclaimed together.

Reece pulled at a blade of grass beside his boot. "Getting married is what killed Pa and our new Ma."

Clara nodded. "We don't want that to happen to you and Miss McKenna, too."

Nonplussed, he gladly let Helen handle that one. She hugged Trent tight. "Oh, darlings, nothing bad is going to happen to your uncle and me just because we are getting married. Tell them, Quinn."

A single nod was all he could manage. He wasn't worried about Helen. She would be fine. She didn't know how far below her due in terms of status, intelligence and sophistication she was marrying. He wasn't going to tell her, either. Not now. Not ever if he could help it. He wasn't afraid of facing the consequences of his decision to reach for far more than he deserved—not since he knew how much it would benefit the children. If something did happen to him as a result, at least they would have her.

"What happened to your folks was an accident." Helen wiped Trent's tears away with a soft-looking handkerchief. His brown eyes watched her intently as she spoke. "We may not know the reasons why it happened. However, we do know getting married doesn't mean you're going to die immediately."

Reece's face was full of cautious hope. "How do we know that?"

"Look at all the married people still alive just in this town—not to mention the whole world. There's nothing for y'all to worry about." She placed a hand on Quinn's knee as her eyes sent a silent encouragement for him to assure them. "Is there, Quinn?"

"Not a thing." He made sure to look the children in the eye as he said it. All the while, he tried to ignore the warmth spreading from Helen's hand into his knee.

"Your uncle and I are going to be perfectly fine. We'll be better than fine, actually, because we're all going to be a family…if you'll have me."

Reservations gone, Clara gave Helen a hug including Trent out of necessity. "Of course we will."

Quinn cleared his throat. "What do you say, Reece? Are you going to make your aunt feel welcome?"

"Yes, sir!" Reece's enthusiasm was reflected in his grin.

"Trent?"

The silent boy gave a grave nod.

"Good. Now, let's drop off Miss McKenna at the boardinghouse and get ourselves on home." He set Olivia on her feet so that she could toddle toward the wagon with the other children. "Helen, I sure am sorry about how they responded at first."

"It ended well and that's all that matters."

"I reckon you're right." He stood and reached down to help Helen to her feet. He made sure to release her as soon as she was steady. He'd told the children that there was nothing for them to worry about. There wouldn't be so long as he remembered that he was marrying Helen to be his children's mother—not his wife. That would be a whole lot easier if he kept his distance.

Helen waved goodbye to the Tuckers. Quinn tipped his hat and sent her a quick grin before leaving her behind on the sidewalk in front of the boardinghouse. She barely resisted the impulse to break into a jig right then and there. Wonder of wonders! She was getting married! Not to just anyone, but to Quinn Tucker—a man with a ready-made family. It felt as if she had wandered into her favorite daydream. She could only hope to be lost in it forever.

"Who was that?"

Helen yelped at the sound of Isabelle Bradley's voice. She'd been staring after the Tuckers' wagon so fixedly that she hadn't heard her friend's approach. "Where did you come from?"

"The post office." Isabelle's narrowed green eyes didn't waver from the retreating wagon. "Was that Quinn Tucker? I heard he got a haircut, but goodness me who knew it would make such a difference. He actually had a face under all that wild hair and a handsome one at that! It was nice of him to drive you home. Violet told me about the school-board meeting. What happened?"

Helen leaned against the cold rod iron of the Bradley's waist-high fence to push it open for her friend. "The other members of the board made Mr. Etheridge apologize."

"Good for them." Isabelle trotted up the porch steps and opened the door for Helen. "So does that mean you no longer have to worry about keeping your position?"

"Yes and no. I resigned." She had time to place her schoolbooks on the front desk and her coat on the rack before Isabelle's shock wore off.

"Why," Isabelle began, extending that one word into several syllables, "did you do that?"

Helen shrugged. "You have to resign if you're going to get married."

Isabelle's mouth dropped open then curved in an incredulous smile. "You're getting married? To whom? When? Why do I never know about these things? Helen!"

She laughed. "Yes, I'm getting married. On Saturday, I think. You're the first to know besides the school board and his children."

"His children?" Isabelle's eyes widened and flashed in the direction Quinn's wagon had gone. "Quinn Tucker's children?"

She nodded. "All four of them."

"But, I didn't even know the two of you were courting."

"Well…" She leaned against the front desk, straightening the stack of books she'd brought home. "We didn't court…exactly."

Isabelle sat on the stool behind the desk. "What does that mean?"

Helen rolled her eyes. "It means we didn't court at all, but it doesn't matter. There will be plenty of time for that after we marry."

"Well, then." Isabelle lifted a brow. "Would it be safe to guess that this isn't a love match?"

She shrugged. "It is in a way. I love his children."

"But you don't love him."

"I could. I will…one day. I'm certain of it. He's kind, Christian, hardworking—"

"—suddenly handsome—"

Helen laughed. "I was attracted to him even before the haircut and shave. Besides, he makes me feel…"

"He makes you feel…?"

Whole. He makes me forget that I'm a little bit damaged. She smiled and settled for, "Pretty."

"You are pretty."

"Thank you. Besides, what *is* love, anyway? It isn't just a feeling. It's a commitment. It's endeavoring to understand and appreciate someone for who they are. Even if it was just a feeling, feelings are controllable." She shrugged at Isabelle's doubtful look. "Perhaps I come at it from a different perspective than most. You see, my parents had an arranged marriage and they love each other very deeply now. I don't see why I should expect anything less."

"What can I say to that? As long as you're sure, Helen. I'll support you."

"I'm sure, and I'd like you to be my maid-of-honor."

"I'd love that."

Suddenly realizing that retrieving and sorting the mail was normally Amy's job, Helen froze. "Oh, Isabelle, Violet told me about Amy. Have y'all had any more word from her?"

Isabelle shook her head. "Nothing as yet. Father has gone to search for them mostly to assure himself and Mother that Amy's new situation is suitable—whatever that means. Mother seems hurt that one of her daughters would do such a thing—hide a relationship and then run off like that. Violet is all aflutter thinking she's in an Austen novel or some such nonsense."

"I never should have lent her my copy of *Pride and Prejudice*. All through dinner she explained to me the parallels between this situation and Lydia's with Wickham. I believe Violet has convinced herself she's Kitty." She laughed at her friend's grimace then regarded Isabelle seriously. "And how are you dealing with all of this?"

"To be honest, I'm more than a little annoyed with Amy, as much as I love her." Isabelle sighed. "Amy's elopement isn't a problem for Amy. It's a problem for me. My parents are determined not to make the same mistake twice, so I'll be the one facing more restrictions and tougher discipline. In the meantime, I'm trying not to be offended by mother's suspicious looks."

"You really had no idea?"

"Amy didn't confide in me on this one at all." Isabelle shrugged. "What's done is done. It's a good reminder that each decision we make not only effects ourselves but may have unintended consequences in other's lives. I suppose we just have to pray about our options, follow God's leading and be ready to live with the consequences of our choices whether good or bad."

"You have a good head on your shoulders, Isabelle.

I'm sure your parents will recognize that once the excitement dies down."

"I hope so." Isabelle frowned as she went back to sorting the mail.

"I guess I'll see you at supper." Helen hurried from the foyer down the hall to her room. She closed the door behind her, but couldn't shut out the wisdom of Isabelle's words.

Pray about our options...follow God's leading... be ready to live with the consequences. She hadn't prayed about the decision to marry Quinn. How could she have with everything happening so quickly? That didn't mean she wasn't following God's leading. After all, how many times had she prayed for a husband and children of her own? Well, not that many because she hadn't thought it possible. However, this was a blessing—an undeniable, pure, simple blessing. She'd be a fool not to run full speed toward it and Helen McKenna-soon-to-be-Tucker was no fool. She'd be more than happy to live with the consequences of her decision. They could only be good ones even if she didn't know her husband very well yet. Or, have much experience running a home. She'd been a teacher for almost half of a semester. How much harder could it be to be a wife and mother?

Chapter Four

"**D**early beloved, we are gathered here in the sight of God and in the presence of these witnesses to join to-gether this man and this woman in holy matrimony..."

Those sure were some highfaluting sounding words. Thankfully, all Quinn had to do was make sure he said *I do* at the right time and he'd be married to a woman too sweet, too intelligent and too attractive for his own good. He swallowed against the nervousness roiling in his stomach. He pulled at the fancy shoestring tie that went with the rest of his getup.

He wished someone had prepared him for how expensive it would be to buy a ready-made suit. Of course, that was only a drop in the bucket compared to what it would cost to feed and clothe four children until they were grown up and on their own. And it could be even more than that if he and Helen added to their brood.

He winced, hoping God hadn't heard that last thought. How could he and Helen have children if he was half afraid to touch her hand for fear of making the Almighty angry? The deal was that Helen would be a mother—not a wife. The distinction was already blurring in his thoughts and the ceremony wasn't even over.

Maybe he ought to have gotten a better handle on that before he asked Helen to marry him. Maybe he ought to have figured a lot of other stuff out, too. Like how to read. Fat chance of that happening, though.

He'd managed to get her to fill out the paperwork for the marriage license by pleading poor penmanship. He'd even put off signing the license in front of her so she wouldn't see that pitifully written signature comprised of only his first name. That didn't bode well for the future. What if he got too comfortable around her and let his secret slip? How would she react if she found out the truth about him?

He shook the thoughts from his head. He didn't even want to consider such a thing happening. Especially not in the middle of the ceremony. But it was already too late. His heart started racing. His palms began to sweat. Maybe he'd keel over right now and be done with it. Helen would take care of the children even if they hadn't been officially married.

He slowly became aware of the oppressive, awkward silence filling the church. Pastor Brightly cleared his throat. "You *don't* wish to take Helen to be your wife?"

"I—" He stopped and stared at the preacher realizing that wasn't the question Quinn had prepared himself to answer. "What?"

"You shook your head. I thought…"

"Oh, no." Quinn waved his right hand dismissing the action he'd done during his lapse of concentrate.

Helen's left hand slipped from his as the preacher's brow furrowed in confusion. "'No' what?"

Quinn frowned at Helen and took her hand in his

again as a nervousness seemed to spread from him to the folks gathered in the chapel. Helen wasn't going to leave him at the altar, was she? "Where are you going?"

"I'm not—" Her words stumbled to a halt. She looked flat out bewildered. "Quinn, are you going to marry me or not?"

"Well, I'm trying to, honey. The preacher here can't seem to get the question right."

A chuckle sounded from the audience. Quinn turned in time to see Ellie Williams smack her husband on the shoulder for the outburst before glaring at her sister-in-law, Lorelei, who sat on her other side shaking with silent laughter. Quinn glanced at his best man for help. Rhett just shook his head. Helen leaned into Quinn's side to whisper, "Pastor Brightly already asked you once."

"Oh." He almost admitted he'd been distracted then stopped himself in time to keep from getting into more trouble. He nodded at Pastor Brightly. "I reckon you'd better ask me again."

Pastor Brightly looked decidedly nervous as he cleared his throat. "Will you take Helen Grace McKenna to be your wedded wife—"

"I will."

"—to live together after God's ordinance in the holy estate of matrimony—"

"I will."

Pastor Brightly took in a deep breath and somehow managed to say the rest without pausing even a second for Quinn to answer. "Will you love her, comfort her, honor and keep her, in sickness and in health, and forsaking all others, keep yourself only unto her, so long as you both shall live?"

Finally, realizing he'd been interrupting the minister, Quinn hesitated before adding one final. "I will."

It was Helen's turn. She answered Pastor Brightly only once and not until the end, but the surety in her voice was worth the wait. Then it was time to exchange rings. He made sure to pay close attention so that he could say *I do* at the right time to endow all of his worldly goods upon Helen—such as they were. Quinn's heart had managed to calm down somewhat by the time Helen slid the ring he'd picked up at the mercantile onto his finger…until he realized there was only one thing left to do.

"I now pronounce you husband and wife. Quinn, you may kiss your bride."

He froze in panic. Sending a quick glance heavenward, he turned to his bride. *What else is a groom to do? It's expected.*

He glanced down at her smiling lips and wished more than anything that he'd kissed her in the schoolhouse first, lighting bolt or no lightning bolt. Now he had an audience and no idea how he was supposed to do this. He leaned down slowly to make sure he had the right trajectory. He brushed his lips across hers. That didn't seem quite right. He tried again, lingering this time. She tilted her head and did the rest.

A lightning bolt hit him, all right. It traveled from his lips down to his soul. It blocked out everything in a flash of light and heat except for the woman before him. He pulled away to stare down at her. A hundred questions battled for answers within him. Had she felt the lightning, too? More important, who had taught her to kiss like that and how soon could he get his hands around that man's neck? Finally, maybe if Quinn was real good about everything else, would God mind if he tasted lightning at least one more time before he died? He wasn't anticipating a long wait seeing as he had not only chased after but caught more than he was entitled to.

Nope. A wedding kiss was acceptable. He'd better play it safe from here on out. That's what a smart man would do. He'd never professed to be one before, but he'd married the schoolmarm. He had to at least try to use his wits if he wanted to keep her.

And he did. For the children. *Only* for the children.

Sean and Lorelei O'Brien had insisted on keeping the children at their neighboring farm overnight. Helen sorely missed their company, for the evening seemed to stretch on interminably without them. She tried to present a picture of unselfconscious comfort by tucking her feet under her and snuggling into the settee with a copy of Jane Austen's *Persuasion*, but an undercurrent of unease seemed to crackle in the air along with the soft roar from the logs in the fireplace. Even the crisp notes of Quinn's banjo couldn't drown it out, though he wasn't above trying—bless his heart.

After announcing that he hadn't had much of a chance to practice lately, he'd settled on the rug-covered floor across from the settee and started playing... and playing...and playing. It seemed as though he'd been strumming for hours, pausing for only an instant between songs, if that. At first, she'd enjoyed it. He was a very talented musician, after all. He'd even gotten her toe tapping a time or two. Now, she was getting concerned and a bit frustrated.

It was their wedding day, for goodness' sake! Didn't

he even want to talk to his new wife? She certainly wanted to talk to him. She'd been counting on this time to get to know the acquaintance she'd just married. She'd be downright mad at him for ignoring her if he wasn't so attractive while doing it.

Book abandoned, she stared at him, since he wasn't paying her any mind, anyway. The firelight caressed his jaw with golden fingers that swept up to his cheek and back down again as he bobbed his head in time with the music. His strong arms curved around the instrument while his left hand slid back and forth across the neck of the banjo and his nimble fingers coaxed music from the strings. His brow furrowed slightly in concentration. She bit her lip to hold back a sigh. *Talk to me.*

He glanced up and caught her watching. His fingers stalled. She smiled her entreaty. His lips curved upward in response. He went back to playing. She closed her eyes in annoyance then opened them to find his gaze fixed on her again. Progress! She'd better do something while she had his attention. His piercing cobalt eyes rendered her mind a complete blank. She reached for something sensible or meaningful to say then dared to speak over the music. "This is a nice room."

Really? That's the best that I could come up with?

It seemed to take Quinn off guard a little, too, for he glanced around as though with new eyes. The furnishings of the living room weren't fancy, but they were comfortable and of good quality. The floors were the same rather worn oak that seemed to stretch through the entire house. The burgundy rug on top of it reflected the red brick of the fireplace, which was cooled down by the hunter green and dark blue in the settee and matching chairs. Having finished his inspection, Quinn offered her a nod. "I'm glad you like it."

Her mind scrambled for something else to say. What could she talk about? The ceremony? She wasn't eager to discuss the fact that he'd made her a nervous wreck by originally accidentally refusing her. The children? All she could think about was the fact that they wouldn't return until tomorrow. Leaving her alone. With her husband. Who had only just discovered that she was in the same room with him.

Realizing they hadn't stopped staring at each other while he played, she wanted to look away but was afraid she wouldn't get his attention again. To be honest, she was tired of trying. It had been such a busy few days with her finishing up at school, packing her things and moving them into her new home. She was worn out. Perhaps she ought to just call it a night and hide until the children returned. She stood.

The music stopped. Quinn looked up at her expectantly. Her mouth opened then closed as she realized that, though she was ready to turn in, she had no idea where to turn in *to*. She'd been so distracted by laying out the wedding supper their friends had sent home with them that she hadn't seen anything of the house besides the kitchen and living room. After supper, Quinn had been too involved with his banjo to offer a tour. He stood, watching her with a concerned frown. "Something wrong?"

"No." Without her permission, her gaze strayed to the banjo which he still clung to rather tightly. "I'm just tired, that's all. I'm ready to go to bed, but I'm not sure where I'm supposed to sleep."

He carefully laid the banjo in its case. "I already put

your trunks in my room. It's the first door you'll come to in the hallway."

"*Your* room?"

Her words were infused with just enough panic and disconcertion to jerk Quinn's head up. His eyes were already widening when they connected with hers. A flush spread just above his well-shaven jaw. "I didn't— I mean—I'll be sleeping in the boys' room from now on."

"Oh." A wave of relief washed over her, but ebbed with confusion. He'd asked her to marry him because he needed a mother for his children. However, since he'd never specifically said that their marriage would be in name only, she'd assumed it would become like any normal marriage after they fell in love. Was he ruling out that prospect? If so, did that mean he was also ruling out the far more important possibility of falling in love with her?

She really ought to ask him to clarify the issue. After all, she had a right to know exactly what she'd gotten herself into. She paused with the question on her lips. Did she want to know the truth? Absolutely. Did she have the nerve to ask? Certainly not.

Instead, she wished him a good night and easily found the right bedroom. The door was heavier than she'd expected so she pushed it open only far enough for her slim frame to slip through. Readying herself for bed, she tried to sort through the myriad emotions tangling in her chest. This marriage had not started out at all as she'd imagined it would. Even the ceremony had been a bit flubbed. She had to admit that Quinn had been rather frustratingly adorable in that moment. He'd been so serious, so confused, so desperate to make things right. He'd even called her "honey." Then he'd kissed her and she'd felt a sensation similar to the one she'd felt at the circus when she'd placed her hand on a glass ball that conducted static electricity—only more powerful. Of course, he'd followed all of that up by ignoring her the whole evening.

One labored sigh later, she slid under the covers of her new bed. At least, she tried to slide in. Her legs would only go so far. She kicked and pushed and wiggled to no avail until one overenthusiastic effort sent her careening toward the floor. She landed with a loud thump, clamping her lips shut a second too late to smother a startled scream. She groaned in a mixture of pain from her soon-to-be-bruised hip and pure, honest-to-goodness frustration. The pounding of bare feet sounded in the hallway. The door flew open, setting off a popping sound as an avalanche of rice covered her concerned husband.

Helen burst out laughing. Quinn ignored the sticky rice clinging to his body in his hurry to kneel by her side. "Are you hurt?"

She shook her head even as she winced at the stitch in her side that came from laughing too hard. "I just hit the floor a little hard."

He helped her up. "How did you end up down there?"

"Try to get in the bed."

He glanced from her to the bed then down at himself. "But I'm covered in rice."

"Doesn't matter. Go ahead and try." She smirked as she watched him lift the covers as though they were going to bite him. "Scaredy-cat."

He narrowed his eyes at her then jumped under the covers. His long legs had nowhere to go. He fell out of the bed, but managed to control his fall with catlike grace. He grinned up at her from the floor. "Helen, I reckon we've been shivareed."

"I hope that's the extent of the troublemaking." She shook her head. "Interesting how it isn't quite so fun when you're on the receiving end. I think I'd better get a broom."

"You can put the rice in the slop pail for the pigs. Meanwhile, I'll see how they rigged up the bed and undo it."

By the time she returned, he'd pulled back the quilt completely from the bed to reveal their saboteur's handiwork. The fitted sheet seemed untouched, but someone had tucked the top sheet into the head of the bed so that it looked like the fitted sheet. They'd then doubled it over so that it also appeared to be a normal top sheet. Lastly, they'd tucked in the sides so the sheet became sort of an impenetrable envelope.

Quinn quickly remade the bed correctly, shaking his head the entire time. "I made this bed myself this morning with new sheets and all. It kind of gives me an eerie feeling to know someone was prowling around the place, causing mischief when I was gone. I've a mind to go into town on Monday and get a better lock for the doors around this place. There. All fixed. I'll take the trash you have with me when I leave."

"Thank you for coming to my rescue." She swept the last of the rice into the dustpan and emptied it into the slop pail.

"I'm just glad you aren't too badly hurt."

She watched him plump the pillows for her as she sat on the edge of the bed. "You don't have to do that."

He shrugged. "I'm done now. Good night."

"Good night." She moved to the head of the bed as

he grabbed the slop bucket, broom and dustpan. She'd just blown out the lamp when the sound of him softly calling her name made her turn to find the silhouette of his broad-shouldered, slim-hipped frame lingering at the door. "Yes, Quinn?"

"You looked beautiful at the wedding today. I hope I told you that."

He hadn't and she hadn't realized how dearly she'd missed the compliment until now. The sincerity in his voice caused a small smile to curve at her lips. "Thank you."

"I'll let you get some sleep." He stepped away from the door.

She moved to the far end of the bed. Clutching the footboard, she called his name. He reappeared in an instant. She bit her lip. Somehow the darkness helped her find her courage. It didn't stop the blush from rising in her cheeks. "Quinn, I think it's only fair of you to explain what you meant when you said you'd be sleeping in the boys' room 'from now on.' Does 'from now on' mean forever?"

His shoulders tensed as she spoke, and his gaze dropped to the path of light that led toward her. "I don't know, Helen. Maybe. Probably."

She nodded then waited for him to close the door behind him before sliding under the covers. She even went so far as to pull them over her head. It wasn't enough to shelter her from the doubts that stalked her thoughts.

She'd married Quinn thinking that it would be easy to fall in love with him one day. However, she hadn't considered the possibility that he might not be inclined to return the favor. Judging by tonight, that might very well be the case.

It would be wise to guard her heart and not place too much faith in love making the difference. If he did fall in love with her and they decided to have a normal marriage, how long would it be before he figured out there would be no baby coming? Would he realize she'd known she was damaged all along? That she'd hid it from him?

It didn't matter. It *wouldn't* matter. Quinn had married her to take care of the four children he already had. Surely her worth as his wife was secure in that. She didn't need to think that far ahead, anyway. Right now, their marriage was only a matter of convenience to him—no matter how much more it might mean to her.

Chapter Five

The dusky-blue light of dawn crept down the hall-way where Quinn paused outside what used to be his bedroom. He tapped on the door and listened for any sounds of his wife stirring. Hearing none, he tapped a little harder. Still nothing. With a frown, Quinn eased the door open and immediately wished he hadn't. Something just didn't seem decent about being in a lady's bedroom while she was sleeping. Yet, he couldn't take his eyes off her as he rounded the corner of the bed and knelt beside it.

She was cuddled under the covers with her hand resting beside her cheek on a hunter-green linen pillowcase. The color complemented the roses in her cheeks and lips. Her rich brown waves tumbled over her shoulder. Quinn felt his brow furrow in confusion. How on earth had he convinced this beautiful creature to marry him?

He'd be a lot more comfortable with this situation if she were a little more plain, slightly dumb or just flat-out boring. She wasn't, though. He'd never been more aware of that than when he'd found himself alone with her for an entire evening. He wasn't completely dense.

He knew that his banjo playing had bordered on excessive. He'd felt the annoyance rolling off his bride in waves. He just hadn't known what to do about it. He was afraid to talk for fear that she'd realized she'd been bamboozled into marrying a man so much dumber than her. He was afraid to look at her because that made him forget he didn't deserve her. Touching her was completely out of the question.

He'd lain awake for hours with his thoughts spinning in circles inside his head. They mostly revolved around the fact that he barely knew the woman he'd just given his last name. He knew plenty *about* her, but he didn't know her personally. He could count on one hand the number of times they'd spoken to each other and most of those conversations had occurred within the past week. That should make for an interesting married life, especially since he had little idea about what one was supposed to be like. His mother had died when he was Trent's age and his father hadn't remarried, which meant Quinn had never seen a marriage modeled in his own home. Townsfolk in Peppin seemed pretty fascinated by making matches and marrying people off, yet no one ever said anything about how to build a good marriage after the match was made.

He wasn't sure how long he'd been kneeling beside the bed thinking and watching Helen sleep before her sooty lashes began to flutter. He suddenly realized how close he was to her and tried to move away, but he was too late. Her eyes opened, locked on his and widened. Gasping, she bolted upright in bed and scrambled away from him. "Were you watching me sleep?"

Quinn figured his best tactic was evasion. "I was just about to awaken you. We've got chores to do."

"Chores?"

He nodded. "I need you to milk the cow, feed the chickens and gather the eggs. We'll have to hurry to get everything done, dress, pick up the children and still be on time for church."

She blinked. "Milk the chickens?"

She must be one of those folks who was slow to wake up. He didn't even try to hide his grin, though he quickly rubbed it away. "I'd like to see you try that."

"Try what?" She corralled her hair so that it pooled over one shoulder.

"Milking the chickens."

The teasing in his voice must have gotten through her sleep-fogged state, for a dangerous glint of humor warmed her brown eyes. "I bet you would. Repeat the list for me again."

He braced his elbows on the edge of the bed and ticked off each chore on his fingers. "Milk the cow. Feed the chickens. Gather the eggs. The milk pail and egg basket will be on the worktable in the barn with the bin of chicken feed beside it. All of that will be on your left side as soon as you walk in. You can't miss it."

She nodded. "Right."

"No, left." He pointed to his left, which he realized too late would be her right.

She tugged his hand down with a laugh. "No. I meant, 'right,' as in 'I understand.'"

"Oh, right." He glanced at her hand still covering his and wondered how the deal he made with God applied when she was the one reaching out. Yes, sir. He and God had some things they needed to hash out. Until then, he'd better not chance it. He disengaged his hand from hers as he stood. "Better get moving. The animals don't like to wait."

* * *

The man had no shame. It was obvious that he'd been watching her sleep for some time, yet he didn't even have the grace to look the slightest bit embarrassed at being caught. Then, as if she hadn't been disoriented enough by awakening in an unfamiliar place, he'd knocked further off balance with his teasing before delivering the final blow to her sensibilities. Chores.

She should have known that living on a farm would mean that she'd have farm chores. She'd just gotten so wrapped up in the idea of being a mother and having her impossible dream come true it hadn't crossed her mind. That and the fact that chores had never really been something she'd ever had to consider before. Growing up, she'd been responsible for keeping her room tidy. However, the maids had taken care of any real cleaning. And there had been no animals to care for.

Her move to Bradley's Boardinghouse hadn't necessitated any real change on her part since the Bradley family handled most of the mundane responsibilities for their boarders. Of course, she'd been in charge of keeping the schoolhouse in order. That had consisted of encouraging the children to clean up after themselves, giving the floor a good sweep and cleaning the chalkboard. There was nothing too strenuous or demanding about that.

Still, how hard could it be to take care of a few basic farm chores? She was an intelligent woman, after all. Surely she'd catch on to her responsibilities quickly. She tied her hair back with a ribbon, put on a light coat and buttoned up her boots. There would be time to dress later. The important thing was to heed Quinn's admonishment to hurry.

The sound of Quinn splitting wood behind the house

rang through the brisk autumn air as she stepped outside. She gave a little shiver and gathered her coat closer
before setting off across the open field toward the barn.
Her right hip reminded her of last night's unfortunate
tumble out of bed by protesting each step she took with
that leg. It didn't help that she continually had to jerk
the heels of her kid-leather boots out of the thick grass.
By the time she arrived at the door of the large red barn,
the hem of her nightgown was wet with dew and clinging uncomfortably to her bare legs. Next time, the animals would have to wait for her to dress more warmly.

The smell of the barn stopped her in her tracks. It
was a mixture of sweet hay, musk from the animals
and the sharp, acrid scent of dung. She rubbed her cold
nose. It wasn't so bad. Surely she'd get used to it in a few
moments. Since she was already in the barn, it made
sense to milk the cow first, so she grabbed the milking pan. Two horses neighed as she passed their stalls.
She couldn't tell whether it was a welcome or a warning. Finally, she found the right animal.

Whoa. She'd seen cows from a distance before, but
she'd never gotten this close to one. She hadn't realized
they were quite so…large. The animal swung its head
toward her and stared. Not threatening exactly—just
slightly intimidating. Helen bent her knees to get a look
at the teats attached to the bulgy sack on its stomach.
In theory, that's where the milk came from. She knew
that. She just wasn't entirely sure what was required to
procure the milk from that into the bucket. Oh, well.
What had she told her students? Learning begins with
the decision to try.

She unhooked the gate, closed it behind her and did
exactly that. She tried…and tried…and tried to milk

that blasted cow. It wasn't as easy in reality as it was in theory. That was for sure. Even when the cow stood still long enough for Helen to set up the stool and reach under its belly to get a hold of its bulgy contraption, nothing came out. Out of breath from the chase as much as the struggle, Helen decided that the cow just didn't want to share her milk today, so she traded in the milking pail for the chicken feed and egg basket.

The chicken coop was on the right side of the barn, closer to the house. She walked into the caged-in yard with confidence. The chickens would be far more manageable than the cow, if only because they were smaller. Plus, there was no fancy equipment on a chicken. It would all be very straightforward. Feed them. Gather the eggs from their nest. No problem.

At her approach, six hens and a rooster rushed out of their little house like children after a long day of school. Helen benevolently spread the feed across the yard as the clucking hens gobbled it up. The rooster seemed far more inclined to follow her around crowing and pecking at the feed that fell near her feet. Sometimes he missed the grain completely and accidentally pecked her boots. He was a pretty thing with his iridescent red-orange body and black-feathered bottom. He seemed to know it, too, from the way he strutted and crowed. The more she watched him, the more he began to remind her of her ex-fiancé in Austin.

She was just throwing the last of the feed when she realized that the rooster either had consistently bad aim or his target had, in fact, been her foot the whole time. She took a large step away from him. The next thing she knew, the rooster was hopping, flapping its wings and chasing her around the closed-in yard. The chickens squawked their disapproval. That caught the rooster's attention and he veered toward the loudest complainer with dubious intentions.

Helen ducked for cover inside the chicken coop, closing the door firmly behind her. With a sigh of relief, she surveyed her surroundings only to find that she was not alone. Two chickens had not left their roosts. Soon all the eggs lay safely in the basket except for the ones the hens were hiding. She approached the white one first, crooning, "Sweet little chick. Aunt Helen needs you to move aside. That's a good girl."

The white chicken clucked her sad tale and backed farther into her nest to let Helen take the precious egg. Helen couldn't help beaming. "Thank you. Now, don't let that mean old rooster scare you. You go on out and eat when I open the door. *If* I open the door. Maybe you could cause a diversion for me so I can get out of here."

She turned to the red chicken. "Time's up, honey. You need to move out the way."

Helen edged closer, but the hen didn't move or stop watching her with beady eyes. Helen extended her hand toward the nest. Perhaps she could just slide her hand under the seemingly frozen bird and… The bird launched out of the nest right toward Helen's face in a flurry of feathers, squawking and screeching. Helen let out a scream that sounded a little too similar to what was coming out of the hen as something scratched her cheek. She tried to ward it off with the feeding pan but only ended up hitting herself in the face. All of a sudden she realized the hen was gone. She'd been fighting the egg basket swinging from her arm.

Her panic faded, leaving her gasping for breath. She searched for her assailant, only to find the red hen clucking at the door as though it would open by her command. Helen gritted her teeth. She plucked the egg from the nest and placed it beside its rattled counterparts, then let the hens out the door. Helen peered out in search of the rooster and found it eating placidly near the door of the chicken coop—waiting for her, no doubt. She braced herself then ran for the exit.

Her peripheral vision told her the rooster was hot on her trail. The red hen appeared in her path, blocking her way out. Helen shifted to the right. Her hip protested. She stumbled. Glancing back, she saw the rooster go airborne with his claws outstretched toward her. Suddenly, she left the ground, too. The world spun. She landed firmly on her feet—unharmed, with her eyes clenched shut. Opening them, she saw the most beautiful sight.

Quinn was waving his arms at the rooster and chasing it into a corner away from her. His strident voice was music to her ears. "Back off! You know better than that!"

She didn't stick around to see the rest. She slipped out of the chickens' yard to await her husband out of harm's way. Her cheek was stinging from its encounter from the basket. Her lip was starting to fatten where she'd walloped herself with the feeding pan. She anxiously sifted through the eggs in the basket, looking for damage. She was so involved in her task that she didn't hear Quinn approach until an instant before he lifted her chin with a gentle touch. His gaze explored her face as a frown marred his. "What happened to you?"

She felt her eyes flash with indignation. "Your chickens attacked me. That's what happened."

"My chickens did this?"

Her gaze dropped from his for an instant. "I might have helped them out a bit. Still, they were the cause."

"I'm not sure what that means, but you'd better wash your face. This scrape on your cheek is bleeding." The concern in his tone, without even a hint of mockery, was just the balm she needed for her wounded pride.

She found herself leaning closer to him, hoping he'd wrap her in his arms if only for a moment. "Thank you for saving me *again*."

"Glad to do it." He chuckled. "I was on my way to the barn to feed the livestock and muck out the stalls when I heard you scream. Did you get a chance to milk the cow yet?"

"I tried, but there's no milk."

That frown was back. "No milk?"

She shrugged. "I guess the cow didn't want to give any today. Maybe there'll be some tomorrow."

A strange look appeared on his face. Confusion? Suspicion? Disbelief? She couldn't quite tell. He ran his fingers through his short hair. "I'll deal with it. You go on inside and take care of yourself. I should be in by the time you have breakfast ready."

"Breakfast. Right. That sounds good." She backed away, smiling and nodding the whole time. She could fix breakfast. No problem. After all, how hard could it be to scramble a few eggs?

Quinn had married into trouble. The knowledge had come upon him gradually at first. Now, with the day drawing to a close, he could no longer deny the truth. He'd suspected it when he'd found his wife running from the rooster, but he'd been willing to give her the benefit of the doubt because it was a fact that roosters could be territorial, especially with new people. As soon as she'd said that piece about the cow, he'd known he had a problem. The cow wasn't dry. She couldn't be. In fact, he had to milk her twice a day just to keep up with her production. However, it wasn't until the disaster of a meal she'd called breakfast that realization had come hard and swift like a knee to the stomach.

His wife knew nothing about housework. What was worse, he wasn't sure she was aware of the fact of just how little she knew. She attacked everything with an optimistic vivacity that remained unfazed despite her missteps throughout the day. It truly boggled his mind how a woman so obviously intelligent could be so clueless about the most basic things. He needed to talk to her. He'd been trying to all day but hadn't managed it yet.

It wasn't that he'd been speechless. He could think of a lot of words to say. He just knew that saying them was going to get him into trouble, which is why he'd initially kept his mouth shut. Then they'd picked up the children from the O'Briens and hadn't had a moment alone since.

Having completed the evening chores, he heaved a sigh and trekked from the barn into the house. Sunday had become the night when he put everyone to bed early—including himself. A fact he realized he'd forgotten to mention to Helen when he found the three older children enthralled by the book she was reading to them in front of the fire. Olivia had long since succumbed to sleep and so had Quinn, though he'd somehow managed to stay on his feet. He waited until Helen paused to take a breath before interrupting. "It's past time for bed, you three. Go on now."

Clara, usually the only one he could count on to

obey and enforce his rules on the others, rebelled with a groan. "Please, just a few more minutes, Uncle Quinn."

"I'm almost to the end of the chapter." Helen smiled as if that should solve everything.

The boys added their pleas, Reece verbally and Trent with his puppy-dog eyes. Quinn wavered—not because of their resistance but because he was contemplating the idea of going to bed now and leaving Helen up to put the kids to bed alone. She ought to be able to manage that since Clara and Reece knew what to do even if she didn't. Quinn would talk to her in the morning. After all, the situation wouldn't change before then.

Quinn nodded. "All right, then, but morning comes early and we don't want to be late for school, so y'all had better finish up soon. Good night."

He ignored the hint of surprise in their voices as they returned his farewell. The bedroll he stretched out on in the boys' room was no worse accommodation than it had been during the two years he'd traveled from ranch to ranch helping with brandings and roundups in Texas cattle country, saving up money for his own spread. It was comfortable enough for him to drift to sleep immediately…until a pint-size foot landed square on his chest. Quinn opened his eyes to find Reece grimacing down at him. "Sorry, Uncle Quinn. I slipped. Just trying to blow out the lamp."

"No problem. I'll do it," Quinn murmured with a sleepy slur as he stood and glanced over to make sure Trent was in the bed that the boys shared. The boy's small form was burrowed completely under the covers in preparation for the coming darkness. Quinn wasn't sure what to do about the boy's fears, since leaving a kerosene lamp burning all night would be a safety hazard. He could only hope that eventually Trent would realize he was perfectly safe.

The lamp had only been out a few seconds before Reece's voice broke the quiet. "Why are you sleeping in here and not in your own room?"

Quinn slid back into his bedroll. "It's your aunt's room now. That's why."

"That's not fair!" The boy leaned over the edge of his bed. "It was your room first. She ought to share. I share with Trent, and Clara shares with Olivia."

"Get back in bed before you hurt yourself."

Reece obeyed, then there was a thoughtful silence that could only mean trouble. "How come we have to share with you if she doesn't?"

Oh, boy. He needed to play his cards right or he'd find himself sleeping in the barn. "It isn't about sharing. Ladies need privacy."

"For sleeping?" Reece's tone said he wasn't buying what Quinn was selling.

The barn was getting more attractive by the second. "Yes. Now, go to sleep."

"But why?"

Quinn rolled onto his side, feeling the hardwood floor through the thin padding. "I'm tired, Reece. If I don't get some sleep tonight, I'll be dragging the whole week. Now, I don't want to hear any more questions from you tonight."

"What if it isn't a question?"

Quinn smiled even as he rubbed a shaking hand over his face. He should have known better than to try to go to sleep before the boys were dead to the world. He stood and edged toward the door. "Go to sleep. I'll be back in a minute."

He passed the door to the girls' room then Helen's, but he didn't stop at either of them. He kept going until he walked out the front door, down the porch steps and toward the wooded hills. He made it to the middle of the clearing before the invisible weight pressing on his shoulders dropped him to his knees. He battled the urge to pray. What good would it do to cry out for help? He'd done that once. Now it seemed that he had even more of a challenge on his hands than before.

He lifted his confused gaze heavenward then couldn't look away. The dark sky was clear, showing off the innumerable stars shimmering above. It was an awe-inspiring sight. More than that, it was fearsome. It served as a blatant reminder of his insignificance and the power of a God big enough, calculating enough, to create it all. Pastor Brightly had preached about it at church this morning. "And he is before all things, and by him all things consist." Of course, the pastor had tried to put a positive spin on that verse, but Quinn knew the truth about God's power. Nana had made sure of that.

Her body may have been growing weaker during those last few days of her life, but her fervor for sparing him from the fires of damnation had been stronger than ever. He could almost hear her wispy voice as clearly now as he had when he'd knelt at her bedside. *You've got to work out your salvation with fear and trembling, boy. You hear me? Your father and brother succumbed to that heathen greed and left me to die. I don't want to be the only one from my family in heaven. You've got to make it there, too.*

She'd spent the last of her strength instructing him on how to do that as if she hadn't drilled it into him long before that. Then the woman who'd been so afraid of being alone had left him behind. He'd been fourteen. Twelve years later, he was still doing his best to follow her advice. That's why he'd lived life hoping that if he left God alone, God would let him alone. Then he'd gone and messed everything up by asking for help.

"Quinn?"

He closed his eyes at the sound of Helen's soft voice. "I'm fine, Helen. You can go back inside."

She didn't move. Silence stretched between them until it broke with her whisper. "I know you aren't fine, Quinn. Just as surely as I know I'm at least one of the reasons why."

He finally turned his head to look up at her. She was bathed in moonlight. Her dark hair fell to her waist, a shiny backdrop to the turquoise Sunday-best gown she still wore. Forgetting for a moment that all of heaven was watching, he caught her hand and guided her down to the grass in front of him. "Why didn't you tell me that you didn't know anything about living on a farm or doing chores?"

"I thought you knew that I hadn't lived on a farm before."

He shook his head, realizing again just how little he actually knew about the woman he'd married. "Even so, some things like cooking don't require a person being on a farm to learn."

"Breakfast was terrible, wasn't it? I can see why you accepted the O'Briens' invitation for dinner and insisted on cooking supper yourself." He could see her blush even in the moonlight. "I'm afraid there's a lot I didn't learn growing up. You see, my family had servants to handle pretty much everything regarding the household."

"Servants?" The word was foreign to him, like something out of a fairy story he couldn't read. How wealthy did a person need to be to have everything done by servants? He couldn't even fathom it. He stiffened. "Wait. What do you mean *everything*?"

She gave a hapless shrug. "I mean the housework."

"Like cooking, cleaning, washing clothes, mending…" Her every nod filled him with more trepidation and confusion. Why had God sent Helen if she couldn't be the helpmeet he needed?

The question must have shown on his face, for Helen reached up to cradle his jaw with her hand, riveting his attention back to her. "I'll learn, Quinn. I promise you that."

"I'm sure you will." They didn't have a choice. She had to learn—and as quickly as possible. He caught her wrist and gently tugged her hand away so that he could think clearly as he made his own promise. "I'll show you what little I know. What I don't know, we'll have to find someone to teach you."

She smiled. "I already asked a couple of my friends for help at church. They agreed to give me a few lessons this week. See, Quinn? It will turn out all right."

He was relieved that she seemed to be eager to learn. Did that mean God intended her to turn out to be a helpmeet, after all? Or a hindrance? Or just plain temptation? Maybe all three options were right. Perhaps He'd sent Helen as some sort of test. If so, Quinn wouldn't falter. He wouldn't start caring about her as anything more than the helpmeet she was supposed to be. Not that he'd ever had a chance with her, anyway. That much had been made even clearer tonight for, despite her frustrating lack of practical skills, she was so far beyond him on every other level, it made his proposal and subsequent marriage almost laughable. Somehow he didn't find it funny—only confusing. He'd prayed for a helpmeet and God had given him a princess. How in the world could Quinn even endeavor to deserve that?

Chapter Six

Helen drew back the faded curtains from the window in her room the next morning to see the orange haze of daybreak stealing across the tops of the farm's eastern hills. That was the only sign of morning as she gave herself one last cursory check in the mirror. The reflection of determination on her face couldn't replace the memory of seeing Quinn sink to his knees on the fog-covered ground last night. She wasn't ignorant about the frustrating lack of skills she'd exhibited yesterday. Nor had she been unaware of the gradual strain it had seemed to be placing on her husband. However, she hadn't realized its true impact until that moment.

She was prepared to put her best foot forward today. The shadows under her eyes spoke of how much thought she'd put into doing exactly that last night. She grabbed the short stack of index cards she'd had the foresight to take to church with her yesterday and tiptoed across the hall into the living room. She stopped short at the sight of Quinn sleeping in a bedroll near the hearth where a banked fire dimly glowed in the fireplace. When he'd said he would be sleeping in the boys' room, she'd assumed that meant in a bed. Apparently not. He worked too hard to be relegated to the floor. Something would have to be done about that. She just wasn't sure what.

She stoked the fire in the cookstove, silently thanking Nathan Rutledge for teaching her how to manage the cantankerous stove in the schoolhouse. Next, she turned to the first index card, which happened to be written by Nathan's wife, Kate. It was entitled, How to Make Coffee. She followed the directions carefully and quietly. She taste tested the resulting brew and was pleasantly surprised to find it quite tasty. She closed the stove's damper to keep the brew warm for Quinn. Now to conquer the chickens…

A few minutes later, she set the egg basket near the door to the chicken coop and laid out most of the feed in one area of the yard before opening the door. A couple of tosses showed the chickens where the feed was, which freed her to ward off the aggressive rooster with a few nudges of the broom, as Ellie Williams had suggested. He soon grew bored and left her alone. Confidence growing, she picked up the basket and entered the coop to find the red hen stubbornly sitting in her roost.

Helen made sure to keep to the side as she reached under the troublemaker. This time when the hen launched from the roost, Helen was out of its trajectory. She gathered the rest of the eggs and was soon headed back to the barn unscathed. She was standing outside the cow's stall with a rope and the milking bucket contemplating her next move when Quinn's deep voice eased into her thoughts. "What exactly are you planning to do to Bessie?"

She turned around to find him standing behind her with his arms crossed and a half amused, half concerned smile on his face. She lifted a brow in response. "I'm going to milk her, of course. The rope is to keep her from moving around the stall."

He frowned. "She is usually pretty content to stay in one place when I milk her."

"Well, I was probably doing something wrong."

"Probably." He gave her a wink then returned the rope to the tack room before setting the milking pail and stool in place for the chore. He beckoned her into the stall with a quick tilt of his head. He crouched down beside her once she was seated. "First thing you want to do is to prod or rub the udder so she'll know it's time to let the milk down."

"Down from where?" She tried to follow his example, but the cow sidestepped at her touch. "See? That's what happened last time."

He narrowed his eyes thoughtfully. "Give me your hands."

"What? Why?"

He took one of her hands in both of his and began to rub it. "They're too cold. That's something you have to watch out for the closer we get to winter. Although, I've been thinking that I should keep doing the milking since dealing with the chickens, cooking breakfast and getting the children ready for school is a lot for anyone to handle in the mornings."

She spoke over the sound of her heart thundering in her ears. "You did all of that and more before I got here."

"Which is why I know it's a lot to handle. Besides, it will go faster if I do it." He switched his ministrations to her other hand. "You should still learn how to milk the cow, though. It's an important skill to have on a farm."

"Did you find the coffee I made?" She asked the

question to the top button of his shirt, which she discovered was a far easier feat then looking into his eyes at such a close distance.

"Sure did. It was nice and hot. Thanks for making it. I also saw that you collected the eggs. How did the rooster treat you?"

She shrugged, wishing he'd hurry up and finish with her hands. "I handled him."

"I don't doubt it." He chuckled then lifted her hands to his cheeks to test their warmth. "Better."

She froze. Her gaze drifted upward to meet his. How could he be so completely unaffected by her when she could hardly even think? It didn't seem fair. Her thoughts must have shown in her face, for his eyes widened then deepened. She felt his jaw tighten beneath the day-old stubble. He abruptly released her hands. His words seemed directed more to the ceiling than her. "Sorry. I guess you could have done that yourself. I wasn't thinking."

"It's fine." She turned to face the cow. "What now?"

She nearly winced at the sound of her breathless voice. She was embarrassing herself. He'd made it clear that he wasn't interested in her as anything more than a mother for his children. There was no need to turn into a ninny just because he deigned to warm her hands. Quinn's arm brushed hers, jolting her from her reverie as he demonstrated the proper hand position for milking. "You're going to want to squeeze from top to bottom to draw out the milk. Don't pull or you could stretch out the teat. Stay alert. You don't want the cow to kick you or the milk pail."

"No, I certainly don't." She copied his movements

and jumped when a stream of milk hit the ground. "I did it!"

He grinned. "You sure did. Just try to get the next one in the pail. Once you're comfortable, try milking two teats at once by alternating."

After two or three minutes, she'd developed a slow rhythm. She glanced at Quinn, who still hovered a bit too close for comfort. "Quinn, I thought you had a real bed to sleep in."

He seemed a bit taken aback by the sudden change of conversation. "A bedroll will do just fine for me."

"You work too hard to be relegated to the floor. Can't something be done about it?"

He rubbed his jaw. "I was thinking about expanding the house. I could add another bedroom. I also thought a room for the kitchen might be nice instead of just a corner in the house. Then we could put the table in there and have more room in the living space. What do you think?"

She paused to glance up at him, both surprised and impressed by how much thought he'd already put into solving the problem. "You know how to do that? Build part of a house, I mean?"

"Sure I do. I traveled around Texas doing whatever honest work I could find until I saved enough to buy my own piece of land." He shrugged. "It made me one of those jack-of-all-trades folks are always insulting."

She laughed. "I guess you must have seen a fair bit of Texas with all that traveling."

"That's a fact. Of course, nothing beats this place." His lips stretched into a lazy grin. "Want to know why?"

"Why?"

"Because it's mine."

She smiled. "That's a good reason."

She focused on the milking again and was proud that she seemed to be picking up speed. "After all that traveling, how did you end up settling down here?"

"I was passing through Peppin in between jobs and heard that the man who owned this place was looking for a farmhand. He was an older widower who was having some trouble running the place by himself, so he hired me on. About a year later, he decided to move a few towns west of here to live with his older son. I bought the place and most of the furnishings from him." His gaze turned curious. "What about you? You didn't need to work, so why did you leave home to become Peppin's schoolmarm?"

Her mind blanked then raced into action. What could she tell him? That she'd fled the embarrassment of a broken engagement? What if he asked who'd broken it off and why? "Helen?"

She blinked, focused a blithe smile on him and lifted one shoulder in a shrug. "I became a teacher for the joy of it. This is where I was placed. I think I'd better go start breakfast and awaken the children."

A furrow appeared on his brow. She wasn't sure if it was a result of her abrupt explanation or the idea of her fixing breakfast. She didn't stick around to find out.

Mrs. Helen Tucker was hiding something. At least that's what Quinn believed after their conversation yesterday morning. He didn't doubt she was telling the truth about why she had become a teacher, but the flash of pain in her eyes and the flush of pink on her cheeks had told him there was more to the story than she was letting on. He was actually kind of glad that she'd kept whatever it was to herself for the moment since he was still adjusting to that last revelation of his wife living the life of a fairy princess story. Until she'd married him, that is.

He had to hand it to her, though. Whatever she had written on those little cards of hers sure seemed to be making a difference. It helped that as a rule she was eager to learn and willing to take initiative. Each meal she'd made over the past two days had been an improvement over the last. That was a good thing, since she'd moved the spices out of the order he'd created for them in the cabinet. He'd lost all hope of being able to tell one identical-looking package from the other without a taste test first. How odd would it look if she caught him doing that?

It had occurred to him belatedly that hiding his illiteracy was probably worse than her failing to mention she didn't know how to do housework. However, that didn't make him any more eager to divulge his secret. He'd done a fair job of hiding it so far. Of course, he'd nearly had apoplexy the first time he'd walked into the house to find Reece reading a recipe aloud to her while she cooked just like the boy had done the few times Quinn hadn't been able to avoid trying a new dish. Thankfully, Helen hadn't seemed to think there was anything out of the ordinary behind Reece's efforts to be helpful. That was all Reece thought it amounted to as well so Quinn's secret was still safe.

Quinn's horse stumbled slightly, reminding him that he was supposed to be paying attention to his surroundings. Today, he'd been riding the fence line of his property fixing any areas with sagging barbed wire. This was the first time he'd been able to survey the state of his farm since the children had come. Having Helen to watch the young ones while the older ones were in school was a huge help to him. Yesterday, he'd gotten more work done in the field than he usually did in a week. The winter wheat was growing steadily though the lack of rain lately had become a concern.

Upon returning to the house, he wasn't too surprised to find that his wife had company since she'd told him that several of her friends had agreed to teach her some household chores. He just hadn't realized that the author of the Bachelor List, Ellie Williams, would be Helen's instructor today. The women's quiet voices and soft laughter told him that Olivia and Trent must be taking their afternoon nap. How the children could sleep with the lingering sweet, spicy smell emanating from the kitchen was beyond him. His stomach gave a rumble almost loud enough to wake them in the other room.

Ellie was the first to spot him. Her green eyes lit up with a calculating gleam that told him he'd be wise to walk right back out the door. "Quinn, you're just the man I was hoping to see."

Uh-oh. His gaze slid to Helen for some clue to what he was in for, but she gave him a guileless smile that set him at ease. Or perhaps it was the smudges of flour on her cheeks and all down the front of her apron that made him think perhaps he could handle himself with the two forces of nature before him. "Good to see you, Ellie. Did Lawson come with you?"

"No. He had to stay and work with the horses." She tapped her booted toe looking downright impatient to skip the preliminaries and get the bee out of her bonnet. "I rode Starlight over here by myself then set her up with some water and a stall in your barn. I hope you don't mind."

"Certainly not."

Helen must have seen him eyeing the door for she stepped forward with a plate of golden cookies that were sprinkled with some kind of red powder. "Try a snicker doodle cookie. The children helped us make them."

"Thanks. I don't mind if I do." He selected two large misshapen cookies and sat down to await his fate. Hopefully it would involve more cookies. He couldn't remember the last time he'd had one. It had to have been at a church picnic or barn raising because he'd certainly never tried to make them on his own. He was starting to think there was something to be said for this marriage deal, after all. Catching Ellie's narrowed eyes on him, he lifted a brow. "Something on your mind, Ellie?"

She nodded as she wiped her hands on her apron. "I was talking to Rhett the other day. He seemed to be attributing your marriage to the Bachelor List, which is ridiculous because Helen lost the list. Right?"

Helen exchanged a glance with him. "Yes, I lost it. The funny thing is… Quinn found it."

Quinn nodded. "Sure did."

"I see." Ellie swallowed. "But, y'all didn't get married just because of a silly list I made."

Quinn bolted upright. "*Silly* list?"

Helen hushed him with a furtive glance toward the hallway that led to the bedrooms. "If you wake the children too soon they'll be cranky the rest of the day."

"Well, I'm sorry, but that list isn't silly." He frowned at Ellie who seemed to grow a bit paler with each word from him. "It's one of the main reasons I married Helen along with the fact that she loved the children."

"And because you love each other…?" When Ellie's hopeful prompt was met with uncomfortable silence, she grabbed onto the table for support. "Oh, dear. I had no idea people would take my list this seriously when I made it. I don't like the idea of people following it so unquestioningly. It isn't infallible, you know, and neither am I."

"It doesn't have to infallible for God to use it to bring people together." Helen pulled out a chair and urged her friend to sit down. "Now, there's no need to get in such a dither about things. Quinn and I know what we're doing."

Ellie bit her lip. "Well, I suppose if y'all are happy then I'm happy. I would like the list back, though. Y'all certainly don't need it anymore."

"If that's true, then I guess you don't need it, either." He leaned his chair back onto two of its legs. "Seeing as you're married and all."

Helen's mouth dropped open. "Quinn, the list belongs to Ellie. She should be able to have it back if she wants it."

"It seems to me that since it's called the *Bachelor's* List it belongs to the bachelors who need it."

Ellie lifted her chin. "It's the *Bachelor* List—as in a list of bachelors. There is no apostrophe *s* to make it belong to anyone but me."

A pasta—what? That thought nearly spilled into words until a quick glance at Helen told him he somehow ought to know what Ellie was talking about. He settled for an ineloquent, but less revealing, "Huh?"

"Will you give me back my list?"

"I'm afraid not."

"Helen, talk some sense into your husband."

Helen looked purely ticked as she crossed her arms and gave him a look that somehow mixed a glare with puzzlement. "We haven't been together long enough for me to know how to do that yet."

Quinn grinned at Helen then gave Ellie's hand a quick perfunctory pat. "I'll take good care of it until the next fella is ready to receive it, and I've got a good idea who that man will be. I believe the list fell into my hands as a result of divine intervention. There's nothing you or anyone else could say to convince me otherwise. Anything good or bad that comes from it is God's responsibility—not yours."

Ellie sighed. "Well, if God's in it, it's bound to turn out good."

For whom? He wanted to ask, but kept his mouth shut because he believed every word he'd spoken. Of course, he'd questioned why God had sent Helen at first. He still wasn't sure he entirely understood all of the reasons. One thing he did know was that, after a few days of marriage, Helen was beginning to be downright helpful. Between the chores, children and ladies visiting he hardly ever saw her alone. That suited him perfectly because it helped him remember that she didn't belong to him so much as she did to the children. He'd be just fine if they could keep this up for another twenty years or so. After that…well, he wasn't sure what he'd do.

Chapter Seven

"**W**ell, darlings, let's hope that's the last of it," Helen said the next day as she entered the living room where she'd left Olivia and Trent a few moments ago to gather the laundry. She'd discovered that the children had come to Quinn with a relatively large wardrobe of good quality clothes. Of course, that meant more work for her because all of them were dirty. She glanced up as she began to separate the clothes into piles. She found Olivia sitting on the rug playing with a doll. However, Trent's watercolors and paintbrush sat abandoned near his latest masterpiece on the kitchen table. "Trent, come back here and show me your painting!"

Silence—thick and suspicious—permeated the house. That didn't mean the boy wasn't close by. She hadn't heard Trent make a sound since she'd arrived. From what she'd heard from his siblings, Trent's silence was a relatively new development and one that she found greatly concerning. Quinn had told her that Doc Williams had examined the boy but hadn't found anything physically wrong. The doctor also said the silence was probably induced by the stress of losing his parents and was most likely a temporary condition. That left room for hope, which was far more than her family's doctor in Austin had given her after her riding accident.

She froze realizing that another minute or two had passed without any sign of Trent. She left the clothes on the floor once more to search for the boy. She went through each room, searched every potential hiding place and concluded that Trent was not in the house, after all. Reining in her mounting panic, she set Olivia on her hip and headed outside to the only logical place for him to have gone in such a hurry. The outhouse door was wide open showing an empty interior. She spun to scan her surroundings causing Olivia to squeal in excitement at the sudden motion.

"There's no need to panic. He couldn't have gotten far. He's probably just in the barn with those gentle and mammoth animals like Bessie who could step on him or kick him or..." She shook her head to stop the flow of thoughts. "Quinn will find him if I can't. Of course, I'd have to find Quinn first. Only I don't know where he is because he's been working on the fences. How long can it take to fix fences?"

Trent wasn't in the barn. She ran outside and glanced toward the wheat fields. The burgeoning stalks weren't tall enough to hide a four-year-old. Perhaps he'd gone back to the house. She trotted from the barn toward the house which set Olivia giggling. Helen started up the porch steps calling, "Trent?"

"He's right here." Quinn's deep voice stopped her in her tracks. She turned to find Trent holding on to Quinn's hand as they rounded the far corner of the house—the one area she hadn't been able to see during her frenzied search. "I was breaking sod for the new addition and he must have seen me through the kitchen window. He was sitting on a nearby log watching me work. I didn't even see him there at first."

"I only left the room for a few minutes. When I came back he was gone. I knew he couldn't have gotten far but still…" She shook her head and covered her heart as she walked down the porch step.

Quinn rubbed his jaw, the look in his eyes slightly guilty. "I guess I should have warned you this fella has a talent for disappearing at the drop of the hat."

She glanced down to find Trent watching her with his deep brown eyes. She set Olivia down then kneeled over to wipe the smudged of dirt from his face with the hem of her apron. "You must have had quite an adventure before sitting on that log to be so messy, young man."

A reluctant little quirk of his lips was his only response.

"He has a talent for that, too," Quinn admitted.

She lifted her brow at the men. "A talent for having adventure or for getting messy?"

"Both."

Helen sank to her knees in front of her nephew so that she could look him in the eye. "Well, I'm all for having adventures and even for getting messy once in a while. However, when you're with me, you are not to go off by yourself without my permission. Is that understood?"

He understood. She could see that in his eyes. He just didn't agree. She could see that, too. She was narrowing her eyes, trying to figure out how to handle it when a shout ruined the moment. "Hello, the house!"

She stood in time to see Rhett Granger wave at them as he drove a wagon practically onto their front porch.

Isabelle sat beside him, her hands gripping the sides of the conveyance. Helen couldn't tell if she was hanging on for dear life or preparing to jump out. Apparently, it was the latter because her friend stepped out of the wagon almost before it stopped. "Helen, never let your children ride with that man. He cannot drive."

Rhett set the brake and hopped down to join them. "Now, that's gratitude for you. There I was shoeing a horse next to the livery when I overheard Miss Adventure here trying to convince the livery owner that she should be allowed to take out her father's buggy by herself. Quinn, ask her how many times she's driven a team of horses."

Quinn frowned. His tone was unnecessarily grave. "How many?"

"Father let me take the reins a few times."

Rhett nudged Quinn in the side with his elbow. "Ask her how she planned to move these heavy boxes she brought with her."

"How did—" Quinn must have seen Helen shaking her head at him for joining in his friends' antics for he stared down at his boots as though they were the most interesting things in the world.

"For your information, *gentlemen*, I was going open the crates and carry the books in stacks to the buggy then get Quinn to help me carry them into the house when I got here." Isabelle popped the top off the crate on the back of the buggy. Taking the first book in hand, she tested its weight as though preparing to throw it at Rhett. "Now, I'm getting a better idea of what to do with them."

Rhett quirked his brow. "Ladies and gentlemen, I give you the gentler sex."

Quinn did a very poor job of hiding his laughter which only made Rhett's grin broaden. Helen frowned at them both. "Rhett, I'm beginning to think you're a bad influence on my husband. Let's get these things inside—although I don't really know why you're giving them to me, Isabelle."

"These are from your parents. The postman dropped the boxes off at the boardinghouse. He said he didn't want them taking up room in his office forever and a day which they surely would since Quinn never checks his mail."

Everyone looked at Quinn who flushed a nice shade of red. He shrugged. "Only family I've got is right here. No one else would have cause to write so why bother?"

"That isn't true, Quinn." Helen smiled at his befuddlement. "When we married I didn't just become part of your family. You became part of mine. You have in-laws and they're pretty lovely people if you ask me."

"In-laws. Now, isn't that something? I reckon I could stop by the post office now and again if they'll be writing you."

"Not just me—us."

"Us," he repeated. A flash of worry crossed his face. Before she could question it, he was lifting a crate from the wagon and carrying it toward the house. "Rhett, I can take Isabelle back to town when I pick up the kids from school."

Rhett followed suit with the last crate. "I'd appreciate that, Quinn. I have a lot of work to do back at the smithy."

The men deposited their burdens in the living room before Rhett said his goodbyes. Quinn took the children with him to "help him dig" the foundation for the addition. Helen was pretty sure that just meant they'd be playing in the dirt, but appreciated him watching the children while she learned how to wash clothes. First, though, she and Isabelle delved into the crates of books to see what treasures her parents had sent. "Thanks for bringing these out, Isabelle."

"You're welcome." Isabelle stacked a few children's books on the table.

Helen gave her friend a sideways glance. "It was nice of Rhett to drive you."

Isabelle grimaced. "He just wanted a chance to ask about Amy."

"He asked about Amy?"

"No, but he would have if I hadn't been complaining about his driving the whole way. The more I complained the worse he drove." Isabelle pursed her lips and narrowed her eyes. "This seems highly suspicious now that I think about it."

Helen's smile quickly sobered. "What is the latest on Amy?"

"Father wired home to say he found her in a small town near Dallas where her husband is from. Violet said she wanted to visit them so mother forbade us to leave the house. Thankfully, I was able to convince her that wasn't practical. Stop laughing. It isn't funny and I have nothing further to say on the matter." Isabelle glanced around the living room. "Where should I put these books?"

Helen followed her friend's gaze. "Hmm. I hadn't realized that there aren't any bookshelves in this room. Or, anywhere else in the house now that I think about it. We'd better put these back in the crate for now. I'll figure out what to do with them later. I have some water heating in the stove's reservoir for the wash."

"We'll probably need a pot or two more. It looks like you have quite a few loads to do." Isabelle put the last of books back in the case. "So Quinn isn't a big reader then?"

"I suppose not." Helen found her largest pot and pumped the faucet to fill it. "He's more interested in his music. Besides, he stays so busy that he'd hardly have a chance to read if he were so inclined."

Isabelle leaned onto the large farm sink beside Helen. "I thought farmers had more free time in the winter with harvest over and planting season not until the spring."

"Well, he has a crop of winter wheat in the ground. He's also working on an addition to the house."

Isabelle took over the pumping for her. "Really? What is he building?"

"Another bedroom and maybe an extension on the kitchen." She carried the heavy pot to the stove, careful not to slosh it.

"Another bedroom? Are y'all planning to add to your family immediately?"

Helen lost her grip on the pot. Thankfully, it was close to the surface of the stove so it settled with a loud bang and only a small splash. Like unexpected pressure on a bruise, pain made her eyes well and prompted her to answer honestly. "The bedroom is for him."

Isabelle was quiet for so long that it seemed Helen could almost hear the thoughts racing through her friend's head. "That sounds…permanent. Are you all right with that?"

"Yes." She blinked away her unshed tears as she mopped up the water on the stove with a clean rag.

Isabelle squeezed her arm. "This from the girl who was certain she'd fall in love with her husband without a problem?"

"I forgot to factor in the possibility that he might not be willing to fall in love with me."

Isabelle's mouth dropped open. "Did he say that to you?"

"He might as well have." Helen reached for the cookie jar. "Take one. The children and I made these yesterday."

"You can't shut me up with a cookie even if they do smell delicious. Why does Quinn get the final word on this? You have every right to fall in love with your husband and seek his love in return. In fact, I'm pretty sure y'all promised to love each other before God and a handful of witnesses not even a week ago."

"I can't control his feelings."

"Perhaps not, but you can't give up, either."

Helen felt her temper rising so she forced herself to take in a deep breath and calm down. She usually wasn't a short-tempered person, but this had been a trying week. As in she had been trying really hard to be who she needed to be for the children and Quinn. She was suddenly realizing that some things had fallen by the wayside during that process. Important things, too. Things like Trent's silence and the fact that her husband was building for a future that didn't include her. Meanwhile, he didn't even have a bed to sleep in.

Isabelle had made an erroneous assumption. That's what made Helen so mad. She hadn't given up on her marriage such as it was. She just hadn't had time to think about it. That needed to change. First, she had to figure out how to do the laundry. Second, she had to cook supper. After that, she had to help the children with homework and put them to bed. Then, once all of that was done and Quinn was avoiding her as usual, she'd come up with some sort of solution to at least one of these problems. She just had to.

Late that evening, Quinn watched the flames in the fireplace abate with grim satisfaction. Something about watching a fire dance always brought to mind things like damnation, the coming judgment and a lake of fire. Nana had become more concerned about those things after his father and brother had gone searching for "fool's gold" as she'd called it. As a child it had terrified him. Eventually, he'd learned not to show that fear for it only seemed to prompt her to add more detail to her descriptions. If the fear of the Lord was really the beginning of all knowledge, those formative years should have left him a lot smarter than he'd ended up.

He speared the wooden logs with a metal poker and a bit too much force. His arms, sore from breaking ground for the new addition, protested the motion. He'd known he was overdoing it at the time, but he couldn't seem to slow down once he'd started—not when every splice of sod was meant to demonstrate his acceptance that he wasn't good enough for Helen. Surely, God would appreciate his efforts.

Satisfied with the glow of the banked fire, Quinn set the poker aside to lay out his bedroll. He found it wasn't where he'd left it that morning or anywhere else in sight. He'd been married less than a week but already knew that nothing was truly lost unless his wife couldn't find it. He went to knock on her bedroom door only to discover someone else had already beaten him to it.

Helen's voice sounded through the partially open door. "And just what are you doing out of bed, little lady?"

Clara's giggle induced him to peer through the gap in the door just as Helen swept the seven-year-old onto her lap. Clara tilted her head back to use what Quinn called her "pleading doe eyes" on Helen. It was hard to deny the child anything when she pulled that weapon from her arsenal. "I was hoping you might read a little more of *Treasure Island* to me. It's so exciting."

Quinn barely quelled a groan that would have given his hidden position away. Books. Why was his whole family suddenly fascinated by books? It used to be they were happy if he had time to play them a few songs after supper. Now, the three older children weren't satisfied unless Helen read about pirates and buried treasure. It was a wonder they settled down to sleep at all with that nonsense filling their heads. Yet, they enjoyed it so much that he couldn't speak against it. It would have been highly suspicious for him to do so, anyway. More suspicion was the last thing he needed after Helen's discovery that there was not a single bookshelf or book in the house besides the ones that her parents had sent. There was his Nana's Bible, of course, but if he mentioned that she might wonder why she never saw him reading it.

Clara's lips pouted slightly. "Please Aunt Helen? I like to hear you read."

The girl was being a scamp, but he couldn't argue with her choice of flattery. Helen was a good reader. No, she was a *great* reader. She made a person feel like they were part of the story. So much so that he'd found himself caught up in the fantasy, too. That scared him a little. He didn't want to find books interesting because that just meant there was more that he was missing out on. As if the notification he'd originally received about his brother's death, his own marriage certificate and any letters from his in-laws weren't enough.

"Thank you, darling. I'm glad you're so eager to hear more, but you know I can't do that. It wouldn't be fair to the others." Helen lifted an eyebrow and added a hint of mystery to her voice. "There's another reason, too. I'll tell you what it is if you can keep a secret."

"I can keep a secret. What is it?"

Helen whispered rather loudly. "It's past your bedtime."

"That isn't a secret!"

Helen placed a finger over her own mouth. "Perhaps if you're very quiet, Uncle Quinn will carry you back to your room."

Caught, Quinn could do nothing but smile as Helen met his gaze. Clara, at least, was surprised at his presence so he winked at her. "Say good night."

"Night." Clara kissed Helen's cheek then rushed toward him. He lifted Clara into his arms and carried her down the hallway to the girls' room.

Clara automatically started to whisper once they entered her room so as not to wake Olivia. "Uncle Quinn, I don't want to go to sleep. I want to stay awake with you and Aunt Helen."

"But we're going to sleep, too," he whispered as he pulled back the covers and set her on the bed.

Her mouth scrunched into a sideways pout. "It isn't fair. I don't get to see Aunt Helen as much as Olivia and Trent do because I have to go to school. It isn't nearly as fun there without her."

"Well, tomorrow is Thursday. Starting on Friday,

you'll have the whole weekend to spend with her." He knelt beside her bed and tucked in her recalcitrant form. "The fastest way to get to tomorrow is to sleep."

"But I'm not finished with today yet." Her long dark lashes closed in a drowsy contradiction.

"Oh, yes, you are." He leaned over to kiss her forehead. "Good night, Clara. Snuggle in tight and tomorrow will be here before you know it."

Her words came out more as a heavy sigh than a whisper. "Good night."

He closed the door behind him quietly and found Helen waiting in the hallway. "Did she settle down?"

"Yeah, she's practically asleep already. By the way, I seem to be missing my bedroll. Have you seen it?"

"I took it apart and washed all of the blankets for you. I was about to bring them out to you." She led the way into the bedroom and grabbed the stack of blankets from the top of the dresser. "You know, Quinn, I still don't like the idea of you sleeping on the floor. This room is plenty big enough for the both of us. We could fit another bed in here across from mine. Perhaps under the window? We could put up a changing screen for a bit more privacy. That way you'd have a real bed to sleep in until the addition is done. Or, if it worked out well enough, you may not have to build anything extra. What do you think?"

The idea of having his own bed and a little privacy again was more than enticing. To tell the truth, sleeping on the floor was getting old fast. It was cold—not to mention uncomfortable—and he had a long way to go on the addition to the house. He'd broken the sod, but that was only step one. He'd need to dig down to the house's foundations, gather stones to lay a new one, build the frame for the floor and the floor itself, the framing for the wall… The list went on and on. It would be expensive, too. He'd known that from the get-go and had been willing to put down the money to secure Helen's place as the mother to his children. Or, had it been out of self-preservation? For his own protection against whatever penance the Almighty might demand for such a blessing? Whatever his motivation, he'd still be building onto the house if he accepted her offer. He just wouldn't have to sleep on the floor while doing it.

He nodded. "I reckon we could try it out, Helen. It will probably take me the weekend to make the bed-frame and stuff a new mattress. My first night in here would probably be Monday. Does that work for you?"

"Certainly."

He took a step back toward the door. "Well, I guess I'd better get on back to the floor for now. Thanks for washing these for me. Have a good night."

Quinn determinedly pushed away his misgivings as he reconstructed the bedroll in the living room. God would understand the change of plans. As he drifted to sleep, Quinn repeated that assurance to himself until he began to believe it.

Chapter Eight

After Quinn left her room with the blankets, Helen finally had the time and privacy she needed to read the letter Isabelle had brought from Helen's parents. She picked it up from her nightstand and sat at the small desk Quinn told her had belonged to the cabin's original owner. She'd never seen him use it so she doubted he'd mind if she did. She opened the lone drawer in search of paper and ink. All it held was a dusty Bible and a jumbled assortment of papers so she shoved the drawer closed, gathered writing materials from her trunk and settled back at the desk to read the letter.

From the start of her parents' letter, it was obvious they were shocked by the announcement of her marriage. She'd sent the news by letter, telling them that the wedding had been planned so quickly that she hadn't had time to invite them. She grimaced. That wasn't entirely true. She hadn't told them until after the fact because she hadn't wanted to take the chance that they might try to discourage her from going through with it. They might have humored her by helping her get the teaching job; however, they hadn't hidden their belief that she'd soon tire of it and come home where she belonged. Instead, she'd gotten married.

She was somewhat relieved to find that their only protests seemed to be directed not at the marriage itself, but rather the fact that they hadn't been notified in time to attend the ceremony. Her father didn't try to hide his disappointment at not being able to walk her down the aisle. Her mother, on the other hand, tried to disguise her hurt and confusion at not being invited by offering cautious congratulations. Helen grimaced, feeling downright guilty as those words became more genuine as the letter progressed.

I know that only the deepest love could have moved my daughter to act so quickly to secure it.

"More like the deepest desperation," Helen whispered. "And fear. Fear that I'd never have the chance again."

I remember all too vividly the night your first engagement ended.

Helen froze, seeing the memory play out even as her mother described it.

While your father sent the guests home, I held you and you cried as I have never heard you cry before. It was only then that I realized how deeply that riding accident had scarred you—not just physically, but emotionally.

Helen rubbed her hand across her lower abdomen. She hadn't realized it until that moment, either. Thom-

as's rejection has confirmed what she'd known since
the accident. As normal as she looked on the outside,
she was broken on the inside in ways that could never
be fixed. Tears filled her eyes as the emotion of that
night rushed back to her. She blinked away the blurri-
ness to keep reading.

> *Oh, how feeble my attempts to comfort you
> seemed then when I told you that he existed—the
> man who would love you for everything that you
> are. I cannot express how satisfying it is to see
> my words come true.*

The words hadn't come true. Not yet. The room par-
tition she and Quinn had decided on was a step in the
right direction. He would be physically close by, but
what good would that really do? They'd shared a house
for a week and were still closer to being acquaintances
than they were friends or sweethearts, let alone spouses.

> *I am so proud of you, my darling, for being a
> woman of integrity. It would have been so easy
> not to tell Thomas Coyle the truth. Yet, you did.
> God saw that and blessed you for it by giving you
> what you truly desired all along—a husband and
> children whom you love and are loved by. What
> an amazing testament to His goodness!*

Helen stared at those words until a heavy tear fell
and landed on the paper and caused one word to blur.
Integrity.

She'd always thought of herself as what her mother
had described "a woman of integrity," but could she re-

ally make that claim now? While she might have told Thomas the truth, she hadn't extended that same courtesy to the man who actually mattered—her husband. Why should she when everything she'd longed for was finally within her reach?

Perhaps because the secret had begun to weigh on her soul. She was so afraid that her faults might make her undesirable as a woman or undeserving of being a mother. No matter how hard she tried to suppress it, it was always lurking in the back of her mind.

Suddenly, she knew. She was going to have to tell Quinn the truth. Her heart slowed to a steady rhythm. For the first time all week her mind cleared. Her eyes widened as she realized what she was experiencing. Peace. She couldn't remember how long it had been since she'd felt this way. Perhaps not since she'd agreed to marry Quinn.

She swallowed hard at the implications of that. She knew that marrying him had been the right thing to do. She *knew* it. Of course, she hadn't exactly asked for God's input or help since then. Now, she was freely admitting she needed help. She might need to tell Quinn the truth, but she didn't want to be foolish about it. She'd pick the opportune time and place for that to happen. To her way of thinking, a few things had to happen first—like them falling in love. And…well, that was pretty much it.

She set her parent's letter aside then dipped her pen in the ink well and began to write out her response. She thanked them for their congratulations before telling them truth about her marriage—that it was a matter of convenience not love. At least, not yet. She carefully blew the ink dry as she contemplated how to finish it.

> *Quinn doesn't know about the accident and*
> *I don't plan to tell him until I'm certain he loves*
> *me. I'm sorry if I've disappointed you by sharing*
> *this. I just wanted you to know so that you might*
> *pray for me—and for Quinn and the children. I*
> *have a feeling this road may not be an easy or a*
> *smooth one. However, I am holding on to the hope*
> *that it will be worth it.*

She signed the letter and couldn't help noticing how much better she felt having confessed everything to her parents. Somehow in doing so, it made the task before her seem less insurmountable.

She'd figured out the household chores this week. Maybe she wasn't doing them all perfectly but it was enough to build on. Now was the time to enjoy her family and past time to get to know the man who had become her husband. The man her mother had talked about in the letter. The one who would love her for everything she was—in spite of what she wasn't. Once she knew he did, she would tell him everything. She would. Even though the mere thought of it made her want to run back to the safety of her parents' arms.

Monday evening, Quinn paused outside door of the room he was supposed to share with Helen for the first time. He wasn't at all sure what to expect from her since they'd hadn't been alone with each other since they'd come up with the idea of sharing quarters. He'd made sure of that—not wanting to give her, himself or God the wrong idea about what this move would mean for their relationship. If the perplexed looks she'd been sending him lately were any indication, she'd certainly taken note of the increased distance between them. Hopefully, that distance would make things easier for them both tonight.

The sound of his knock seemed to echo through the heavens as thunder rolled in the distance promising some much needed rain for Quinn's crop of winter wheat. His misgivings swelled as Helen bid him enter, but he did so, anyway. There was no sign of her until he spotted a hint of movement behind the changing screen.

"Quinn, is that you?"

"Yep." He felt heat crawling up the back of his neck. He chanced a glance over his shoulder to find her watching him with a lifted eyebrow as she belted her dark pink dressing gown at her waist. He offered what he hoped was a passable smile. "Are you done in there?"

"It's all yours."

"Thanks." He grabbed his sleep shirt then waited for her to move aside before he slid past her and behind the screen. These things weren't meant for men. He could tell that by the flowery fabric and the fact that it barely came up to his chin. Feeling a little foolish, he changed clothes before leaping under the blanket of his bed as nonchalantly as possible. He stared at the ceiling for a long moment then couldn't resist peeking at Helen again.

She was brushing her hair with a frown on her face. Perhaps she was as ill at ease with this situation as he was. He cleared his throat. "If you're uncomfortable with me being in here, I can leave."

She set the brush aside and turned to face him. "Why should I be uncomfortable? You are my husband, aren't you?"

He felt his jaw tighten. "I reckon so."

"Do you? That's funny. You've been acting more like a stranger than anything else."

There was no way he was going to get into that with her. Not even if she was right. Obviously, this sleeping arrangement had been a mistake. He could only hope that God wouldn't hold it against him. Mindful of Helen's watchful gaze, he grabbed his pillow and a blanket. He only got halfway across the room before she caught his arm. "Where do you think you're going? We aren't finished with this conversation."

"Yes, we are." He shook his head, unable to reconcile the woman standing before him in defiance with the sweet-tempered woman he'd married. "*What* has gotten into you?"

She blinked her long dark lashes then loosened her hold on his arm until it became gentle and disturbing for an altogether different reason. Her tone softened though it retained an underlying strength and thoughtfulness. "I don't know, Quinn. Maybe it's the way you've been avoiding me for the last three days. Even before that, we hardly ever had any real conversations. And now… now, you can't even look at me."

All the charges she laid against him were true except one, so, of course, he needed to focus on that one. "What are you talking about? I'm looking right at you."

"No." She slowly shook her head. "You aren't looking *at* me. You're looking *through* me. You aren't really seeing me at all."

He wished he could say that she was speaking in riddles, but he knew exactly what she meant. He'd been trying to block her out of his senses. It had worked moderately well so far… Well, except for the fact that it had eventually made his normally even-keeled wife madder than a cat caught in a rainstorm. He needed to smooth things over, but how? He could apologize. However, that would probably require a subsequent change in his behavior, which would make it a whole lot harder to stay on the straight and narrow concerning his arrangement with God.

"You're still doing it." Helen crossed her arms and tilted her head. "You're still looking through me."

"Right." He searched his mind for something to say that would make her happy. Thinking wasn't really his strong suit. It was even harder now with her looking at him like that. "Let's sit down and, uh…talk."

He led her to the nearest object, and then hopped back up when he realized that object happened to be her bed. He settled on her vanity stool. That was still closer to her than he wanted to be, so he stood and started to pace. She must have mistaken that for an attempt to escape, for she dashed to the closed door and pressed her back against it to thwart him. Panic tightened his shoulders as she narrowed her eyes at him and seemed to be waiting for something to happen. *Oh, what does it matter? Either way, I'm not getting out of this unscathed, so I might just as well be done with it.*

He let out a short puff of air, braced his feet shoulder width apart and closed his eyes. His ears filled with the sound of the rain's rhythm drumming against the house. That's when he became aware that the scent of his room had changed. It smelled like her. It was a mix of the spiciness of snicker doodles, the clean scent of soap with an underlying trace of some kind of exotic perfume. No doubt it was expensive.

The rain drove harder against the house as he pushed that thought away.

Opening his eyes, he saw the caution in hers. They weren't just ordinary eyes, though. They were the kind he could stare into for hours and still not fully discover all of the mysteries they hinted at. His gaze fell to her lips, so often curving into a smile when she interacted with the children. Now they were pursed slightly to one side in challenge. Her delicately arched eyebrows lifted in a silent reminder that she was waiting on him.

He shook his head. "You're wrong. I may not have been looking, but I couldn't help seeing you...in glimpses."

"Glimpses?"

He stepped toward her. "I've seen your determination and persistence when it comes to the chores."

"You have?"

"Yes." He stepped closer again. "More important, I've seen love, compassion and patience with the children."

Her gaze clung to his. "I do love them."

"Yes, you do, and every day you make life better for them—for me, too." With most of the distance erased between them, he figured he was close enough—probably too close for his own good—so he stopped moving. "I *have* seen you, Helen."

She tucked her hair behind her ear. "Then why don't you show it?"

He frowned. "How do you want me to show it?"

"Let us get to know each other, actually have a relationship."

Thunder crashed above them. It couldn't drown out the sudden aloofness Quinn heard in his own voice. "We agreed to marry for the children's benefit not our own."

"Why do those two things have to be mutually exclusive? It would be to their benefit to have a healthy marriage modeled in their home."

Everything within him quieted at that. He tried the idea on for size and liked the way it fit. It wouldn't work, though. He hadn't asked God for a healthy marriage. He'd asked God for a helpmeet and hadn't even deserved to get that. He glanced up at the rafters shielding them from the storm raging overhead. "What we have will be enough. Mutual respect, shared goals, our love for them…" He trailed off as she began to shake her head. "What, Helen? What more do you want from me?"

"Exactly what I thought I was getting when I married you. A chance for companionship and caring. Perhaps one day even love." The hope that filled her eyes was destined to be disappointed.

No matter how much he found himself longing for the same thing, it couldn't happen. "I can't give you that."

She paled slightly then covered his mouth with her fingers. "Please don't say that, Quinn. You can't mean it. Leave me a little bit of hope."

He took both of her hands in his so that she couldn't keep him quiet. "I do mean it. The truth is I'm n—"

—*not worth hoping for,* he would have finished if she hadn't kissed him square on the mouth. The rest of the world faded away until it only comprised Helen, him, this moment. Yet, in the back of his mind, he *knew* she was only doing it to shut him up. That frustrated him to no end. Their kisses shouldn't be like this. They ought to be real and true and meaningful.

When she would have ended it, he gathered her closer and kissed her back, the way she *should* be kissed. She caught her breath in surprise then melted against him as the kiss turned into something far warmer, sweeter and gentler than she could have intended it to be. He pulled away once they were both good and breathless. "Look at me."

He waited until her dark lashes swept upward and her eyes focused on his. "Maybe I've no right to tell you what you can and can't hope for, even if I'm certain you'll be disappointed. However, I do have a right to tell you something else, so I want you to listen to me." He lowered his voice and kept his tone gentle yet firm. "This isn't a game between us. If you ever kiss me again, you'd sure as shooting better mean it. Understand?"

That infernal light of hope leaped into her eyes again. That's when he knew he'd done something wrong. It came to him as a flash of lightning illuminated the room. First, he shouldn't have kissed her back. Second, after kissing her he should have backed away, apologized and repented. He hadn't done any of that. Instead, he'd implied that another kiss was inevitable and acceptable. To make matters even worse, he'd done it out loud for God to hear and take notice. He groaned, "What have I done?"

A loud pop and the sound of shattering glass exploded through the room. Reflexively, he shielded Helen's body with his own until he determined that the danger had passed. He turned in time to see something roll across the floor toward him in the candlelight. He knelt down to find it was a clear orb of ice the size of an apple. His gaze reversed its path to the broken window above his bed while the popping sound surrounded the house. "Hail. It's a hailstorm."

Pounding sounded on their bedroom door. Helen

opened it to reveal Reece and Clara standing hand in hand. Clara threw her arms around Helen's legs. "We're scared!"

Reece rolled his eyes then jumped at a crash of thunder. "I'm not scared, but Trent is curled up in a ball and won't move. I promised to get a grown-up."

"I'll go." Quinn put the hailstone in Helen's washbasin before grabbing his blanket and pillow that had fallen to the floor at some point in their exchange. He handed them to Reece. "Hold on to these, son. Helen, get Olivia. We'll wait it out together in the hallway where there aren't any windows."

Quinn found Trent just as Reece had described him. The window was on the opposite side of the room from the bed, which put Trent in the direct trajectory of anything that might burst through it. Quinn situated himself between the boy and the possible danger before rubbing Trent's back. "Hey, cowboy, we're all going to camp out together in a safe place until this nasty ol' storm blows over. We're going to sing some cowboys songs, too. Would you like that?"

The little boy managed to nod.

"How about pretending I'm your horse so we can ride on out of here?" Quinn let out a sigh of relief when Trent uncurled himself to latch on. They cantered out of the bedroom into the hallway where Helen was getting everyone comfortable and warm. Olivia sat on her hip with eyes alternately widening and drooping from loud noises and sleepiness. Quinn sat down with Trent in his lap. Reece huddled closer to them. Clara moved closer to Reece. Helen and Olivia snuggled in next to Clara.

Helen leaned forward to look down the line. "Is everyone warm enough?"

Reece nodded. "We're getting there."

Trent threw his head back to look at Quinn expectantly. "Trent wants us to sing. What'll it be, folks?"

Clara reached for his hand. He was pretty sure the other one was holding Helen's. "'Old Chisholm Trail,'" she said.

Quinn cleared his throat and began to sing over the sound of the storm. "'Oh, come along, boys, and listen to my tale, I'll tell you all my troubles on the ol' Chisholm trail.'"

Reece and Clara immediately joined in on the chorus. Helen soon caught on and sang in a rich alto that blended nicely with his baritone. The song ended up being a great choice because there were many verses to it. It kept the children so distracted from the storm that they didn't seem to hear the window break in the kitchen or the living room. However, as five minutes turned to ten then twenty without any letup from the hail, Quinn found it increasingly hard to sing.

The wheat crop had been destroyed for sure. There was no doubt about it; and he had only himself to blame.

Chapter Nine

Helen leaned her head back against the wall in the hallway to listen to the hail peter out a good thirty minutes after that first ball of ice had crashed through the bedroom window. This night had not gone at all as Helen had hoped it would. She'd envisioned that she and Quinn would have a nice heart-to-heart chat then go to sleep in a companionable silence. Instead, all the emotions she'd stored inside from her talk with Isabelle, her mother's letter and Quinn's avoidance had swirled together to create a storm that had rivaled the one raging outside. The tension in that room had been palpable, leading up to the argument. It was then that everything Helen had wanted to say for days tumbled out in all the wrong ways.

She could hardly believe she'd been foolhardy enough to try to kiss him into silence. But in the moment, she'd been too desperate to think of anything else. And if she hadn't, she was certain she would have heard him proclaim that he could never love her. She refused to believe that. Besides, *never* was such an ugly word. It created a life empty of hope—one that was filled with desperation and fear. She knew that firsthand. Her fingers slid toward her abdomen only to encounter Olivia's slightly rounded tummy instead.

A smile tugged at Helen's lips as she leaned down to place a kiss on the sleeping child's head. She peered down the line to find that the children had all fallen asleep curled up together like a litter of newborn kittens. Her focus shifted past them to her husband. He sat with his head in his hand and his elbow braced on a propped-up knee. Her gaze traced the strong lines of his profile. She'd been trying to ignore it since he'd laid down the ground rules for their marriage, but the man was far too handsome for her peace of mind.

He turned his head slightly and pinned her with his cobalt stare. She ought to be embarrassed at getting caught staring at him. She wasn't. After all, what was there left for her to be ashamed of? She'd already all but begged him to give love a chance and had been turned down flat.

His gaze trailed down to her lips before returning to her eyes. She couldn't help remembering that, while she may have started their kiss, he'd finished it with an intensity that her left her breathless. She'd thought he'd experienced the same thing, but that was before remorse had filled his eyes and he'd muttered those simple words of regret. *"What have I done?"*

She kept her voice low so as not to awaken the children. "The hail may be over, but the storm doesn't seem to be letting up. Rain may be getting into the house through the broken windows in our room."

Our room. His slight wince at those words told her all she needed to know about his intentions of sharing it with her after their argument. He pulled in a deep breath, ran his fingers through his close-cropped brown curls and nodded. "Stay put. I'll inspect the house for damage."

She waited while he checked the children's rooms first then knelt beside her. "It looks like their rooms were spared because their windows didn't face the brunt of the storm. Let's get them back to bed and go from there."

After somehow managing to get all the children tucked in without waking a single one, Helen peered around Quinn's broad shoulder to stare into *her* room. The lantern he held aloft revealed the gaping black hole where the window should be, while a deluge of rain angled through the opening. "Oh, Quinn, your new mattress!"

She rushed forward to save it from being rained on. Quinn's arm snaked around her waist, lifting her off her feet and back to the threshold. "The floor is covered in glass. The last thing we need tonight is for someone to get cut."

She glanced down at her bare toes planted right next to his. "Shoes. They're in the living room by the front door."

"Stop." He caught her arm as she tried to dash away. "Let me check it out first. I think I heard a window break in there, too."

The living room window had shattered completely. Large pieces of glass mixed with rainwater, leaves, broken branches and hailstones to litter the floor from the front of the room by the settee all the way to the kitchen area in the back. Helen shook her head. "What a mess."

"We have to clean it up fast and good. I don't want the children to so much as walk through this on the way out the door until that glass has been taken care of. Or you, either. At least not without shoes, so hold still."

"Quinn." Her protest was soft and ineffectual, for they both knew someone would have to wade through that mess to get their shoes. She held her breath as she watched him pick his way across the floor toward the front door and put on his boots without incident. He grabbed hers and the children's, as well, before crunching over glass to meet her back in the hall. Before she could reach for her shoes, he was down on his knees guiding her feet into them as he'd often done with the children.

She placed her hand on his shoulder for balance and felt his muscles tense beneath her fingers. This was her problem. He was just so blasted sweet and gentle that it was hard to stay upset with him. She'd never really seen him riled until tonight. It had been a powerful thing to behold, yet not even for an instant had she felt threatened or scared by his strength. She swallowed. "Thank you. So, uh, what are we going to do about the windows? I mean, how will we keep the rain out?"

He stood and walked back into the living room to don his coat. "I'll need to board up the windows."

"Tonight?"

He must have heard the worry in her voice, for he allowed a hint of a smile to reach his lips and reassure her. "Right now. There's no use cleaning up the room if the weather is just going to keep making it a mess."

"How can I help?"

He frowned. "As much as I wish I could turn down your offer and keep you out of the weather, I'll need someone to hold the boards in place while I nail them.

I'll go get the supplies from the barn and meet you back here."

"Wait. Perhaps I ought to sweep up the glass first. If the children wake up, they'll come looking for us again and step on the glass."

"You can start sweeping while I get the supplies. In the meantime…" He slipped past her into her bedroom and returned lugging his mattress, which he used to block off the children's rooms. "That should slow them down or make them yell for us. Since they slept through the last of the hailstorm, hopefully they'll sleep through me pounding a few nails. Besides, this won't take long."

He was right and that was a good thing because the rain never let up for a moment while she held the boards in place for him. With the broken windows sealed up, they hurried back toward the front door. Helen suddenly realized Quinn wasn't behind her anymore. She turned to find he'd stopped halfway up the steps of the small porch. "Quinn?"

"I'm going to check the fields."

Her eyes widened. "Now? Can't that wait until morning?"

"I need to know." His gaze dropped to the porch steps. "I need to know what we're up against, if there's anything left."

"Oh." She stared in the direction of the fields as realization washed over her. How could it never have crossed her mind that all of Quinn's hard work and their family's livelihood was at stake? What would the impact of this be if the winter wheat crop was indeed lost? She had no idea where they stood financially. She should know. She should have asked. Here, she'd just criticized Quinn for not trying to get to know her, but had she truly taken an interest in anything that mattered to him beyond the children?

"Helen?"

She glanced back at him, saw the worry wrinkling his brow and nodded. "Go. I'll check on the children."

He returned her nod then hurried into the night. Helen found the children still sleeping, seemingly undisturbed by the activity around them, so she changed out of her sodden clothes and built up the fire in the stove to replace the heat that had been lost through the open windows. Her teeth had just stopped chattering, when a blast of cold, wet air announced Quinn's return. He closed the door behind him and leaned against it as rainwater dripped off his clothes and puddled around him. He had to see her standing near the fire, for she'd lit both of the lamps in the living room, but he seemed reluctant to look at her.

Silence stretched between them. It didn't matter. The grim look on his face said it all. They'd lost the crop.

She crossed the living room to meet him at the door. "You must be soaked and frozen through. You should change before you do anything else."

She hesitated only a moment before removing the slouch hat from his head and setting it on the hat rack. She felt his gaze on her as she unfastened the metal buttons of his slicker. He caught her wrist and she glanced up to find regret, guilt and even a hint a fear in his eyes. "I'm sorry, Helen."

"Why? None of this is your fault."

His lips firmed into a straight line. She recognized that look as the one she'd seen on Trent's face when she'd told him not to wander without her permission— stubborn disagreement. He released her wrist to shrug out of his yellow slicker and hang it on the coatrack. "I'll put on some dry clothes."

When he returned, he sat on an armchair near the fire, so she sat on the footrest in front of him. "Tell me."

He ran his fingers through his damp hair and sighed. "It took most of my savings to buy this property and fix it up to the standard it's at today. I invested what was left in the ground with the wheat I planted last spring. It wasn't a big crop, but the fall harvest was good. I reinvested much of the profit from that into the winter wheat. It's gone. All we have is what's left from the fall harvest."

"Will that be enough to last us until the spring?"

"I'll only be planting in the spring. We won't have any real income until I harvest the crop in the fall."

"I see." Her gaze shifted to the fire in the fireplace as she tried not to let her alarm show on her face. "Will we have enough until the fall then?"

"If nothing else goes wrong, if we're thrifty, if we have no other major expenses, we should be fine."

"That's a lot of *ifs*."

"Well, one thing is for sure, there won't be any additions built to this house. At least, not this year. And tonight's arrangement isn't going to work. I'll put the new mattress on the floor out here at night and back in the room during the day."

She'd expected as much so she signaled her agreement with a nod even though he didn't seem to be asking for it. "So we should be fine *if…*"

"Pretty much." He rubbed his stubbly jaw. "I know you aren't used to dealing with anything like this. I don't want you to worry. I'll do whatever is necessary to take care of this family."

"I know you will, Quinn."

He seemed to soak in her confidence before surprising her by reaching down to squeeze her hand. "Good. My family may never have the fancy things in life, but we won't ever have to go without the basics like food, clothes or a solid roof over our heads. I've kept that promise to myself ever since I got my first job working as an errand boy. I'm not going to break it now."

Her eyes widened as compassion filled her heart at the possibility of Quinn as a little boy being hungry or cold. He must have read the questions in her eyes, for he bristled. His jaw tightened as he released her hand. He warded off any comments with the shake of his head. "Forget I mentioned that."

She didn't want to forget it. However, she didn't want to make him uncomfortable, either, so she lifted her brow and offered a smile to ease the moment. "You may be glad to hear that I know a sight more about finances than I did about housework. My parents may be wealthy but they're still careful with their money. They make a budget each month that allows them to run the household, factor in all their expenses and set money aside for—" She froze, blinked. "Me. They set money aside for me. Quinn, I'm such a fool!"

"What? Why?"

"My dowry. It's quite extensive. I need to remind my parents to send it. Our marriage happened so fast and I've been so busy that I forgot about it completely. I guess they did, too." She grinned up at him. "I do believe that solves our problem, Quinn."

"A dowry?"

She narrowed her eyes. "Please, tell me I didn't lose you all the way back there."

"No, it's just… I don't want us taking any handouts from your parents."

She straightened her back and lifted her chin. "It isn't a handout. It's the money my parents have been saving for me since I was born. When we got married, what's mine became yours. So legally it belongs to you, too. We have every right to use it, especially if it's to help take care of the children."

He paused, seeming to consider this. "Well, I reckon if it already belongs to us, it's all right, then."

She opened her mouth to argue, only to close it upon the realization that he'd agreed far easier than she'd expected. Finding him watching her with a slow smile tugging at his lips, she lifted her chin. "Why are you laughing at me?"

"I'm not laughing." The statement was ruined by his chuckle. "I'm just coming to the realization that I married a woman with some fire in her bones. I wasn't really expecting that from you since you're so—"

"Prim, proper and perfect?"

"Yeah." He smiled at the reminder of the interaction that seemed so long ago now, though it had only been about two weeks.

"Well, I don't know about that. However, I suppose I can get fired up about certain things—like my family." She wanted to add, *And I might even be able to get fired up over you, if you'd let me,* but didn't dare. She'd already pushed him too far too fast during their conversation before the storm. That didn't mean this was over. She wasn't giving up. Somehow she'd get to know her husband, secure her place in his heart and tell him the truth. Right now, however, they had another obstacle to overcome. "I'll write to my parents about the dowry.

In the meantime, we'd better finish cleaning up if we want to get any sleep tonight."

Helen was so sure her dowry was the answer to all their problems. Quinn understood that their problems went deeper than that. Or rather, higher. He glanced up at the sky that was still gray and foggy after last night's thunderstorm. Quinn slapped the reins to urge the team down the field. The pressure of the plow caused the matted remnants of his wheat crop to give way to moist brown dirt beneath it, covering the signs of what he suspected might very well be God's punishment for Quinn's impetuous decision to kiss Helen.

He also had a feeling the effect of that kiss on his relationship with Helen would not be so easily or neatly buried beneath the surface as the ruined wheat was. Something essential had change between them. There was a new awareness…connection…openness… He wasn't entirely sure how to describe it, but he was certain that it was going to get him into more trouble. He couldn't afford that. Financially, Helen may have found a way to ease things for their family. Spiritually, Quinn figured he had a lot of work to do to get back on the Almighty's good side. Otherwise, it would all come to naught in the end.

"God, I'm sorry for kissing her." He frowned, realizing that wasn't entirely true. He might as well be honest since God knew his thoughts, anyway. "Well, let's just say that I'm sorry kissing her made me go back on our deal. I repent. If You'll forgive me, I'm more than willing to go back to our agreement."

"What agreement?"

Quinn choked on air at the sound of Helen's voice.

He turned to find her trailing after him with Olivia on her hip while Trent lagged a good distance behind, hopping across the upturned mounds of dirt in a game of his own making. Quinn suddenly realized he was no longer holding the reins, so he rushed around the horses to grab their bridles. He gathered the reins and tied them to the plow before turning to face his wife. "You shouldn't sneak up on a man working with horses. It's dangerous."

"I'm sorry." Her lashes lowered innocently. "I would have spoken sooner if I hadn't heard what you were saying."

He squared his shoulders as he sized her up, sass and all. She looked unapologetically feminine in a purple dress with little lacy black bows down the front. Her hair was half up and half down, which seemed to fascinate Olivia, since the girl's tiny fingers were tangled in the shiny brown locks. The wonder on the child's face told him Helen was in trouble. He stepped forward just in time to stop Olivia from giving a mighty yank to the hair in her grasp. "That was a private conversation between me and God."

"About kissing me."

Quinn stared down at her, then cleared his throat nervously. "Did you need something, Helen?"

"Dinner is ready, but I need you to answer my question." She narrowed her eyes and stepped even closer. "What agreement do you have with God and how exactly does it concern me?"

He ought to just go ahead and tell her. In fact, it would probably make things easier for him if she knew. Maybe she'd stop thinking the future could be any different than the present. Since he'd promised to stop ignoring her, it would be great if she could stop being so frustrating, attractive and inquisitive. "I've always done my best to be a good man, to fear the Lord, to make as little trouble for myself with the Almighty as possible. The children came and I found out that it wasn't enough. *I* wasn't enough. I needed something that I had no real hope of getting on my own. I asked God for a helpmeet. He gave me you—and because I knew I didn't deserve you, I promised in exchange that you would be here for the children and only for the children. I went back on that promise by kissing you."

He gestured to the desolate field around them. "You see? All of this *is* my fault. It happened because I was weak. I gave in to…"

"Temptation," she finished for him.

He felt the color rising in his face and he glanced toward the house. "I reckon I should have told you all of this before. I just didn't realize how high the stakes were."

She was quiet for a long time—a really long time. At least, it seemed that way while he was waiting in silence. When she spoke, her words were not at all what he expected to hear. "Quinn, you need to read the Bible."

Everything within him froze. His heart pounded in his ears. "What makes you think I don't read the Bible?"

"Pretty much everything you just said."

Stay calm. Just because she figured out you haven't read the Bible doesn't mean she's figured out that you can't read at all. He swallowed hard. He'd gotten quite adept at tuning out preachers over the years. A habit he'd picked up from so many Sundays trapped in the pew during the fire-and-brimstone sermons his grandmother's favorite minister had preached. Still, he made the only claim that might help at the moment. "I go to church."

Helen touched his arm. "I know you do, but that doesn't replace the need we have as believers to read the Word for ourselves. Why don't you?"

He carefully picked his words. "It's a little hard for me to understand."

She nodded. "That King James English can seem a bit antiquated at times, I will give you that. I have an idea, though. How about we read it together?"

How about let's not? He gritted his teeth to keep those words inside. "I don't think so."

"Please, Quinn. You need to hear the truth about God. He isn't anything like what you described. He isn't trying to punish you. He loves you. I can prove it to you with the Bible. Besides, I haven't been as connected to God lately as I should be, so this would benefit me, too."

He rubbed his jaw as he considered her words. Was it possible that Nana and her minister had been wrong? He didn't like to think so. Nana hadn't always been the easiest person to live with. However, she'd been pretty much all he had growing up with his mother dead, his father and brother gone, and the teasing he'd received for being slow at school leaving him without many friends. Her opinions had been the deciding factor in his life. Was he supposed to abandon all of that because Helen said it was wrong?

Then again, if he was being honest, Helen wasn't the first one to make him question his perspective on God. The few times he'd paid attention in Peppin's church, he'd heard things that hadn't lined up, either. He'd just attributed it to the difference in denominations. What if it was something other than that? Something more important?

"Quinn, what do you say? We can read the Bible this evening after the children go to sleep. Although, it would be nice if we included them in it once a week."

Oh, boy. She had it all planned out now. However, that bit about the children gave him an idea. He watched her carefully to see if his words aroused any suspicion in her. "I suspect you might be able to make it more exciting if you read it out loud like you do those adventure books."

"Then that's what I'll do."

He took a deep breath then nodded. "I suppose we could do it, then."

A slow smile blossomed on her lips and she threw one arm around his neck in a hug. He started to wrap an arm around her waist to pull her and Olivia closer— then settled for just lightly patting her back. Until he was certain what the truth was concerning God and His expectations, he'd better play it safe. He didn't want to get his hopes up that God wouldn't mind him caring for his wife. He just hoped he hadn't set himself down the path to destruction concerning the reading problem. If Helen found out the truth about that, even God's approval might not be enough to make this marriage work.

Chapter Ten

The boarded-up windows left the kitchen and living room about as dim as Helen felt that evening. In her resolve to find love with her husband, how had it never occurred to her that they weren't connecting spiritually? Her parents had often talked about how praying together had been one of the things that had helped draw them closer during the first few months of their arranged marriage. They'd also encouraged her to read the Bible every day, which was a habit she'd somehow lost after she'd moved to Peppin. Hopefully, all of that would change now.

Reece's heavy sigh drew her attention as she checked on the batch of dinner rolls baking in the oven. "Did everything go well at school today, Reece? No trouble from Jake?"

"Nah. He minds Miss Etheridge because their pa told her to spank Jake if he gives her any trouble." He made one final mark on his slate then glanced up at her. "I'm done. Will you check it for me?"

"Certainly." She added a pinch of salt to the pot of stew then left it to simmer on the back burner of the stove as she looked over the list of math problems. "You're doing great, honey. Look at the third one once more, though."

He glanced up with a sheepish smile after going through the steps again. "I forgot to carry the two, but I fixed it."

"Excellent." She gave in to impulse and kissed him on the forehead. He ducked his head a second too late to hide his smile. Helen glanced at Clara, who was working on her penmanship. The little girl must have been satisfied with her efforts, for a little smile curved her lips even as faint lines of concentration stretched across her forehead. Trent and Olivia imitated their older sibling by drawing on their own slates. Trent's strokes were slow and deliberate. Olivia's were pure abandonment.

"What?" Clara asked.

Helen blinked, realizing the older two were looking at her curiously. She grinned. "Y'all are so cute."

Clara giggled.

Reece groaned and made a face. "I'm not cute."

"Oh, yes, you are." She slipped into a nearby chair then leaned forward and lowered her voice to capture all of the children's attention. "In fact, I think you have about three seconds before the cuddle monster attacks."

All of their eyes widened. Clara and Reece exclaimed as one, "Cuddle monster?"

Helen nodded. Olivia's shoulders rose in anticipation at the playfulness in Helen's voice as she began to count. "One…"

Clara slowly backed her chair out from under the table and edged toward the living room, whispering loudly, "Reece, you'd better get Olivia out of her chair."

"Two…"

Reece jumped out of his chair and removed Olivia

from her high chair then urged her toward the living room. "Trent, run!"

Trent just stared at her with a serious look on his face that pulled at Helen's heartstrings. *Lord, please let him play. He needs it as much as the others, if not more.*

"Three!" She rounded the table, reaching for Trent. He slipped beneath the table and crawled to safety. She laughed with relief. "Clever boy! I'll get you yet, but first..."

Olivia was toddling toward her rather than away from her, so Helen lifted the girl into the air then kissed and tickled her until she screamed with laughter. Setting Olivia down, she managed to catch Reece next. He was too big for her to pick up, but she hugged him tight then blew a raspberry into his neck before tickling him until he went limp with laughter and ended up on the floor.

"What is going on in here?" Quinn's voice made everyone freeze. They'd been so noisy they hadn't even noticed him come inside for supper.

Clara rushed over to hide behind his leg. "Save me! Aunt Helen turned into the cuddle monster."

"She did?" Quinn lifted an eyebrow at her. Helen blushed and was ready to explain herself, when he gave her a quick wink. "That's funny. So did I."

Clara squealed as Quinn lifted her into his arms, spun her around, dipped her backward then kissed her cheeks. He set the girl down but kept ahold of her so she could regain her equilibrium. "Who's next?"

"Trent." Helen turned to find him slowly crawling toward the door. At the sound of his name, the boy picked up his pace. She was closest to him, so she hurried over to him. He tried to evade her grasp by wiggling like a little worm. "Oh, no, you don't."

She sank to her knees and dragged him back toward

her. Trent let out a screech of laughter. She barely had time to pull in a silent gasp before Quinn was on his knees in front of her. Their eyes met, sharing a wealth of hope, desperation and disbelief in an instant. Quinn began tickling the boy, whose hoarse laughter echoed through the otherwise silent room. Then an equally hoarse little voice said, "Stop! Stop!"

Quinn froze at the sound then sat Trent up. Helen couldn't resist taking the giggling little boy's face in her hands to plant a few kisses and raspberries. When she let go, he turned his bashful face into Quinn's chest as his uncle wrapped him in an embrace. Helen felt a small hand on her shoulder and glanced up to find Reece staring down at his little brother. Clara sat beside Quinn, pulling Olivia down to sit in her lap. Trent peeked out curiously as if wondering why everyone was so quiet. Reece sat down beside Helen and captured his brother's gaze. "Trent, you talked!"

Trent froze. His eyes widened in shock then filled with fear. He buried his face in his little hands and began to sob. Helen reached over to touch his knee. "Don't cry, honey. That's a good thing. A very good thing."

Clara inched closer, disturbing Olivia enough for the girl to seek out Helen's lap. "Yeah, Trent. It's good. Say something else. Say my name."

"No, say mine," Reece insisted.

Quinn hushed them both before gently asking, "What's wrong, Trent? Why haven't you been talking to us?"

Between the hoarseness and the crying, it was hard to understand him. "I wasn't supposed to make a sound."

"Why?"

"Mr. Jeff said so."

Helen looked to Quinn. "Who is Mr. Jeff?"

Reece answered instead, clearly in full-on protective big-brother mode. "Jeffery Richardson. He was Pa's assistant. He's the one who brought us here. Why'd he tell you that, Trent?"

"I heard him talking about our inherance."

"Inherance?" Helen narrowed her eyes. "Do you mean inheritance?"

Trent nodded. "He said not to make another sound unless I wanted my brothers and sisters to go away like my parents did. So now…now, you're all going to die!" The last word ended in a wail.

Quinn frowned. "No, we aren't. He can't hurt you— any of you. I won't let him. Besides, he's long gone and good thing, too, because if he wasn't, I'd teach him a lesson he'd not soon forget."

Helen sniffed at the funny smell wafting through the room then gasped. "The rolls!"

She set Olivia on the floor then jumped to pull the baking tin from the oven. Grimacing at the burnt rolls, she set aside the few worth saving as Quinn joined in the kitchen. "What do you make of all of this, Quinn?"

"I don't know anything about an inheritance. It's never been mentioned before. Not by Richardson or the children."

"I hate to say this, but my first thought was that this Mr. Richardson might have stolen it."

He grimaced. "Mine, too. Why else would he want Trent to keep quiet about it?"

"What should we do?"

"I don't know yet." He watched the children with a furrowed brow. His expression was so fierce, so protective, so loving that she couldn't look away. He glanced at her and his eyes widened before he reached into his pocket to pull out a thick envelope. "Oh, I almost forgot. I stopped by the post office today. They had this for you."

"It's from my parents. Maybe they sent my dowry." She opened the letter to find that a check had been included. She glanced at it before handing it to Quinn so she could investigate the rest of the contents. "It's made out to both of us, so you should be able to deposit it without any problems."

She heard him suck in a quick breath. "Helen, this is too much. Surely your father can't spare this."

"Nonsense. I told you they've been saving it for me." She was surprised to find one sheet of the letter was addressed to Quinn individually while the rest was intended for her. She spared a quick glance at her husband and seeing he was still somewhat dazed by the amount of the check, she scanned his page to make sure her parents hadn't given away her secret. She was relieved to find it was simply a newsy letter welcoming him to the family. They expressed the hope that he would correspond with them so that they could get to know their new son-in-law. It also asked if it would be possible for the family to come to Austin for a reception in Helen and Quinn's honor. "Quinn, they wrote to you."

"They did?"

"Yes, here. They want us to come for a visit." She handed him the page and realized there was another sealed envelope inside the original one. Her name was written on the front of it. She froze as she recognized the handwriting from the myriad little notes they used to exchange despite living in the same city. It was from Thomas Coyle, her ex-fiancé. Why would he write to her after all of these months and why would her parents include his letter with their own? She glanced at

Quinn, who seemed engrossed in his own letter. "I'll be right back. I just want to read this really quickly."

"Go ahead." He tucked his part of the letter into his pocket. "I'll get the children to wash their hands and move their schoolbooks for supper."

"Thank you." Moments later, she closed her bedroom door and leaned against it to read her parents' letter for some explanation. She found it toward the end.

I know you will be surprised to find the other letter we've included here. Thomas came to us quite desperate to explain himself and begging for your address. We did not feel it wise to give it to him. However, we promised to include his letter with one of our own. You are, of course, under no obligation to read the letter, but I thought it might help on the off chance you needed closure as much as Thomas seemed to. If not, forgive us for interfering.

Helen set her parents' letter on the desk then sat in the chair to stare at her name printed in Thomas's succinct handwriting on the outside of the envelope. Were her parents right? Did she need to hear from Thomas to be able to put the past behind and move on? She broke the seal on the letter.

A knock sounded on her bedroom door. A hoarse little voice called from the other side of it. "Aunt Helen, we're hungry!"

She smiled. Tossing Thomas's letter in the desk drawer, she closed it firmly. She didn't need closure. The past was over. Her future was on the other side of that door and she wasn't about to ignore it.

Chapter Eleven

Anticipation thrummed through Quinn's veins as he watched Helen flip through the thin leaves of her Bible later that evening. He leaned forward in his chair by the fireplace when her finger trailed down one of the pages and stopped. She glanced up with a hint of nervousness in her smile. He returned it and, though he knew he was on shaky ground when it came to getting through this with his secret and his pride intact, he wanted to ease her mind. "No need to be nervous about this. I want to hear what you have to say."

Relief lowered her shoulders. "Thank you. It's just— I'm no expert here, so I may not have all the right words or the right answers."

"You don't have to." He gave her a supportive nod. "Go on now."

"First, I want to make sure that I understood you correctly when we spoke earlier. It seemed to me that you were saying God had punished you for taking advantage of a blessing not meant for you by sending that hailstorm."

"That's about right."

She nodded. "Well, then. Punishment only comes after someone is condemned, or in other words, judged to be guilty. Right?"

He frowned. "What do you mean?"

"Wouldn't you make sure that one of the children really did something wrong before punishing them for whatever they were accused of?"

"Of course."

"Keep that in mind as I read this. It's from John 3:17. Jesus is speaking and he says, 'For God sent not His Son into the world to condemn the world, but that the world through Him might be saved. He that believeth on Him is not condemned...' Now, you believe that Jesus is the Lord, don't you?"

"Yes, I do."

"Then God is not condemning you, which means you won't experience the consequences of condemnation."

His brain had a bit of trouble wrapping around that. "Why did the hailstorm happen right after I kissed you, then?"

"Quinn, that hailstorm would have happened whether we'd kissed or not. I'm sure the storm had more to do with the season changing from autumn to winter than anything else." Helen tapped the Bible. "God's word, on the other hand, never changes. It says He isn't trying to punish you. In fact, I think He's trying to show how much He loves you."

He gave her a doubtful look. "By allowing our crop to be ruined?"

"Perhaps." She lifted one shoulder in a shrug. "After all, it did bring you here to this moment where you could hear the truth."

He tried real hard to think that through, but he couldn't help being distracted by the vision sitting across from him. There was something so beautiful about Helen in this moment. Perhaps it was the eagerness on her face, the soft upturn to her lips or the way her pink dressing gown brought out the same shade in her cheeks. Was it talking about the Bible that had put that sparkle in her eyes, or had it always been there?

"Oh, and by the way, Quinn…" She lifted an impervious brow. "I kissed you first."

He tensed as Helen moved from the settee to sit on the footrest in front of his chair the way she had the night of the storm. He really needed to move that thing. He tried not to stare at the Bible in her hands. Surely she wouldn't make him read it. "What does that have to do with anything?"

She gave him a look that made his heart ram against his rib cage. "It means 'the blessing' was not taken advantage of."

"You weren't?"

"No, and, if you insist on thinking of me that way, I won't complain, but there is something you ought to know about God's blessings."

"What's that?" Maybe if he kept her talking she'd forget about the book. Nope. She opened it and flipped a couple of pages over. His hand clutched the arms of the chair, his knuckles turning white. "Helen, you've given me a lot to think about. Maybe we should call it a night."

"One more verse then I'll leave you alone." She angled the book toward the light from the fireplace and began to read. "'Or what man is there of you, whom if his son ask bread, will he give him a stone? Or if he asks for a fish, will he give him a serpent? If ye then, being evil, know how to give good gifts unto your children, how much more shall your Father which is in heaven give good things to them that ask Him?' To whom does the Father give good things?"

"Huh?" He'd been too panicked to pay attention.

"Listen." She read the verse again and asked the same question.

"He gives good things to them that ask Him."

She closed the Bible, much to his relief. "Who asked God for a helpmeet, a mother for his children?"

"I did," he said quietly.

She responded in the same volume. "So to whom did God give good things?"

"Me. He gave them to me."

Silence stretched between them as they stared into each other's eyes. He wasn't at all sure at what point he'd leaned forward during their conversation, but his face was dangerously close to hers. Or, *was* it truly dangerous if God wasn't out to get him? Yet, how did that new information or anything else that Helen said account for the misfortune that had fallen upon his father and brother? He suddenly realized it didn't. They'd done it to themselves. It had been a consequence of reaching out for something they didn't deserve. He would be doing the same thing if he closed the distance between him and Helen.

He leaned back in his chair. Her lashes swept down to cover her eyes, so if she was disappointed it didn't show. Patting his knee, she stood and placed the Bible on the end table next to him. "Now I'm done. Good night, Quinn."

"Night, Helen."

She went to her room without looking back once, which left him free to try to rub at the warm impression her hand had left on his knee. His mind kept replaying that last verse, "how much more shall your Father which is in heaven give good things." It was a nice idea even if it was contrary to what he'd thought he'd known. Imagine—God going above and beyond on his behalf. Was that why God had given him a princess for a helpmeet?

If so, it wasn't fair to Helen or him. Quinn was no prince. Far from it. He'd lived much of his life dirt-poor. Now he made his living out of the dirt as a farmer who might not have made it to his next harvest without an influx of money from his wife's wealthy parents. He was a Christian man who apparently knew very little about his faith. If that wasn't enough, he was uneducated and illiterate.

He set the Bible on his knee. It opened to a place bookmarked by a thin red ribbon. His rough fingers smoothed over the delicate page filled with words. It was a code he'd never learned to crack. He'd always told himself he didn't mind, that it didn't matter. He could no longer pretend. It was torture having so much knowledge, life and truth at his fingertips yet totally unreachable.

At least he now knew that God wasn't waiting to strike him down for his next mistake. That was a relief. However, it didn't really change anything about who he was or what he should expect out of life. He would never measure up to the man he wanted to be— the man Helen deserved. That was the truth, too, and there was no changing it.

"Mama."

Helen turned her mount toward the distant call. Peering through the thick forest surrounding her, she waited for it to sound again. This time it came as a terrified scream. "Mama!"

The horse leaped forward as Helen galloped through the trees, chasing the child's cry. Low-hanging branches slapped against her face, painting angry red welts upon her skin. The cries grew louder. She was close. Suddenly, the ground disappeared before her. The horse reared backward, searching for stable ground and throwing her from the saddle. She sailed through the air.

Crashing through prickly bushes, she rolled to a stop at the base of a tall oak tree. Pain lanced through her body. She couldn't move. She couldn't breathe. She could only stare at the branches overhead that were wide and thick as they entwined to block out the sky.

Footsteps crunched through the dead leaves and stopped. Quinn stood over her. He was so tall, so strong. His gaze bored into hers with an intensity that made her shiver. His gaze trailed to her lips and stayed there as he knelt. She thought for sure that he would kiss her. Instead, his hands began to probe her abdomen with enough force to make her eyes smart with pain. His voice was rough, harsh, unyielding. "Damaged. Damaged. Damaged."

"No," she whimpered. "Help me. Please."

His lip curled in disgust. "I can't help you. No one can. You did this. You brought it on yourself with your own recklessness."

She grabbed his arm as he stood. "Please, Quinn—"

"No." His gaze was steady. "I don't want you. I will never love you. Now, let me go."

Stunned, she released him. He disappeared, leaving her alone and broken in the silence.

Helen jolted awake, gasping for breath. Her shaking fingers searched the night table for a match. Lighting the lamp beside the bed, she turned it up as bright as it could go to dispel the murky darkness surrounding her. The light couldn't take away the memory of the

dream as she lay in bed examining each aspect of it as
one might pick at an old wound.

Mama. A child had called her "Mama." Tears pooled
in her eyes and spilled down her cheeks. Not even in
her dreams had she been able to reach that which she so
longed for. Then to somehow confuse the sentiments of
her family's doctor concerning her injury with Quinn's
face, form and unspoken words. It was too much to bear.

A soft knock sounded on her door. No doubt it was
Quinn coming to awaken her as he did every morning. Dashing the tears from her cheek, she called, "I'm
awake. You—"

The door opened.

"—don't need to come in."

Seeing she was awake, Quinn stopped in his tracks.
"Sorry, I didn't— Hey, are you all right?"

"I'm fine." She threw back the covers then splashed
her face with water from the pitcher and bowl on her
nightstand to remove the traces of tears from her face.
"I just had a bad dream."

"It must have been pretty awful. You look…shaken."

She met his gaze in the mirror as she patted her face
dry with a towel. For a moment, the whisper of his
words from the dream seemed to fill the room. *Damaged. Damaged. Damaged.*

She couldn't seem to stop the tears from filling her
eyes again, so she closed them. She felt his hand on
her arm an instant before he turned her toward him
and enveloped her in his arms. She rested her cheek
on his firm chest, allowing the reality of his strong
arms around her to chase away the sinking feeling in
her stomach. Of course, if he knew the truth about her,
his reaction might be closer to what it had been in the
dream. Or, at the very least, closer to Thomas Coyle's.

"Do you want to tell me about it?" His deep voice rumbled in her ear. "That always seems to help the children if they have a nightmare."

She shook her head. "I'll be fine."

He pulled back enough to look her in the face. "You're sure?"

"Yes," she said, though she avoided meeting his gaze. "I'd better get ready. Are you putting in the new windows today?"

"Yep, Rhett is coming by to help me with it this afternoon."

"That's good." She gathered clothes for the day and saw her finished response to her parents sitting on the desk in the corner. Thomas's letter was still in the drawer where she'd tossed it. Perhaps that's what had brought on the dream. That letter she hadn't read. Well, she certainly wasn't going to read it now. "I'd like to mail the response to my parents' letter today."

He scratched the shadow he'd yet to shave from his cheek. "I, uh, haven't written mine yet. I probably won't have time to do it until after I install the windows."

"That's good. You can mail it when you pick up the children from school, then."

He nodded. "Well, I'll let you get dressed."

For an instant, she thought she saw a pensive look on his face. She turned to question it, but he was already out the door, so she let it go and focused her attention on getting ready for the day. Hopefully, it would only get better from here. How could it get any worse?

That odd feeling was back—the one he'd had after Helen had explained why she'd become a teacher. Of course, anyone who'd seen her after the nightmare she'd had this morning would have come to the conclusion that something was bothering her. Whatever it was, she wasn't telling. Not that Quinn had any room to be offended by her secrecy since he was currently holed up in the tack room with her parents' letter. Still, he was concerned and it was distracting him from a very important task.

"Anything else you want me to add to this letter?" Rhett sat on a stool in front of the thin workbench where he worked as a somewhat reluctant coconspirator in the mission to keep Quinn's illiteracy a secret.

"I'm not sure." Quinn left his post near the door where he was supposed to be keeping watch to look at the piece of paper his friend had been writing on. "You're using your best penmanship, aren't you? Helen's folks are fancy people. I want to make a good impression."

Rhett seemed genuinely confused. "I thought you wanted me to be as sloppy as possible so they wouldn't want to write you again."

"Not funny."

"You asked for it."

"Save the jokes for later. Can you read what you've written so far?"

"Sure." Rhett leaned his elbow onto the workbench for a closer look at the letter.

Dear Mr. and Mrs. McKenna, Thank you for the letter. It was kind of you to welcome me to your family. Helen and I accept your invitation to visit—

The distinctive sound of the barn door closing made them both jump. Quinn's heart skipped a beat then made up for lost time by pounding in his chest. He rushed to the partially open tack-room door to peer into the barn. No one was there...which meant someone had been. Maybe Trent had been wandering again. But if so, the boy would have come right into the tack room. That meant the person had probably been… "Helen."

"You don't know that."

"No, but I'd better find out." Quinn jogged through the barn then into the barnyard. The children were playing in the nearby meadow and Helen was walking at a fast clip toward them in a direct line from the barn. Dread slammed into his chest with enough force to ease the air from his lungs in a groan. The sound made Helen hesitate then stop. Slowly, she turned to face him. He swallowed hard, forced himself to close the distance between them, all the while controlling the urge to run the other way.

Use your head, man. Play it safe. Maybe she didn't hear everything. Maybe you can explain it away. He couldn't quite make himself meet her eyes, so he stared at the ground between them. "Were you in the barn just now?"

Her voice was soft. "Yes."

"Did you need something? I was in the tack room. You should have called out. I would've—"

She placed a hand on his arm, mercifully stopping his flow of word. Feeling his jaw tighten, he finally lifted his gaze to meet hers. The surprise and confusion lingering in hers told him she'd heard more than enough to know the truth. "Why didn't you tell me, Quinn?"

"I… I never tell anyone." He gestured toward Rhett, who was giving them wide berth en route to the children. "Well, I had to tell Rhett because I needed someone to read the Bachelor List for me."

"You couldn't read the Bachelor List." The tone in her voice and the widening of her eyes told him that she was finally beginning to understand the immensity of his limitations.

"No, I couldn't." He stepped backward out of her grasp. "Well, now you know."

Turning away, he strode toward the field. Be it pity, disgust, disillusionment or outright laughter; he didn't want any part of whatever might come next from her reaction. At least, not right now. Not while he felt so naked, so ashamed.

"Quinn, wait." That was all the warning he had before she caught his arm and slid in front of him. He stumbled into her and had no choice but to pull her close to keep them both from going down. She frowned up at him. "You've got to stop walking away from me when we have a problem."

He shook his head. "This isn't your problem. It's mine."

"It doesn't matter. We'll face it together. Please, don't walk away from me." Her plea ended in a near whisper as her eyes glistened with unshed tears.

He stared at her in disbelief. How could it be that after finding out the truth about him she had run toward him rather than away? It didn't make sense. Yet, she stood before him looking concerned and hurt. He wasn't at all sure how to respond. "Helen, I need to walk. I need to think."

She looked at him for a long moment then gave a single nod before releasing him. He walked a few steps alone then took a deep breath and did one of the bravest things he'd done since asking her to marry him. Turning toward her, he held out his hand. "Are you coming?"

Chapter Twelve

Without hesitation, Helen slipped her hand into Quinn's grasp. Relief softened his features, prompting a hint of a smile on his lips. She followed his troubled gaze to the wooded hills surrounding the farm. The trees bedecked in sable, orange and yellow leaves contrasted sharply against the somber gray sky. She knew neither of them was truly concerned with the view and merely needed time to gather their thoughts.

The wail of Rhett's harmonica sounded above the wind, reminding Helen of why she'd gone into the barn in the first place. She'd wanted to find out if the men would play together for the children. She hadn't been trying to eavesdrop. However, it had been impossible not to hear what Quinn and Rhett were saying as she'd approached the tack room.

Momentary shock had rooted her in place long enough to grasp a full understanding of the situation. Needing time to figure out what she should do next, she'd left the barn only to have Quinn follow her.

She had many questions but didn't want to make the situation harder for him by asking them. She was relieved when he broke the silence between them, even if his tone was defensive. "I can't read. So what? Not everyone can. I've managed just fine until now."

If it didn't bother him that he couldn't read, he wouldn't have kept it a secret. She knew that from experience. However, it would hardly help the situation to make him admit his obvious fear and embarrassment. "I know that not everyone can read and write, but why can't you?"

The question seemed to catch him off guard, so she waited while he mulled it over. She saw the moment he settled on an answer, for his features clouded with pain then resignation. He stopped walking, took her other hand in his and looked her in the eye. His voice deepened in all seriousness and sincerity. "Well, Helen, the truth is... I'm just plain stupid."

Her mouth fell open. She stared at him, blinked, shook her head. "What? You don't really believe that."

"I *know* it. Granted, I've gotten pretty good at hiding it over the years, but I am not a smart man. That's just a fact."

"That is *not* a fact."

He released her hands to comb his through his close-cropped curls. "Look, you've got to accept—"

"No, I don't, and neither do you, because it isn't true." She started walking again. "No, there has to be another explanation."

He sighed as he caught up with her. "There isn't. I just couldn't figure it out."

"What do you mean? No one just figures it out. You have to be taught. Did you go to school?"

He grimaced. "Yeah, I went a couple of times. That was enough for me. I hated it."

"Why?"

"After my ma died, Pa couldn't seem to find the strength or will to take care of himself or his sons, so I was a ragged, dirty little thing when I first started going. The other children picked on me incessantly because of it. Meanwhile, the teacher seemed to take an instant dislike to me. Once she discovered reading didn't come as easy to me as arithmetic, she began making pitying remarks about my 'lack of intelligence.' She'd finish my lessons for me because I was 'too slow' even if I was going at the same speed as the others. The other children picked up on it and it only made the teasing worse."

"That's just...*abhorrent*. As a former teacher, I can't imagine doing that to one of my students." Helen shuddered at the thought. Yet, hearing his story gave her insight as to one of the reasons why Quinn had been so passionate about taking proper care of his nieces and nephews. He didn't want them to experience what he had as a child. That brought to mind Reece's attempts to protect Clara from being teased. "What about your brother? Did he try to stop them from teasing you?"

"My brother was six years older than me and had already had his fill of being teased at school himself by that point. After a couple of weeks, I followed his example in refusing to go. That worked until my grandmother came to live with us. She fussed some sense into Pa, cleaned us up and sent me back to school. Nothing at the schoolhouse had changed, so I started skipping again. Pa eventually figured out what I was doing and said if I didn't go to school I'd have to get a job, so I went to work."

Concern furrowed her brow. "How old were you then?"

"Eight or nine."

Her eyes widened. Their lives had been so different.

At that age, her only concern had been what dessert the cook would serve at dinner or how to convince her parents to have a tea party with her. Meanwhile, Quinn had been taking on the responsibilities and work ethic of a grown man. "And you never went back to school?"

"Never set foot in one again until the children came to live with me. My brother taught me a bit more arithmetic, but I refused to even attempt the reading and writing. My grandmother tried to teach me when I was older. She couldn't see too well by that point, so I ended up more confused than I'd started out."

"See?" She lightly nudged his arm with her shoulder while not even attempting to temper her triumphant smile. "I told you it didn't have anything to do with intelligence. The problem is that you've never studied with a proper teacher."

It was as plain as the scowl on his face that he knew exactly where she was going with this. "I suppose you think you're the proper teacher for me."

"Well, I am certified to be a teacher even if I wasn't one for very long. As for being proper..." She tilted her head and shrugged. "I do believe you've described me that very way several times in the past."

He caught her arm and, with gentle force, turned her to face him. His pure blue eyes deepened as he searched hers—for what she wasn't sure. However, what she found in his was unmistakable. She saw the pain of old wounds hidden but unhealed, shame at a past foisted upon him then adopted as part of his identity and a desperate hope for something unattainable. In his eyes, she saw a reflection of herself. Yet, even in the face of his compelled honesty, she dared not reveal just how much she could empathize with his struggle, for there was one major difference. He had the ability to change his circumstances. She did not.

Still, he held back, though his scowl softened to a frown as he shook his head. "I appreciate the offer, but nothing doing."

"Why not?"

"It wouldn't work."

She tilted her head as she considered him. The decision to learn had to be his or he would have neither the confidence nor the will to succeed. "Quinn, not once in my weeks of knowing you and living with you has the word *stupid* even crossed my mind concerning you. Don't cheat yourself into thinking that's only because you were good at hiding it. I would have seen the signs of that just as surely as I did for this, even if I didn't know how to interpret them."

He frowned. "You were suspicious?"

"No, but I probably would have been soon enough." She paused, wondering if she'd been inadvertently giving away hints that she had a secret, as well. At least there was little chance hers would be revealed so long as Quinn continued sleeping in the living room. She displaced the thoughts with a quick toss of her head. "That is neither here nor there. What matters is that I've seen you just as you said you'd seen me the night we— The night of the storm."

A worried look returned to his face. "What do you see when you look at me, Helen?"

"I see an *intelligent* man." She dared to smooth the worry lines from his brow. "A man who is steady, kind, self-sacrificing, talented and…"

He must have noticed the color she felt warming her cheeks, for he cocked his head and edged slightly closer. "And what?"

The word *handsome* hovered on her lips, but she replaced it with a secretive smile before settling on a different word altogether. "Brave. Brave enough to face the mountain of illiteracy and make it a mere stepping stone. I can help you do that if you'll let me."

Though obviously listening intently, he'd glanced away to stare into the distance while she spoke. He released a heavy breath. Finally, he met her gaze again. Reluctance had changed to a hunger she suspected would only be sated by knowledge. Whether he knew it or not, he'd just reached a decision.

If he didn't get his nerves under control, Quinn was sure he was either going to pass out or lose his supper. The sight of Helen spreading out her teaching supplies on the kitchen table sure didn't help his efforts to calm down. He reminded himself that he needed to man up if only because he couldn't take another blow to his pride after being found out yesterday. That on top of needing to ask Rhett for help again and needing Bible lessons from his wife... Well, come to think about it, he didn't really have much pride left to protect. What little was left probably wouldn't survive the night.

Helen had been eager to get their reading lesson under way once the children had fallen asleep. The reading lessons he'd agreed to for reasons he couldn't fathom. As if her knowing about his illiteracy wasn't bad enough. Now she was going to experience his lack of intelligence firsthand. Her words to the contrary had been sweet and inspiring if not entirely accurate. The ways she'd described him had bolstered his courage— perhaps a little too much. Particularly that talk about being brave, since he was pretty near sure she'd been about to say something else entirely.

He couldn't get that secretive little smile or her blush out of his mind. It wrestled for dominance with all the memories of the times he'd tried to learn to read and failed. Well, he hadn't tried that many times, but that was for good reasons. Reasons Helen seemed bent on discovering as she slid a piece of paper and pencil his way. He stared at them. Quinn hadn't asked God for anything since he'd been given Helen. Now might be a good time to try out what he'd recently learned about God's giving nature.

He closed his eyes. *God, I don't think Nana was wrong about You knowing my every thought, even if she was wrong about some other things. The Bible says You give good things to those who ask. It would be a real good thing if You could give me some help...or a way out. I'm not choosy. Please, Lord, I'm asking You to help me.*

He took a deep breath and felt his pounding heart begin to slow to a more relaxed rhythm. This wasn't the end of the world. It was just learning with a new teacher. He could do this. He *would* do this. At least until Helen gave up.

He opened his eyes at the sound of Helen dragging a chair closer to him. She squeezed his shoulder then settled in beside him. "Ready?"

"Yes." *No. Maybe.* He attempted a smile, which she returned eagerly. She was enjoying herself already and the lesson hadn't even begun.

"Before we start, you should know this is going to take time. Don't expect to learn everything overnight. Be patient with yourself."

He wasn't expecting to learn much of anything, so

he'd have no problems there. He nearly groaned. Who was he fooling? He wanted to learn to read—desperately. That's why he'd agreed to this crazy scheme. He wanted to know once and for all if there was something truly lacking in him or if, as Helen had suggested, he only suffered from lack of proper instruction. "How much time would it take for me to learn to read?"

"As much or as little as you need. It also partially depends on what you know so far."

"I can write my first name." He demonstrated.

"That's good! Can you tell me the names of the individual letters that make up your name?"

He touched the pencil point to the paper beneath the first letter. "*Q-u-i-n-n*. Quinn. That's it. That's all I know. No. Wait. I don't know what this letter is called, but it's how your name starts. I remember because it sort of looks like a longhorn."

She laughed. "I've never thought about it before but you're right. It does. That's an *H*."

"How many other letters are there?"

"There are twenty-six letters in the alphabet. They look like this." She wrote them out across the top of the paper for him.

He gave a low whistle. "How am I ever going to remember all those?"

"You already know a few of them. Can you find the letters in your name among the others?"

"Yep." He pointed each of them out as he found them. "That's strange. The *Q* doesn't seem to be here."

"This is the *Q*."

"Why does it look different?" He couldn't hide the alarm in his voice. "Have I been writing it wrong all these years?"

"You've been writing it correctly. Each letter comes

in two forms—uppercase and lowercase. We usually use the uppercase form to start a sentence or a name. That's why these are both *Q*." She wrote the uppercase letter directly over the lowercase then did the same with *H*. "These are both *H*."

He stared at the paper, wondering what the other uppercase letters looked like. First… "Show me the rest of the letters in your name."

She did so, filling in the uppercase forms of those letters as she went. Then he asked her to do the same with the names of Reece, Clara, Trent and Olivia. There were still some letters to uncover, but he slid his paper toward Helen. "Can you write our family's name all together in one place?"

She smiled and slid the paper back toward him. "I think it would be better if you did. I'll spell them out for you. Remember that with names the first letter will be uppercase and all the rest will be lowercase. You already have your name written down, so suppose we start with mine."

It must have taken a while with her telling him the letters, him finding them on the list and then learning how to write them. However, before he knew it, he had all of their names written on his paper. The letters were big and a little misshapen. Yet he couldn't help feeling a sense of pride while looking at them. He sent a self-deprecating smile to Helen. "It's kind of sloppy."

She returned his smile with tears in her eyes as she shook her head. "It's beautiful."

"What about the other letters? There are still a lot of them I don't know and I want to see their other forms."

"Then let's go over them." She went through the alphabet, filling in their uppercase counterparts and teaching him how to write both forms of the letters.

By the time she was finished, Quinn felt himself drifting toward confusion. "I'm never going to keep them straight even if I manage to remember them."

"Sure you will, because I have a song that will help."

"A song?" He couldn't help perking up at that.

She winked. "I thought you'd like that. It's called 'The Alphabet Song.' As you sing, I want you to focus not just on the melody or sequence of the letters, but on remembering what each looks like. Got it?"

"Yes, but will I be able to play it on my banjo?"

She laughed. "I have no idea. Maybe. Now listen, repeat after me and do as I do. Ready?"

"Yep."

She touched the appropriate letter when she sang it. He repeated after her, copying the melody and her actions as she walked him through the song. They did the same thing twice more. Then they sang it together. Finally, he sang it on his own. She clapped for him when he finished, though she did so softly so as not to disturb the sleeping children. "Bravo, my good man."

He managed a small bow even though he was seated at the table. "Thank you. What now?"

"That's all for tonight. You've accomplished a lot and I don't want to overdo it on our first lesson. However, you should know that I am thoroughly impressed with you."

"You are?"

"Most definitely." She yawned and he realized that he'd been so involved with the lesson that he hadn't noticed how late it was getting. "You catch on quickly."

"I do?"

Her heavy lashes blinked drowsily. "You do. Now it's time for sleep. Morning will come early and you'll want to be rested for our lesson tomorrow. Good night."

"Wait." He stood with her then lifted her chin so

that her gaze focused on his. "I said it earlier in jest. I want to say it again from the bottom of my heart. Thank you. I never thought I'd be able to learn even this much. Now I'm beginning to think that maybe I can do this, after all."

"Then you'd be right."

It would be so easy to taste the sweet smile blossoming on her lips, but he doubted that she'd want him to. Sure, she'd kissed him once before, but that had only been to shut him up. Besides, as wonderful as she had been about his illiteracy problem, it had to have lowered her opinion of him—even if she didn't show it. In fact, she probably *wouldn't* show it so as not to make him feel worse about himself. That was just the kind of thing she would do because she was smart and patient and far too good for him.

Pulling in a deep breath, he released her chin and let her retire for the night with nothing more than a softly spoken good-night. He sat back down at the kitchen table to stare at the papers on the table—papers on which he'd written letters he now recognized. Something within him quickened. He may not deserve Helen now, but if he could learn to read…perhaps he could earn her.

Why hadn't he thought of that before? Surely, if he made himself a better man, he'd deserve better things and he wouldn't have to worry about ending up like his father and brother. It would need to be more than just learning to read, though. He'd need to become a better Christian, father and husband. It wouldn't be an easy task. Yet, if it would give him a chance to earn Helen, then he had to take it.

Chapter Thirteen

Two weeks after Quinn's first lesson, Helen cleared the books and paper he'd been using from the kitchen table to make room for breakfast. She'd just set them on the end table by the settee when he clomped in from outside with an armful of wood for the stove. He stacked the logs in the wood box. "Sorry about that, Helen. I meant to move them before I left."

"No problem." She returned to the stove and began cracking eggs into a bowl. "How late did you stay up last night?"

He scratched his jaw. "I think I went to sleep about one."

"Quinn—"

"I know. It's just that I get caught up in practicing what you teach me, then I look up and hours have gone by." He gave her a confident grin that set his dimples winking. "Did you see my handwriting? It's improved a lot, hasn't it?"

"It certainly has." How could she chide him when he was so eager to learn and please? He was blazing through the process so quickly that she was afraid he'd burn out. Every spare moment not consumed by the children or the farm was spent in her teaching him or him reviewing what he'd learned. There seemed to be a lot of spare moments lately with the winter wheat no longer in the ground. He also hadn't made any mention of adding on to the house though there were plenty of funds for him to do so. However, rather than finding encouragement in that, Helen suspected it was only a side effect of his determination to conquer reading and writing.

Helen reveled in his every accomplishment and enjoyed seeing the confidence he was gaining in those subjects spread to other areas of his life. Yet she couldn't shake the nagging fear that she'd relegated herself to becoming merely a teacher in his eyes. She wanted to be more than that, but she didn't feel as though she was making much progress in that respect. She was getting impatient and frustrated with herself. After all, how long had they been married? Shouldn't they be further along in their relationship than this?

"I'll awaken the children."

She nodded, deep in thought as she whisked the eggs together with some seasoning. A month, she realized. They'd been married for one month today. It wasn't that long. Just long enough for her to become a little discouraged that she'd never be able to convince Quinn to love her. Maybe she needed a change in her perspective or just a change of scenery. She hadn't left the farm except to go to church on Sundays since she'd married Quinn. If she gave in to this sudden craving for a few moments to herself, would she be a horrible wife and mother?

She certainly felt like one during breakfast when she announced her plan to go to town alone. The children from oldest to youngest followed their uncle's lead in set-ting down his fork to stare at her. Quinn wiped his mouth with a napkin and frowned. "There's no need for that. I'd be happy to go to town to get whatever you want."

"I know you would, but I'd like to get it myself." Particularly since she hadn't decided on what exactly she'd be getting yet.

Clara leaned across the table with dancing blue eyes. "Will you bring us back a surprise, Aunt Helen?"

"I certainly will."

Quinn's acquiescence was a bit grumbly. "I'll saddle one of the horses."

"Actually, I'd rather drive the wagon than ride." The doctor had ordered her not to ride again after that fateful accident. Out of concern, her parents had enforced that rule. Helen wouldn't feel comfortable enough to ride to town alone on a horse even if she'd wanted to—which she didn't. Thankfully, Quinn didn't find the request odd. He just nodded and that was that. Soon Helen put on her hat and coat then kissed the children goodbye before walking to the wagon Quinn had readied for her. He helped her onto the seat then handed her the reins. "You won't be gone too long, now, will you?"

"I'll be back before you know it."

"We'll be waiting." He backed away to watch her go. She glanced back as she neared the turn that would soon hide the house from view. The sight of Quinn waving at her with the children lined up beside him made her want to turn the wagon around right then and there. How could she leave them, if only for an hour or two?

No, she was being silly. She'd cure her case of cabin fever and be back home in no time at all. She answered Quinn's wave with one of her own then focused on the winding road before her. It wasn't long before she strolled into Peppin's bustling mercantile. The owner's daughter, Sophia Johansen, welcomed her with smile. "Hello, Helen. What can I do for you?"

"I'll take twelve ounces of candy corn."

"Sure thing."

Isabelle sidled up to the counter beside Helen. "Sophia, do you have any of my mother's favorite tea in the back? There's none left on the shelf."

"I'll check." Sophia handed Helen the candy corn in exchange for payment.

"Thank you!" Isabelle turned to Helen as Sophia disappeared into the stockroom. "This is a nice surprise. What are you doing in town?"

Helen shrugged. "Cabin fever set in."

"You made it about a month. Not bad for a former city girl." Isabelle glanced around the mercantile. "Where are your husband and the little ones?"

"I left them at home."

Isabelle smirked. "She said guiltily."

"I feel awful." Helen grimaced. "You should have seen them when I left. It was as if they thought I would never come back."

Isabelle only had time to make a sad face in sympathy before Sophia returned with her order. At that instant, Helen felt a soft touch on her back and turned to find Ellie grinning at them. "So many of my good friends all in one place. Why didn't anyone tell me there was going to be a party?"

Helen laughed. "It wasn't intentional."

"Says who?" Sophia asked. "Whenever I'm bored, I pray for company then wait to see which one of my friends will show up."

Isabelle gestured to the busy counter where Sophia's father, Mr. Johansen, and brother, Chris, were dealing with customers. "It looks like you have a lot of friends, Sophia."

"That's why my father keeps me around." Sophia winked as Isabelle paid her bill. "What can I do for you, Ellie?"

"Not a thing. Lawson is the one with the list and I think Chris is helping him. Hey, all of us being in one place is too good an opportunity to pass up. Why don't we go across the street for some of Maddie's pie and coffee."

Helen and Isabelle quickly agreed. Sophia declined since she had work to do. After Ellie arranged to meet her husband later at his parents' house, they settled in at a table in Maddie's Café. Ellie's warm green eyes focused on Helen first. "So you're in town alone?"

"Yes." Helen shot a quick glance at Isabelle, who patted her arm.

"And she feels guilty about it. Ellie, tell her she shouldn't."

"Why don't you tell her, silly?"

"She's more likely to believe you because you've been married longer than her."

"Just a minute." Helen set her cup of coffee down with mock indignation. "Ellie only beat me to the altar by a week."

Ellie waved off her protest. "Listen to some advice from a mature, married woman." She waited until they finished laughing before she continued. "Actually, it isn't from me, but from my sister Kate who's been married more than ten years. It's permissible to take some time for yourself every once in a while—healthy, even. Stop feeling guilty, Helen."

"Yes, ma'am."

Maddie brought them three slices of pecan pie and the conversation lulled as they dug into it rather enthusiastically. Ellie set her fork aside long enough to ask, "Helen, what's it like being a mother to four children from the get-go?"

She felt herself beaming. "It's more wonderful than I ever dreamed. It's also harder than I imagined. Just keeping up with all of them can be a challenge sometimes. Each one has their own little personality that's so fun to see developing. Reece is the protector. Clara is just a sweetheart to everyone. Trent is the deep thinker of the group, even at four years old. Baby Olivia is always a smiling little ray of sunshine."

Isabelle smiled. "They think the world of you. I can tell that just from seeing y'all together at church."

"Well, I think the world of them, too."

"Aw. That is very sweet," Ellie said, then tilted her head. "What about Quinn? How are things going with him?"

"He's doing well." Helen sorted through what she could and couldn't say since she wasn't sure he'd want anyone to know she'd been tutoring him. "We've been able to spend more time together recently, so that's been nice."

Isabelle shook her head. "It seems like everyone is getting married all at once. First, you, Ellie. Then Amy. Then Helen. All back to back. I have to admit, y'all have me curious as to what all the fuss is about."

Helen lifted a brow. "Curious enough to try it yourself?"

"Perhaps one day. Of course, there is a little matter of finding the right groom. None of the boys in town seemed the least bit interested in me when Amy was around. There was something about her that drew them like bees to honey."

Ellie nodded. "I think you're right about that, but she's gone now. That ought to change things."

"I think it did." Isabelle blushed.

Helen's mouth dropped and she exchanged wide-eyed glances with Ellie before turning back to Isabelle. "You've got a beau. Who is it? Rhett?"

"What? No! I don't have a beau. If I did, it certainly wouldn't be Rhett. Why would you guess him of all people? Everyone knows he was in love with Amy."

Ellie just smiled and ignored the protests. "Helen, what made you think of Rhett?"

"He drove Isabelle to my house once and I detected a certain something in the air."

Isabelle rolled her eyes. "Manure most likely."

"Methinks the lady doth protest too much," Helen murmured over her coffee.

Ellie shuddered. "Please, no Shakespeare. It brings back memories of a certain pig farmer who shall go unnamed."

Helen sent a sly grin to Isabelle. "Which is funny because the quote is from *Hamlet*."

"You, stop it." Ellie glared then turned to Isabelle. "Who did you mean if not Rhett?"

"I only meant that men in general seem more interested in me now that Amy is gone. Now, let's change the subject. So, Ellie, how is married life?"

"Beyond amazing."

"How so?" Isabelle asked with a laughing glance

to Helen. They both knew Ellie wouldn't have let Isabelle off so easily if the conversation had changed to any other subject.

"I thought my relationship with Lawson was special when we were just friends, but it can't even compare to this. That isn't to say that it hasn't been an adjustment. Learning to live with someone, sharing everything, has been challenging at times. However, at the end of the day, there's nothing like being held by the man you love and knowing beyond a shadow of a doubt that you are loved in return."

Helen felt her breath hitch painfully in her chest. The pie might as well have turned to dust in her mouth. She washed it down with a sip of coffee. Isabelle's concerned look only made it worse. Ellie was oblivious in her dreamy state and kept going.

"The best thing is seeing how that has affected both of us. It's—" Finally realizing the mood had changed, Ellie stopped and looked back and forth between her friends before settling on Helen. Dismay parted her lips. "Oh, Helen, I'm sorry. I didn't mean to—"

"There's no need to be sorry. Why did you stop? I was listening." Helen realized she was fooling no one when Isabelle handed her a handkerchief. "I'm not going to cry. Or, at least, I wasn't until you gave me this silly thing."

"Lawson and I have been praying for y'all ever since my visit."

Isabelle nodded. "So have I."

Ellie tilted her head. "I asked a question earlier I think bears repeating. How are things with Quinn? Give us the real answer this time."

"It isn't bad. Truly, it isn't. At first, I thought that falling in love would be easy for us. After I found out he wasn't inclined to allow that to happen, I guess I thought I could make him love me. The problem is, I don't really know how to do that." She shrugged. "He cares for me, I think. That's about as far as it goes. I keep hoping that circumstances will draw us closer and they seem to in the moment, but there is no lasting change as far as I can tell. Like I said, I don't know what to do."

Ellie reached over to cover Helen's hand. "Will you take some advice from a fellow newlywed?"

"Of course."

"Stop trying." Ellie softened her words with a smile and shook her head. "You can't *make* someone love you."

Helen stared at her. "Then you're saying it's hopeless."

"No. I'm saying stop trying to do this on your own. God can and will help if you let Him. In fact, we can take our lessons of love from Him. He proves His love over and over, but He doesn't force anyone to accept it. He just…loves them. That's it. End of story. That's all you can do with Quinn. Focus your thoughts, attention and time on loving him. Stop trying to *make* love happen and *let* it happen through you."

Helen stared into her nearly empty coffee cup, trying to ingrain Ellie's words on her memory. "Stop trying. Let it happen through me. I think I understand."

Ellie tilted her head, then narrowing her eyes, she searched Helen's face. "*Do* you love him, Helen?"

"Do I…" Finding she wasn't ready to answer that question, she asked another instead. "Why do you ask?"

"Because it isn't fair to ask him for something that you aren't willing to give in return." Ellie's smile was gentle yet her words revealed a hard truth that Helen couldn't deny.

She didn't want to love Quinn. Not yet. For no matter how much she'd convinced herself love would make the difference, she'd never be completely sure until he did, in fact, love her. She'd been guarding her heart without even making the conscious decision to do so, waiting for Quinn to fall in love first. It was the smart thing to do. She now realized it was also selfish. What's more, it wasn't working.

Stop trying. Let love happen through you.

It was good advice, but was she brave enough to use it?

Quinn leaned forward in the church pew soaking in every word of Pastor James Brightly's sermon the next day. The man was less than ten years older than Quinn's own twenty-six years of age. Yet his style had a dynamism that reminded Quinn of a tent revivalist his grandmother had taken him to many years ago. Without the fire-and-brimstone flare, that is. The past two weeks Pastor James had been preaching things that Quinn had never heard—or, at least, paid attention to—before.

"How does God see us now that we have been restored to him through faith in Jesus Christ? Are we still enemies of God as we read earlier in Romans 5:10? Not at all! If you'll turn with me to Ephesians 5:25, we find that he sees us as a groom might see his bride. It says, 'Husbands, love your wives'—now, I could teach a whole sermon on that."

While chuckles echoed through the church, Quinn glanced down the pew to where Helen sat with Olivia in her lap three little fidgeting bodies away. Loving her had never really been part of their deal. Yet he suddenly knew that was exactly why he'd been working so hard to be a better man. He'd wanted to level out things between them so that they could have a chance at love. *Turns out that's a pretty good thing since the Bible commands me to do it.*

Quinn refocused on the pastor as the man continued, "'Even as Christ also loved the church, and gave himself for it, That he might sanctify and cleanse it with the washing of water by the word.'"

Quinn flipped through the Bible clutched in his hands wondering where he might find the scripture. Ephesians started with an *E*. Was the next part an *F* or a *PH*?

"Notice it is Christ who is doing the sanctifying and cleansing. It isn't something we are able to do on our own no matter how hard we might try. It's by God's grace and comes through Christ with the washing of water by the Word. And what is the Word?"

"The Bible," Quinn called out before realizing this wasn't a tutoring session with Helen and the question had been rhetorical. Folks turned to look at him while he shot a wide-eyed look at his wife. She looked just as surprised at his outburst as he was. Her shoulders lifted in tandem with her eyebrows as she tried to suppress her amusement by pressing her lips together.

The pastor had no such compunction on containing his grin as he moved from behind the pulpit to point at Quinn. "Exactly! The Word of God. Every time you read the Bible you are allowing Christ to wash you in cleansing water. But why? Is He doing this just for the sake of doing it? No! There is a purpose."

Pastor James took up his Bible. "It's revealed in the

next verse. 'That he might present it to himself a glorious church, not having spot, or wrinkle, or any such thing, but that it should be holy and without blemish.'"

Quinn sighed, realizing he had a lot more Bible reading to do if he wanted to be part of the glorious church the scripture talked about. Still, he enjoyed hearing about God's free, all-encompassing love for him even if he was having some trouble adjusting to the idea—especially since he hadn't had much experience with that type of love before. Perhaps he'd seen shades of God's kind of love from Helen. Not that she loved him, but she accepted him and was helping him overcome his limitations. That had to mean something. Whether it did or not didn't change the fact that the Bible commanded him to love her. How was he supposed to go about that exactly? It wasn't as if he had much experience wooing a woman. All right, so he hadn't had any experience.

He was jolted from his thoughts when Pastor James shook his hand heartily on the way out. "Quinn, I sure do appreciate you participating in the sermon. It really helps to know someone is listening and as involved with what I'm saying as I am. I pray your enthusiasm spreads to the rest of the church."

Quinn wasn't sure how to say his participation had been more of an accident than anything, so he just murmured something in agreement as the man moved to the next parishioner. Seeing Helen's arms were free since all of the children had rushed outside to play, Quinn offered her his arm. She took it as they strolled toward the door. "It looks like you started something, Quinn."

He shook his head. "All because I forgot I wasn't at our kitchen table."

"I thought that was it." She laughed. "Maybe I've been testing you too much."

"No. It's good for me." He held the door open for her to precede him outside. It was warm for November. Quinn wouldn't be surprised if it was seventy degrees. His nieces and nephews seemed to revel in the fair weather as they played on the church lawn with the young Rutledges.

Helen paused. "Oh, there's Kate Rutledge. I'd better make sure Ellie told her sister she invited us all over to the ranch for dinner."

"Go ahead. I've been meaning to talk to the sheriff about what Trent said a while back about Jeffery Richardson."

"That's a good idea. You'll let me know what he says?"

"Of course." Quinn waited until she left before making a beeline for Ellie's brother.

His neighbor listened carefully as Quinn related Trent's tale. "Hmm. That does sound suspicious. I'll contact law enforcement in Alaska to see if they have any information about Jeffery Richardson or what might have happened to your brother's estate."

"I'd appreciate that." Quinn took a deep breath then pushed aside his inhibitions. "This isn't related to what we've been talking about, but I was wondering if you could give me some advice."

"I can try. What do you need advice on?"

"Marriage."

Sean lifted a brow. "I don't pretend to be an authority on the subject since I've only been married about a year and a half. Still, I'd be happy to share what I've learned."

Lawson appeared at his brother-in-law's side. "Sorry for butting in. I was passing by and heard you mention needing advice on marriage, so of course, I had to stop. I figure I'd probably benefit from whatever Sean had to say, too."

Sean combed his fingers through his dark blond hair and grimaced. "Great. No pressure. So what's the problem, Quinn?"

"I wouldn't say there was a problem exactly. It's just that verse about husbands loving their wives made me think. Helen and I got married pretty quickly, so there was no wooing period for us. Now I believe that maybe there should be, only I don't know how to go about it."

Sean nodded thoughtfully, then said, "There are the general things like finding something that you enjoy doing together."

"I think we have that." He was pretty sure she enjoyed teaching him and he enjoyed learning from her. "What else?"

"You can do small things to show her that she's special and you're thinking about her, like giving her genuine compliments and giving her flowers."

Despite the warmer weather today, most of the flowers had long since faded. He wasn't sure simply saying she looked nice would have the result he wanted. "I can try those things, but I want us to become closer, more connected to each other."

Lawson tilted his head. "Chemistry. Is that what you're talking about? You want to build chemistry?"

"I think so."

Sean grinned. "That's a whole other animal. Lorelei and I had sort of a love-hate type of thing going on between us at first. We were both too stubborn and afraid to admit we were attracted to each other. We traded barbs whenever we were forced into each other's company. Once we fell in love, those barbs changed to banter. It can get pretty spirited at times. Anytime I want to spice things up I use that. It's always good for a kiss or two."

"Ellie and I started out from a completely different place than Sean and Lorelei since we'd been good friends for a long time," Lawson contributed. "I guess that's why she seems to get a kick out of flirting with me. Truth be told, I feel the same way."

"Banter and flirt." Quinn grimaced. "It sounds complicated."

Lawson shrugged. "My matchmaker of a wife once told me that every couple has a unique chemistry. You just need to find out what works for you."

"Remember, at the end of the day, a woman just wants to feel loved," Sean added. "There are a lot of ways you can show her you care. Have fun with it. Be creative. You may be surprised by what you can come up with."

Even as he agreed to try, Quinn wasn't so sure it would work. He was attracted to his wife. He just wasn't sure she felt the same about him. He might not know much, but he was pretty sure that mutual attraction was an important part of courting someone. She'd seemed open to deepening their relationship that night of the storm. However, a lot had changed since then.

He wanted the type of closeness he saw between these men and their wives now that he knew God wouldn't punish him for it and now that he was endeavoring to deserve her love—a love that didn't yet exist. It would go on not existing unless he did something about it. A sense of foreboding settled on his chest right there in the church yard. Was God trying to warn him that he was heading straight for trouble just like his brother and father before him? Had they felt this same way before they'd started their journey—excited and nervous all at the same time? If so, they'd pushed on, anyway…as Quinn intended to do.

Of course, they'd ended up dead. Quinn would just have to be more careful than them if he didn't want to get hurt in some way. He knew just how to do it, too. He wouldn't even broach the subject of love until he was certain he deserved her. Surely that would make things easier for both of them. Or, at the very least, safer for him.

Chapter Fourteen

As if Helen wasn't nervous and edgy enough from her talk with Ellie and Isabelle yesterday, now she had to deal with Quinn sending her inscrutable glances as he drove them to the Rutledge ranch for dinner. Her nieces and nephews had chosen to ride in the wagon with the four Rutledge children, leaving nothing to fill the air between her and Quinn except a rather uncomfortable silence. At least, it was uncomfortable to her. She wasn't entirely sure whether or not Quinn noticed since he seemed unreachably deep in thought.

She supposed she couldn't fault him for that since she'd been doing more than her share of deep thinking lately. She'd arrived at the conclusion that she would follow Ellie's advice and allow herself to fall in love with Quinn. However, she'd also realized there was a big difference between deciding on a course of action to take and actually starting down that path. To put it plainly, she was scared out of her wits. What if she fell in love and he didn't? Or, they both fell in love but it wasn't enough? Or, what if love was enough for the meantime but not enough later when the truth finally came out?

It was impossible to know for sure that he'd never resent her for her inability to bear children.

"Helen, we're here."

She glanced down to find Quinn waiting to help her down from the wagon. She blinked. "Oh. I guess I was woolgathering."

Ellie appeared at Quinn's side with a large picnic basket in hand. "It's too nice of a day for that, Helen."

"Are we all going on a picnic?" Helen asked as she made it safely to the ground.

"No. You and Quinn are going on a picnic alone."

"Alone?" Alarm widened Helen's eyes. She had been counting on the company of the group to ease the tension within her. "But the children—"

"The older ones are already heading to the hay fort my brothers built in the barn and the younger ones will be inside with Kate and me. They'll have dinner with us later, so you two will have plenty of time alone."

Helen narrowed her eyes at her friend. "You were planning this when you invited us over here, weren't you?"

"Of course." Ellie's green eyes sparkled. "I'm just glad the Lord provided such good weather for it."

A hint of a smile tugged at Quinn's lips as he took the picnic basket Ellie offered. "Where is this picnic supposed to take place?"

"The creek probably has the best view. See that little break in the tree line? The path there will lead you straight to it. Go on now. There won't be many more days like this, with it being November." Ellie's wink encompassed them both. "Best make the most of it."

"Thanks, Ellie." Quinn caught Helen's hand and tugged her toward the tree line. "We'll see you later."

Helen sent him a suspicious sideways glance as she followed him. He seemed awfully eager all of a sudden, and he was holding her hand instead of letting her take his arm as he usually did. What was going on?

She hadn't figured it out by the time the path ended in a clearing where a thin veil of bronze leaves covered the ground. Water cascaded down a short waterfall to make the creek's surface a rippling mirror of the blue sky overhead. Meanwhile, an intermittent breeze set the leaves in the trees trembling as they provided a golden backdrop. Awed by the sight, Helen stood near the banks of the creek and pulled in a deep breath then wrapped her arms around her waist. "I had no idea this place would be so breathtaking in the daylight."

"Hey, this is where it started." Quinn came to stand slightly behind her.

"This is where what started?"

Warmth filled his deep voice. "Us."

She turned to face him and the gentleness in his eyes made her heart lurch, shaking the walls she'd built to guard it. She tilted her head. Allowing a smile to touch her lips, she lifted a brow. "You mean, this is where you dragged me into a freezing creek."

He chuckled as he eased even closer. "I thought you looked pretty all mussed up."

"I looked half-drowned which I was." She swallowed. Was that really her voice sounding all soft and breathless?

"No, I remember distinctly. You had a trace of mud right here." His fingers traced a light trail across her cheek.

"I did not."

"No, I guess you didn't." He let his hand stray toward the loose chignon at the back of her head. "Well, I know for sure that your hair was more like this…"

She noticed the mischievous look in his eye only an instant before she felt one of her hairpins being tugged free. She batted his hand away and covered her hair while retreating a few steps from the creek. "Don't you dare, Quinn Tucker."

A lazy grin revealed his dimples. "You were the most beautiful woman I'd ever seen."

She froze and stared at him. "I was?"

"Yes, even though you weren't very nice to me that night."

"I was, too."

"No." He crossed his arms, which somehow only made them look more powerful. "You said I reminded you of a bear and desperately needed a shave and a haircut."

She kept her tone solemn even as she felt her eyes begin to dance. "But you *did* remind me of a bear and you *did* desperately need a shave and a haircut."

He growled.

She held up one finger. Widening her eyes, she glanced at the woods surrounding them in fear. "Did you hear that?"

"Hear what?" His entire body tensed while his boots spread into a protective stance as he scanned their surroundings.

"I don't know. It almost sounded like…a bear." She waited for his gaze to snap back to hers, watched his eyes narrow and his jaw twitch. Her lips already curving into a smile, she pressed them together to keep from laughing. A giggle slipped out, anyway.

"That's strange. To me, it sounded like someone asking to be thrown in the creek."

Her eyes widened for real this time. She held up her hands, backing away from him as he stalked her every move. "Now, Quinn. Be reasonable. Don't do anything I'll make you regret."

"Oh, I won't regret a single thing, darlin'." He grabbed for her. She evaded him by dashing behind a tree. He ran around the other side to cut off her escape. She faked left then went right. He caught her arm then channeled her momentum to spin her around so that she ran right into his hard chest. The impact hardly rocked him as he locked his arms around her waist. "Better prepare yourself. It may be warmer today, but that water is still going to be cold."

She tilted her head back to search his face. He wouldn't really throw her in the creek, would he? Suddenly, she wasn't so sure. There was a playful glint in his eyes that she didn't trust. She worked her hands between them in an effort to push her way out of his arms. He wasn't cooperating, which made the task nigh on impossible. "An honorable man would allow me a forfeit."

"What kind of forfeit?"

"I'll let you wash the dishes for me tonight."

"I don't think you understand how forfeits work. You're supposed to do something for me." His voice deepened. "Or…give me something I want." His attention flickered down to her lips before returning to her eyes.

Her breath seemed to get lost in her chest. Perhaps he'd forgotten that he'd ordered her not to kiss him again unless it meant something. She hadn't forgotten. In her book, that meant the next person to do any kissing would have to be him. She lifted a brow. "I have a better idea. How about I apologize and you let me go?"

"Not a chance."

He said it so gravely that she had to smile. Sliding her hands up to his shoulders, she clasped them behind his neck and rose on tiptoe to place herself more securely in his arms. She took care to speak tenderly so as not to rile him as she whispered, "Please, Bear."

"No." He whispered, and then eased her backward in a slow dip that shifted her to the center of his embrace. He finished the smooth movement by lifting her just enough to meet his kiss. Her equilibrium, already struggling to compensate, was completely lost. She clung to him as the kiss deepened and intensified. She could feel the walls she'd built around her heart catching fire with her, tumbling into ashes, floating away on the wind that teased her senses with the faint scent of Quinn's bay rum aftershave.

She was left vulnerable and exposed as her fears melted away. They would return. She was certain of that because there would be no getting him out of her heart after this. He would stay there no matter what his reaction was to her secret. That meant she could potentially be hurt deeply—as deeply as she allowed herself to love him. She didn't want to get hurt, but it was too late. What she hadn't wanted to admit before was clear to her now. She was well on her way to loving Quinn already. In fact, she probably had been from the very beginning. Otherwise, she wouldn't have been so eager to accept his offer of marriage no matter how many children he had.

He allowed them both a free breath before he sealed his kiss with a softer, briefer one. When he released her waist, she stumbled a few dazed steps to stare at him. She pressed the back of her hand to her lips then trailed it upward to smooth her hair. She tried to speak, but what came out was little more than the last half of a sigh.

"That was…" Quinn slowly shook his head as he stared back at her in wonder. After a moment, determination set the angles of his chiseled jaw. "Now, for your forfeit."

"My—what was the kiss, then?"

"A kiss." His smile told her he knew it had been far from just an ordinary kiss. "You still owe me a forfeit." He chuckled as she set her hands on her hips and glared. "Don't worry, darlin'. All I want you to do is answer some questions for me."

She tilted her head and narrowed her eyes. "What kind of questions?"

"Questions about you. On the drive over here, I realized that you know so much about me—even down to my deepest darkest secret. Yet, I know hardly anything about you. Why is that?"

"I'm not that interesting."

He gave her a disbelieving look. "I think you are. What's more, you've helped me with all of my problems, from needing a wife, to finances, to reading. I'd like to help you like you've helped me, but you've never even mentioned having any problems except that time you had a nightmare."

Her heart started racing for an entirely different reason. "I guess I do tend to keep my problems to myself."

"Then you'll tell me more about yourself?"

"What do you want to know?"

He stepped forward to take her hands in his. "Everything."

"Everything?" She swallowed hard. She couldn't tell him *everything*.

He nodded. "Start at the beginning. What were you like as a child?"

She pulled in a calming breath. She could do this. She could tell him about herself without betraying her secret. She just had to be careful. Something akin to conviction pricked her conscience. She struggled to salve it. After all, it wasn't as if she was lying. She was just leaving a few things out…for now. She forced a laugh. "That may take a while. I'm sure you'll find out plenty about me when we visit my parents, but I'd be happy to tell you about the distracted little daydreamer I used to be. Why don't we sit down and have our picnic while we talk."

"I almost forgot what brought us here in the first place." He gave her a little wink that caused her heart to skip like a rock. "Come on. Let's see what Ellie packed for us."

He led her toward the picnic basket and she followed him—followed her heart even as it brought her closer to her day of reckoning. She tried to convince herself that she was making more out of this than she needed to since they had four children already. Surely that would soften the blow for him as it had for her. However, there was still the possibility—or, perhaps, *probability*—that he might resent being sold damaged goods as much as Tom had. In that case, the best thing she could do was enjoy these moments with Quinn so she would have them to cherish later if things ever changed. What else could she do now that she'd thrown down the shield around her heart like a gauntlet to both love and heartache?

* * *

Ten days later, Reece and Clara had finished their last day of lessons before the Thanksgiving break, which, Quinn discovered, somehow gave them boundless energy. Trent and Olivia seemed to take their cue from their older siblings, so he found himself blindfolded during a fourth game of blindman's buff after supper. A small hand tapped his leg. He turned toward it slowly enough for whoever it was to get away, earning Olivia's giggle as a reward. A snicker that sounded like Reece came from his left just as a breeze passed by on his right. It stirred the air enough that he caught Helen's scent.

She was close. He froze, listened carefully enough to discover the almost-silent rhythm being beat out on the floor. Of all the gall…she was dancing! In fact, she probably had been for a while, though how she'd evaded his searching outstretched arms all this time was beyond him. She was too easy a mark now that he knew, but he couldn't help joining in with a little jig of his own.

Laughter came at him from all sides while someone gasped. It must have been Clara, because she spoke up from behind him. "He's been able to see all this time!"

"No, but I can hear real well." He spun toward her. She yelped. He gave her a head start as she dashed away. However, her steps were heavy with panic and she was easy to track down. He caught her arm and reeled her in. "Who could this be?"

"Cla—" Trent's yell was muzzled; probably by Reece, who'd been particularly frustrated by his brother's inability to remember the blind man had to guess his captive's identity correctly to win.

"I think it's Clara." He removed his blindfold to glance down at her.

She pouted. "You hunted me down."

"You bet I did, sweetheart, because I needed one of these." He lifted her into the air high enough to place a smacking kiss on her cheek before setting her down. "We'll pick up with Clara the next time we play."

The children's protests at ending the game were immediate and fierce. It was getting close to bedtime and they needed to calm down, so Quinn shook his head. "Sorry, that's it. I'm done. Y'all wore me out. See?"

He collapsed onto the rug. One at a time his family took their cue from him by wilting down to the floor. However, instead of landing on the rug, they all ended up on him or each other until he felt like the floor in a game of pick-up sticks. After more laughter and a few grumbles, they seemed content to relax, so Quinn didn't have any room to complain or to move. He didn't mind, though. Especially since Helen's head came to rest on his left shoulder.

Ever since that kiss at the creek, she somehow seemed even kinder and sweeter than she'd been before. He hadn't kissed her again because he didn't want to presume too much, but he'd been thinking about it a lot. Perhaps more than he should. To get his mind off of it now, he asked, "Are y'all excited about our trip to Austin tomorrow? It sounds like Helen's parents have a lot of fun things planned for us."

"Yes," Reece answered. "I just feel bad because we'll have to leave Charlie all alone. Can't we take him—Ouch. Clara!"

Quinn wasn't sure what Clara had done to Reece, but

her fierce whisper was easy to hear. "You weren't supposed to tell about Charlie. Now he'll have to go away."

Quinn and Helen sat up at the same time, which
forced the children to do the same. He barely got the
question out before Helen. "Who is Charlie?"

Trent was wide-eyed and obviously confused. Olivia frowned at them all. The older two looked guiltier
than he'd ever seen them. Finally, Reece explained as
if it was the most natural thing in the world. "He's our
friend who lives in the woods."

"What woods, Reece?" Helen asked.

"The woods around our house."

Quinn frowned in concern. "What is Charlie? A
child? A dog? What?"

Clara shook her head. "He's a man. A full-growed
man."

"Full-grown," Helen corrected then shook her head
as though unable to process the children's meaning.
"Wait. So there's a strange man living on our property?
And y'all knew and didn't tell us? How long has this
been going on?"

Clara lifted her chin. "He isn't strange."

"Yeah, he's nice."

Quinn waved off their words. "Answer your aunt's
questions. How long?"

Reece shrugged. "I don't know. We met him last
week when we were playing outside. He gave us some
cookies like our ma used to make. Our second ma, I
mean."

Trent's little body stiffened. "You had cookies, and
you didn't tell me?"

"Cookie?" Olivia looked around as though expecting them to materialize from thin air.

Clara patted Trent's knee. "I wanted to, but it was *supposed* to be a secret."

Reece grimaced. "Land sakes, Clara, I'm sorry. What more do you want from me?"

Trent glared. "I want my cookies."

Olivia held out her hands, with chubby fingers grasping the air. "Cookie!"

"That's enough." Quinn stood and set the three oldest side by side on the settee. With Helen at his side holding Olivia, he looked them in the eye one at a time. "I want y'all to listen to me very closely."

Trent looked near to tears. "I didn't do anything!"

"I know that." Quinn knelt in front of the settee and covered the boy's cheek. "I'm not angry at you. Or you, Clara. Or you, Reece. It's just important to me that y'all understand what I'm going to say. That's why I want y'all to stop bickering and pay attention to me. Understand?"

He waited until the three of them nodded then extended his hand to Helen. Once she took it, he turned back to the children. "Your aunt and I love each one of you more than we could ever hope to express. We want you to be safe. That is why it is important for you to watch out for—what should we call them? Tricky people."

Clara frowned. "What are tricky people?"

"Tricky people are grown-ups who ask you to keep secrets from your aunt and me or from each other. They tell you it's all right to do things without our permission. That includes taking things they offer you, going places with them or doing whatever they're asking you to do. Grown-ups who ask you to keep them safe are also tricky people."

Helen squeezed his hand in support. "So what should the children do if they think they're dealing with a tricky person, Quinn?"

"Get away from that person. Find me or your aunt. Tell us about it. Understand?"

They all nodded. Reece put a protective arm around Clara's shoulders. She frowned. "Charlie is a tricky person?"

"I'm afraid so." Quinn allowed Helen to finish up the conversation. As she helped them deal with the emotional part of it, he was already planning his next course of action. He wanted to take care of this before they left for their trip tomorrow afternoon. Since it was already dark, he'd best wait for first light to start canvassing the woods for the trespasser. Perhaps he'd swing by the sheriff's place first to get his help.

During the past ten days, Sheriff Sean O'Brien had been persistent in searching for information regarding Jeffery Richardson and the children's inheritance. However, the sheriff hadn't been able to make any progress on either issue. The local officials in Alaska seemed to resent any kind of outside interference. It was frustrating, to say the least. Meanwhile, Quinn wouldn't stand for anyone messing with his family. The trespasser would find that out soon enough. So would Richardson.

Quinn couldn't shake the feeling that he was missing something important pertaining to that situation, but what? The answer came to him later that night just as he finished reviewing Helen's reading lesson. Richardson had sent Quinn a letter notifying him of Wade's death. It was still in the desk where Quinn had put it because he couldn't read. Well, he could read now. Surely the letter would offer some information about what had happened to Wade's assets even if what it said was false.

He wanted to be able to give the letter to the sheriff at daybreak, which meant he'd have to go into Helen's room while she was sleeping at some point. He might as well do it now. He'd just have to be quiet about it. He opened Helen's door, wincing as it creaked. So much for being quiet.

He found her pushing to her elbow with sleep lading her thick lashes. She spoke almost as slowly as she blinked. "Is it morning?"

"No, I—"

"Must be the children, then." She didn't even bother with her house robe. She just took the blanket with her as she stood. "They were still a little upset when I read them. I mean the book." She gave her head a minuscule shake. "What?"

He really ought to tell her to go back to sleep, but it was hard to do anything other than watch her be adorable. "Are you asking me or yourself?"

"I'm not sure." She stared up at him until her eyes focused. "Which one of the children needs me?"

He aimed her back toward the bed when she tried to walk past him. "There's nothing wrong with the children. You go on back to sleep now. I just came in here to get something from the desk. I promise I won't disturb you again tonight."

She made a humming noise and was already sleeping by the time he grabbed everything out of the desk drawer. He spread his loot out on the kitchen table. He discovered that many of the papers he'd saved over the years on the off chance he'd learn to read were nothing other than advertisements for products he'd never use or need. He ignored everything except the letter on top with its seal flap facing up. He opened the envelope and sat down to read aloud in case he needed to sound out any words.

He went straight to the body of the letter, which was written in a smooth, precise script.

I never stopped loving you. I cannot tell you how much I regret letting you go the night of our engagement.

It took a second for the words to process. He read them again, frowned and glanced at the header. "Dearest Helen"? Was this a love letter? From whom? Unlike the rest of the letter, the signature boasted fancy curves in the cursive style of writing Quinn had yet to learn.

How long ago had it been written? There was no date on the letter. However, the paper had a stiffness to it that suggested it had been recently transcribed. Stranger still, there was no stamp on the envelope. Did that mean this person lived around here? Was that why Helen had insisted on going into town by herself?

He barely resisted the urge to crumple the paper in his fist. Instead, he folded it and slid it back into its envelope. He didn't want to read any more. Whatever was written there wasn't intended for his eyes. Besides, it was far too painful. He'd been trying so hard to be a better man so that he could be worthy of his wife's affections. He'd never considered he might also be competing for them.

He'd asked Helen to tell him everything that day at the creek. She'd told him about her growing-up years and the silly society gatherings she'd been expected to attend. She'd never once hinted at a former romance—certainly not a former fiancé. He'd been too involved with what he'd considered the beginning of their own courtship to even think to broach the subject. Well, he had questions now. Plenty of them.

He started to rise with the intention of going to Helen's room, then sat back down after remembering that he'd promised not to disturb her. Besides, it would be better to approach the problem with a cool head in the morning, so he'd let her sleep. Tomorrow, however, he intended to get some answers.

Chapter Fifteen

◄━━

Quinn was gone when Helen awoke the next morning. A note on the kitchen table told her that he'd gone to get the sheriff and search the woods. She was supposed to bar the door until he returned. Bar the door? She'd been hoping to get her chores out of the way quickly so that she'd have more time to prepare the children for their trip. As much as she'd anticipated seeing her parents again, the date of departure had sneaked up on her. She'd had to make several arrangements at the last minute. One of them being arranging to have some formal clothes made for Quinn in Austin.

He had none to take with them, save the suit he wore to church every week. As handsome as he looked in it, it just wouldn't be enough for the events her family had planned. She'd told him about it, hadn't she? Maybe not. Everything had been so hectic. She'd make sure to tell him when he came in for breakfast. She'd better start fixing it now. She'd learned that the smell of it was often enough to awaken the children. Perhaps an early start for them would help her get a jump on the rest of the day.

After remembering to bar the door, she accidentally knocked over the stack of papers Quinn had left on the table in her haste to return to the kitchen. She bent to pick them up then hesitated, realizing that mixed among his assignments was the contents of what she'd come to think of as her desk. She suddenly remembered that he'd mentioned needing something from the desk as the reason for coming into her room last night. What could he have wanted with all of this junk? That's all it was, too, since she'd had the foresight to burn the letter with her mother's references to that dreadful night she'd almost become publicly engaged to Thomas. She gasped. "Tom!"

She'd completely forgotten about his letter. Dread filled her as she sorted through the papers looking for the note she'd never read. She winced when she found it. It had obviously been disturbed. Was that because Quinn had read it? Or was it simply from her knocking it onto the floor? Oh, why had she been so careless with it? If Quinn had read it, then she needed to, as well.

She set the other papers in a stack on the table then opened the letter to read it just as someone pounded on the front door. She froze. Thinking something might have happened to Quinn, she stuffed the letter into her apron pocket and rushed to the door. She was ready to unbar it before she realized it might not be the sheriff or Quinn at all. It might be Charlie. The pounding sounded again. She swallowed. "Who is it?"

"Quinn. I've got Sean with me. You can unbar the door. It's safe."

A wave of relief flowed over her then ebbed into tension as she realized she still had that blasted letter in her pocket. However, she couldn't leave the men out there. She moved the wooden bar out of the way and opened the door to let them in. Almost immediately, she wished she hadn't because Quinn's mattress was still on the parlor floor. There was no way the sheriff could miss it. It was too late now. At least the bed was made. "Come to the kitchen. I was just about to put on some coffee."

"Thanks, Helen," Sean said. "I may not have time to drink it, though. I've got to head into town soon. Quinn and I just wanted to let you know how it went."

"Y'all said it's safe? Does that mean you found Charlie?" Helen glanced up from adding water to the coffee-pot in time to see Quinn move his stack of papers to the end table. Nothing in his expression told her whether he'd seen Thomas's letter or not.

Sean picked a chair that faced away from the parlor. "No. We found the place where he'd been camping, but the man himself wasn't anywhere on the property."

"Hopefully, he's moved on." Quinn settled at the corner of the table with a frown. "It strikes me as strange that he gave the children cookies, though. Usually vagrants don't just happen to have sweets around to offer children."

Sean frowned. "You think he befriended them for a specific purpose?"

"I don't know. I hope not."

"Well, I'll keep an eye on the place while you're gone. I was planning to, anyway. Meanwhile, I'll look into any new clues I can gather from the letter."

Helen whirled toward them. "What letter?"

"The one Richardson sent to notify me of my brother's death. I'd forgotten that I had it." There was something in his eyes that she hadn't seen before. An underlying steel. She had a feeling that meant he'd read Thomas's letter. What if that also meant he knew the truth about her?

The room swayed. Her stomach roiled. She leaned back onto the counter to steady herself. She struggled to sound normal "What did it say?"

"It said all of Wade's assets had been turned over to the state because he'd made no will."

Sean nodded. "That should be easy enough to check. I'd better head into town now. Y'all have a nice trip. Don't worry about anything."

After seeing Sean to the door, Quinn returned to the kitchen and held up the empty envelope with her name on the front in Thomas's handwriting. "Who is writing you love letters?"

She blinked. He didn't know who had written her. Was there a chance he also didn't know her secret? "You didn't read it?"

"Only enough to know what it is. The name was written in cursive. Who is this man?"

"His name is Thomas Coyle. He was my fiancé for a few days before he jilted me at our engagement dinner. Officially, it was never announced, but everyone knew."

"How long has he been writing you?"

"That was the only letter I received. He gave it to my parents and they enclosed it in their letter. I didn't answer it. I didn't even read it. I was going to just now, but you came in." She swallowed. If he didn't already know the truth about her, she didn't want to give it away. However, she had to know how much of her past Thomas had revealed. "Did he say anything you think is important? Anything we need to discuss?"

He stared at her for a long moment then shook his

head. "No. He didn't say anything important to me. Although, I do think he was headed toward an apology."

The pressure building in her chest eased out with a long, slow exhale. Her secret was safe for now. Her relief came a moment too soon, for Quinn asked, "Why didn't you tell me you'd been engaged?"

"It only lasted a few days. It hardly counts."

His eyes narrowed. "Did you love him?"

She shrugged. "I thought so at the time."

"Then it counts. I'm not saying you had to tell me every detail because I don't expect that. Still, it would have been nice to find out from you and not from his letter." His jaw clenched. "Will we see him in Austin?"

She frowned. He didn't sound upset about the prospect. In fact, he sounded downright eager. Did he want to ask the man why he had jilted her or just punch him in the nose? "I doubt it. He ought to know better than to think I want to see him since I'm married and never responded to his letter."

Quinn turned the envelope over in his hands. "Why would your parents send such a thing to their married daughter?"

"I'm sure they didn't read it. They probably assumed he was apologizing, which I guess he did. My mother thought it would be good for me to have a definite ending to what happened between us." She shrugged. "For me, it ended with the engagement."

She found him searching her face as he approached her, and she wondered if he could see the wariness within her. "So that's all there is to this?"

"Yes, that's all there is to the letter."

"May I have it?" He waited until she pulled it from her frilly apron pocket to place it in his hand. As soon as she did, she wanted to take it back. What if he read it again? He might have missed something Tom had written about her secret the first time, but he surely wouldn't miss it again. Her worries vanished an instant later when her husband tossed the letter and its envelope into the fiery belly of the stove.

Pure relief filled her as she erased the distance between them with a single step and slipped her arms around his neck for a hug. "Thank you for understanding and believing me."

"Well, I'm still a little confused, but I do believe you." He hugged her closer then released her, though he kept ahold of her arms. "What about Coyle? Am I going to have to compete with his memory?"

She stared at him in confusion. "Compete with his memory? For what?"

"For your heart."

"You…you want my heart?" Did he hear the awe in her voice? It must have been hard to miss, for he grinned.

"Seeing as I'm your husband, don't you think I should?"

"Oh." Happiness wrestled with disappointment. He wanted to win her heart. That was good. However, it wasn't because he loved her and wanted to be loved in return. It was only because he felt obligated to do so as her husband. "Don't worry about Thomas. He isn't going to be a factor. Now, I'd better get breakfast ready and the children up if we want to make it to the train on time. Austin awaits."

Quinn could almost feel the tension emanating off Helen as the train chugged to a stop at the station in

Austin. It was easy to recognize her anxiety since he was more nervous than he'd been since Helen had discovered his illiteracy. That situation had ended far better than he could have hoped. He was resolved the same would be true in this case. It wasn't an altogether different situation, for he'd mentally designated this trip as a test of sorts.

Surely if he could make it through four days in a house, society and role so far above his means and come out unscathed, then he ought to be set for the rest of his life. He could stop looking over his shoulder waiting for trouble to catch up and just live his life. No, not just live it. Enjoy it. He wasn't there yet, but he could be soon. He just needed to get a little help from God, keep thinking on his feet and continue to find new ways to better himself.

He'd been doing well so far. The reading lessons were getting progressively more challenging. However, he was determined to learn as much as possible. The children seemed far less gloomy than they had been when they'd first come to him grieving their parents. That meant he and Helen had to be doing something right. Helen seemed more engaged with him, so his wooing must be having some effect. However, he had hoped for more of a reaction to the news that he wanted to claim her heart. Her excitement had quickly died. That wasn't exactly encouraging.

As for Helen herself, the longer he knew the woman, the more he was discovering that she was an enigma wrapped in warmth, beauty and fancy clothes. How many more mysteries did those deep brown eyes of hers hold? She revealed another one as they gathered their belongings in preparation to disembark. "Have I mentioned this is the first time I've been to Austin since I left only a few weeks after my engagement dinner with no engagement?"

"Apparently there's a lot you haven't mentioned." His comment brought them both up short. She paled. He grimaced. "I'm sorry. I don't know where that came from."

"I do. You have every right to be angry at me for not telling you about…" She let the sentence fade and he realized that the children's gazes were bouncing back and forth between them.

"I'm not angry." Even that came out a little gruff.

Of course, Reece had to call him on it. "You sound angry."

"No, he doesn't." Clara shifted Olivia to her other knee and patted Quinn's arm. "He's just grumpy because the train ride was long."

They began to bicker about whether Quinn was grumpy or angry. The truth was, neither. He was jealous. He had been since he'd found out that Helen had at one point thought she was in love with that city fellow. What would it be like, Quinn wondered, for Helen to think she was in love with him?

"I'm grumpy, too." Trent crossed his arms while Olivia covered her ears and frowned at Clara and Reece.

Helen sent him a panicked look. Suddenly, Quinn realized they were frighteningly close to someone having a temper tantrum. Deciding it wouldn't be him, he transferred Olivia to Helen's care and ushered the older three children into the aisle that had cleared during their tableau. "No one is angry or grumpy. We are all very happy. What's more, we are excited to meet Helen's parents and will be on our best behavior."

By the time he finished his speech, they had stepped

off the train onto what might very well be Quinn's proving grounds. He checked to make sure they were all accounted for as Helen scanned the busy station for her
parents. Olivia was in Helen's arms. Clara was holding
his hand. Reece stood beside Clara. Trent was…

Quinn turned in a circle, dragging Clara with him
as he raked the area with his gaze and came up empty.
Panic tightened his throat. "Where's Trent?"

Helen whipped around to face him. "I thought you
had him."

"So did I." Just then a porter moved a huge cart of
luggage and Quinn spotted Trent down on all fours at
the edge of the platform next to the train wheels. "What
in the world? I see him, Helen."

Those last words to Helen were thrown over Quinn's
shoulder as he raced back to the train. He snatched up
Trent just as the boy reached toward the train wheels.
Setting him away from the track, Quinn knelt in front
of Trent. He ignored his still-racing heart to speak in a
reasonable tone. "What do you think you're doing, son?"

"I wanted to see what makes it go." Trent made a vain
attempt to dodge Quinn's efforts at wiping mysterious
black marks off his face.

"You cannot get that close to a train unless your aunt
or I are with you. You could have been hurt."

"How?"

"You could have gotten your fingers caught in the
wheels or fallen on the track. Your aunt and I didn't
know where you were, so we might not have been able
to find you before the train started. Remember, we
talked about this? You aren't allowed to go off on an
adventure without permission from your aunt or I. Understand?"

While Quinn had been talking, the boy had gone from fascinated to appalled, to downright sober. Finally, Trent nodded. "Yes, but we need to go on more adventures."

"That's a deal." Quinn turned Trent to face the train and explained as best he knew how the steam-powered engine made it move, before herding the boy back to the others. Seeing that Helen's parents had joined the group, the nervousness he'd forgotten in his panic at losing Trent returned full force.

It did Quinn a world of good to see Helen smiling proudly as she introduced him. "Mother, Father, may I present my husband, Quinn Tucker?"

Helen's mother was the same height as her, though a bit plumper. She'd given Helen the shape of her large doe eyes, delicate bone structure and oval face. The woman's hazel eyes sparkled. "I am delighted to meet you, Quinn! You must call us Lucille and Robert."

"Thank you, Lucille. I've been looking forward to meeting you both." He turned to Robert, who had passed his dark hair and eyes on to Helen.

The man had a smile on his face. However, the look in his eyes was not exactly friendly. His handshake seemed an attempt to assess Quinn's strength. "Not as much as I've been looking forward to meeting you."

Well, that doesn't sound the least bit threatening. He looked Robert straight in the eye to let it be known that he wouldn't cower before any man. Then Quinn gave a single nod to communicate his recognition, acceptance and respect of what the man was—a protective father. Not just any father, though. This was Helen's father and, by law, his own. It would be nice to have a father again. For now, Quinn would just appreciate not having this man as an enemy.

Quinn glanced down when Trent tugged at his hand. Following Helen's example of a formal introduction, Quinn said, "May I introduce my nephew Trent Tucker? Trent, this is Mr. and Mrs. McKenna."

Quinn stared in surprise as Trent wrapped one arm in front and the other in back to bow. "How do you, Mr. and Mr. McKenna."

Helen's parents returned Trent's greeting. Lucille waved her handkerchief. "Now, let's dispense with formalities because I am just dying to hold my grandniece. Do you think Olivia would let me?"

After Olivia went willingly, Robert ushered them all around the corner of the train station to the place where their luggage was being loaded onto not one but two waiting carriages. There wasn't enough room for all of them in one, so the men rode together in one and the ladies in the other. Robert made the ride enjoyable for them all by pointing out the interesting sights of the city through the carriage window.

The trolley cars, wagons, carriages and horses thinned out once they passed the domed Capitol building to ride through quiet boulevards. Towering oak trees, spindly crape myrtle and yellow mimosas stretched out their branches to the mansions interspersed between them. The carriage finally rolled to a stop in front of a Queen Anne–style house of sea foam green with moss-colored embellishments. They followed a winding brick path leading from the curb to the house's wide porch steps, which, like the rest of the house, sat on the vast green lawn at a diagonal angle to the street. Quinn paused long enough to glance up to the turret on the third floor before pulling in a deep breath and steeling himself for what was sure to come next.

The entrance room was only a little smaller than the entire living room and kitchen area of his house. It had mahogany floors and archways that gleamed in the soft sunlight spilling from the windows. A grand staircase split to allow access to two sides of the upper floor. An antique grandfather clock that looked older than America itself clanged as though announcing the hour of his doom. No way would he ever deserve the love of a woman who grew up in a place like this. If this was just the beginning, he'd better turn around and keep on walking until he made it back to Peppin.

Escape became impossible when a man whom Quinn sure hoped was in the McKennas' employ obligingly and almost soundlessly made off with Quinn's hat and coat. Meanwhile, the children vanished up the stairs with Helen and her mother. Robert urged him to follow them with a rather strong slap on the back. "Better go up. The tailor is waiting to do a final fitting."

"Tailor?" His voice echoed through the corridor with enough grandiosity to match the surroundings.

A faint smile quirked Robert's mouth. "Our wives arranged for you to have a few things made so that you'll be comfortable during your stay here."

"Are you sure *comfortable* is the right word?" he asked, glancing at the man's current attire. It looked like a more fashionable, higher-quality version of Quinn's Sunday go-to-meeting clothes. He knew from experience that those weren't comfortable in the least.

He earned a chuckle from his father-in-law. "Believe me. Being inappropriately dressed at a society function would be a far more uncomfortable experience than wearing whatever clothes our wives deem necessary. Besides, don't you want to make Helen proud to be escorted by you?"

"Of course."

"Then up the left side of the staircase you go."

"Yes, sir." The echo made his heavy sigh sound excessively dramatic. Once he made it up the stairs, he followed the sound of voices to find his family.

Lucille was introducing the children to a nanny she'd hired to see to their needs during their stay. Quinn waited until his nephews and nieces followed the nanny into the nursery, which would function as their bedroom, before protesting, "You didn't need to go to the trouble of hiring a nanny, Mrs. McKenna. Helen and I can handle them and they're usually very well behaved."

"It's Lucille and I'm quite certain everything you said is true. I just thought this visit would be more restful and smooth for all of you this way. It was quite easy to arrange because the nanny was recommended by a dear friend of mine." Suddenly, dismay widened Lucille's eyes. "Oh, dear. I do hope I haven't offended you by hiring her. I know you and Helen are perfectly capable of seeing to them on your own."

He wanted to tell her that wasn't what he'd been thinking, but it was *exactly* what he'd been thinking. Why was he being so sensitive about everything today? He shook his head. "I just don't want you to feel that you have to go out of your way for us."

Now she looked offended. "Of course I'll go out my way for you, young man. You're family now, and that's how this family operates. Isn't that right, Helen?"

Helen grinned. "Yes, indeed."

"All right, then. Thank you, Lucille."

"You're welcome." She reached out to squeeze his hand and met his gaze with a smile. "Truly, you are welcome here. I hope you will come to think of this house as your second home."

"I'd like that." He relaxed a little and gave her hand a gentle squeeze in return. "By the way, Robert said something about a tailor?"

Lucille gasped. "Oh, dear. I completely forgot. He should be waiting in your room."

Quinn moved to follow the woman as she hurried down the hallway, but Helen tugged at his arm and moved closer to speak in a low tone, "I'm sorry. I meant to tell you about this. I realized a few days ago that you didn't have any formal clothes besides the ones you wear to church, so I sent Mother your measurements. She had a few things made for you by Father's tailor, who is one of the best in the city. Everything should be ready for the final fitting."

He nodded slowly as he processed everything. She was right about him not having clothes—at least, not the right kind for this setting. That much was obvious now. "I should have thought of it myself. It's a good thing you arranged it since I wouldn't have known how."

Relief softened her features before worry once more marred her brow. "I really did mean to tell you sooner…"

"Don't worry about it anymore." He stared at her hard to let her know he meant more than just the clothes. "I know you've had a lot to handle in making this trip happen. I appreciate that. It's all just a little…"

"Overwhelming?" she asked with a smile. "I imagine it must be akin to what I felt those first few days on the farm. I thought I'd never measure up to being the woman you and the children needed me to be. I might have seemed confident on the outside, but I was quaking on the inside."

"You measured up just fine, Helen."

"Thank you." She placed a comforting hand on his chest. "So will you, Quinn. I know it."

Her confidence in him meant more to him than her parents' fancy carriages, Texas-size mansion and expensive clothes. If she believed in him, then he had an honest-to-goodness shot at making a success of this visit. More important, he had a chance at becoming the kind of man he wanted to be. The kind of man who could win her heart.

Chapter Sixteen

In contrast to the cozy and immensely enjoyable Thanksgiving dinner Helen's family had partaken of on Thursday, Saturday's reception was a crush. Most of her father's associates had shown up, including the governor, a state senator, a few state representatives and many prominent businessmen. Their wives made up her mother's close-knit social circle. Each one of them made a point to welcome Helen back into their society's embrace with hugs, cheek kisses, compliments and an entire litany of the most recent gossip.

Her old circle of friends approached her a bit more cautiously, which she knew was no one's fault but her own. She hadn't corresponded with any of them after she left. Many had also been Thomas's friends, which added an undercurrent of awkwardness to their interactions. She didn't ask about him nor did anyone mention him. However, more than once a conversation suddenly hushed as she passed.

She'd been looking forward to this event if for no other reason than that she would no longer be thought of as a jilted fiancée but as a contented wife and mother.

Now she found that their opinions meant little, their conversations were shallow and she longed for nothing more than to escape upstairs to the nursery. That wouldn't help, for the children were surely fast asleep at this hour.

Realizing she'd been standing alone for a few minutes, she glanced around in search of Quinn. She finally spotted him in a conversation with several men, including her father and the governor. Clad in a jet-black tailcoat with a white waistcoat and white necktie that accentuated the broad width of his shoulders and slim hips, he looked far more at ease than she'd expected him to be. He also seemed to be enjoying himself more than she was.

He caught her watching him and sent her a wink that made her eyes widen in panic. Polite gentleman simply did not wink at their wives in public. Thankfully, it had not been so brazenly done that anyone else noticed. She meant to send him a scolding frown but found herself smiling and shaking her head slowly instead. The governor placed a hand on his shoulder, stealing back his attention.

She decided to take a break from the crowd. Despite being one of the honorees at the reception, no one stopped her as she slipped out of her parents' ballroom. She told the butler that she'd be in the sunroom for a few minutes if anyone needed her. She went directly there after borrowing a candle from a nearby wall sconce. The circular room was chilly, but the view it provided of the night sky was worth the discomfort. She'd just placed the candle on an end table when she heard movement from the far corner of the room. "Who's there?"

A man stepped closer to the flickering circle of candlelight. He was dressed as though he was a guest at the party, although he most certainly was not. He toasted her with the silver flask in his hands but didn't bother to bring it to his smirking lips. "Good evening, Helen."

She gasped. "Tom."

He edged toward her, capping the flask in his hand with a bit of difficulty. His gaze raked over her dress. His speech was unmistakably slurred. "You look ravishing. That dark shade of pink was always my favorite color on you. Did I ever tell you that?"

"You're drunk."

He waved her comment away with a broad sweep of his hand. "Don't be rude."

"How did you get in here?"

"I—" his fingers made a crawling motion in the air "—sneaked in."

"Well—" she copied his motion "—sneak right out again."

"No." He rubbed his hands over his face, pulled in a sobering breath and shook his head as though to clear it. "I am in full possession of my faculties. What's more, I have things to say. I'm not leaving until I say them."

"Then I will." She rounded the furniture to head toward the door.

He cut off her escape path and her attempts to get around him. "Please, don't leave. I'm trying to tell you that I still love you."

"I don't care. Let—" She froze, stared at him in disbelief. "What did you say?"

"I love you. I can't stop thinking about you. All my life my father has ingrained in me the importance of passing our fortune to the next generation. I couldn't do that with you. However, I believe I might have been a bit hasty in ending things between us."

She shook her head as she tried to reconcile this with

everything she'd told herself about love making the difference for her when Quinn found out. But if Tom had loved her, and still rejected her when she told him of her condition, did that mean that love wouldn't be enough for Quinn, either? "I don't understand. What are you trying to say? That my inability to have children doesn't matter to you now?"

He stepped closer. "No, it matters. So does my love for you."

"Actually, it doesn't, because I'm married to someone else." She swept a hand toward the ballroom. "It's sort of the reason we're having this little party."

"I know." He erased the distance between them. "That doesn't mean we can't see each other from time to time. You can't have children, so no one would know—"

He caught her arm when she would have slapped him. She tried to wrench from his grasp, but he wouldn't allow it. "How dare you even suggest such a thing? Let me go. If someone should see us like this—"

He jerked her closer. "You mean, if your *husband* should see us like this. Why do you care? You only married him for his children."

"That isn't—"

"Uh-uh." He shook his head. "That's the funny thing about lying, my dear. It doesn't change the truth. You're using him just as some common fortune hunter would use an heiress—to get something you couldn't have on your own. Money or children. What's the difference?"

He was right and she knew it. He must have sensed it, for he grinned. "Come now, Helen. Drop the righteous indignation. We both know you don't love him. How could you?"

She felt her eyes flash as his words illuminated the truth within her. "You're wrong. I do... I do love him."

His green eyes bored into hers, examining and recognizing her feelings for what they were. Hurt unfurled in his gaze then hardened into something vengeful. He tilted his head. "Ah, but have you told him? Have you told him what you told me? No, I can see you haven't. It's written all over your face. Perhaps I ought to tell him myself. Clear the field, so to speak."

Desperation and panic froze her in place. "Tom, you wouldn't."

"I might." His mouth tilted into a wry smile. "The funny thing is, I'm not sure if he'd care with the overabundance of children he already has. That was smart on your part. What worries me are the lies you must have told and the truths you must have covered up. That's what drives a man crazy. He'd wonder again and again what else he didn't know, what else you may have lied about."

Any fight she had left within her drained away. Her gaze lowered. She'd seen that very thing happening already.

"Poor fellow. I almost feel bad for him. Not quite so bad that I wouldn't steal his wife. Or, can you steal what never belonged to someone else in the first place?"

Her words came out in a near whisper. "He's my husband. Of course I belong to him."

"No." He smiled. "You belong to me. Always have. Always will. My only mistake was in thinking I had to marry you. You, my dear, are best suited for other purposes."

She gasped. Searching his face for the man she'd

once wanted to marry, she found only resentment and anger instead. "How can you say these things?"

"I say them because they are true. I love you in spite of all your damage. No, *because* of it. That is something your husband will never do." He leaned closer to whisper in her ear, "When he rejects you—and he will—you know where to find me."

The moment he let her go, she ran for the door. She reached it just as Quinn entered the room. He caught her arms when she stumbled into his chest. Startled, he looked down at her then across to Thomas. Releasing her, Quinn crossed the room in two strides. One solid punch across the jaw sent Thomas stumbling backward until he hit the back wall of glass then slid down to rest on his backside. Quinn stood over him menacingly. "Who are you, and what have you done to my wife?"

Thomas didn't bother to get up. He moved his jaw to see if it still worked. Satisfied, he glanced at Helen with wicked mischief in his eyes. She held her breath. Would he go through with his threat to tell Quinn the truth about her? He smiled up at Quinn. "We were just talking, friend. Just talking."

Quinn's gaze fell to hers as she tugged on his arm. She needed to separate them before Thomas changed his mind. "Helen, did he hurt you?"

Emotionally and mentally? Yes. Physically? "No."

"Who is he?"

"Thomas Coyle." She felt Quinn's muscle bulge with tension beneath her hands. "Please, let's go. He's leaving now, too."

Quinn ignored her, growling, "What did you say to her?"

Tom lifted a knowing brow. "Nothing she'd want you to know."

"What is that supposed to mean?"

Helen answered before Tom could. "It means he told me he loved me. I told him I didn't care."

"Is that all?"

"That's all that mattered."

"May I get up now without you sending me right back to the floor?" At Quinn's short nod, Tom stood. He brushed himself off. Edging to the door, he paused long enough to smirk and lift his flask in a toast. "Many happy returns to the lovely couple and if not…"

She interpreted his meaningful glance to her to be an echo of his earlier words. *You know where to find me.*

For Quinn's benefit, he finally said, "So much the better."

This time he drank deeply of the flask as he disappeared. Her relief was momentary as she realized he might be heading straight for the ballroom. She grabbed Quinn's arm. "Make sure he doesn't go into the reception."

Quinn rushed to the door and peered out. "He went down the side hall toward the back door. You're sure you aren't hurt?"

"Yes, I'm sure."

"Did he take liberties with you? If so, I'll—"

"I'm fine. Please, don't ask any more questions. Not right now." He reached out a hand to stop her, but she evaded his grasp to walk out the door. "I don't think I feel up to returning to the party. Give my excuses to Mother."

His plea came soft and low. "Helen."

She shook her head and hurried up the stairs to her room with Tom's words nipping at her heels. They were waiting for her as she swept down the hallway to her bedroom. *When he rejects you—and he will—you know where to find me... I love you in spite of all your damage. No, because of it. That's something your husband will never do...*

His words wouldn't be so pervasive, so effective, if she didn't already believe them to be true. Nearly everything he'd said was an echo of a thought that had filled her mind at some point in the past. The others—the vile ones—she knew couldn't be true. Yet they felt true because they fell in line with all the others. Now she not only felt damaged but dirty.

A knock sounded on the door. Her heart began to pound. She couldn't face Quinn right now. Not in this state and not until she gathered herself. Her mother's voice filtered through the door. Helen hesitated only a moment before letting her in. Lucille closed the door behind her. "Quinn sent me to check on you. What happened? What did Tom do to you?"

"He said some pretty nasty things, which I'd rather not repeat." She moved to the vanity table to remove her earrings.

Lucille came to stand behind her. "It might help to tell someone."

"Not this time." She turned her back to her mother and placed her hands on her hips. "Will you unbutton me?"

"Yes, but how can you be so calm about this?"

"I'm not calm. Just a little numb, I guess." With the dress's back undone, Helen stepped behind the changing screen. "Besides, I refuse to cry over or because of some man who is not my husband." She froze as she buttoned the collar of her nightgown. "I can and *will* thank God in my prayers tonight that he isn't my husband. He might have been if he hadn't shown his true colors once he learned about my problem."

"Your problem." A frown filled her mother's voice. "I've been thinking about that lately. Maybe we should get a second opinion."

Helen rounded the changing screen to stare at her mother. "A second opinion from whom? I was attended by Dr. Whitley after my accident. He's the most respected doctor in Austin. Once he issues a diagnosis, all the others defer to it. That's why he is our family doctor in the first place, because he's the best there is."

"Yes, I know." Lucille sighed. "I just wish there was some way for me to fix this for you."

Helen sat at the edge of the canopy bed to take her hair down from its fancy chignon. "Some things can't be fixed, Mother. Things like me."

"You are not a thing," Lucille said fiercely as she sat beside Helen. "You are a person. You are my daughter, your father's little girl, Quinn's wife, an aunt to your nieces and nephews. That is what defines you, along with your faith, your spirit, your personality—not your problem. Not unless you let it. So stop letting it."

She stared at her mother in disbelief. "Do you think that I *want* to feel this way about myself? Do you think I would *choose* this? Choose to be the way I am? To pretend that I'm normal, all the time knowing there is something wrong with me? Knowing that the person I..." She choked on a sob. "The person I love more than anything could reject me for it once he finds out?"

"That isn't going to happen. Quinn isn't Tom. He's a different kind of man. A better man. He isn't going to reject you."

"You don't know that."

"Neither will you unless you tell him."

Helen pulled in a deep, calming breath. "I just… I wanted to wait until he loves me. I think he's close. It will be easier then."

Lucille shook her head even as her tone gentled. "Darling, he may grow to love you more, but you aren't going to love him any less, so it won't be any easier. You need to tell him soon. Do it for your own peace of mind, if nothing else."

"I know." She slid her fingers into her loose hair and sighed. "I will, but not tonight. I need to think, gather my courage…"

"Pray."

She nodded. "Pray."

"Meanwhile, I'll make your excuses to the guests and hint that it's time for everyone to go home. Get some rest, sweetheart." Lucille hesitated near the door. "One last thing to remember, Helen. Quinn already has four children. Four. That's enough of a handful for any man. Unless he's expressly said anything different, he might not want any more. Good night."

That's what Helen had counted on in the beginning. Somewhere along the way she'd lost sight of that because she'd wanted him to love her for herself—not just accept her because having his own children made her tolerable. Yet, how could he truly love her if she'd never revealed how broken she really was? If he was falling in love with her as she hoped, then he was falling in love with the illusion she'd created.

She'd have to take the risk of losing whatever affection he may have developed for her by telling him the truth. She could see that now. Shutting her secret into a dark corner of her heart had only allowed it to grow and spread until its shame poisoned her thoughts and actions. Of course, bringing it into the light might only make it worse. How would she bear it every day for the rest of their lives if she saw pity in his eyes or disgust or disillusionment? She'd have the children's love. That would certainly help, but she wanted more. She wanted Quinn. She hadn't realized how much until tonight.

She burrowed under her blankets as though the extra padding could somehow insulate her from everything that had happened that evening and everything that would come. "I'll tell him, Lord, as soon as we return home. Will You prepare the way? Give me the right moment. Please work things out between us. I'm asking because You're the only one who can straighten out the mess I've made of my marriage, the mess I've made of me. Amen."

After saying goodbye to Helen's parents at the train station the next morning, Quinn made sure his family had settled comfortably into their seats before glancing out his window for what would be his last glimpse of Austin until they arranged another visit. The city had been Quinn's proving ground just as he'd expected. It had proven him to be a fool. In all of his efforts to measure up to the standard of what he thought Helen's husband was expected to be, he'd failed to be the husband she'd needed. He'd seen her staring across the ballroom at him, looking a little lonely despite the crowd of people. He'd seen the entreaty in her eyes for his attention. And he'd put off answering her silent call because he wanted to look important. He'd wanted to *be* important.

Somehow he'd gotten confused enough to think that meant swapping stories with the governor about the different places they'd each been in Texas. He wasn't confused anymore, but it was too late. Helen had left the ballroom by herself last night. If he'd been with her, she wouldn't have had to face Coyle alone, and whatever had passed between them wouldn't have happened. As it was, other than gaining favor with his in-laws, the only meaningful thing Quinn had received for reaching above his station was increased distance between him and his wife.

He glanced across the train aisle to where she sat in a smart sapphire-blue dress that served to make her large brown eyes look even richer. She was smiling as if everything was normal, for the children's sake, but there was a pensiveness lurking beneath the surface that she couldn't hide from him. She must have felt him watching her, for her gaze touched his then abruptly dropped away. He wished he was sitting beside her so that he could take her hand and try to bridge the gap between them. It would take some serious maneuvering of the children to manage it. He wasn't at all sure she'd appreciate his efforts, so he stayed put.

As the train began its sluggish crawl out of the Austin station, Reece gasped and lunged toward the window. "Hey, look! It's Charlie."

"What?" Alarm had Quinn out of his seat before the question made it past his lips. "Where?"

Quinn scanned the crowd as Clara squeezed in front of him to press against the window. "He's walking alongside the train, Uncle Quinn."

"I see him." The man was nothing if not average in height, build and looks. He wore a brown suit and matching bowler hat. The train picked up speed. Charlie didn't. Stopping at the edge of the platform, the man met Quinn's gaze and tipped his hat. Quinn watched him fade into the distance then sank down to his seat. "He just stood there and tipped his hat like he'd come to see us off."

His concern was reflected on Helen's face. "Did you recognize him?"

"I've never seen him before, which means he must have kept his distance on purpose."

"You think he's been following us around the whole time we were in Austin?"

"He must have been."

"But why?"

Quinn just shook his head, at a loss for any reasonable explanation. Trent climbed onto his lap. "I'm scared."

Too late, Quinn realized they shouldn't have been discussing this in front of the children. He wrapped one arm around Trent and pulled Reece closer to his side. Helen did the same to Clara and Olivia. "Hey, we're all safe. We're all together. Let's not worry about anything."

"Your uncle is right. How about each of us shares their favorite part of their trip to Austin? Who wants to go first?" Helen soon had them thoroughly distracted in reminiscing about the fun they'd had.

As the train ride lengthened, the younger two were lulled to sleep by the rhythmic clack of the rails, while the older two read the books Helen had brought along for them. Even Quinn was yawning by the time the train stopped in Peppin. Making sure everyone was accounted for once they exited the train was easier this time since Trent was sleepily clinging to his hand. He glanced at Helen, who had Olivia in her arms, while Clara and Reece stood close by. "I'll get the wagon from the livery and load our luggage in it then stop by the sheriff's office. Perhaps you…"

He faded off when he realized Helen's gaze was resting beyond him. "No need. I think the sheriff is coming to us."

He turned to find Sean approaching with his wife, Lorelei. The man reached out to shake hands. "Welcome back, y'all. I'm glad I caught you, Quinn."

Caught was probably a good word. It certainly appeared as though the couple had been lying in wait. Quinn glanced at Helen before sending a questioning look to the sheriff. Was something wrong?

"You're just the man I was hoping to see," Quinn said. "Do you have a moment to talk?"

"Sure thing. I've already arranged for your luggage to be set aside. Why don't you let Lorelei take the children to my office while we take a walk."

Lorelei leaned down to whisper to the children conspiratorially. "We'll have some hot cider and sugar cookies."

Reece glanced to Quinn. "Is that all right, Uncle Quinn?"

"Sure. Y'all go ahead." Once the children were a good distance away, Quinn turned to Sean. "What's happened?"

Sean swept his hat forward to indicate they should leave the train station. "Let's head toward the courthouse and I'll tell you."

The sheriff had definitely been planning ahead for this conversation, but why? Momentarily forgetting Helen's earlier distance, he reached for her hand. Thankfully, she didn't pull away as they followed Sean down the street to the courtyard, where he slowed the pace to a leisurely stroll. "Did you want to tell me that you'd seen Charlie in Austin?"

Quinn exchanged a confused glance with Helen. "Yes, how did you know?"

"He sent a wire to let me know y'all were on the way." Sean veered onto the path that led toward the courthouse. "That's how I knew to meet your train."

Helen frowned. "Why would he do that?"

"Charlie is actually Charles Powell. He's a private detective who was hired to protect your family."

Quinn stopped to stare at the sheriff. "Protect us from what?"

"Hired by whom?"

"To answer Quinn's question, it was a preventative measure in case Jeffery Richardson doubled back—which he didn't. He was caught by authorities in Mexico two days ago."

"That's great news." Quinn glanced at Helen to share a relieved smile before they started walking again. "What about the children's inheritance? Was it recovered?"

"Much of it was. However, that ties back to Helen's question."

Curiosity filled Helen's voice as she repeated it. "Who hired Charlie?"

Sean nodded toward the front of the courthouse, which came into view as they turned the corner. "There's your answer."

A couple rose together from where they'd been sitting on the courthouse steps. The man descended quickly at first, then slowed to a stop a few feet away. Quinn could do nothing but stare, frozen in place by the man's searching, deep blue eyes. A dimple appeared in his cheek. "Hello, little brother."

Chapter Seventeen

Quinn barely registered Helen's gasp behind him as he stared at the taller, broader version of the brother he remembered. "Wade, is it really you?"

"Sure is, partner. I'm a little worse for wear. You, on the other hand…" Wade's smile faltered with regret. "You're all grown up now. It's been a long time. Too long."

Quinn was having as much trouble as Wade in reconciling the boy he'd known with the man standing before him. Quinn had missed his brother fiercely those first few years after Wade and their father had left. However, with age, the memories of their time together had become something pleasant yet distant. He couldn't help feeling some of that distance now. Especially since no communication had passed between them and so much had happened after they'd said goodbye.

There had been Nana's death and their father's death. Wade had become a father through his first marriage then widowed and remarried. Quinn, of course, had gotten married, as well. Quinn struggled through his shock to find his voice again. "You're not dead. I mean I thank God you aren't, but how?"

"Believe me, I've been thanking God, too. I'd be happy to share the story with you and the children. First, let me introduce my wife, Charlotte." Wade held out a hand to the flaxen-haired woman who descended the last few steps with graceful ease. Her dark green eyes mimicked the color of her dress, which looked fancy enough that she could have borrowed it from Helen's closet in Austin.

"This is truly a pleasure, Quinn. After all the good things Wade has shared about you, I feel as though I already know you."

"Thank you. It's a pleasure to meet you, too." Realizing he'd never had occasion to introduce Helen before, he placed a hand at the back of her waist as he looked down at her. "This is Helen, my wife."

She blinked as though coming out of a daze at the sound of her name. She offered her in-laws a smile that was pure graciousness. "I'm so glad to meet you both and that y'all are alive and well."

She didn't look well. She looked pale. Suddenly, he realized why. Wade and Charlotte hadn't just come to visit him. They'd come to take the children away. As much as Quinn had come to think of his nieces and nephews as his own children—as much as he loved them as he would his own—they weren't. They belonged with their parents. Their *real* parents.

As glad as he was that his brother was alive and as wonderful as it was to be together again, Quinn's heart felt heavy at the prospect of the children leaving. Still, he knew what must be done. "Let's go tell the children."

* * *

Helen couldn't breathe. She could hardly think. If it wasn't for Quinn's hand at the small of her back guiding her toward the sheriff's office, she'd probably still be standing at the base of the courthouse steps in total shock. She rejoiced in the fact that Wade and Charlotte were alive. This was without a doubt the best thing that could have happened for her nieces and nephews. She knew that. Yet, somehow that didn't ease her heartache at losing them.

They'd decided on a similar plan to what the sheriff had done to break the news to the children, so Helen and Quinn entered the sheriff's office while Wade and Charlotte stayed outside. Sean waited right inside the door for his cue to open it. Lorelei offered a compassionate smile in greeting. The children glanced up from where they sat surrounding the sheriff's desk with their cups of cider and a cookie apiece. The sight of them was enough to fully pull Helen from the fog of shock that had fallen over her with Wade's first words.

"Thanks, Miss Lorelei." Reece swallowed the last bite of his cookie. "Are we going home now?"

Quinn mussed the boy's hair. "Actually, we have a surprise for you."

Clara's blue eyes widened with immediate interest. "What kind of surprise?"

"Where is it?" Trent asked, already pushing his chair back to stand.

Helen forced the cheery words past the lump in her throat. "It's the best kind of surprise there is. First, I want everyone to stand in the middle of the room and face me. Clara, you bring Olivia. Good. Now, we're all going to close our eyes and count to three."

With the children safely away from the steamy cups of cider, their backs facing the door and their eyes closed or covered, Helen met Quinn's gaze. "One."

He nodded to the sheriff, though his eyes didn't shift from hers as he came to stand beside her. His deep voice joined hers to say, "Two."

Helen watched the sheriff's door ease open silently for Wade and Charlotte to slip inside. Wade's chest swelled visibly in a gasp at the first glimpse of his children in months. Charlotte pressed a hand to her lips as tears filled her eyes. Helen swallowed. Quinn squeezed her hand and took over the count. "When I say the next number I want y'all to look straight at me. Understand?"

They nodded.

"Three." Quinn waited until their eyes were on him to grin. "Your parents are *alive*. Turn around. They're right behind you."

The children gasped and turned to run into their parents' waiting embrace. Pandemonium broke out between Trent's screams of joy and Clara's heartfelt sobs. Olivia's delighted giggles were punctuated by the occasional "Papa" or "Lotte." Reece kept murmuring, "I can't believe it." There wasn't a dry eye in the room or a face without a smile by the time the children calmed down enough to start asking questions.

Wade pulled one of the chairs over for Charlotte to sit. Clara immediately climbed onto her lap. Reece stood beside the chair and put an arm around the woman's shoulder. She, in turn, slipped one around his waist. Meanwhile, Wade sat in another chair with Olivia on one knee and Trent on the other. "I promised your uncle and aunt the story of what happened. If y'all listen closely and don't interrupt, most of your questions will be answered."

Trent nodded as he put an arm around his father's neck. "We'll listen good."

Wade smiled then turned to address Quinn and Helen. "My bride and I decided to spend our short honeymoon on our sailboat off the coast of Alaska. We left the children in the care of my assistant, whom until that point had been a close personal friend and a man I trusted to handle many details of my life. I believe you met Jeffery Richardson."

Quinn nodded but didn't interrupt, so Wade continued, "Our sailing trip was nearly over when we noticed the wind whipping up. Since it was earlier in the season than they normally occur, we didn't realize we were caught in a windstorm until we'd been completely blown off course. The mast broke and the ship began to sink, so we escaped into the lifeboat."

Charlotte shook her head as she gazed into Wade's eyes. "We nearly drowned many times that night. It was all we could do to keep the lifeboat out of the sea and try to keep warm. By morning, the worst of it was over."

"Yes, but we'd only had time to grab a few provisions. They barely lasted us past the first day. There was no sign of shore in any direction, so I could only row in the general direction of where it should be. On the second day we saw what appeared to be a shoreline. We thought we might be able to make it there by nightfall or early the next morning." Wade's frown turned into a smile. "We had just run out of water when we saw a small fleet of kayaks headed toward us. A tribe of Eskimos met us halfway and towed us to shore. We could only understand a little of what they said, which was about how well they could understand us. However, they welcomed us into their village where they took care of us for the next three and a half weeks because I had the misfortune of coming down with pneumonia.

"It took another five days for us to make it back home to Juneau by dogsled. Once there, we discovered that we'd been presumed dead, which I suppose is understandable since we hadn't been able to send word that we were alive. We were devastated to find out that our children had disappeared along with Jeffery. Apparently, he'd seized the opportunity of our supposed deaths to sell my fur-trading post and everything else I owned to the highest bidder. He took the proceeds along with all of the money I'd left to the children in my savings account." He shook his head and ran his fingers through his hair. "We're still in the process of trying to put our lives back together in Alaska."

Charlotte nodded. "Meanwhile, we managed to find out he'd talked about bringing the children to their uncle in Texas."

"The question was, where in Texas?" Wade focused his dark blue eyes on Quinn. "I've been searching for you a long time. I even hired private detectives to find you. They never could. You're a hard man to track down, little brother."

Helen glanced at Quinn, who gave a wincing grimace. "Sorry about that. I know I traveled a lot. Didn't leave much of a paper trail, either."

"You sure didn't. I finally decided to search for you my own way since the professionals couldn't find you. By that time, I had children, so I couldn't just leave them or take them cross-continent to look in person. I spent several years investigating by mail and telegram.

Toward the end, Jeffery joined me in the search. We built your history from the time I left and followed your path by contacting each successive employer. I knew we were getting close. He must have found you while I was gone. It took us a while, but we followed his trail to you. Then the authorities asked us to wait until they found and captured Jeffery before contacting y'all."

Quinn smiled. "It sure means a lot to know you were trying so hard to find me, Wade. I wish we'd been able to reunite earlier and under different circumstances. Then again, I guess this is pretty good, seeing as we found out that you and Charlotte are alive, after all."

Charlotte nodded. "God was looking out for us even when it didn't seem like it."

Helen waited until they'd told the children about Charlie's role in all of this and Jeffery Richardson's capture before asking Wade, "So what are y'all planning to do from here?"

"We're going back to Alaska."

Quinn placed a hand on her shoulder. "When are y'all leaving?"

"Our train leaves tomorrow afternoon. I know it's soon, but we need to arrive in Alaska before winter really sets in."

Helen had expected as much. Still, a protest rose up within her. Did they have to go so soon? Then again, why draw out the pain? The children were leaving. Whether that happened tomorrow morning or a week from now, it wouldn't change the inevitable. Dread pooled in her stomach as she realized the same principle applied to her secret. Yet, how could she find the courage to tell Quinn the truth after everything that had just happened? Then again, how could she not?

* * *

It was decided that they would all go to the farm to help pack the children's things. Once it became clear that the men would only be in the way until there was some toting to be done, Wade had requested a tour of the farm. Quinn was happy to oblige and spent the next twenty minutes showing his brother around and explaining all the improvements he'd made. Wade didn't seem to notice the cold breeze shifting through the trees as they stopped halfway up a nearby hill to look down at the farm spread out below them. "This is beautiful land, and you've done a great job with it. I'm proud of you, Quinn."

The words made Quinn stand a bit taller, and it was hard to hold back a grin. He suddenly felt like an eight-year-old again. Back then, he would have climbed to the top of any tree, jumped across any mud hole or captured a Texas-size toad to earn the attention and approval of his brother. Especially during the years their father hadn't been inclined to give it. He cleared his throat. "Thanks, Wade. It means a lot to hear you say that."

Wade's gaze shot to his. "It does?"

"Of course. I always looked up to you. You were smart as a whip, stronger than most of the boys we hung around with and you always made me feel important." Noticing the puzzlement on his brother's face, Quinn frowned. "What? Don't you believe me?"

Wade shrugged. "It's just… I got the impression that you resented me for leaving with Pa."

"As I remember, Pa didn't give you much choice in going with him. How could I resent you for that?"

"Then why did you refuse to write to me?"

"Wade, you know I couldn't read or write back then.

I'm only learning now because Helen found out I was illiterate and wanted to teach me."

Wade frowned. "You mean, the tutor didn't help you?"

"What tutor?"

"The one I asked Nana to hire for you a few years after I left."

Quinn's jaw nearly dropped in shock, and it took him a minute to formulate a reply. "You wrote to Nana?"

"Sure, I wrote to her—not to mention sending money home every month." Wade narrowed his eyes. "You didn't know, did you?"

"I had no idea." Quinn sat down on a nearby log as his mind raced to keep up with the implications of what Wade was saying. "I'm sorry to say that I never saw any letters. I certainly never had a tutor. Although, Nana did try to teach me a little around the time you say you wanted her to hire one. The only money I knew of was what I brought in myself."

"I don't understand. Why would she keep all of that from you?"

Quinn sighed. "I can think of a hundred different reasons. Of course, we'll never know what motivated her. Maybe one. Maybe all."

"What kind of reasons?"

"She definitely resented y'all for leaving, so it could've been her trying to punish you for that. She didn't want me to leave her like y'all had, which she probably thought I would as soon as I was old enough to follow if I knew you still cared about me, and that I'd be welcomed. She didn't want me to get any fancy ideas about what I could accomplish in life. She might have wanted to protect my soul from the influence of too much money. Need I go on?"

"No." Wade bit out the response and began to pace. "Pa and I couldn't send that much money at first, but it increased over time. Once he died, it dipped because I was the only one working. I knew I needed a better-paying job, which is why I jumped at the chance to go to Alaska when I heard how much I could make in the fur-trading business. I kept sending money until the letters came back saying no one lived at that address. It must have added up over the years. What did she do with all of that money if she wasn't buying food or hiring a tutor like she was supposed to do?"

Quinn smiled wryly. "Knowing Nana, she probably gave all the money to the church."

"I can't believe this!"

"I can." Quinn sighed. "I'm sorry she did it because we could have used that money. Although, now that I think about it, twice when things got desperate I came home to find a church lady had dropped off some groceries. Nana hated accepting charity, so I'm guessing that 'church lady' was actually your money at work."

"That's some consolation, but not much." Wade stopped pacing, turned to Quinn and stared as though trying to peer into his brother's soul. The anger in his tone was replaced with concern. "Forget about the money. What about you? How did you fare living with her?"

"Uh…good, I guess." At Wade's doubtful look, he shrugged. "It was difficult at times, but I loved her and I'm sure she loved me, even if she was a little flawed in expressing it."

"I'm not questioning that. You're a good man and

she raised you, so she must have done something right. I just hope you realize that a lot of what she said about me, about God, probably even about you and the things you should expect out of life wasn't right."

Quinn stared at his brother. "How do you know what she told me?"

Wade sat beside him, straddling the log to look at him. "I know because she said the same things to me before I left. In fact, the last words she ever spoke to me were from Galatians 6:8. 'For he that soweth to his flesh shall of the flesh reap corruption.' It was as though she thought I was leaving out of rebellion to sow wild oats. All I did was obey Pa by going with him to find higher-paying work. We were trying to make life better for our family."

"She said y'all were going to look for gold."

"Where exactly would we find it? The last gold rush was way back in '59." Wade rolled his eyes and shook his head. "The point is, her words stayed with me for years until I read the last half of that scripture. 'But he that soweth to the Spirit shall of the Spirit reap life everlasting.' Don't let anything she said haunt you like it did me. Live your life based on God's truth—not our grandmother's."

Scratching his jaw, Quinn frowned. Did that include her warning about getting hurt or killed if he reached out for more than he deserved?

Wade placed a hand on his shoulder. "I can tell there is something bothering you. What it is?"

Quinn took a deep breath and explained what had been plaguing him.

"You think I went through all that trouble because

I reached above my station for something I didn't deserve?"

"Can you find any other explanation? I mean, look at everything that happened. You got caught in an act of nature on your honeymoon and almost died. Your wife almost died. Your children were placed somewhere you might not have been able to find them. You lost everything you owned because it was stolen from you. Need I go on?"

Wade was quiet for a long moment. Just when Quinn thought he'd stumped his brother, Wade spoke. "I doubt I'll ever be able to say for sure why all of that happened to me. However, I know it wasn't some form of punishment."

"How can you be so sure?"

Wade pulled in a deep breath. "I'm alive. My wife is alive. I found my children. Everything else I called mine can be replaced or rebuilt. I didn't lose it all, Quinn. In fact, I found something I might not have otherwise."

"What's that?"

"You." Wade smiled. "I don't regret the trouble I went through. I see it as God's grace working through fallible man in a fallen world. Life is too short to live always looking over your shoulder for trouble. It's coming. It always is. But God's power and love and grace are already right there with you. That's what you focus on, little brother. Nothing else."

Quinn swallowed hard against the emotion building in his chest before giving a low whistle. "You should've been a preacher."

Wade laughed. "Stare death in the face a few times. You might find yourself thinking an unusual amount of deep, poetic thoughts, too."

"No, thanks. I'll just take it from you." Quinn would, too, because it was good advice. Especially since most of what Nana had said seemed to be a slanted version of what Quinn had been reading in the Bible lately. Why did he cling so tightly to that one adage of hers when he'd forsaken so many others?

Perhaps because it fit everything he believed about himself. It made perfect sense to him that a man who wasn't smart, literate, handsome or rich should have a life just as lacking as he was as a person. Yet Quinn wasn't that man anymore. He still had a long way to go with his reading and writing, but he'd made enough progress to prove to himself he wasn't as stupid as he'd always thought. While he may never be particularly handsome or rich, he'd discovered something of far more worth—a deeper relationship with God.

He certainly wasn't perfect. That had been made evident by his inability to protect Helen from whatever cruel words her ex-fiancé had spoken. However, he'd like to think that he'd made himself into a far better man than he had been when he'd first married her. Did that mean he could stop looking over his shoulder for trouble, as his brother had suggested? Would he actually be able to enjoy the life he'd been working so hard to deserve?

It was going to look different now that his nieces and nephews would no longer be a part of it in the way he'd anticipated. Of course, different didn't have to be a bad thing. With the children leaving, perhaps Helen would be open to moving forward in their marriage. Surely, she could tell that he cared for her deeply. If she cared for him even half as much, maybe she'd be willing to start a family of their own.

Chapter Eighteen

This wasn't the final goodbye to her nieces and nephews. Helen knew that. Why then, was it a struggle to keep back the tears? She'd see them off tomorrow afternoon at the train station. That would be the real test. Now she should savor the last glimpse of them as they rounded the curve in the hillside that would take them out of sight after what had been a surprisingly enjoyable afternoon and evening.

She'd found a new friend in Charlotte, who'd expressed a desire to correspond often and promised to share news about the children. Wade's delight in finding his children and his long-lost brother in one place had been almost palpable in a way that Helen had found endearing. Watching the interaction of the reunited family had been as sweet as the applesauce cake Charlotte had taught her to make.

With a final wave and a heavy sigh, she returned to the house with Quinn trailing after her. He closed the door behind them with a slight thud that seemed to echo excessively in the empty cabin. She slowly became aware of the fact that she was well and truly alone with her husband. He had been a comforting and supportive presence during the day, but he had to know as surely as she did that everything had changed. She wasn't sure she was ready to deal with that within herself, let alone together.

Grateful for any distraction, since they would surely be few and far between tonight, she tied on her apron and went to work on the supper dishes. She fully expected Quinn to pull out his banjo or delve into his studies, so she was more than a little surprised when he chose to roll up his sleeves and join her at the sink instead. It had been Clara's chore to help Helen with the dishes. They'd talk about their day and share a giggle or two before reading or music time. Sharing the chore with Quinn was an altogether different experience.

He said nary a word as he took the sudsy dishes she handed him to rinse. The area in front of the sink was too small for both of them, so his arm kept brushing against hers. Each time, the urge to hide her face against his broad chest grew stronger. Would it be wrong to give in to that, knowing he might not want to have anything to do with her once she revealed the truth about herself?

When he rejects you... Tom's words whispered through her thoughts. The plate she'd just cleaned slipped back into the soapy water. She braced her hands on the side of the sink for support. In that moment, all she could see was the image presented in her imagination. The one from her dream where Quinn's hands examined her abdomen as the doctor had so many years ago while he pronounced the words she'd heard then. *Damaged.*

That's what she was. Damaged. With the children gone, there would be nothing to soften the news when Quinn found out. She'd been counting on love, but the word hadn't been mentioned between them since the night of the storm when he'd denied even the possibility of it happening. That meant there would be nothing to make up for her inadequacies.

She stiffened when Quinn stepped behind her, wrapped his arms around her waist and eased her back against his chest. Her breath caught in her throat as he pressed a kiss against her hair. The gentleness of that kiss released the sobs that had been building in her chest since she'd first realized she was losing the children, along with even deeper ones created by the awful encounter with Tom. Turning in Quinn's arms, she rested her cheek against his chest and let them all out.

Quinn rested his chin on the top of her head while he rubbed circles on her back. "I know, darlin'. I know."

But he didn't know. Not really. That only made her feel worse. She tightened her grip on the front of his shirt and pulled in a shaky breath. "Oh, Quinn."

"It's a hard thing to take." His deep voice rumbled in her ear. "We'll miss them terribly, but we can…" Leaning back slightly, he lifted her chin so that he could see her face. "We can start a family of our own someday, if you're willing."

She stared at him as her mind raced with the implications of what he was saying. He wanted a full, complete marriage. Did this mean…? Could he possibly love her, after all? Her hand instinctively covered his heart. "What are you saying?"

"I'm saying I think it would be good to have children of our own. I don't mean as a replacement to our nieces and nephews. They would be their own people." His eyes strayed from hers and took on a faraway look as if he could see into the future to the children she couldn't possibly have. "They'd be even more special to us because they'd be made up of you and me. No one would ever be able to take them away from us. We'll have as many as you want. If we have a boy, I'll teach him how to farm and we can expand—"

"Stop." The word came out in a near moan, but it was enough to capture Quinn's attention. She had to tell him. She had to tell him *now*. "There won't be any children. Not for us."

He searched her gaze. "You mean you don't want to have children with me?"

"I mean I *can't* have children, Quinn."

"I don't understand. Why not?"

"I had a riding accident when I was sixteen. The doctor said I'll never be able to have children. That's why I agreed to marry you. You already had four and…" She ran out of words when his face blanched. His arm dropped from around her. Turning away, he sank onto one of the kitchen chairs. She leaned back against the sink for support as raw, heavy silence stretched between them. Despair rolled over her in waves, washing away any trace of hope that he wouldn't reject her. Her voice sounded distant to her ears as she whispered, "Say something."

After a long moment, he glanced up with devastation written all over his face. "What do you want to do?"

She stared at him. Do? About what? Her condition? No. Their marriage.

He was asking her what she wanted to do about their marriage now that the reason they were together had been stripped away and she'd revealed the truth about herself. What *could* be done? They were legally married. That hadn't changed. "I'm not sure."

Something in his blue eyes hardened along with his

tone. "Well, I'll not hold you here. You can go back to Austin if you like. Take the dowry your parents sent. I won't need it and it really belongs to you."

That was all she needed to know. She closed her eyes to hide the pain that cut through her chest. She forced her voice, her face, to remain impassive. "I suppose that would be best. I'll finish the dishes in the morning. Good night."

She closed the door to her room behind her but made no effort to get ready for bed. Instead, she sat on her bed with her hands buried in her hair and wept a silent torrent of tears. She tensed as she heard Quinn's footsteps in the hall, then relaxed when she realized he was retiring to the room where the boys used to sleep. She was physically, emotionally and mentally exhausted from everything that had happened, but sleep wouldn't come. Her tears faded as hurt slowly turned to anger. Soon she was pacing the floor of her bedroom with her hands clenched into tight fists. She paced until the walls seemed to close in on her, then she knew she needed to get out of the house and into the fresh air no matter how dark or cold that air might be.

She quietly crept from her room since another confrontation with Quinn was the last thing she wanted tonight. Or was it? She stomped into her boots while sending a glare down the hallway toward the room where he slept. She grabbed her coat and stepped into the night. The dark hills silhouetted by moonlight loomed around her. Innumerable stars shimmered above. A mockingbird's call drifted down from the woods. Yet, all Helen's mind could focus on was one question that continued to bother her. If Quinn didn't love her then why had he wanted to change their arrangement?

"He's just like Tom, that's why." Picking up a pine-cone, she sent it spiraling toward a tree, which absorbed the blow with a satisfying *thwack*. Even as her words settled into the air around her, she knew they weren't true. Quinn was nothing like Tom, which was why his reaction had been so hurtful. She hadn't been sure what to expect from him, but she'd certainly hoped for more than just his silence. Once that had ended, all she'd gotten was a kindly put command to get out.

What she'd really wanted was for him to sweep her into his arms and profess his love. She'd wanted him to beg her to stay. She'd wanted him to tell her that he didn't think less of her because she'd injured herself in a moment of recklessness on a high-strung horse. She'd wanted him to contradict every word Tom had spoken and sweep away the self-deprecating thoughts that so often filled her mind. He hadn't done that. In fact, his action made her wonder if the doctor and Tom had been right all along. Perhaps it was time to fully accept that she was everything they'd said or intimated her to be: *permanently damaged*.

Something rose within her that she'd never felt before. Courage, strength, determination, temerity—whatever it was, it came out in one steely spoken word: *"No."*

Suddenly, a rush of what she could only describe as clarity overtook her. Let Dr. Whitley say her injury was caused by recklessness rather than pure accident. Let Tom try to convince her that she wasn't intended to be an honorable woman. Let Quinn return her to her parents as he would damaged goods to a mercantile. That didn't mean it was true. It certainly didn't mean she had to accept their view of her as something on which to base her identity, her thoughts or her plans.

She didn't need anyone to contradict words she knew weren't true. She couldn't wait for someone to come along who could clear her mind of cruel thoughts. She could—she *would* do it herself. In fact, it wasn't something anyone else could do for her. It was something she needed to overcome with God's help and Word and grace. He certainly didn't look at her and see damage. He saw His Beloved. How had she lost sight of the importance of that? The answer was simple. She'd focused on the opinion of others rather than God.

"Helen?"

She stiffened at the sound of Quinn's voice. The brittle scales of the pinecone she hadn't realized she was holding bit into her hand. She dropped it and pulled her coat closer. "Yes?"

"What are you doing out here? You'll freeze."

What did he care? She spun to ask him exactly that. The sight of him leaning against the door frame stilled the words on her tongue before they reached her lips. He lifted the lantern he held in what must have been an effort to see her better. For her, it only served to illuminate the concern marring his brow and the mussed curls that could only come from fitful sleep. His deep blue eyes were too tired to be guarded. She saw gentleness there, which was altogether confusing in the aftermath of their last conversation.

Her anger abandoned her, leaving her feeling vulnerable. It would have been easier to hold on to those feelings if she didn't love him so. Everything he'd done until earlier tonight had made her feel whole and even cherished. She'd thought he was beginning to care for her. Hadn't he said he wanted to win her heart? Could the truth about her really have changed that so quickly?

Afraid she'd do something or say something to reveal how close she was to throwing herself into his arms and begging him to let her stay, she lowered her eyes to the porch steps as she mounted them. Her intent was to quickly edge past him into the house, but he took his time in shifting his weight away from the door frame. His arm came up to block the entrance when she tried to move past him. Surprised, her gaze automatically locked with his, which was a mistake. Surely her tangled emotions were written on her face. Any hope that they weren't shattered as a frown deepened on his face.

Had she no pride? Just because she'd had a breakthrough concerning her condition didn't automatically alter Quinn's view of her. She was damaged in his eyes. Yet, she wasn't sorry for telling the truth. If she hadn't, she wouldn't have found the strength to face it or the courage to choose not to let it define her. She lifted her chin. "Excuse me, please."

A moment passed before his arm dropped. She edged by him and down the hall into her bedroom where she pulled in a heavy sigh. She wouldn't be able to sleep tonight, so she might as well start packing. It wouldn't do either of them any good for her to stay here longer than necessary. Yet what was the point of leaving? They'd still be married even if they were leading separate lives.

Didn't that mean that there was still hope for them? Perhaps he'd change his mind over time. Surely he'd get lonely out here all by himself. Eventually, he might ask her to return. She sighed. Was she truly prepared to spend months, years or even a lifetime waiting for such a thing to happen when he obviously wanted a way out of their marriage? Perhaps the only fair thing to do would be to let him go. She just wasn't sure how she could.

* * *

Quinn awakened the next morning feeling completely disoriented. Then he remembered he'd spent the night in the boys' room because the children had gone with Wade and Charlotte to the hotel in town. Children. Helen. He sat up in Reece's old bed and dragged his hands through his mussed hair as every painful detail of the past twelve hours rushed over him. Helen couldn't have children. The news had been disappointing in itself because he'd enjoyed being a father to his nieces and nephews. However, that hadn't compared to the devastation he'd felt when he'd realized how much more it mattered to Helen that she couldn't be a mother.

It had mattered enough that she'd married a man she didn't love—probably had no hope of loving—to obtain the children she wouldn't have been able to have on her own. And then they were taken from her. Now she was left with him. A man she'd never wanted in the first place. A man she must have known all along didn't deserve her. No wonder she was heartbroken.

He'd felt her pain along with his own. Yet he knew his wound had been inflicted by his own stupidity. He'd gotten so caught up in trying to be a better man, he'd forgotten that only one thing had truly qualified him to be her husband. It didn't have anything to do with him or the Bachelor List. It was that she'd loved his children. Now the children were gone, and he couldn't give her any more. He had nothing to offer that would be of any worth to her.

An image came to mind of Helen standing in the cold with her coat wrapped close around her. He still couldn't figure out what she'd been doing out there in the middle of the night and she hadn't deigned to explain. In fact, he couldn't recall that she'd said more than a few words to him during that exchange. She hadn't needed to because her eyes had spoken volumes—most of which didn't make a lick of sense.

Longing, hurt and something he might dare to call caring had replaced the pure apprehension that had stared back at him after she'd divulged the true reason she'd married him. The apprehension he'd understood. Why wouldn't she fear being stuck with him alone for the rest of her life? He'd done his best to let her know he had no intention of keeping her captive just because their names were on the same marriage certificate. He'd offered her a way back to the life she deserved. The one where she'd be able to live in a gilded mansion and never have to scrub dishes or milk a cow or avoid an ill-tempered rooster.

His plan had been to stay right here where he belonged. That would spare them both unnecessary pain—hers at being stuck with a man she'd never really wanted, and his at wanting a woman whose heart he'd never be able to win. However, the look she'd given him on the porch was not that of a woman whose heart was completely untouchable. He couldn't fathom why she'd want anything to do with someone who had nothing to offer, but what if she was amenable to changing her mind? Could there be some small part of her that wanted to stay?

The answer came to him as soon as he passed by her doorway and saw her struggling to buckle a nearly overflowing suitcase. Not only did she want to leave, but she couldn't wait to get away from him. The sight made him downright ornery even though he knew he had no right to feel that way. He felt a muscle in his jaw twitch. "Are you planning on leaving today?"

She jumped a little at the sound of his voice, then spared a quick glance his way. "I have a few things to do in town first, then I should be able to leave on the same train with the children."

Dandy. His whole family would be leaving him at one time. That ought to make things around here nice and lonely. Still, he could hardly protest since it was a smart plan. He crossed his arms. "Good. I don't like the idea of you traveling alone."

"Well, I won't be." The buckles finally snapped closed. "We'd better hurry if we want to finish the chores and make it into town in time to have breakfast with the other Tuckers."

The "other Tuckers" were already waiting for them at Maddie's Café—which meant the story of Wade and Charlotte's survival was probably winding its way through town with record speed. As soon as they finished eating, Charlotte took the children to the schoolhouse to say goodbye to their friends while Helen left to take care of a few things on her own. Realizing this would probably be the most privacy he'd get with his brother, Quinn decided to make the most of the opportunity. "Helen will be traveling as far as Austin on the train with y'all. Will you look out for her for me?"

"You know I will." Wade paused as Maddie refilled their cups of coffee before he continued, "You aren't going with her?"

Quinn felt a wry smile tug at his lips. "That would kind of defeat the purpose. She's going there to live with her parents."

Wade frowned. "You two are separating? For how long?"

"I don't know. Forever, I guess. I suppose I should have expected as much as soon as I found out you were alive." Quinn quickly explained everything to his brother from his original prayer for a helpmeet to the Bachelor List and all that came after.

"I had no idea," Wade said once Quinn had finished. "So you're just going to let her go?"

Quinn grimaced. "I can hardly force her to stay. That would be selfish since she deserves so much more than I can give her. Besides, I hardly think I'd stand a chance with her."

Wade shook his head. "That's Nana talking. Not you. At least, I hope you don't really believe that."

"I believe what you said about Nana's warnings not being true. In fact, I'm pretty sure most of what I learned from her was plain wrong. I've also read my Bible enough to know that God's promises for His children are good. It just doesn't seem like they're intended for me."

"Why not?"

"I'm not the kind of man who has great things happen to him. At least, not the kind that last. I thought that would change if I made myself into a better man. Well, I've changed a little, but not enough to make a real difference. Until I do…" He shrugged. "I don't deserve anything more than what I've always had."

"It kind of sounds like it's more about identity than anything else."

"Identity? What do you mean?"

"It's like this." Wade set aside his coffee and leaned forward. "You're saying because you're this person, you don't deserve certain things. This may sound strange and I know we've only recently reconnected, but I can already tell you aren't the person you think you are."

Quinn gave his brother a quizzical smile. It *did* sound a little strange, but Quinn was intrigued. "Who am I, then?"

"I'm afraid that's something you've got to figure out for yourself."

Quinn thought about it, then asked, "You wouldn't happen to have a Bible in town, would you?"

"As a matter of fact, I do." Wade settled the bill with Maddie then led Quinn to his hotel room where he placed a Bible in Quinn's hands. "I'm supposed to meet Charlotte at the mercantile. You'll have this room to yourself for a while. Make yourself comfortable."

Quinn wasted no time in doing just that, sitting in an armchair by a window that overlooked Main Street. The activity below faded away as he flipped through the pages of the Bible at random. The words seemed to jump out at him as they never had before. How had he missed this verse declaring him a new creature? Or this one saying that God would give him a double portion of honor in place of the shame he'd endured? Or another declaring that God wanted to give him a future and a hope? The more he read, the more he realized that his worth was based not on what he could do, but on what God had already done.

Even so, something about all of this didn't make sense.

Why would God do this for him? He leaned back in his chair to think over everything he'd read, everything Helen had shown him, everything he'd heard Pastor Brightly preach, and arrived at one conclusion. It was because God loved him. And that changed everything.

Well, perhaps not everything. Helen was still going to get on the train and never look back. After all, his newfound freedom didn't mean he should chain her to a life or a man she'd never wanted. She'd made her decision. He needed to respect that even though he prayed with all his heart that she'd change her mind.

Chapter Nineteen

Quinn grimaced as a hollow whistle announced the arrival of the westbound train. Steam hissed through the cold air while a few passengers disembarked and the large steel doors of the luggage car slid open to receive his family's bags. Quinn sneaked a sideways glance at Helen, who looked as proper and composed in a cranberry-colored traveling suit as she had the first time he'd seen her standing at the front of the schoolroom a few months earlier. She was clutching what appeared to be a scroll wrapped in brown paper and tied with string. Whatever it was had garnered more of her attention than he had since she'd joined the rest of them for a quick dinner at the hotel.

Wade clasped him on the shoulder. "Everything is loaded up. It's time to say goodbye."

Quinn's heart sank as everyone turned to look at him. Helen's goodbyes to Wade, Charlotte and the children wouldn't be necessary until she reached Austin. He pulled in a deep breath to steel himself. This was going to hurt. He had no doubt about that. Clara stepped forward and he lifted her into a hug. She threw her arms around his neck. "You're the best uncle in the world and I love you."

"You are a precious young lady and I love you, too." He held her tight then kissed her forehead before setting her down.

Trent was already tugging on his leg for attention. "I've got something important to tell you."

"Is that right?" Quinn swept the boy into his arms. "What do you have to say for yourself, young man?"

Trent hid his face on Quinn's shoulder with a sudden attack of shyness, which made his words a bit muffled. "You're my second-bestest buddy besides Reece."

"I am? Well, 'second-bestest' is good enough for me, cowboy." He jostled the boy slightly so they could grin at each other before they exchanged a hug. Charlotte handed him Olivia next. He told the little girl goodbye with a kiss on the cheek that she promptly returned, much to everyone's amusement. Reece was next. As they hugged, the boy admitted, "I'm going to miss you and Aunt Helen something awful. I wish we could all be together."

"We'll miss you, too, Reece. You'll be in our thoughts and prayers no matter how far apart we are. Distance doesn't stop family from being family." Quinn glanced up to find Wade watching and smiled. "Your pa taught me that."

After saying goodbye to Charlotte, Quinn offered his hand to his brother. Wade brushed it aside and went for a hug instead, which ended with them both pounding each other on the back. When they stepped apart, Wade put a hand on Quinn's shoulder. "I hate that we're saying goodbye again when it seems we've just said hello."

"So do I." A lump made its way into his throat even

as his eyes began to smart. He fought back the feeling with a smile. "I can't tell you how much this has meant to me or how much you've helped me in the short time you've been here."

"It's meant the world to me, too. I only wish I could have been here a long time ago. We've missed so much." Wade shook his head and swallowed hard before turning away. "Charlotte, children, let's get on the train. Helen, we'll save you a seat."

Quinn pulled in a deep breath then slowly turned to face his wife. She offered a tremulous smile that soon vanished. He cleared his throat, rubbed his jaw and tried to form the words to say goodbye. They wouldn't come. He slipped his hands into his pockets. "Your parents will be waiting for you in Austin?"

"Yes."

He nodded. "Send me a wire to let me know you've arrived safely."

"I will."

"Good." Silence stretched between them until it was broken by the conductor's call of "All aboard." Quinn's heartbeat ratcheted up in his chest. This was really happening. She was actually going to leave. "I guess this is it."

"Yes, I suppose it is." There were tears in her eyes when she met his gaze for the first time all afternoon. "Thank you, Quinn. Thank you for giving me the chance to be a mother even if it was only for a short time. It was everything I dreamed it would be. Now, all you have to do is sign this and return it to Judge Hendricks. He'll take care of everything else."

"What are you—"

She rose on tiptoe to kiss him deeply. Startled, it took

him a moment to respond, and when he reached out to pull her closer, she was already disappearing onto the train. All she left behind was the package she'd been so fascinated with all afternoon. Was this what he was supposed to sign and return to the judge? He ripped the brown paper away to reveal the official-looking document inside. "'Petition for an-nul…annul-ment.'"

Everything within him froze. He couldn't seem to breathe as he examined the pages that would legally make it as though his marriage had never taken place. Helen had already filled everything out and signed her name on the last page right next to the blank spot where his was supposed to go. This was far different than just letting her live with her parents in another city. This would mean letting go of her and any hope of reconciliation. It meant he'd most likely never see her again. *This* was what she wanted?

His hands fisted, crumpling the papers in them as he stared at the train that hissed out more steam as it began a slow chug out of the station. Well, annulment wasn't what he wanted. He was sick of this. He was sick of living his life expecting the worst then letting it play out right in front of him as though he had no choice or strength to change things. If God wanted him to have good things, an abundant life, a hope, a future, then why should Quinn be content to settle for anything less?

Helen was the best thing that had ever happened to him. He didn't deserve her. That was true. He didn't deserve God's love, either. That didn't mean that it didn't belong to him…just as Helen did in the eyes of God and the law. She was his wife. He was her husband. He suddenly realized that meant it was no longer a question of whether he deserved her. The true question—the only question that mattered was, did he love her?

The answer was undeniable. Yes, he did. He just hadn't dared to accept it or acknowledge it for fear that something would happen to take her away from him. Now what he'd feared was happening. Still, he had a choice. He could let her go or he could fight for her. It might not change the outcome of what would happen. However, for the first time in his life, he intended to try.

The train bellowed a whistle that sounded like an outright challenge, causing Quinn to realize his deep thinking had allowed the train to ease out of the station. It was gaining speed in an effort to leave Peppin behind. Without a second thought, Quinn jumped from the platform onto the track. He took off running after the train, ignoring the yells from the folks at the station questioning his sanity along with every misgiving and fear that rose up to tell him he was being a fool.

Quinn Tucker was chasing after more than he was entitled. What's more, he planned to catch her. Once he did, God willing, he'd never let her go again.

Helen rested her head against the train window and fought back tears as the train picked up speed. Her seat's window faced the opposite side from the center of town, so she'd have no last look at the place she'd called home or the man she'd called her husband. Perhaps that was for the best. Her conversation with the county judge had yielded a way of escape for Quinn. Maybe he would find someone else in time. Someone he wouldn't think of as damaged.

Meanwhile, she'd find a way to be content on her own while cherishing every memory of the eight weeks she'd been his wife. She could only imagine what Austin society would say when she turned up only a few days after her wedding reception husbandless. Right now, she really didn't care. The only thing that mattered was that she'd left her heart back in Peppin with a man she'd probably never see again.

Helen slid forward in her seat as the train abruptly slid to a stop. Her hand shot out to keep Trent, who sat next to her, from doing the same. She exchanged an alarmed look with Charlotte as Wade stood to peer out the window. He spoke over the confused murmurs coming from the other passengers in the train car. "Maybe there's something on the tracks."

Reece squeezed in between his father and the glass. "Maybe it's outlaws."

That brought Trent out of his seat. "I don't see anything."

"Boys, sit down." Charlotte's voice was commanding enough to make even Wade comply. Meanwhile, the folks across the aisle began opening their windows, allowing the cold to seep in along with the conductor's irritated voice. "That brake is for emergencies only. This does not constitute an emergency."

"It does to me."

Helen felt her eyes widen at the sound of the deep, familiar voice. A gasp eased through her lips and her heart thundered in her chest as she hurried down the aisle toward the door. It eased open from the outside and she found herself staring down at Quinn. He froze, with his hands braced on either side of the doorway as though ready to jump inside and…do what exactly?

Hope battled with alarm and uncertainty as they stared at each other for a long, drawn-out moment. His searching gaze traced her every feature before returning to hers. He must have seen something he liked, for his blue eyes deepened while his dimples flashed in a reckless grin she'd never seen before. A strange weakness filled her knees. His strong hands caught around her waist and hers automatically braced on his shoulders as he swung her down to stand in front of him. Her fingers slid from his shoulders to push away from his chest once she found her bearings. It did little good since he didn't release her. "What is going on? What are you doing here?"

He ignored her questions completely. "Helen, please don't go."

She was dreaming. She'd fallen asleep on the train and was dreaming. "What did you say?"

He spoke louder, as if that would somehow help her understand. "I want you to stay."

Before she could think of a response, a collective "aw" sounded above her head. Helen glanced up and her eyes widened. All the passengers on her car had crammed together at the open windows. They weren't the only ones. People were hanging out the windows down the length of the train to watch. The engineer had climbed down from his station to stand in the tall grass with his hands on his hips. Even a few folks on the platform of the train station a good distance away had stopped what they were doing. "Land sakes, Quinn. You stopped the train."

"Yeah, I sure did." He didn't look the least bit repentant about it, either. Nor did he seem fazed by all the attention they were garnering. He led her a short distance off and positioned her so that she faced away from the train. Suddenly, it felt as though it was just the two of them beneath the wide Texas sky. His gaze had lost none of its intensity. "Did you hear what I said, Helen? I don't want you to go to Austin. I want you to come home with me."

It was exactly what her heart was aching to hear. Well, not exactly. Still, it was the closest he had ever come to a profession of love. Even so, it didn't change anything. She slid out of his one-armed embrace and took a step back. "Quinn, as much as I would like it to work out between us, I don't think it will. It's better that you file the petition for annulment. Where *is* the petition?"

His jaw tightened at the mention of the annulment before his lips settled into a smirk that was entirely too distracting. "Don't know. Don't care. Why wouldn't it work?"

She glanced away, rubbed the nape of her neck and pressed her lips together.

"Helen." That one word issued a command impossible to ignore.

"It's going to be hard enough to stop thinking of myself as damaged. If I was living with a husband who saw me that way, it would be nigh on impossible. I can't do that to myself."

A blank look was followed by one of pure confusion. "What are you talking about? Damaged how?"

"The accident. I can't have children." She frowned when his confusion didn't ease. "Quinn, I told you this."

"I know you told me. I just don't understand where you're getting the idea that any of that matters to me. I never said that made you damaged. I never even thought it."

She stared at him in disbelief. "Then why did you look so devastated?"

"I thought you were saying you had no use for me. You married me for the children. The children were gone and I couldn't give you any more. You thought it was…?" He shook his head. "Not at all. I mean, sure I'm disappointed that we won't be able to have any children. However, if I looked devastated, it was because I knew I was about to lose you."

"It was?"

"Yes, it was. It seems we've both been a little confused. Let me clear something up for you right now. You are not damaged." He eased closer, his hands cradling the loose fists she hadn't even realized she'd made. "You are intelligent, beautiful and caring, among so many other qualities, all of which make you an incredible woman. So much so that I almost let you go because I know I have no hope of ever deserving you."

"What changed your mind?"

"I fell in love with you. I'm pretty sure it happened the night of Ellie and Lawson's shivaree. If not then, it might have been when you thought I wanted you to milk the chickens, or when your kiss caused a hailstorm, or seeing your determination and patience in teaching me to read, or the time you called me Bear. I'm not sure. However, as I stood on the platform with that petition in my hands, watching as you rode out of my life, one thing became clear. I love you, Helen Tucker. I'm asking you to give me a chance to show you how much. I'm asking you to come home."

Those were the words she'd been longing for him to say. Hearing them spoken was like stepping into a daydream. She was afraid she'd blink and all of this would vanish. She'd find herself back on the train, staring out the window wishing for something she'd never have. Yet, he stood before her with his heart in his eyes confirming his words. She couldn't contain her smile. It started in the depths of her soul and spread until it reached her lips. He traced the upturned corner of her mouth. "Does this mean yes?"

"It means I love you, too."

"You—" Surprise gave way to searching. "You really love me?"

"With all my heart."

A grin spread across his face. "And you'll come home?"

She nodded. "And I'll come home."

He whooped. Catching her waist again, he lifted her into the air and whirled her in a tight circle, much to the delight of the onlookers, who let out a cheer of approval. She laughed and clung to Quinn's hand as he led her back toward the waiting train. Wade stood beside the conductor with a grin on his face and her luggage sitting in the grass at his feet. Her nieces and nephews raced toward her. She knelt down to receive their hugs, kiss their cheeks and tell them goodbye. Her in-laws each gave her a hug before ushering their children back onto the train. The conductor gave them one last scowl that reluctantly changed to a smile as he shook his head. Mumbling something about Peppin being a crazy town, he signaled the engineer and hopped back on the train.

Helen waved at the children and shouted, "Thank you!" in return to the strangers calling out well-wishes as the train lumbered down the tracks then sped away. A quick glance at the station told her most of the folks had gone about their business. Awareness rushed over her and she turned to find Quinn already watching her with an expectant smolder in his eyes. A blush warmed her cheeks. He might be ready for a kiss or two, but she had important business to take care of first. Placing her hands on her hips, she tilted her head and lifted a brow. "Quinn Tucker, what is that you said about not deserving me?"

"No idea."

She narrowed her eyes. She erased the distance between them until they stood toe to toe before poking him in the chest. "Hey, focus for me here. This is important."

"I'm listening." He caught her wrists and guided her arms up so that they encircled his neck before wrapping his arms around her waist.

She gave him a doubtful look but continued, anyway. "You said you were going to let me go because you didn't think you deserved me. Why would you think such a thing?"

"I may be a little smarter than I originally thought. Still, I'm not rich or handsome or..." He must have realized it would not be wise to continue. Perhaps her glare clued him in.

"How dare you say those things about my husband? You certainly are smarter than you think. Book learning is not the only measure of intelligence. While you are excelling at that, you are also intelligent in other areas such as practical wisdom, life experience, human nature, musical ability. I could go on and on." She leaned back in his arms. "As for finances, you don't give yourself enough credit for going from a child with a hungry belly to a man who owns his own land. Besides, I've lived rich in money. I'd a thousand times rather be rich in love."

"I believe you. Now you don't have to tell me I'm handsome."

"You make my knees weak."

He lifted a brow. "I make your knees weak?"

"Remember how I sort of stumbled the first time I saw you with your new haircut and a shave?" She smoothed the collar of his gray coat even though it didn't need fixing.

"Yeah."

"Well, right after that I…" She bit her lip then shot a glance heavenward before letting out a small sigh. "Truthfully, I sort of swooned. Just a little."

"I made you swoon." He grinned, looking all too pleased with himself.

"And when you gave me that look just a minute ago I could hardly breathe."

"What look?" he asked. She gave him her best rendition of his earlier smolder, which only made his blue eyes darken. "I see what you mean. So…what happens when I kiss you?"

"Now, that's a hard one." She gave him a mischievous smile. "I can't seem to remember…"

Recognizing her invitation for what it was, he lowered his forehead to hers. "I do. Lightning."

Then he set out to prove it.

Epilogue

One year later...

Helen was certain she must be dying. There was no other way to explain the peculiar way she'd been feeling of late. She'd tried to downplay her illness to Quinn, but there was no mistaking the mounting concern in his eyes. She'd come to town alone today, hoping a visit to the doctor would provide her some insight and tell her things weren't as hopeless as she feared. Tension filled the air as Doc Williams finished the examination. "I'd say you have about seven months left."

Dread filled her sensitive stomach. Tears filled her eyes. Her mind began to race. How on earth was she going to tell Quinn? They'd been married—truly married—for little over a year. They'd thought they had an entire lifetime to spend together. She'd had no idea that lifetime would be so short. "Seven months. That's such a small amount of time."

"Yes, and it will go by even faster than you think." He was far too intent on flipping through a calendar to notice the quiet sob that caught in her throat. "That puts your due date around the end of July."

She blinked. "Due date? I thought that term was only used for women who are expecting, not someone who is…" She couldn't say the word. Not yet. She swallowed. "Someone who has so little time left as I do."

Doc Williams straightened in his chair and peered through his glasses at her as alarm filled his distinguished features. "Mrs. Tucker, I never meant to give you the impression… I thought you already knew about your condition and were just coming to me for confirmation."

"I was."

"No. I don't think you understand." He removed his glasses and took her hand. "Seven months from now you're going to deliver a baby."

"A baby?" The world spun. If not for the man holding her hand, she might have toppled right off his examining table onto the floor. "That's impossible."

"I assure you it is not only possible but inevitable."

"No. There must be some other explanation." She told him of her riding accident and the doctor's prognosis afterward.

He listened intently, alternately nodding and frowning until she finished. "I see. Well, your body doesn't lie. It has all the symptoms of a woman in the family way. I am quite sure your family doctor's prognosis has been proven most decidedly wrong."

"I don't understand how that could be possible. He was so certain. As certain as you are now."

"The female body remains mostly a mystery to those practicing medical science. Unfortunately, that can breed a level of what I can only describe as ignorance in even the most respected of doctors. Some think that recklessness or personal misbehavior is the main cause of infertility in ladies. It would seem that your family doctor subscribed to that school of thought."

"You don't think that's the case?"

He shook his head. "The numbness and pain you described that took place following your accident aren't unusual for such trauma. From your description, it sounds as though those feelings went away with the rest of the bruises you acquired in your fall. You've never missed a month until recently, right?"

"Right."

He shrugged as though that settled everything. "It seems to me that everything is progressing normally. We'll keep a close eye on you to make sure there aren't complications. However, I don't anticipate there being any. You are a healthy young woman who is about to welcome her first child."

She couldn't seem to catch her breath, couldn't seem to get past the shock. "I'm going to have a baby."

Doc Williams grinned as he helped her down from the examining table. "Congratulations, Mrs. Tucker."

"Thank you." She walked from his office into the waiting room in a daze. She blinked, realizing Charlotte had rushed forward to meet her. "I'm sorry, Charlotte. Did you say something?"

Helen's in-laws had returned to Peppin with the children only a week after their train had pulled out of town. Wade said they'd realized if they were essentially going to have to start over, they ought to do it here in Peppin with their family. Quinn had been ecstatic and so had Helen. The two families were constantly in and out of each other's houses, sharing meals and laughter. Charlotte had become one of Helen's dearest friends. That was why Helen had asked her sister-in-law to accompany her to the doctor without revealing the reason for the Saturday-morning appointment.

Charlotte watched her in concern as she looped her arm through Helen's and guided her out the door. "I asked if you were all right. You looked so scared when you went in and now you look sort of stunned."

"I am stunned." They paused beside the wagon Helen had parked outside the doctor's office. "I'm fine, though. Better than fine. I… I need to go home. I need to tell Quinn."

A knowing smile slowly tipped Charlotte's lips. "I see. Are you sure you're up to driving right now?"

"Yes. Oh, Charlotte." She hugged her friend tightly then left her in the dust. Helen barely made it out of town before she let out a very unladylike squeal of joy. "I'm having a baby. I'm having a *baby*! Thank You, God! Thank You! Thank You! Oh, I can't wait to see Quinn's face when I tell him."

There was another squeal, some laughter and a hundred more "thank-Yous" before she set the brake outside her house. She forced herself to pull in a calming breath, which had absolutely no effect before she flew up the porch steps into the cabin. The door shut behind her with a bang. Pulling off her gloves and shrugging out of her coat, she tossed them aside. "Where, oh, where is my Bear?"

"Right where you left him," Quinn called back.

She followed his voice to the girls' old room, which had been converted into a study with an ever-growing library. He'd added a fireplace to the wall the room shared with their bedroom so it was nice and warm. As usual, rather than sitting at the rolltop desk or in one of the two comfortable chairs, he'd stretched out on the thick rug in front of the hearth. Before he could stand to greet her, she knelt behind him and wrapped her arms around his shoulders in a quick hug. "Have you been reading all this time?"

He caught her arm to keep her there as he sat up then glanced at the clock on the mantel. "I guess so. With no need for a winter crop, since the fall harvest went so well, I have a lot of time to improve my mind. Besides, what else was I supposed to do left all by my lonesome for ages?"

She rolled her eyes. "I've been gone little more than an hour."

"Felt like ages." He lifted her hand to his lips for a kiss. "Listen to this. It made me think of you. It was written by a fellow named Marlowe. 'Come live with me and be my Love, And we will all the pleasures prove, That hills and valleys, dale and field...'"

It wasn't very surprising that a man who loved music would find an affinity for poetry. Still, it was a delightful development. Speaking of delightful developments, she had one of her own to share if she could just get his nose out of that book. She leaned forward to kiss his cheek, hoping it would make his dimple appear. It did, so she did it again. He snapped the book closed, snagged her waist and brought her around so that her back rested against his propped-up knee. He'd perfected the smoldering look that had originated almost a year ago and had no qualms about using it on her now. "You are *the most* distracting woman."

He kissed her and she got a little distracted herself until he finally let her breathe again. She sat up but didn't go far. "Quinn, I went into town to see the doctor."

The fire in his blue eyes banked in concern. They'd both been afraid to speak of the frequent episodes of what she now knew was merely morning sickness until now. "What did he say?"

"He said…" Her fingers traced the curve of his jaw as her lips betrayed her serious tone with a smile. "You and I are going to have a baby."

His mouth dropped open even as his brow furrowed in confusion. He shook his head. "That can't be right."

"That's what I told him." She filled him in on Doc Williams's explanation for her previous diagnosis and his expectation that she'd have a normal pregnancy.

Quinn still looked a little stunned when she finished. He blinked, searched her gaze. "Are you serious? We're really going to have a baby?"

"I'm serious. You're going to be a father."

Shock faded to awe. His mouth opened and closed without him finding any words. Standing, he lifted her up with him then tugged her into his embrace. She tried to pull back to see his face, but he wouldn't let her go even that much. She mumbled into his chest. "Are you happy?"

She felt him nod.

She giggled. "Are you sure?"

He caught her face in his hands and kissed her. Cradling her cheek, he stared into her eyes with a look so joyful, so loving that it took her breath away. "I love you."

"I love you, too."

"I can't wait to meet our baby." He pulled her close again. His tone turned deep and reverent. "I don't know what to say except thank You, Lord, for answering my prayer and blessing me beyond anything I could have imagined."

She joined in from the depths of her heart. "Amen."

* * * * *

Jan Drexler enjoys living in the Black Hills of South Dakota with her husband of more than thirty years and their four adult children. Intrigued by history and stories from an early age, she loves delving into the world of "what if?" with her characters. If she isn't at her computer giving life to imaginary people, she's probably hiking in the Hills or the Badlands, enjoying the spectacular scenery.

Books by Jan Drexler

Love Inspired Historical

The Prodigal Son Returns
A Mother for His Children
A Home for His Family
Convenient Amish Proposal

Amish Country Brides

An Amish Courtship
The Amish Nanny's Sweetheart

Visit the Author Profile page
at LoveInspired.com for more titles.

A HOME FOR HIS FAMILY

Jan Drexler

Lay not up for yourselves treasures upon earth, where moth and rust doth corrupt, and where thieves break through and steal: But lay up for yourselves treasures in heaven, where neither moth nor rust doth corrupt, and where thieves do not break through nor steal: For where your treasure is, there will your heart be also.

—*Matthew* 6:19–21

To my mother, Veva (1929–2014).

Thank you for teaching me to love stories.

I miss you more than words can say.

Chapter One

Deadwood, Dakota Territory
May 1877

"Sorry for the delay, folks. There's a bull train on the trail ahead of us, and they're hogging the road. It won't be long until we're moving again." The stagecoach guard acknowledged Sarah MacFarland and Aunt Margaret, the only ladies in the cramped stage, with a tip of his hat. Water sluiced off the brim onto the feet of the male passengers. "The good news is that we're only a few miles from Deadwood, and the rain is easing up a bit."

"Thank you." Sarah answered him with a nod, but kept her face classroom-firm. She had already learned women were few in this western country, and men were eager to take even a polite smile as permission to overstep the boundaries of propriety. Aunt Margaret had the notion Sarah might find a husband out here in the West, but Sarah had no such dreams. Twenty-eight years old put her firmly in the spinster category and she was more than happy to remain there.

"Excuse me, ma'am." Mr. Johnson shifted his bulk and reached under his seat. The man's cigar jammed between his teeth had bothered Aunt Margaret the entire journey from Sidney, Nebraska. "If you'll oblige, I'll take my bag. Since we're this close to the camp, I might as well walk the rest of the way."

He grabbed his satchel and squeezed out of the crowded coach. The other men spilled out after him like a half-dozen chicks from a grain sack.

"Are they all walking to Deadwood from here?" Aunt Margaret adjusted her hat as she peered through the open door.

Peder Swenson pushed himself up from his spot on the floor. "I'm not. But I am going to stretch my legs and see what's going on." The blond eighteen-year-old had kept them entertained with stories of his native Norway on the long journey.

As Sarah watched Peder stride away on his long legs, she couldn't sit still another minute. "I am, too."

Aunt Margaret grabbed her sleeve. "You will not. Who knows what you'll find out there? We've seen enough of those bullwhackers along the trail to know what kind of men they are."

Sarah held her handkerchief to her nose. Rainy weather kept the heavy canvas window covers closed, and even with the men gone, the heavy odor of unwashed bodies was overwhelming. "I'll be careful. I have to get some fresh air. I'll stay close by, and I won't go near the bull train."

Aunt Margaret released her sleeve, and Sarah climbed out of the stagecoach, aching for a deep breath. With a cough, she changed her mind. The air reeked of dung and smoke in this narrow, serpentine valley. She held her handkerchief to her nose and coughed again. Thick with fog, the canyon rang with the crack of whips from the bull train strung out on the half-frozen trail ahead. She pulled her shawl closer around her shoulders and shook one boot, but the mud clung like gumbo.

A braying sound drew her attention to a wagon a few feet from the coach, leaning precariously close to the swollen, rocky creek at the side of the trail. She stepped closer to get a better look and nearly laughed out loud at the sight of a black mule tied to the back of the covered wagon. The creature sat in muddy slush as it tried to pull away from the rushing water and noise.

A tall man, soaking wet and covered in mud from his worn cavalry hat down to his boots, grabbed for the mule's halter. "Loretta, if you break that rope again, I'm going to sell you to the first butcher I find."

The mule shook her head, and he missed his grab, landing flat on his back and sliding down the slope toward the edge of the creek. As he fell, the animal flicked her gray nose toward him and snatched his hat in her teeth.

A giggle rose in Sarah's throat at the sight, and her shoulders shook as she fought to keep it in.

The man rolled over, lurching to his feet as he grabbed his hat from the mule. "You stupid, dumb, loco..." He muttered all kinds of insults at the animal, who only tossed her head as he slapped the hat against his legs in an effort to clean the mud off it.

A young boy appeared at the back of the wagon, pulling the canvas cover open. He couldn't have been older than eight or nine, with a straw-colored cowlick topping his forehead. Would he be one of the students in her new academy? Uncle James had written that several families lived in and around Deadwood and that some of the parents were desperate for a good school. Sarah had brought a trunk full of books and supplies for boys just like this one, and for the poor young women trapped in the saloons. She smiled at the thought. Dr. Amelia Bennett would be so proud of her.

The boy caught her attention again, shaking his head as he watched the man and the mule. "She was only trying to help."

"Charley, the day that mule helps me do anything will be the day I eat my hat. I've never seen a more useless…"

"Not Loretta." Charley's voice rang with boyish confidence. "She knows exactly what she's doing."

The man leaned one gloved hand on the corner of the wagon box while he raised a boot to dislodge the mud with a stick. "Then why does she keep fighting me every time I try to get her to do something?"

"Because she's smart. She doesn't want to go any closer to this creek."

The man stomped his foot back onto the ground and lifted the other one. "The horses don't have any problem with it."

Sarah glanced at the four-horse team at the front of the wagon. They stood with their backs hunched as the rain gave way to a cold wind that threatened to snatch her hat away. She pushed it down tight and turned back to the scene in front of her.

"The horses are stupid."

The flabbergasted expression on the man's face as Charley pronounced his judgment triggered another giggle. Sarah slapped a gloved hand over her mouth, but a snort of laughter escaped between her fingertips.

"Ma'am." The man locked eyes with her, then released his foot, stomping the heel on the ground. "I'm happy to see we amuse you."

"Oh, I'm…" She snorted again. "I'm so sorry. But the mule, and you and those poor…" She couldn't talk through her laughter. "Those poor horses. I think the mule is right."

"See, Uncle Nate? I told you."

"Charley, get back in the wagon." The boy ducked inside as the man called Nate strode across the few feet of trail toward her. "So you think the mule is right?"

Sarah's laughter died. No answering smile lit his dark eyes and his lips formed a thin, tight line. She was the only one who had found the incident funny, but he didn't need to condemn her. She lifted her chin. "You drove into a precarious spot. One misstep and your wagon and all its contents could end up in the creek."

"You think we ended up there on purpose? The stagecoach…" He looked at the coach, and then at her. "*Your* stagecoach about ran us off the road."

Sarah's face heated in the cold air. A muscle in one of his stubbled cheeks twitched. "I apologize. I should have realized you were at the mercy of the crowded trail."

He pulled his hat off and wiped a weary forearm across his brow. "Yes. The crowded trail, and the rain, and the forty freight wagons all trying to head into Deadwood today and the cold." He turned away, gazing into the fog-shrouded pines looming above them at the edge of the canyon, and then faced her again. "And now it's my turn to apologize. I'm letting my frustrations get the better of me."

Sarah observed him as he waited for her reply. His apology had turned the corner of his mouth up in a wry grin.

"Of course, you have my pardon." She smiled, breaking her self-imposed rule. "Anyone would be hard-pressed to let a day like today not frustrate him."

As he smiled back, a gust of wind ruffled his short dark hair.

"You and Charley are on your way to Deadwood?"

"Yes, ma'am, we are."

Sarah searched his eyes for that wild gleam of gold fever—the look that made the men she had traveled with lose all their common sense—but his brown eyes were calm and clear in spite of the tense lines framing them that spoke of exhaustion and many days on the trail. He met her gaze with his own interested one. Something foreign fluttered in her stomach.

"My uncle has started a church in town, and I'm a teacher. I'll be opening a school soon, and I hope Charley will be able to attend."

His smile disappeared. "Wouldn't count on us, ma'am. We'll be busy getting settled."

The flutter stilled. "But you can't let a boy like Charley grow up without any education."

"I don't intend to, miss. The children will get all the education they need."

Sarah pressed her lips together. Did this cowboy truly think a child could get a decent education while mining for gold or running wild in the streets?

Her reply was interrupted as the stagecoach driver climbed back up onto his seat. "You'd better take your place, miss," he said over his shoulder. "We have a way cleared and are going on into town now."

"Yes, all right." As she turned to the coach, Charley's uncle reached out to open the door for her. As he leaned near, she caught the scent of leather and horses.

"Thank you, Mr...."

"Colby. Nate Colby."

He smiled as he offered his hand to steady her climb into the coach.

"I hope we'll be able to continue discussing Charley's education at another time."

He waited until she was seated and then leveled his gaze at her. "I think we've finished with that subject. The children's schooling is already taken care of."

Sarah opened her mouth, ready to deliver the stinging words that would put this cowboy in his place, but as her eyes locked with his, the argument died in her throat. He smiled, nodded to Aunt Margaret and closed the door. He was gone.

"Why, Sarah." Aunt Margaret began, straightening Sarah's skirt as she took her seat. "Who is that man? You promised you would stay away from the bull train."

Sarah rubbed at a splash of mud on the hem of her skirt, turning away from her aunt. She was certain her face held a telltale blush. "He was driving an immigrant wagon and has his nephew with him."

And he had mentioned children, so more than only his nephew.

"But still, you haven't been properly introduced. We don't know anything about the man, and you're letting him…"

"I allowed him to be a gentleman and open the door for me. It isn't as if he is courting me." She patted Margaret's hand in assurance.

The driver called to the six-horse team and cracked his whip. She fell back in her seat as the coach started off with a jolt. The opposite door flew open, and Peder jumped in.

"*Uff da*, I made it!"

As Peder launched into his description of the stalled bull train for Aunt Margaret, Sarah turned in her seat and lifted the corner of the canvas window cover. Nate Colby stood in the center of the muddy trail, his feet planted far apart and his arms crossed over his chest, watching the stage. She let the curtain fall and braced herself against the rough road. He certainly wasn't the kind of man she had expected to meet in the notorious Deadwood.

Nate shook himself. He had no time to stand watching a stagecoach wind its way along the muddy trail between the freight wagons, even if it did carry the most intriguing woman west of the Mississippi. He had a family to take care of.

He turned to the wagon, tilted on the bank between the road and the creek, and that stubborn mule still pulling on the halter rope with all her might as if she could keep the whole outfit from tumbling into the water.

Olivia appeared in the opening of the wagon cover. At nine years old she was the image of her ma, from her upturned nose to her golden hair. "Uncle Nate, are we almost there?"

"We should be in town this afternoon." Nate tied down a corner of the canvas that had pulled loose in the rising wind. "You get back in the wagon and take care of Lucy. I've got to get us off the creek bank and back up on the trail. It's going to be bumpy."

Eight-year-old Charley popped his head up next to Olivia's. "Who was that, Uncle Nate? I've never seen a prettier lady."

Olivia gasped. "Charley, you can't say that. No one was prettier than Mama."

"Mama was a mama, not a lady."

Nate tightened the end of the canvas. "Your mama was a lady, Charley," he said, drawing the opening closed with a tug. "She was the prettiest lady who ever lived."

"I told you so."

Nate hardly heard Olivia's words as he moved around the wagon, checking every bolt, tightening every rope. She was right; no one had been prettier than Jenny, and no one had been happier to have her as a sister-in-law than him. But if anyone came close to Jenny, it was that girl from the stage. Instead of Jenny's golden light, she had the beauty of a rare, dark gem, with black curls framing her face. Her eyes had seemed nearly purple in the gray afternoon light, but no one really had purple eyes.

Olivia's voice drifted through the canvas cover, singing Lucy's favorite song. Nate pushed against the familiar worry. Lucy would get better soon. Once they were settled, she would get back to the bubbly and energetic five-year-old she had been before the fire. All she needed was a safe and secure home with her family, and she would be back to normal.

But how long would it take until they had a home again? He went through the steps in his head.

Find his land. Good land with plenty of meadow grass for the horses. That was first. Then file the homestead claim. Next would be to build a house, outbuildings, make sure water was accessible.

Nate worked a wet knot loose and pulled the canvas tight before tying it again. He moved on to the next knot.

Find more mares for his herd. Some of the mustangs he had seen here in the West had descended from quality stock, he could tell that. And with some work and gentling, they'd make fine broodmares. Their colts, with his Morgan as the sire, would make as fine a string of remounts as the US Cavalry could wish for.

Test the next tie-down. Loose. He pulled at the soaking knot. The plan had to work. What would become of the children if this chance didn't pay out?

He retied the rope, tightening the wet cover against the rising wind. The plan would work if it killed him.

Nate pressed his left cheek against the damp, cold canvas, easing the burn of the scars that covered his neck and shoulder and traveled down both arms to the backs of his hands. The constant reminder of his failure to save Andrew and Jenny. The reminder of what his cowardice had cost the children. A chill ran through him. What if he failed again? He couldn't. He wouldn't.

Olivia's song filtered through the canvas, a song of God's protection and care.

With a growl, Nate pushed away from the wagon and headed toward the horses. When had the Lord protected them? When he was nearly blown to pieces in Georgia during the war? When Ma and Pa died in '64, leaving Mattie alone to fend for herself? When Jenny and Andrew were burning to death? When three children were left homeless and orphaned?

He could live without that kind of protection. God had His chance, and He hadn't come through. They would just have to get along on their own.

And they'd get along without any busybody schoolteacher stepping in. As if he'd let some stranger take care of Andrew and Jenny's children. It didn't matter that the scent of violets curled like tendrils when he stepped close to her, pulling him deeper into those eyes.

He shook his head. The children were his responsibility, and he'd make sure they had everything they needed.

When he reached the team he checked the traces, and then each horse. Pete and Dan, the wheel horses, stood patiently. Ginger, his Morgan mare, tossed her head as he ran his hand over her legs. At just three years old and growing larger with her first foal, she had the lightest load of them all, but she'd have to throw her shoulders into the harness to get the wagon back on the trail. She could do it, though. Morgans were all heart.

Last was Scout. The stallion rested his nose on Nate's shoulder, mouthing at his neckerchief as Nate scratched behind the horse's left ear and smoothed the forelock back from his eyes. This horse had saved his life more times than he could count during the war and carried him all over the West as he had searched for Mattie the years since then. Nate owed him everything.

Scout nudged his shoulder.

"Sorry, boy. No carrots today. We've got work to do." He stroked the dark cheek under the bridle strap, holding Scout's gaze with his own. The horse understood. He would get the wagon back onto the trail.

With shouts from the bullwhackers and the crack of whips, the train started out. Nate called to his team, "Hi-yup, there!"

The horses strained, the wheels turned in the mud and the wagon lurched up and onto the road. But as it did, Nate heard a sickening crack. Halting the team, he stooped to look under the wagon, dreading to confirm his fears.

The front axle was splintered and twisted along a narrow crack from one end to the other. A stress fracture. But it was still in one piece. He'd have to try to drive the wagon into Deadwood for repairs.

He stamped his feet to get some feeling back into them.

The weather was turning bitter, and fast. He had to get the children into some sort of shelter for the night. The wind seemed to take a fiendish delight in whistling down the length of the canyon. If he didn't know better, he'd think this weather was bringing snow behind it. But this was May. They couldn't have snow in May, could they?

He'd have to walk to keep the strain off the axle. He glanced up at the wagon. Should he have the children walk, too? He shivered and buttoned the top of his coat. No, they'd be better off in the wagon, out of the wind. He pulled at Scout's bridle, and the horses started off.

Glancing upward, he breathed out a single word. "Please." As if he really believed someone would hear him. The wind pulled water from his eyes, and he ducked his head into the blast. When the gust eased, gathering itself for another onslaught, he looked straight up into the pewter sky, at the light breaking through the gray clouds in golden rays. He had to keep the children safe. He had promised.

"Oh, not again!"

Sarah caught hold of the branch of a juniper shrub as her boot slipped on the muddy creek bank. The night spent in the snug cabin Uncle James had built when he came to Deadwood last summer had been a welcome relief after days in the stagecoach, but she was quickly getting chilled and miserable again on this afternoon's mission of mercy.

"Are you all right?" Aunt Margaret puffed as she tried to keep up with Uncle James's pace.

"Yes, I'm fine." Sarah pulled at the juniper until she was on the trail next to her aunt again and brushed a lank strand of wet hair out of her face. Uncle James reached out a hand to steady her, shuddering as a gust of wind struck them.

"This storm is getting worse, and it's starting to snow. We need to be getting home." Uncle James took Aunt Margaret's arm.

"I'm glad we went, though. Mr. Harders would have been frozen solid by morning in that cold cabin with no fire." Sarah buried her chin in her scarf.

"The poor man." Margaret clicked her tongue under her breath. "If he was this sickly, he should never have come to Deadwood."

James tucked her hand in the crook of his arm. "His doctor told him to come west for his health."

"And this place is healthy?"

"Wait until the weather clears, my dear. I know you'll love it as much as I do."

Sarah took her aunt's other arm. "Let's hurry and get home where it's warm."

"Wait." Margaret clutched at James. "What is that? An Indian?"

Sarah peered through the brush along the creek. "She doesn't look like a Sioux, unless they wear calico skirts." Sarah started toward the girl, who was now bending to dip a pail in the creek. A few steps took her around the bushes and face-to-face with the barrel of a shotgun.

"You stop right there." The gun barrel wavered as the eight-year-old boy holding it stepped into view. The same boy she had seen yesterday afternoon, peering out of the covered wagon. Charley, wasn't it? She looked past him to the empty trail. Her stomach flipped at the thought of seeing Nate Colby again.

"Young man, put that gun down right now." Margaret's voice was as commanding as if she was reprimanding one of the Sunday school boys.

"Uncle Nate said to keep a gun on any strangers coming around, and that's what I mean to do." Charley squinted down the barrel and raised it a bit higher to aim at Margaret's head.

This was getting nowhere, and Sarah was wet and cold.

"Come, now, surely you can see we're no threat." She smiled, but Charley only swung the gun barrel around to her. The gun wavered as he stared at her. "I know you, but I don't know them." He turned the shotgun back toward Uncle James.

"Charley, what are you doing?" The girl with the water pail came up the path behind him, and the boy tightened his grip on the gun.

"Keeping a gun on them, just like Uncle Nate said."

The girl, half a head taller than the boy and a little older, eyed Sarah as she pulled a dirty blanket tighter around her small body.

"Are you two out here alone?" Sarah smiled at them. "Where is your uncle?"

The children exchanged glances.

"No, ma'am, we aren't alone," the girl said. "Uncle Nate went hunting, but he'll be back soon." She pulled at her brother's sleeve. "Come on, Charley. We have to get back."

Charley let the gun barrel droop and backed away.

"There aren't any cabins around here." James sounded doubtful, as if these children would lie.

"We have a wagon. We've been traveling the longest time."

Charley turned on the girl. "Olivia, you know Uncle

Nate said not to talk to strangers." His voice was a furious whisper.

"They aren't strangers. They're nice people." The girl's whispered answer made Sarah smile again.

"Why don't you bring your family to our cabin for a warm meal? You can wait there until this storm blows over."

The two looked at each other.

"Uncle Nate said to stay with the wagon." Sarah could hear doubt in the boy's voice.

His sister pulled on his sleeve again. "Lucy is already cold, and night's coming. It's just going to get colder."

"We have stew on the fire," Sarah said. The thought of the waiting meal made her stomach growl.

"Why are you even asking them?" Margaret stepped forward and took each of the children's hands in her own. "Now take us to your wagon, and let us take care of the rest."

The children looked at each other and shrugged, giving in to Margaret's authority. They led the way to the covered wagon, listing on a broken axle, at the side of the trail. The canvas cover whipped in the wind. So Mr. Colby had made it almost all the way to town before breaking down. Another half mile and he would have reached safety. But where they were now... Sarah glanced at the bare slopes around them, peppered with tree stumps.

As they drew close, Olivia dropped Margaret's hand and ran to the wagon.

"Lucy! Lucy, where are you?"

A curly head popped over the side of the crippled wagon, and a young girl with round eyes stuck her thumb in her mouth and stared. Sarah guessed she looked about five years old.

Out here, away from the shelter of the trees and brush along the creek, the wind roared. Sarah marveled at its fury, and the children huddled against the gust.

Margaret stepped to the end of the wagon and looked in. "Is this all of you? Where is the rest of your family?"

Olivia's teeth chattered. "There's only Uncle Nate. We're supposed to wait here until he gets back."

Sarah stamped her feet to warm them. Mr. Colby should know how dangerous it was to wander around this area alone. Uncle James had warned her and Margaret to never go anywhere outside the mining camp without him after they had arrived last evening. Between claim jumpers and Sioux warriors scouring the hills, even visiting a sick neighbor was a risk.

She stepped forward and put her own warm cloak around Olivia's shoulders. "He can find you at our cabin. We need to get in out of the weather, and you need a hot meal."

Charley looked at her, his lips blue in the rapidly falling temperatures. "How will Uncle Nate find us?"

"I'll leave him a note."

Olivia and Charley exchanged glances, and then Olivia nodded. "All right, I think he'll be able to find us there, if it isn't too far."

Sarah scratched a brief message on a broken board she found near the trail and put it in a prominent place next to the campfire. She raked ashes over the low coals with a stick and stirred. The fire would die on its own.

She took Olivia's hand in hers as Margaret lifted Lucy out of the wagon. Uncle James untied the horses,

Charley took his mule and they started up the trail toward home.

Sarah's breath puffed as they climbed the steep hill, her mind flitting between worry and irritation with the children's uncle Nate. These children needed her, no matter what their uncle said. Somehow she would see that they received the care and education they deserved.

As the snowfall grew heavier, obscuring the distant mountains, Nate gave up. He'd been wandering these bare, brown hills since midmorning and hadn't seen any sign of game. He and the children would just have to make do with the few biscuits left from last night's supper.

When the wagon axle had finally broken yesterday afternoon, he thought the freight master would have helped them make repairs, but the man had only moved the crippled wagon off the trail and then set on his way with the bull train again.

"We're less than a mile from town—you'll be fine until we send help back for you. Just keep an eye out for those Indians."

And then they were gone, leaving Nate and the children alone.

Less than a mile from Deadwood? It might as well be twenty, or fifty, when everything they owned was lying by the side of the road. By the time the gray light of the cloudy afternoon started fading, Nate knew the bull train driver had forgotten them.

They had spent the night on their own with little food and a fitful fire. Morning had brought clouds building in the northwest and he'd hoped he'd be able to find a turkey or squirrel before too long. But here he was coming home empty-handed.

As he hurried over the last rise, Nate's empty stomach plummeted like a stone at the sight of the wagon. The wind had torn one corner of the canvas cover and it flapped wildly. Why hadn't Charley tied that down? Didn't he know his sisters and all their supplies were exposed to this weather?

And why hadn't they kept the fire going? They had to be freezing.

The hair on the back of Nate's neck prickled. The wagon tilted with the blasting gusts of wind. It was too quiet. The horses were missing. Even Loretta was nowhere in sight.

Nate broke into a run.

When he reached the wagon, he closed his eyes, dreading what he might see inside. They were just children. He had been so stupid to leave them. He had let his brother down again.

He gripped the worn wooden end gate and slowly opened his eyes. Nothing. Just the barrels and boxes of supplies. The children were gone.

Why had he taken so long? He should have stayed closer to the wagon. He had been warned about the Indians in the area, attacking any settlers who were foolish enough to venture out without being heavily armed.

He knew why he had taken the risk. No game. No food. He had had to leave them for a few hours.

He turned into the wind and scanned the hills rising above.

"Charley!" A gust snatched his voice away. "Olivia! Lucy!"

A wolf's howl floating on the wild wind was his only answer as he slumped against the wagon box, his eyes blurred with the cold. It had been the same when he and

Andrew had returned from the war, back home to the abandoned farm. The wind had howled that afternoon, too, with a fierce thunderstorm. But they were gone. Ma, Pa, Mattie… Ma and Pa were dead, but Mattie was lost. None of the neighbors knew where she had gone, or even when. Years of searching had brought him only wisps of clues, rumors that this cowboy or that miner had seen her in Tombstone, or Denver or Abilene, but she was gone without a trace.

Nate's legs gave way as he sank to the ground.

The wolf's howl came again, answered by several others. A pack on the hunt? Or a Sioux raiding party?

Nate scrambled to the fire, pulling his rifle with him. He blew the coals to life again and fed the flames with a few small sticks left near the wagon and a stray board that he threw on when the blaze was strong enough. A fire should keep the wolves away, at least until dark. Until then, he could search for some sign of which way the children had gone.

He took a deep breath, shutting down the panic that threatened to consume him. The panic that would make him freeze in a shuddering mess if he gave in to it. Closing his eyes, he whooshed out the breath and filled his lungs again. *Where could they be? Think.*

The wind gusted again with a force strong enough to send the canvas wagon cover flapping. With the rising wind, perhaps the children had gone to seek a better shelter than the crippled wagon. He clung to that hope. The alternative—that they had been stolen along with the horses—was too horrible to consider.

Chapter Two

The walk back to the cabin wasn't more than a half mile, but Sarah's feet were frozen by the time they climbed the final slope up from the trail at the edge of town. The wind pierced her wool dress.

Charley and Uncle James took the horses and mule into the lean-to where they would get some shelter, as Aunt Margaret led the way into the house. Warmth enveloped Sarah as she stopped just inside the door. She took the cloak from Olivia and guided the girls closer to the fireplace.

Lucy watched the glowing coals while Olivia folded the blanket her sister had been using as a wrap and laid it on the wood plank floor.

"You girls must be frozen." Aunt Margaret added a few sticks to the fire and swung the kettle over the flames. "Sit right here while we warm up the stew. Supper will be ready soon enough."

She left the girls to get settled on the blanket while she pulled Sarah to the side of the cabin where Uncle James had built a cupboard and small table.

"What can we feed them? I do wish we had been

able to bring Cook out West with us, and Susan. They'd know what to do."

She wrung her hands, but Sarah stopped her with a touch. "You said you wouldn't complain about leaving the servants behind in Boston."

"That was before I found out we would be cooking over an open fireplace. How can we have guests in conditions like this?"

Sarah put one arm around the shorter woman's shoulders. "We'll put another can of vegetables in the pot and some water to stretch it out. Meanwhile, we'll make a batch of biscuits. That will fill everyone's stomachs."

"I'm so glad you know your way around a kitchen." Margaret glanced at the girls, content to sit near the fire. "I'll learn as quickly as I can, but I don't think I could make a biscuit if my life depended on it!"

"Then we'll do it together." Sarah put a bowl on the table, along with a can of flour and Uncle James's jar of sourdough starter. She squelched the irritation that always rose whenever Aunt Margaret's helplessness showed its face. One thing Dr. Amelia Bennett had expounded upon frequently at her Sunday afternoon meetings was the careless way women of the privileged classes in Boston wasted the hours of their days, while their less fortunate sisters in the mills and saloons longed for the advantages denied them because of lack of education. But with all the education available to her, Aunt Margaret had never even learned to do a simple task like baking.

Sarah took a deep breath. Dr. Bennett wasn't here, but she was. She would help her aunt in any way she could, even if it was only to teach her how to make sourdough biscuits.

While they mixed the dough, James and Charley came in the door, bringing a fresh blast of cold air and stomping feet.

"It's getting even colder out there as the sun goes down." James sat in his chair near the fireplace and pulled off his boots.

"But Loretta and the horses will be safe in the lean-to, won't they?" Charley hung his coat on a hook and joined his sisters by the fireplace.

"Sure they will. Animals can survive pretty well as long as they have food and shelter."

"What about Uncle Nate?" Olivia turned to Uncle James, and then looked at Sarah. "Will he be all right?"

Sarah smiled at her. "We'll pray he will be."

A dull ache spread across her forehead as she rolled out the dough and cut biscuits. Nate's crooked smile swam in her memory. Was he warm enough? Would he be able to find the cabin? She didn't have any choice but to trust God for his safety.

"What made your uncle decide to bring you to Deadwood?" Uncle James asked.

The two children exchanged glances.

"There were some ladies in our church who wanted us to go to the orphans' home," Olivia said. "Uncle Nate said he wouldn't do that. He said he could take care of us."

"They called the sheriff to arrest Uncle Nate." Charley scooted closer to the fire.

"Charley, don't exaggerate. They only said they might. They said will's fare was at stake." Olivia looked at Sarah. "What does that mean?"

Sarah laid the biscuits in the bottom of the Dutch oven. "I think they meant welfare. That your welfare was at stake. It sounds like they wanted what was best for you."

"Yes, that's it. That's what they said. But Uncle Nate said they didn't know the situation and he'd see what was what if they tried to take us away from him."

Aunt Margaret cleared her throat and Sarah saw her exchange glances with Uncle James.

"What was your situation?" Uncle James leaned back in his chair, ready to hear the children's version of the event.

"There was a fire…" Olivia bit her lip.

"Our house burned." Charley picked up the story as Olivia fell silent. "Pa and Uncle Nate got the three of us out of the house and then went back in to get Mama."

The children stared at the fireplace. Sarah set the Dutch oven in the coals and then sat next to Olivia with her arm around the girl's shoulders.

"You don't have to tell us the rest, if you don't want to."

Charley went on. "When Uncle Nate came out of the house, his clothes were on fire." His voice was hollow, remembering.

Olivia hid her face in Sarah's dress. "I could hear Mama," she whispered. "She and Papa were still in the house."

"But Uncle Nate," Charley said, his voice strengthening, "he didn't want to give up. He kept trying to go back inside, to save them, but the neighbors were there, and they wouldn't let him. And then the roof fell down and everything was gone."

"Uncle Nate was hurt awful bad." Olivia sat up and took Charley's hand. "He almost died, too."

"That's when the ladies at church said we should go

to the home." Charley wiped at his eyes. "But Uncle Nate just kept saying no."

"It sounds like your uncle loves you very much." James laid his hand on Charley's shoulder.

Charley leaned against Uncle James's knee. The children fell silent, looking into the fire.

Sarah watched Lucy. She didn't look at her sister or brother, and she hadn't seemed to hear what they had been talking about. She sat on the folded blanket, staring at the flames, lost in a world of her own. During their walk from the crippled wagon to the cabin, the little girl hadn't made a sound, but had passively held Sarah's hand as they walked.

At the time, Sarah had thought Lucy was cold and only wanted to get to the cabin. But now with the others talking and in the warm room, she was still closed into her own thoughts. Could it be that she was deaf? Or was something else wrong?

The biscuits baked quickly in the Dutch oven, and supper was soon ready. Everyone ate in front of the fire, and Sarah was glad to see how quickly the biscuits disappeared, except the ones Olivia had insisted they save for their uncle along with a portion of the stew.

After they were done eating, Lucy climbed into Sarah's lap. The little one melted into her arms without a word, the ever-present thumb stuck in her mouth.

"You stay where you are," Margaret said as Sarah started to put Lucy back on the floor so she could help clean up from the meal. "Her eyes are closing already."

Sarah settled back in her chair, enjoying the soft sweetness of holding a child in her arms. These children had suffered so much, and their story brought memories of her own losses to the surface. How well she remembered the awful loneliness the day her parents had died, even though she had been much younger than Olivia and Charley. She had been about Lucy's age when she had gone to the orphanage.

She laid her cheek on Lucy's head, the girl's curly hair tickling Sarah's skin, pulling an old longing out from the corner where she had buried it long ago. The room blurred as she held Lucy tighter.

All those years in the orphanage, until Uncle James returned from the mission field when she was seventeen years old, she had never had the thought that she would marry and have children. She had changed enough diapers, cleaned enough dirty ears and soothed enough sore hearts to have been mother to a dozen families.

Marriage and children meant opening her heart to love, and she refused to consider that possibility. Loving someone meant only pain and heartache when they died. She wouldn't willingly put herself through that misery again.

She still enjoyed children, but only when they belonged to someone else. Teaching filled that desire quite nicely.

Sarah hummed under her breath as Lucy relaxed into sleep. Charley and Olivia had settled on the floor in front of the fire, where they were setting up Uncle James's checkers game.

Where was their uncle? She prayed again for his safety in the blowing storm.

Nate stood in the abandoned camp. His hastily built fire was already dying down, and the empty canvas flapped behind him. Snow swirled. Before too long any traces of where the children had gone would be covered.

The wind swung around to the north, bringing the smell of wood smoke. A fire. People. Friends? A mining camp?

Or an Indian encampment.

He needed to find the children. He had to take the risk.

Setting his face to the wind, he followed the smoke trail to a line of cottonwoods along Whitewood Creek. He had reached the outskirts of the mining camp, and the thin thread of smoke had turned into a heavy cloud hanging in the gulch. He paused on the creek bank. Ice lined the edges of the water. The children had either been taken away, or they had run off to hide. It wouldn't take long for them to freeze to death on an evening like this one.

There. Hoofprints in the mud. Nate followed the trail up away from the creek until he came to a cabin sheltered among a few trees at the edge of the rimrock. A lean-to built against the steep hill behind the cabin was crowded with horses. Even in the fading light, he recognized Scout and Ginger. Pete's and Dan's bay rumps were next to them, and then the mule's black flank.

Nate tried not to think of what kind of men he might find in this cabin. This was where the horses were, so horse thieves, most likely. But were they kidnappers? Murderers?

He pounded on the heavy wooden door and then stepped back, gripping his rifle.

The middle-aged man who cracked open the door wasn't the rough outlaw he expected. The white shirt, wool vest and string tie would fit in back home in Michigan, but Nate hadn't seen a man dressed this fancy since they left Chicago in March.

"Yes, can I help you?" The man poked his head out the door.

"I'm looking for some children."

"Uncle Nate! That's Uncle Nate out there!"

Charley's voice. Relief washed over Nate, leaving his knees weak.

The man smiled and he opened the door. "Come in. We've been expecting you."

Nate stepped into the warmth. Charley jumped up from a checkers game on the floor in front of the fireplace and ran toward him, wrapping his arms around Nate's middle without regard to his soaking and icy clothes. Olivia joined her brother in a hug, but Lucy stayed where she was, asleep on the lap of...

Nate dropped his gaze to the floor. Lucy was in the lap of the young woman from the stagecoach. Willowy, soft, her dark hair gleaming in the lamplight, the young woman held the sleeping child close in a loving embrace. He couldn't think of a more peaceful scene.

A round woman dressed in stylish brown bustled up to the little group. "Oh my, you must be frozen. You just come right in and change out of those wet clothes. We saved some supper for you."

Nate ran his fingers over the cheeks of both the older children. Yes, they were here, safe, sound and warm. It was hard to see their faces, his eyes had filled so suddenly.

"I thank you, ma'am, for caring for the children like this. I can't tell you how I felt when I got back to the wagon and they were gone."

"Didn't you get our note?"

Nate met the young woman's deep blue eyes.

"Uh, no, miss. I didn't see any note."

"We found the children alone with the storm coming up, so we brought them here." Pink tinged her cheeks as she spoke, her voice as soft as feathers. "I left word of where we were going on a broken plank. I leaned it against the rocks around the fire."

"A piece of wood?" The piece of wood he had laid on the fire when the wolves were howling. He could have saved himself some worry if only he had taken the time. Then Nate looked back at Charley and Olivia, their arms still holding him tight around the waist. If he had lost them, after all they had been through, he would never have forgiven himself.

"No matter. You're here now," said the man. He put his arm around the shorter woman. "I suppose some introductions are in order. I'm James MacFarland, and this is my wife, Margaret."

"Ma'am." Nate snatched the worn hat off his head and nodded to her.

"And our niece, Sarah MacFarland."

She had a name. He nodded in her direction.

"I'm Nate Colby."

"Well, Mr. Colby, there are dry clothes waiting for you behind that curtain. While you're changing, I'll dish up some stew for you." Mrs. MacFarland waved her hand toward the corner of the little cabin where a space had been curtained off.

Nate untangled himself from Charley's and Olivia's arms and ducked behind the curtains. On the small bed were a shirt and trousers, faded and worn, but clean. When he slipped the faded gray shirt over his head, he paused. There was no collar. Nothing to cover his neck.

The children had gotten used to the angry red scars

left by the burns that had nearly killed him, but these people—Sarah… Miss MacFarland—what would they say?

"Uncle Nate, aren't you hungry?" Charley was waiting for him.

Nate pulled the collarless shirt up as high as he could and gathered his wet things. He didn't really have a choice.

Sarah stroked Lucy's soft hair, surprised she still slept after all the noise Olivia and Charley had made when Nate came in. She had felt like shouting along with the children, she was so relieved to see him safe.

When he stepped out from behind the makeshift curtain, Sarah couldn't keep her gaze from flitting to his collar line. When the children had told of how their uncle had been burned in the fire, she hadn't realized how badly he had been injured. Scars covered the backs of his hands and the left side of his neck like splashes of blood shining bright red in the light. Suddenly aware she was staring, Sarah turned her attention back to the girl in her lap, but not before she saw Nate's self-conscious tug at the shirt's neckline, as if he were ashamed of the evidence of his heroism.

"Come sit here, Uncle Nate." Charley directed his uncle to the chair closest to the fireplace and Olivia gave him a plate of stew and two biscuits she had saved for him. Nate didn't hesitate, but dug his spoon into the rich, brown gravy and chunks of potato.

Uncle James pulled a footstool closer to the fire while Olivia and Charley went back to their checkers game on the floor, relaxed and happy now that their uncle was here. Aunt Margaret settled in the rocking chair with her ever-present knitting.

"The children tell us you've had quite a trip," James said after their visitor had wiped the bottom of his plate with the biscuit. "You've come to get your share of the gold?"

Nate reached out to tousle Charley's hair. The boy leaned his head against his uncle's knee.

"Not gold, but land. My plan is to raise horses, and this is the perfect place. When the government opened up western Dakota to homesteading, I knew it was time."

"You've been out here before?"

Nate's eyes narrowed as he stared at the fire. "I've made a few trips out West since the war." He glanced at the children. "It's a different world out here than it is back East. A man can live on his own terms."

"I'm gonna be a first-class cowboy." Charley grinned up at Nate.

When Nate caressed the boy's head, Sarah's eyes filled. No one could question that he loved the children as much as they loved him.

"That's the boy's dream." Nate leaned back in his chair and smiled at his nephew. "Providing remounts for the cavalry is my goal, but I need a stake first. We'll start out with cattle. With the gold rush, I won't have to go far to sell the beef."

"There's plenty of land around here, if you're looking for a ranch." James was warming up to his favorite subject—the settling of the Western desert. "The government has opened this part of Dakota Territory up to homesteading, but with the gold rush going on, not too many are interested in land or cattle."

Margaret rose to refill Nate's plate, her face pinched with disapproval. She hated the greed ruling and ruining the lives of the men they had met on their journey to Deadwood. Would she keep her comments to herself this time?

"Have you struck it rich yet?" Nate asked James between bites of stew.

James glanced at Margaret. His work here had been a bone of contention between them ever since Uncle James had decided to move west. "It depends on what you mean by *rich*. I'm a preacher, seeking to bring the gospel to lost souls."

"If Deadwood is like other gold towns I've heard about, there are plenty of those here."

Margaret let loose with one of her "humphs" and Lucy stirred on Sarah's lap. The little girl opened her eyes and gazed at Sarah's face with a solemn stare before sticking her thumb in her mouth again and settling back to watch Nate eat. There was still no sound from her. Sarah smoothed her dress and buried her nose in her soft curls again.

Nate saw Lucy was awake and winked at her, and then his eyes met Sarah's. His smile softened before he went back to eating his stew.

James went on. "Deadwood is the worst of the worst. Too many murders, too many thieves, too many claim jumpers, too many…" He paused when Margaret cleared her throat. "Ah, yes," he said, glancing at the children, "too many professional ladies."

Oh yes, those "professional ladies." Sarah had heard Aunt Margaret's opinion of them all the way from Boston. There were few enough women in a mining camp like Deadwood, but most of them wouldn't think to darken the door of a church. Sarah shifted Lucy on her lap and glanced at Margaret. What would her aunt do if one of those poor girls showed up on a Sunday morning? Or if she knew of Sarah's plan to provide an education for them?

"Have you had any success?"

"We have a small group of settlers, families like yours, who meet together. I've recently rented a building in town, and now that Margaret and Sarah have arrived, I hope more families will come. You and the children are welcome to join us."

Nate shoveled another spoonful into his mouth.

"Could we?" Olivia looked into Nate's face. "Oh, could we? We haven't been to church ever since…"

Charley gave his sister a jab with his elbow, but Nate, scraping the bottom of his second plate of stew, didn't seem to notice. Aunt Margaret took the empty dish.

What had happened? One moment Nate was discussing Uncle James's work, and the next Olivia and Charley were fidgeting in the uncomfortable silence. Lucy slid off Sarah's lap and crossed to Nate. He took her onto his lap and stroked her hair while he stared at the fire.

"We'll be busy building the ranch," he said, looking sideways at James. "I doubt if we'll have time for church."

He shifted his left shoulder up, as if he wanted to hide the scars, and glanced at Sarah. It sounded as if going to church was the last thing he wanted to do.

Nate woke with a jerk, the familiar metallic taste in his mouth. He willed his breathing to slow, forcing his eyes open, trying to get his bearings. The MacFarlands' cabin. They were safe.

Head aching from the ravaging nightmare, he rolled onto his back, waiting for his trembling muscles to relax. He might go one, or even two, nights without the sight of the fire haunting him. Before Jenny and Andrew died last fall, the nightmares had almost stopped—but now they were back with a vengeance. Whenever he closed his eyes, he knew what he would see and hear: the cavalry supply barn going up in flames. Horses screaming. The distant puff and boom of cannon fire. The fire devouring hay, wood, boxes of supplies, reaching ever closer to the ammunition he had managed to load onto the wagon. And those mules. Those ridiculous mules hitched to that wagon, refusing to budge. Over and over, night after night, he fought with those mules. And night after night the flames drew ever closer to the barrels of gunpowder. And since last fall, Andrew had been part of the nightmare. He stood behind the wagon, in the flames, yelling at him, telling him to hurry…hurry…to leave him…don't look back…

And then Nate would jerk awake, shaking and sweaty.

He glanced at Charley, lying beside him on the pallet in front of the fireplace. At least the boy hadn't woken up this time.

Nate looked around the cabin. Still dark, but with a gray light showing through a crack in the wooden shutters. Close to dawn. Almost time to get the day started.

Above him, in the loft, the girls slept with Sarah MacFarland. He hadn't missed how quickly Olivia and Lucy had become attached to her. Lucy had even let Sarah hold her, something she hadn't let anyone do except himself in more than six months. They were safe here. Safer and warmer than they had been since they left home eight weeks ago.

Was he wrong to bring the children to Deadwood? Was this any place to raise them?

The women of their church back in Michigan had made it clear the only right thing for him to do would be to put the children in the orphanage. The Roberts Home for Orphaned and Abandoned Children. As if they had no one to care for them.

Absolutely not. They would take these children from him over his dead body.

Charley turned toward him in his sleep and snuggled close. Nate put his arm around the boy and pulled him in to share the warmth of his blanket.

The sound of dripping water outside the cabin caught his attention. The wind had died down, and the temperature was climbing. The storm was over, and from the sounds of things, the snow was melting already. And that meant mud. As if he didn't have enough problems.

Shifting away from Charley, Nate sat up. He pulled on his boots and stepped to the door, opening it as quietly as he could. No use waking everyone else up. Standing on the flat stone James used for a front step, he surveyed the little clearing.

Last night, James had told him he had been in Deadwood since last summer, building this cabin before sending for the women back in Boston. He had built on the side of the gulch, since every inch of ground near the creek at the bottom had already been claimed by the gold seekers. This cabin and a few others were perched on the rimrock above the mining camp, as if at the edge of a cesspool. Up here the sun was just lifting over the tops of the eastern mountains, while the mining camp below was still shrouded in predawn darkness.

Saloons lined the dirt street that wound through the narrow gulch. The sight was too familiar. Every Western town he had been in had been the same, and he had stopped in every saloon and other unsavory business looking for his sister. But Mattie's trail had gone cold a few years ago. No one had seen her since that place in Dodge City where the madam had recognized the picture he carried. She had to be somewhere. Could she have made her way to Deadwood? Fire smoldered in his gut at the thought of where Mattie's choices had taken her.

The door opened behind him.

"Oh, Mr. Colby. I didn't realize you were out here."

Nate moved aside to make room for Sarah on the step. The only dry spot in sight. She had already dressed with care, her black hair caught up in a soft bun. Her cheeks were dewy fresh and she smelled of violets. He resisted the urge to lean closer to her.

"I'm an early riser, I guess." He chanced a glance at her. "I heard water moving and thought I'd check on the state of things. Our wagon is still on the trail back there, mired in the mud by now."

"I had to see what the weather was like, too." She smiled at him, and his breath caught. "After yesterday's storm, this morning seems like a different world. I've never seen weather change so quickly."

"That's the Northern Plains for you. It can be balmy spring one day, and then below zero the next."

"I suppose we'll have to get used to it." Sarah pushed at a pile of slush with one toe. She wore stylish kid-leather boots with jet buttons in a row up the side.

They would be ruined with her first step off the porch. "Your children are so sweet. I've enjoyed getting to know them."

Nate rubbed at his whiskers. "They seem to like you, too. You have a way with children. I've never seen Lucy take to anyone so quickly."

"I hope you'll reconsider sending them to school when I open the academy next week."

He shot another glance at her, wary. "They won't have time to attend any school. They'll be with me all day. I'll see they get the learning they need."

She leveled her gaze at him, tilting her chin up slightly. Nate straightened to his full height, forcing her chin up farther. "Mr. Colby, I'm sure you know children do best when learning in a safe, secure environment. Can you provide that for them while you work to find your ranch?"

"I can provide the best environment they need, and that's with me." Nate felt the familiar bile rising in his throat. The busybodies back in Michigan had used the same arguments.

"But what about school?"

"President Lincoln learned at night after a day's work. Charley and Olivia can do the same."

"But surely you don't think—"

"Surely I do think I know what's best for these children. They're my responsibility, and I'm going to take care of them."

She stared at him, her eyes growing bluer as the sun rose higher over the distant hills. And here he'd thought he'd escape these do-gooders when he came west. No one was going to take his children away from him. He slammed his hat on his head.

"I'll be waking the children up now. We need to work on getting the wagon repaired and head on into town."

"You can leave the girls here, if you like, while you and Charley take care of the wagon." She reached out one slim hand and laid it on his sleeve. "You are right, that the children are your responsibility, but that doesn't mean you can't let others help you now and then."

Nate considered her words. She was right, of course. With all the mud and the slogging to town and back to get that axle repaired, it would be best for the girls to stay here and enjoy a day in the company of women, in a clean, safe house. But it galled him to admit it.

He nodded his agreement to her plan. "I'll take Charley with me. But only for today." He lifted a warning finger, shielding him from those gentle eyes. "The children stay with me. They're my responsibility and I aim to do my best by them."

"Of course you want the best for them. So do I."

She turned to look down into the mining camp as it stirred to life in the early-morning light. Somehow, he didn't think her version of what was best for the children would be the same as his.

Chapter Three

"I can help. Let me help." Charley hopped on one foot, a flutter of movement in Nate's peripheral vision.

Shifting his left foot closer to the wagon, Nate shoved again, sliding the wagon box onto the makeshift jack. He ran a shaking hand across the back of his neck.

"Charley, some jobs are just too big for an eight-year-old." Who was he trying to kid? This job was too big for a thirty-year-old. If Andrew was here...

Nate looked into Charley's disappointed face. If Andrew was here, they'd still be living in Michigan, and Charley would still have his pa. But a man couldn't bring back the past, and he couldn't always fix the mistakes he'd made, no matter how much he wanted to.

He squeezed Charley's shoulder. "I'll need your help with the next part, though." Charley's face brightened. "We need to get that broken axle off there and find a new one."

"Loretta can help, too, can't she?"

Nate looked at the mule, tied to the back of the crippled wagon. It flipped its ears back and stomped its front foot in response.

"I suppose she could carry the axle to town."

"Sure she could. Loretta can do anything."

Nate glanced at Charley as he knocked the wheel off the broken axle. Where did the boy get such an attachment to a mule? The animals were outright dangerous when they took it into their heads to go their own way.

He knew the answer to his own question. Andrew had given Loretta to the boy years ago, when Charley was barely old enough to ride. Andrew held that mules had more sense than horses and that she'd keep Charley safe wherever he wanted to take her. Nate had argued, tried to change Andrew's mind, but Loretta became one of the family.

And now? Charley had already lost so much. He wasn't going to be the one to take the mule away from the boy. No matter how much he hated it.

Nate fumbled with the ironing that held the axle to the bolster above it. Sometimes he could use a third hand.

"What can I do? I want to help."

Nate glanced at the boy again.

"Here you go, Charley. Hold the axle up against the bolster while I get it unfastened."

With Charley's help, Nate released the ironings with a quick twist, and the axle was free. He glanced at the mule again. It was wearing the pack harness that Charley used for a saddle. It had come in handy on the trail when Nate needed to bring some game back to camp or haul water. Would the thing carry the axle for him?

Nate approached the mule, hefting one part of the heavy axle in his hands. "Whoa there, stupid animal, whoa there."

The mule rolled its eyes and aimed a vicious bite at his shoulder.

"She knows you don't like her." Charley stood off to the side, watching.

"Of course I don't like her. Help me get these axle pieces on her harness, will you?"

When Charley climbed up onto the animal, Nate was sure the mule winked at him. But it let him load the axle on the harness, and Charley fastened the straps, balancing with his weight on the other side of the mule. Nate looked at Charley's grin as he perched on the pack saddle. In spite of the work still ahead to get the wagon back on its wheels, Nate had to grin back at him. What he wouldn't give to be a boy again.

He fixed his eyes on the trail ahead. Those days were long gone.

Sarah scrubbed the hem of her traveling dress on the washboard. Mud seemed to be everywhere in this place.

"Here's some more hot water for you." Aunt Margaret came out the back door of the cabin to the sheltered porch where Sarah and Olivia bent over tubs of soapy water.

"Thank you." Sarah pushed a lock of hair out of her face with the back of her arm. "It's so wonderful to be able to do laundry in the fresh air this morning." She smiled at Olivia as she took the steaming kettle from Margaret. "I would imagine it was hard for you and your uncle to keep up with chores like this along the trail."

"We didn't take time for anything," Olivia answered, swishing a pair of socks in her tub. "Uncle Nate said we had to keep up with the bull train."

Sarah turned the heavy skirt in the water and tackled another muddy stain. Her thoughts wandered to Nate Colby. Again. Was he having any success with his wagon? Would he be able to get the axle fixed? He'd have to take it into Deadwood to find someone to repair it.

"Did Uncle James say when he was going to show us the building he rented?" she asked Margaret.

Her aunt looked toward the roofs of the mining camp below them. "He said we would go this afternoon although I can't see why we need a building down there."

"Because that's where the people are. And the academy needs to have a place, unless you want the children studying in the cabin."

And with the church and school in the center of the mining camp, she would have ready access to the unfortunate young ladies she intended to find and educate.

Sarah looked up at the towering pine trees that climbed the steep hill behind the cabin. On those Sunday afternoons last winter in Dr. Amelia Bennett's crowded parlor on Beacon Hill, she had never imagined the fire that had been lit in her would bring her to such a place as this.

Dr. Bennett was a pioneer. A visionary. Her plans for educating the women of the docks and brothels of Boston were becoming reality in the opening of her Women's Educational Institution, and Dr. Bennett had urged Sarah to spread the work to the untamed wilderness of the American West, as she had called it. Sarah intended to make her mentor proud.

A sniff was Margaret's only reply as she went back into the house. Lucy stopped playing with the pinecones she had found and stared after her.

Olivia wiped an arm across her forehead. "Is she always so…"

"Disapproving?" Sarah finished Olivia's question. She wrung the water out of her skirt. "My aunt didn't want to come out West. She's trying to make the best of things, but it is hard for her to adjust to this life."

"Why did she come, then? Why didn't she stay at home?"

Sarah looked from Olivia's earnest face to Lucy's wide eyes. Why did any of them leave their homes? "My uncle said God was calling him to preach to the gold seekers." She put one of her uncle's shirts into the warm water. "Aunt Margaret came because he asked her to."

"Why did you come?"

Olivia's question struck deep. Sarah moved the shirt through the gray water and smiled at the girl. "I wanted adventure, and I wanted a purpose in my life. When Uncle James wrote that there were families here with children, I knew what this town would need is a school." A great center of learning, for young and old. That was how Dr. Bennett phrased it.

"Can I go to your school?"

"May I…"

"May I go to your school?"

Sarah thought back to her conversation with Nate. Olivia would be such a charming pupil in the academy, one she would love to share the knowledge of the world with, but could she promise such a thing if the girl's uncle was opposed to it?

"We'll have to see what your uncle says." Olivia's face showed her disappointment as she went back to her scrubbing. "But even if you can't come, I'll certainly share my books with you and help you learn."

"Would you, really?" Olivia's face shone as if the sun had come clear of a swift cloud. "And will you help me teach Lucy to read?"

Sarah glanced at the five-year-old, who had gone

back to her pinecones. It looked as if she was building a house with them. She leaned closer to Olivia. "I've never heard your sister say anything. Does she talk?"

Olivia shook her head. "She used to. Before Mama and Papa…" She bit her lip, and Sarah put an arm around her narrow shoulders.

"She hasn't spoken since you lost your parents?"

At the shake of Olivia's head, Sarah pulled the girl into a closer embrace. There had been a boy at the orphanage who had never spoken, from the time he came to live there until he passed away a few months later. The matron had said he died of a broken heart, but Sarah had known better. He had died because he couldn't face life with no hope and no family.

She watched Lucy put the pinecones in lines, framing the rooms of her house. She put rocks into the spaces for furniture and used small pinecones for people that she walked in and out of the doors.

She could learn to speak again. Surely her life wasn't as hopeless as the boy at the orphanage. Lucy was still surrounded by family, and she was healthy. Surely with love and nurturing she had hope for a normal, happy life. Resolve to assist these children filled her heart.

"I'll help you teach Lucy to read, and we'll make sure Charley works on his studies, too."

Sarah held tight as Olivia's arms squeezed around her waist. Had she just made a rash promise she couldn't keep?

By the time Nate found a wheelwright who could make a new axle, noon had passed. He fingered the coins in his pocket.

"Is there any place to buy something to eat?" he asked the wheelwright.

"The Shoo Fly Café has good pie." The burly man gestured with his head up Main Street.

"What about a grocer's?"

"The closest is Hung Cho's, right across the way there."

"Thank you. We'll be back to pick the axle up around midafternoon."

Nate guided Charley across the muddy street with one hand on the boy's shoulder, making sure he stepped wide over the gutter in the middle. Hung Cho's was a solid wood building with a laundry on one side and what looked like a hotel on the other. Some of the signs were in English, but most had what Nate guessed were Chinese characters.

Charley stared at the short, round Chinese man who approached them as Nate sorted through the wares on the tables outside the store.

"Yes, yes, sir." The man bowed slightly. "You want some good food for your boy, yes? Hung Cho carries only the best. Only the best for our friends."

Nate glanced at the man. He had run across men from China before, but Charley hadn't. Hung Cho's smile seemed genuine, his expression friendly.

He fingered the coins in his pocket again and looked at the items on the table. He recognized some apples, dry and wrinkled from being stored all winter, but apples nonetheless.

"How much for one of these?"

"Oh, these apples. They are very fine. Make a boy very healthy, yes? Only one dollar."

"I only want to buy one, not all of them."

"Yes, yes. I understand." Hung Cho's head bobbed as he nodded. "Apples are very dear. One dollar."

Nate pulled out a dollar coin, along with a two-bit piece. I'll take one. Do you have any crackers, and maybe some cheese?"

Hung Cho leaned forward to peer at the coins in his hand, and then slid his look up to Nate's face. His smile grew wider. "You have coin money, not gold? You are new in Deadwood."

At Nate's nod, Hung Cho reached under the table and brought out two apples in much better shape than the ones he had on display. "For cash money, I give you two apples, one pound crackers and cheese. Nice cheese, from back East."

They followed the little man into the dim interior of his store. The odor of dried fish in one barrel overpowered the close room. Hung Cho squeezed between it and another barrel filled with rice. He scooped crackers out of a third barrel and weighed them in a hanging scale, then sliced a generous wedge of cheese from a wheel behind the counter. He wrapped it all in a clean cloth and handed the bundle to Charley.

"One dollar and two bits, please."

"Why the change in price?"

"Cash money is hard to come by. Bull train drivers want cash from the Chinese instead of gold." The man's smile disappeared as he shook his head. "They do not trust the Chinese. Will not accept gold dust from us for fear it is not pure."

Nate handed over the coins in his hand.

Hung Cho bowed as he slipped the money into some folds in his robe. "Thank you, sir. Thank you very much."

They left the store and then turned right, toward the

center of the mining camp. As they crossed an alley and stepped back up on the boardwalk in front of a row of businesses, Charley tilted his head up to look at him. "Where are we going to eat, Uncle Nate?"

They were passing an empty space between two canvas tents. A couple barrels stood close to the boardwalk. "How about right here?"

They settled themselves on the barrels and divided the food between them. Charley shoved the crackers into his mouth two at a time.

"Whoa there, boy. Those crackers won't disappear. Take your time."

Charley grinned at him and Nate took a bite of his apple as he settled in to watch the traffic on Main Street.

Two doors down was a saloon, and beyond that were signs for several more. Across the street, a large building had a sign, The Mystic Theater, but from the look of the young women leaning over the rail of the balcony, much more than theatrical entertainment was available there. James MacFarland had been right about the saloon girls—they seemed to be everywhere. This must be the Badlands of Deadwood he had heard the bullwhackers mention.

Nate took another bite of his apple and looked closely at the women on the balcony. The youngest seemed to be no more than sixteen, while a couple of them wore the bored look of years of experience in their business. The apple turned sour in his mouth. He swallowed that bite and then offered the rest to Charley.

Mattie, if she was still alive, would be the age of those older women. Did her face bear that same expression? She would be thirty-two years old by now, and it had been almost fourteen years since she had disappeared.

He watched the two women, their mouths red slashes against their pale, white faces. The dresses they wore had been brightly colored at one time, but now looked sadly faded next to the younger girls, like roses that clung to a few blown and sun-bleached petals.

He hoped that Mattie had found her way out of that life.

He sighed and took a cracker. Turned it in his hands. The last time he had searched for his sister and come home again with no news, Andrew had told him to give it up. If she wanted to come home, she'd find her way.

But Andrew didn't live with the memory of her face the night he told her he was running away to join the army. The hard, crystalline planes that shut him out.

"You'll kill Ma and Pa," she had whispered as she tried to wrest his bundle of clothes from him. "And then what will I do?"

He had turned from her, bent on following Andrew, but she had been right. By the time he had come home after the war was over, Ma and Pa were dead, and Mattie was gone.

He looked back up at the balcony of the Mystic. He'd never give up looking, hoping that someday he'd find her before… The cracker snapped between his fingers. He refused to listen to that voice inside that kept telling him it was too late.

When Charley finished his lunch, Nate wrapped up the rest of the crackers and cheese.

"Let's go see what the town looks like."

The street was crowded with men all going nowhere in particular and Nate pulled Charley closer to his side.

Between the coarse language and the open bottles of liquor, he knew this wasn't a place Andrew and Jenny would want their son to be. But this was where they were.

The businesses crowded together between the hills rising behind them and the narrow mudhole that passed for a street. Nate slowed his pace as the storefronts turned from the saloons to a printing office. Next came a general store and a clothing store, with a tobacconist wedged in between. Across the street was Star and Bullock, a large hardware store that filled almost an entire block.

And in the middle of it all, just where the street took a steep slope up to a higher level on the hill, men worked a mining claim. Nate shook his head. In all his travels through the West, he had never seen anything quite like Deadwood.

"Look, Uncle Nate. There's Miss Sarah!"

Charley ran ahead to where the MacFarlands stood at the end of the block. Nate halted, watching Sarah's face as she greeted the boy. She looked truly happy to see him. From what he had seen, busybodies from schools and orphanages never seemed to like the children they claimed to care so much about.

She didn't fit the mold. She didn't fit any mold.

Charley pointed his way and she looked for him. Another smile. The crowded streets seemed to fall silent, and Nate saw several of the men on the boardwalk look in her direction. He hurried to catch up with Charley.

"Miss MacFarland." He found himself smiling, and he turned to the elder MacFarlands. "Mrs. MacFarland. James." Lucy reached for him and he lifted her into his arms.

Sarah's wide skirts swung as she turned toward him. "Was your errand a success?"

"The broken axle is being repaired as we speak."

"We were just on our way to see the new storefront Uncle James rented. Would you and Charley like to come along?"

"Say yes, Uncle Nate. Please?" Charley clung to his free hand, while Olivia hopped up and down. He couldn't say no to them.

"We'll be pleased to accompany you."

They all followed James as he turned down a side street and led the way toward a boarded-up saloon. Nate let Sarah go ahead of him, Charley and Olivia each holding on to one of her hands, while he followed with Lucy. Anyone watching would think they were a family.

Nate let that idea sift through until it soured his stomach. A family? He hugged Lucy close as he carried her. These children were all the family he needed, and he didn't deserve even this.

When they reached the building on Lee Street, a few doors from the corner at Main, Sarah took Lucy's and Olivia's hands while Nate and Uncle James pulled the slats from the boarded-up door. Once there was an opening, Uncle James led them in.

"This is a church?" Olivia let go of Sarah's hand and stepped farther into the room. "It looks like a saloon."

Uncle James cleared his throat as Margaret followed Olivia to the bar that extended from one end of the room to the other. "The latest tenants ran a drinking establishment, and it needs work."

Aunt Margaret stared at him. "You said you had found a storefront."

Lucy tightened her grasp on Sarah's other hand at the ice in Margaret's voice. Sarah gave her small hand a reassuring squeeze. "It does need a lot of work, but I can see the possibilities." She led Lucy to the center of the room to get a feeling for the size of the space. "If that bar is removed..."

"And that hideous mirror behind it." Aunt Margaret waved her hand in the direction of the gold-flecked monstrosity on the wall. A narrow hole in the center radiated spiderweb cracks in all directions.

"There will be room enough for whoever comes to worship." Sarah glanced around the room again. A piano listed to the side in one corner. Perhaps there would be someone in town who knew how to repair it.

She glanced back at Nate, standing in the doorway. He was removing nails from the wood slats, one by one. He didn't seem to want to come any farther into the dusty building.

Margaret sniffed as she ran one finger along the top of the bar and inspected her glove.

"You need to see this place as I do, dear." Uncle James crossed the room to his wife and pulled both of her hands into his own. "With some effort, we can redeem this place for the Lord's work." He turned to look around the room. Sarah had to smile at the grin on his face. Uncle James was a hopeless optimist.

No, not hopeless. He had confidence in the Lord's leading.

"What I see is a den of iniquity." Margaret's voice softened. "But if anyone can make a silk purse out of a sow's ear, it's you, James MacFarland."

"When we started the church in China, we didn't even have a building. Only a stone slab and rubble."

James sighed, the smile still on his face. "Here we have a good roof, a good floor and two large rooms. The Lord has blessed us, indeed."

"Two rooms?" Sarah had planned to teach in this room, but if there was another...

"Right through that door." James nodded toward the far end of the bar.

Sarah picked up Lucy and started across the dirty floor, skirting a broken chair on the way. Olivia and Charley came behind them. When she opened the door, Charley crowding past, she nearly dropped Lucy. A man stood in the center of the room, a white felt hat and cane in one hand and a sheaf of papers in the other. He looked up when she gasped.

"Oh, I'm sorry. I thought this room was vacant." Sarah stepped back, pulling Charley with her.

The man smiled as he took a step toward her. "There's no need to go. I am to meet my client here. A Mr. MacFarland?"

Uncle James was at her side. "Mr. Montgomery." The two men shook hands. "You're early. I was just showing the building to my wife and niece."

"Wilson Montgomery, at your service, Mrs. MacFarland. Miss MacFarland." He bowed his head in Margaret's direction and then in Sarah's. His voice was cultured and his manners impeccable, except that his gaze lingered on Sarah a little too long before he turned back to Uncle James.

"Mr. Montgomery is from the bank. He's handling the lease on this building."

"Why don't we ladies inspect this room while you and Mr. Montgomery attend to your business?" Aunt

Margaret shooed Sarah and the children into the back room and closed the door behind them.

"Well, what do you think?"

Sarah looked around the room. It had its own entrance from the alley on the side of the building, and with a window next to the outer door, the room was light and airy.

"I like it." She walked from one wall to the other, mentally placing benches and a chalkboard.

"No, no. Not the room. Mr. Montgomery." Aunt Margaret's words hissed in a loud whisper.

"Mr. Montgomery?" Sarah eased Lucy down to the floor. Olivia took her sister to the window to join Charley.

"Don't you think he's perfect? James told me about him last night. He's from Boston."

Aunt Margaret ended her pronouncement with a smile. Sarah grasped her aunt's meaning.

"You don't mean you think that he…" Sarah shook her head. "Don't start matchmaking, Aunt Margaret. You know I'm too old to marry, and no man will appreciate a spinster being thrown at him."

"Oh, now," Aunt Margaret sputtered, "I would never throw you at him. He attends the church and is a very eligible bachelor. He is the manager of the First National Bank of Deadwood, and his father is the owner."

As she ended her sales pitch, Sarah sighed. "If he is that eligible, don't you have to ask yourself why he isn't already married? In my experience, once a man reaches a certain age without being married, there is usually a good reason for it."

"In your experience? My dear, you haven't had that much experience."

Sarah watched the children at the window. Charley

had found a spider and the three of them were engrossed in its meal of an insect caught in its web. She would rather not talk about men with Aunt Margaret. Her aunt had been thirty-five when she met Uncle James, fresh from the mission field in China. Since she had married late in life, she held that there was hope for every woman. But a man, at least a good man, was a rare bird.

Nate opened the door between the two rooms and stepped in.

"It's time for Charley and me to head back to the wheelwright's. The axle should be done by now."

Sarah turned to greet him. His timing couldn't have been better. Maybe he would take Aunt Margaret's mind off Wilson Montgomery.

"I'm so glad we met in town so you could inspect the new church and school with us." She crossed the room, slipped one hand into the crook of his elbow and swept the other across the room with a grand gesture. "This is our academy. What do you think?"

His gaze followed the sweep of her hand. "It's a right fine room. But you'll need desks, won't you? And a chalkboard? And books?"

Margaret was watching them, so she leaned a little closer. "I brought books with me, and Uncle James will build benches for the students to use." She looked up at him. "I'm not sure what to do about the chalkboard. Do you have any ideas?" She considered batting her eyes, but she had never done that to any man, and she wasn't about to start now.

He lifted her hand off his arm and stepped away. "I'm sure you'll think of something, Miss MacFarland." When he grinned, a dimple appeared in his chin. She hadn't noticed it yesterday. Shaving certainly made a difference in a man's looks.

Nate walked over to the window. "Charley, it's time to go."

He ushered the boy toward the door leading to the alley and turned to Sarah. The shadow of his smile still lingered. "We'll come for the girls as soon as we get the wagon fixed."

"You'll stay for supper tonight, of course." Aunt Margaret's voice denied any argument.

Nate turned his hat between his hands and looked at Charley. "I appreciate it, ma'am, I surely do. But the children and I need to set up our camp."

Sarah's throat tightened. Once he left with the children, would she ever see him again?

Her face heated with a sudden flush. Where had that thought come from? But still, something made her want to have more time with him. And the children.

"You must eat supper with us tonight." His eyes met hers. "And I think I know where there is a perfect spot for you to camp, right near the cabin."

He glanced at the children, watching him. They were waiting for his decision with bated breath, just like she was.

Finally he shoved his hat on his head. "I know when I'm outnumbered." He turned to Aunt Margaret. "I'm certainly beholden to you for your hospitality, ma'am. I don't know how I'll be able to repay you."

"Pishposh." Aunt Margaret waved her hand in the air. "You don't need to repay anything. We're glad to have the company."

Sarah followed him to the door and stepped outside. Charley wandered toward the front of the building, but

Nate turned to her. Sunshine had chased all the morning clouds away, and it shone brightly into the alley. She shaded her eyes with her hand as she looked up at him.

"I'm glad you decided to have supper another night with us. I would hate to give up the children's company so soon."

"Is it their company, or are you still going to try to talk me into letting them come to your school?"

"You know already that I would love for them to attend and that I think it is the best thing for them." Nate started to turn away, but she stopped him with a hand on his arm. "But I will respect your wishes concerning them."

He looked at her, his chin tilted just enough for her to see she hadn't convinced him, but his teasing grin lingered.

"You won't mention the school, to me or to the children?"

Could she just give up on making sure those children had an education? On the other hand, Nate was their uncle. Maybe she could convince him that they both had the children's best interests in mind.

Without mentioning the school.

"I promise. As long as you promise we can be friends."

One corner of his mouth turned up. "Friends? All right, friend." He stepped backward. "I'll see you at suppertime." He caught up with Charley at the corner of the building and disappeared.

Yes, he certainly was a rare bird.

Chapter Four

Replacing the axle was easier now that Nate had figured out how to work with Charley. The boy's nimble fingers slipped the ironings into place as Nate held the axle against the bolster. Even so, it was late afternoon before he had the horses hitched up and they were ready to drive to the MacFarlands' cabin.

Instead of the shorter route up the steep hill on the north end of Williams Street, James had recommended the more gradual ascent up Main Street to Shine, and then to Williams. Nate and Charley had led the team down that route before picking up the new axle, and it was still going to be a hard pull for the horses with the loaded wagon.

Charley climbed up onto the seat next to him and Nate chirruped to the horses. Before too long they reached the outskirts of the mining camp, where tents crowded along the road. Miners of all description watched them pass. Groups of young men, old sourdoughs, even a couple families. Soon they'd be heading to their claims, now that the snow in the hills was melting. Men who had secured claims along Whitewood Creek were already at work, standing knee-deep in the rushing water with their pans, or shoveling dirt and gravel into rockers.

Nate glanced at Charley, who watched the miners with wide eyes.

"They're sure working hard, aren't they?"

The boy nodded. "I thought gold miners just picked nuggets up off the ground, but what they're doing doesn't look like much fun."

"Mining is dirty, backbreaking work. And not too many find success."

"Then why do they do it?"

Nate watched two men shovel gravel into a sluice. "They're looking for an easy way to get rich, but they're learning the only way to success is hard work. The ones who keep at it will do okay, but others will give up before the month is over."

"That's why we're going to be cowboys, right?"

Nate nudged Charley's knee with his own. "That's right. We'll be working hard, too, but at the end, we know we'll have something to show for it."

They passed the wheelwright's shop and Chinatown. The street was crowded as they approached the Badlands and Nate slowed the horses to a walk, threading their way between freight wagons unloading their goods and the crowds spilling off the board sidewalks into the mud.

Once they moved past the Badlands, the crowds grew thinner and the going was a bit easier. A flash of color on the board sidewalk caught Nate's eye. Three girls dressed in red, yellow and purple silk dresses jostled each other as they paraded down the walk. High-pitched laughter rose above the general noise of the street. With their attention all on themselves, they pretended not to notice the stares they were garnishing from the crowds of men around them.

Nate's stomach roiled, but out of habit he studied each face, looking for the familiar features. He looked again at the girl in red. She was too young to be Mattie, but she looked so much like his sister that he stared. She wasn't laughing along with her friends, but glanced this way and that, a frightened rabbit surrounded by hounds.

Just as the wagon drew close to the girls, the team halted, unable to move past a freight wagon stopped in front of them. At the same time, a large, balding man approached the three women. When they saw him, their laughter died. The girl in red stepped behind her friends.

"Good afternoon, girls," the man said in a loud voice, commanding the attention of everyone in the vicinity.

The girl in purple giggled as the one in yellow, the older one, sidled up to the man, caressing his arm. "Hello, Tom."

The man shrugged her away. "That's Mr. Harris to you, Irene. What are you girls doing out here on the street this time of the afternoon?"

Irene pushed away from him as the purple girl giggled again and dangled a package in front of him. "We've been shopping, Mr. Harris. But we're on our way back to the Mystic right now." She waved at the crowd of men around them. "And maybe we'll bring some customers with us."

Nate turned his head away. The girl was inebriated, or drugged. He had seen her kind too often in his search for Mattie. Past the watching crowd, crossing the intersection of Main and Lee, were the MacFarlands with

Olivia and Lucy. As Sarah stopped to watch the altercation, Nate's attention was pulled back.

"Fern, I want you and Irene to head back to the Mystic right now." The girls did his bidding, pushing past him. Fern and Irene waved to the men as they made their way down the boardwalk toward the Badlands, but Harris reached out and grabbed the girl in red. "Not you, Dovey." He pulled her closer than a man properly should. "I'll escort you back. We wouldn't want you to get lost now, would we?"

The look on Dovey's face as she tried to pull away from Harris was more than Nate could stand. Girls like Fern and Irene were one thing—they seemed to be having a good time—but Dovey wanted no part of Harris's plan for her.

He handed the reins to Charley. "Stay here."

Nate jumped onto the boardwalk, facing Harris. "It looks to me like the young lady doesn't want to go with you."

Over Harris's shoulder, Sarah's face caught his eye. She urged him on with a nod.

Harris looked at Nate and then turned to the surrounding crowd. He laughed with the tone of a man who knew he had the upper hand. "I don't know who you are, but this matter is none of your concern."

Dovey looked at him with Mattie's eyes, pleading. "It's all right." Her voice was almost a whisper. "Don't…"

"Do you want to go with this man?"

Harris laughed again. "Of course she does, don't you, my dear?" His right hand was in his pocket, where the outline of a derringer showed through the fabric. Harris's face grew hard. "And truly, it's none of your business." He held Nate's eyes with his own as he pushed past, pulling Dovey along with him.

The crowd closed around the pair and they disappeared. Nate pulled at the handkerchief knotted around his neck. If it had been Mattie, that confrontation might have been different. He liked to think he would have risked a shot from that derringer to get her away from Harris.

Sarah appeared at his side as the crowds of men dissipated, holding Lucy by one hand. "Do you know that girl?"

Nate picked up his niece and held her close. The little girl snuggled in on his right side, away from the scars. "No. She reminds me of someone, though."

"I applaud you for stepping in like that. Those poor girls need a champion." Sarah had a fire in her eyes he hadn't seen before. She looked down the street where Harris and Dovey had disappeared.

James and Mrs. MacFarland caught up with Sarah, Margaret ushering Olivia in front of her. "Sarah, this just isn't proper. Not at all." Margaret hissed her words, reaching out for Sarah's arm.

"But, Aunt Margaret, this is just the kind of situation Dr. Bennett told us we may run into in this wild town. Can't you see? That poor girl obviously needs someone's help."

Margaret's head switched this way and that, daring any of the men still watching the scene to say anything. "That may be true. But not here, and not now."

Sarah bit her lower lip and Nate smiled. In any other woman, he'd take that to mean that she was unsure of herself. But Sarah MacFarland? She was holding back whatever words were dancing on the tip of her tongue.

James put his arms around both women and turned them toward the city stairs that led between Lee Street and Williams, where the cabin stood.

"We need to go home, ladies. We'll meet you up above, Nate, and we'll lead you to a fine camping place."

Nate touched his fingers to the brim of his hat in answer and climbed back up onto the wagon seat, settling Lucy next to Charley. He'd hate to be on the receiving end of whatever comments were waiting to come out of Sarah's mouth.

Sarah held Olivia's hand as they climbed up the steps leading to Williams Street. Partway up, Olivia stopped to look behind them and clutched Sarah's hand even tighter.

"We're already as high as the roofs on Main Street."

Sarah looked back. Even here the noise and dirt of the mining camp seemed far away. "We need to hurry if we're going to get back to the cabin before your uncle Nate."

Olivia started climbing again, taking one step at a time. "Will we get to stay with you again tonight?"

"I think your uncle will be setting up your camp, but you can eat supper with us." Sarah paused for breath at the top of the steps. Uncle James and Aunt Margaret were far ahead, walking arm in arm past the cabins perched along the trail. Their cabin was farther on, around the bend of the hill.

It was just as well. Arguing with Aunt Margaret about the scene down below wouldn't be fruitful. She let Dr. Bennett's words bolster her strength. *Choose your battles wisely*, she had said many times during the Sunday afternoon meetings in her parlor on Beacon Hill. *We fight against a formidable enemy. One who is not willing that any of these unfortunate souls would slip from his grasping fingers.* Sarah smiled at the memory. What fire that woman had, and what a way with words!

"Is our campsite far away from you?"

Sarah looked down into Olivia's face and smoothed back a wisp of blond hair that had escaped her braid. "No, not very far at all. We'll be able to see each other often."

Olivia smiled at that and turned to follow James and Margaret. She was a sweet girl. Sarah hurried to catch up with her. "We'll have to ask your uncle about the reading lessons. At the very least, I'll be able to loan you some books to use."

"Do you have the Third Reader? That's the one I was reading from at home."

"Yes, I do. How far along are you?"

"Nearly finished. I memorized 'The Snowbird's Song' for our Christmas program, but that was our last day at school."

"I know that poem. It's all about how God takes care of the birds and provides for them."

"Yes, that's right." Olivia fiddled with the end of one braid. "But Uncle Nate said we have to take care of ourselves." She flung the braid back over her shoulder and looked up at Sarah. "Is he right? Won't God take care of us?"

Sarah stopped and faced the girl. "What makes you think He wouldn't?"

Olivia blinked her eyes, as if she was trying to hold back tears. "Mama always said He would, but then she died. If God was taking care of her, wouldn't He have rescued her from the fire?"

Feeling her own tears threatening, Sarah looked past Olivia to the buildings below them. But Olivia took her hand, bringing Sarah's gaze back to her.

"And when Lucy cries, I tell her what Mama always told me, but how can I know?"

Sarah pulled Olivia to a log lying along the trail and motioned for her to sit next to her. "One thing I always hold on to is that God promised He would be with us. Jesus said that in the book of Matthew. And God always keeps His promises." She swallowed past the lump forming in her throat. She remembered questioning God just like Olivia was doing. How did she get past the questions to the faith she had now?

"But what about Mama?"

Sarah smiled and squeezed Olivia's hand. "You can be certain that God is still taking care of your mama. I don't know why she died, and I don't know why God didn't rescue her then, but I do know that He never abandoned her. Sometimes it's very hard to understand, but you can trust that God's ways are best."

"Then Uncle Nate is wrong?"

"I'm not sure I'd say he's wrong, but maybe he doesn't understand about God the way we do."

Olivia frowned as she concentrated on Sarah's words. The sound of a wagon coming up the trail traveled toward them. It had to be Nate.

"Then I should pray for him, right?"

Sarah gave the girl a quick hug. "Yes, you can pray for him, and I will, too."

Olivia grinned and hugged her back. "I hear the wagon coming. We'll have to run to beat them to the cabin."

"Then let's run. I'll race you!"

Sarah ran as fast as she could, but Olivia was ahead of her the rest of the way to the cabin. She collapsed against a tree, breathless and gasping, but laughing at the way Olivia danced around her. Suddenly the wagon appeared around the bend of the hill, and she caught Nate watching her. At the sight of the grin on his face, she straightened up and tried to control her laughter, but she couldn't keep from smiling as Charley jumped off the wagon seat and joined Olivia in a game of tag.

Sarah glanced at Nate again, his chiseled features soft as he watched the children's game. She frowned. Noticing a handsome Westerner was far from the tasks Dr. Amelia Bennett had challenged her with when she left Boston. But Dr. Bennett had never met someone like Nate Colby.

Nate was watching her, that grin still on his face. She felt flushed and windblown from her race with Olivia.

She walked toward the wagon. "This morning Uncle James showed me a spot that might make a good camp for you. It's just a little farther along the trail. I can take you to it."

"Come on up." He patted the seat next to Lucy, where Charley had been sitting.

She climbed into the seat, taking Lucy onto her lap. The little girl stuck her thumb in her mouth and relaxed in her arms.

"Olivia and Charley are fast runners. I'm glad I'm not trying to catch them." She glanced up again. He shifted in his seat and pulled at his neckerchief. Were his scars bothering him?

"They like to play tag, that's for sure. Almost every

night on the trail they'd start a game like that. I don't know where they get the energy."

Nate clucked to the horses, and the team went on up the trail and through a stand of young pine trees.

"There it is, to the left there. Do you see the creek, and the clearing next to it?"

A stream tumbled down from the hills in a narrow gulch of its own before falling over the rimrock and joining Whitewood Creek below. As the creek reached this spot, it slowed, forming a little eddy. A small meadow with lush grass filled the rest of the space.

"Here it is. This is where we get our water. Uncle James says the stream will dry up to almost nothing later in the summer, but it's so much better than going down to get water at the bottom of the gulch."

Nate turned the horses into the meadow and then circled around so the wagon rested parallel to the creek, up against the rising hill behind it.

"This will make a good camp. Plenty of grass for the animals and convenient with the water close by."

Nate jumped to the ground and then reached back for Lucy. Before Sarah could jump down on her own, he turned to help her. She rested her hands on his shoulders, and he grasped her waist, guiding her to the soft grass as she hopped down. As soon as she was steady, he moved his hands away. The place where his hands had rested burned with the memory of his touch.

Sarah stepped away from him, her mind a blank. What had they been talking about?

"This is a lovely sound with the water falling and jumping down the slope." She turned back to look at him. "How long do you think you'll be here?"

Nate started unhitching the horses. "As long as it takes to find a homestead and file on it."

"I'll enjoy having you and the children living close by for a while."

"I know the children will like it, too."

"It will give us all an opportunity to learn to know each other better." She bit her lip. Her words sounded forward, even to her own ears.

Now would be the perfect time to bring up loaning her reading books to the children, and she had promised Olivia. Then she saw something moving on his shoulder. A daddy longlegs spider was creeping toward his collar.

She stepped close to him, and Nate froze. His gaze made her knees quiver. She took a deep breath of leather, pine and horses. Swiping her hand across his jacket sleeve, she brushed the culprit to the ground.

"There," she said, stepping back again. "I was afraid that spider would crawl down your shirt, as fast as he was going."

She cast about in her mind to find the words to mention how she could help the children with their reading, but he turned back to the horses and the moment was gone. Sarah balled her hands into fists at her own cowardice.

"I'll go get the children. I know they'll want to help you set up camp."

She nearly ran back to the cabin, brushing past the young pines at the edge of the trail. What was it about Nate Colby that made her lose her senses when she was around him?

With Charley's and Olivia's help, camp setup was quick. Of course, they had all had plenty of practice on the trail. Nate had built a lean-to for a quick shelter for the horses and the mule while the children set stones in a ring for their fire.

"Since we're going to be camping here for a long time, we can make it look real nice," Olivia had said.

"Do you think it will take me that long to find our homestead?" Nate tied the lean-to poles together with strips of rawhide. No use wasting nails on such a temporary structure.

Olivia had looked toward the MacFarland cabin then, but hadn't answered. She wanted to stay near Sarah for as long as possible, and Nate didn't blame her. He had finished the lean-to in silence, his stomach roiling. If he was ever tempted to look for a woman to spend the rest of his life with, Sarah MacFarland fit the bill. But a woman like Sarah deserved a real man, not someone like him.

The thought came back to him again after supper, while the children helped Margaret with the chores. James had gone back to the mining camp for a meeting with his banker.

Nate and Sarah sat on the bench next to the cabin door. Nate whittled on a bit of pine, watching the evening darken the trail under the trees. As the hour grew later, the noise from the mining camp increased.

Sarah cleared her throat and he turned toward her.

"I was talking with Olivia, and she's anxious to start her schooling again."

"I told you, I'm going to see to their education."

She turned to face him. "Oh, I know. But I can help."

Nate tapped the bit of wood against his knee. These busybodies never accepted his answer, did they?

"The children are going to stay with me." He could feel his teeth grinding.

"Of course they are. What I'm offering is to loan

them books and to help tutor if they need it. Lucy is old enough to start learning to read."

"Do you think she'll ever be able to learn anything?" he interrupted her. Women like her never came up with practical plans. She knew what Lucy was like.

Sarah sat in silence for a moment. "We'll never know if we don't try." Her voice was gentle.

"I've tried everything I can think of, but she hasn't spoken—hasn't hardly noticed anyone else is around—ever since her ma and pa died."

"I know about that. The children told us what happened."

Nate didn't want her pity, but he waited for it. Waited for the condescending comments he had heard from the church people back in Michigan, about how the fire that killed his brother was God's will. He couldn't have done anything. God would help him get through the hard times. He shoved at a pile of pine needles with his boot. What god would put him through this misery?

He waited, but Sarah sat in silence. Glancing at her, he saw that she was watching the ground in front of his foot, and then looked out over the gulch, where tendrils of smoke rose from the buildings and tents on Main Street. She sighed and then looked at his face, and when she saw him looking at her, she gave him a little smile.

"Uncle James always says that when one direction isn't working, maybe it's time to turn around and try something else."

A snort escaped. "Something else? How? What?"

She shrugged her slim shoulders. "I really don't know. But I know who does."

Ah, here it came. The preaching. He braced himself for the argument, but she only laid her hand on his.

"You'll figure it out."

"You're not going to tell me to just pray and the answer will come?"

She shrugged again. "Praying will help, and God will answer, but I'm not telling you anything you don't already know."

He turned back to the pine needles. He had scuffed them aside so that the yellow quartz of the rimrock showed underneath. He knew about God, all right.

"What I know is that I could have done something to save Andrew and Jenny, but I didn't. The children think I tried to go back in the house, but I know better. I could have tried harder—I should have tried harder to rescue them, but I froze. Andrew needed me and I did nothing to help him."

She started to say something, but he kept going. "God stopped caring about me when I abandoned my parents to go to war, and He sure doesn't care about me now." He stood and walked toward the edge of the gulch. Anywhere to be away from those violet eyes. "We're on our own, and the children will survive or not because of me. Me and no one else. They're my responsibility and I'll take care of them." He watched the haze of smoke shift in a fitful breeze.

Somehow, he'd take care of them.

He heard her walk up beside him. "You're not alone, Nate."

Her voice was so soft, he almost missed the words.

"You may think God has left you on your own, but you're here, and we're here." She motioned toward the gulch. "Like it or not, you're part of this community, just because you're here. Anytime you need help, you'll get it." She turned to face him. "And the children will survive, with or without you. They may be scarred, but they're ready to face the future."

He looked down at the town. Rough and dirty, like an open wound cut in the wilderness. Like the open wound in his heart. What future could she see for them?

Sarah pushed some hair back with one hand and twisted it into her bun, all without looking away from the scene below them. She was beautiful. Disheveled from playing with the children, tired from a long day of work, and yet she glowed with beauty. She glanced at him and smiled before turning back to watch the lamps being lit in the mining camp. Lanterns on poles lined Main Street, and one by one they came to life.

A gnawing hunger prodded him. A future? The long-forgotten dream pulled at him. A home. Not just a ranch, not just a cabin in the wilderness, but the kind of home Pa had made when he married Ma. With a woman like Sarah, could a future like that be a possibility?

But how could he even think that when he knew what kind of man he really was? He chafed his arms with his hands, trying to ease the tense muscles. No woman would marry a coward.

"What you did today, with that girl—that was very brave."

"It was foolhardy. That man—Harris—he could have shot me down right there on the street and no one would have thought twice about it. I poked my nose into his business."

She turned to face him again. "You said she reminded you of someone."

"My sister, Mattie." He swallowed. Hard. He had failed Mattie, too.

Sarah laid a soft hand on his sleeve. "Tell me about her."

Nate shrugged, careful not to disturb her touch. "Mattie ran away from home soon after I went to war. When Andrew and I got home again, she was gone. Ma and Pa were in the churchyard. Andrew moved on, married Jenny, started his life. But I couldn't leave it alone."

He paused, listening to the sounds drifting up the hill from the saloons.

"Andrew and Jenny said I'd always have a home with them, but I can't—couldn't—stay in one place. Not while Mattie was out there somewhere."

"Do you have any idea where she went?"

Nate pulled at his neckerchief. "I found out she went with some man to Saint Louis. And then to Saint Joe. And the man abandoned her there. After that she headed farther west, to the mining towns in California, Colorado, Montana."

Sarah listened without a word.

"I'd spend months traveling, searching for any trace of her. I'd show her picture around, and people would tell me they had seen her here or there. Then I'd lose track again and I'd head back to Michigan. But it wouldn't last. A few months later I'd be off looking for her again."

"How long have you been searching?"

Nate thought back over the span of time since the war. "Twelve years, off and on. I lost the drive to look any more the last couple years. I'm afraid I've lost her."

He couldn't say that he feared she must be dead. Gone from him forever.

"And she is a saloon girl?"

Nate managed to get one word past the lump in his throat. "Yes."

Her hand on his arm tightened. "You're just the person I've been looking for."

Nate shook his head to clear the fog of memories. "What do you mean?"

"I've been looking—praying—for someone who feels as strongly as I do about these poor saloon girls. They need my help, Nate. You can be the one to help me contact them, to tell them about the school I'm starting for them."

He took a step back. "You're planning to teach the children and the saloon girls together?"

She laughed, but he couldn't tell if she was laughing at him or at her own ludicrous idea.

"Oh no. Of course not."

Nate felt his shoulders relax.

"I would teach the saloon girls at a different time. Like at night, or on Saturday morning."

"Sarah, you know these girls work at night, don't you?"

She waved her hand in the air. "Don't you think they'd rather go to school and learn a skill that will get them out of that life?"

Nate rubbed at his whiskers. "You're assuming they want to leave the life they have now."

"Well, maybe some of them don't. But you saw that girl this afternoon. The one they called Dovey. You can't tell me she isn't looking for a way out."

Dovey's eyes haunted him. Had Mattie longed for a way out of the trap she ended up in? Had she wished for someone to help her? He sighed.

"What kinds of things would you teach them?"

"Oh, how to read and write, if they don't already

know. And a skill, like sewing or housekeeping. Dr. Bennett says—"

"Hold on there. Who is this Dr. Bennett?"

"She's just the most wonderful person!" Sarah paced back and forth, her hands animated. "Dr. Amelia Bennett is a medical doctor, trained in London. I joined her Committee for the Betterment of Women last autumn and learned so much about the importance of education in a person's life. Not only children, but adults, too. Dr. Bennett says that even the poorest, most unfortunate woman can rise above her circumstances with the right education. She says that the reason there is poverty and disease in the world is because there isn't enough education."

Nate lifted one foot onto a nearby stump and leaned on his knee. "And you're going to fix all the evils of the world by educating saloon girls?"

That laugh again. "Of course not. Only the evils of Deadwood."

"Sarah."

She stepped close enough that he could see her smile in the growing dusk. "Don't worry about me. I know the evils that exist down there won't be eradicated in a year or two. It's a process. But someone has to do something, don't you think?"

Nate gazed down on the roofs of the saloons of the Badlands. If Mattie was down there, he'd be doing something, but he had no idea what.

"I'll help you, but only to give a chance to those girls who want it. Most of them have chosen the life they're in for a reason."

Sarah looked beyond him, down the trail. "Uncle James is coming. Please don't say anything to him, or to Aunt Margaret. Not until I have a chance to make some plans."

"All right, I won't."

She squeezed his arm again, gently this time. "Thank you, Nate. I'd better go inside and see if Aunt Margaret needs help with the children."

Even in the dusky light, Nate couldn't help following her with his eyes as she opened the door and stepped into the cabin. Had he just promised to help Sarah in her wild scheme to help saloon girls? What was it about that woman that made him lose his senses when he was around her?

Chapter Five

Two weeks later, Sarah had nine children enrolled in the academy, all of them between six and twelve years old. Any boy older than twelve was already working on a mining claim, and the girls worked just as hard in stores or in one of the many boardinghouses that had appeared as summer approached and the mining camp's population exploded.

Nine children, even without the Colbys. Nate insisted on taking his children with him on his daily hunts for land, sometimes even camping out overnight if they had traveled too far. When she had protested, reminding him of the dangers, he had assured her that with the finer weather, and the new peace treaty signed with the Indians, the only danger they needed to worry about was going too far up the wrong gulch and having to backtrack.

Still, Sarah smiled to herself. The Academy for Young Children, tucked away down the alley behind the church on Lee Street, was thriving. It might be too early to count the school a success after only one full week of classes, but they were doing well. Very well.

At least, until today. She tapped the end of her pencil on her desk. Only the Woodrow children had come to school this morning. The Fergusons had sent word that their four children wouldn't be attending school until the summer was over, which she could almost understand. The Fergusons had a claim in Two-Bit Gulch, and with the warm weather and long days, they needed all four of their boys to help work. But the Radcliffes, with their two girls, would certainly let her know if something was wrong, wouldn't they?

With only three students, she had given the Woodrow children permission to work their arithmetic problems on the big chalkboard at the front of the room. Laura Woodrow finished her sums first. A bright nine-year-old, she was quick with both reading and arithmetic. Sarah wished there was a way for her to meet Olivia. The two girls would be good friends.

Bernie, Laura's older brother, raced to finish his work as quickly as his sister.

"Slow down, Bernie. You're making too many errors." Sarah leaned over him to erase his last problem, scribbled so quickly she couldn't even read it. "Now, write that one over again. And take your time."

The eleven-year-old sighed but wrote the numbers again.

Seven-year-old Alan, the youngest of the family to attend school, slowly wrote his numbers on the board, his tongue stuck through the gap in his front teeth as he concentrated. When he finished writing the number six, he turned to Sarah.

"Is that right, Miss MacFarland?" His missing teeth gave him a lisp, so when he said her name, it came out "Mith MacFarland."

"Yes, Alan, that's just right. You can go back to your seat now. As soon as Bernie is done, we'll have our history lesson."

Sarah retrieved the history book from the shelf behind her desk and opened it to the page they ended on yesterday. She brought her chair to the front, where she could sit facing the children as she read.

Where were the Radcliffe girls?

Bernie joined his brother and sister on their benches and Sarah started reading. The narrative told the story of the Battle of Hastings in 1066, and the children listened, spellbound.

When she finished the chapter, she closed the book and looked at her watch, pinned to her shirtwaist.

"It's dinner time. I'll see you in an hour."

The children left quietly enough, but as soon as the boys were out the door, Bernie shouted to Alan that he would race him home, and they were gone.

Sarah returned the history book to the shelf and reached for her shawl. She and Uncle James walked home for dinner together. She hoped he was ready.

Just then noise from the front room of the building caught her attention. Someone had come in and was talking to Uncle James. The door between the two rooms opened and Celia and Nancy Radcliffe ran in, followed by their mother.

"Miss MacFarland," Celia said. "We've come to tell you goodbye."

"Goodbye?" Sarah glanced at their mother, Tina, who nodded, her eyes red from crying.

"I'm afraid so. We're going back East and only stopped here to make our farewells."

"But why?" The Radcliffes had only been in Deadwood for a month. Surely they wouldn't be giving up already.

Tina glanced at the girls, who were listening to their conversation. "My husband feels it is best for the girls to live closer to their grandparents." She turned to the girls. "All right, you've said goodbye. Go back to the other room with your pa."

Sarah gave each of the girls a hug. "God go with you both." She smiled as she said it, but she could feel the tears standing in her eyes. She would miss these pupils.

After the girls closed the door between the two rooms, she turned to Tina. "There's more to this story, isn't there?"

Tina nodded and Sarah laid her hand on the other woman's arm. In just a few weeks they had become good friends, and now she had to say farewell so soon?

"What is wrong?"

"There were men who came to our claim last night. I had the girls in the cabin with me, but I could hear them talking to Will. They threatened…" Tina took a deep breath, holding her handkerchief to her lips. "They threatened such awful things if Will didn't give them the deed to his claim."

"You must tell the sheriff about this. That isn't right."

"Will doesn't want to take a chance." Tina leaned closer as she lowered her voice. "Those men work for Tom Harris, the man who runs the saloon in the Badlands. I'm afraid of what they might do if Will fights them."

"Then you must leave. But where will you go?"

Tina wiped a tear off her cheek. "We'll go live with my parents. They still have their farm, and Pa will let Will work with him until he can find something else."

She blew her nose. "We had such dreams when we came here. Times are so hard. There were no jobs in Chicago, and nowhere else to turn. Will thought he could find enough gold to start over. That was all he wanted."

Sarah pulled her friend into her arms. "I'll miss you. And I'll miss the girls."

Tina gave her a swift, tight hug. "I'll miss you, too. I have to leave. I told Will I'd only take a minute to say goodbye. You're a good friend, Sarah."

They went into the front room, where Uncle James and Will were shaking hands.

"I'm sorry to see you go, and your family. Deadwood is a rough place, and we need families like yours to help tame it and make it into a town we can be proud of. But I understand. I'd be going back East, too, if I were in your shoes." Uncle James shook hands with Celia and Nancy, while Sarah gave Tina a last hug.

"Be careful on your way," she said to Will.

"We're traveling with one of the bull trains. It's safer that way."

Sarah stood in the doorway of the church, watching as the family climbed into their wagon and set off down the street. They turned onto Main and were gone from sight.

"Well, that leaves only the Woodrow children in the academy." Sarah turned back inside.

"You're not giving up, are you?"

Sarah shook her head. "We'll keep going. When autumn comes and more families move back into town from their claims, we'll grow again. Until then, the Woodrow children will have me to themselves." Sarah smiled at Uncle James, hoping she looked brave.

Then she remembered. With fewer students, she would have time to plan an institute for the saloon girls.

"Don't worry. I have plenty of projects to keep me busy."

Sarah dressed carefully the next day after their noon meal, slipping her calling cards into her reticule, along with the list Uncle James had prepared for her. There were almost a dozen families in town that had school-age children, and she planned to visit each one in her quest to build up the numbers of students.

She peered at her image in the small mirror and straightened her shoulders. Her green silk day dress might be a bit warm for today, but it was the best she owned. Making a good first impression was paramount. Dr. Bennett had drilled that into her. She pinched her cheeks to bring some color into them and picked up her reticule.

"I'll be back in time for supper, Aunt Margaret," she said as she opened the door.

"I wish I could go with you, but this suit of your uncle's needs to be finished before church tomorrow."

"I understand, and it's all right. I'll be able to find my way around town, and I'll be home long before dark."

Sarah closed the door behind her and started down the trail toward the Lee Street steps. The first of the families on her list were the Samuelsons. Uncle James had given her directions to their house in Ingleside, on the other side of the gulch.

But as she started down the steps she paused. It was still early in the afternoon. Perhaps now would be a good time to call on some of the ladies in the Badlands. She would still have time to visit the names on her list afterward.

She smoothed her skirt and continued down to Main Street. This time of the day would be the best for visiting the Badlands, she argued, trying to convince herself of the wisdom of her plan. The town should be quiet, and the girls would be…unoccupied. Her face heated at the thought she might find one of them working, even at this early hour. But that wouldn't happen. Evil deeds were done under cover of darkness, weren't they? As long as it was still midday, she wouldn't run into any trouble.

As she turned left on Main, toward the Badlands, Sarah took a deep breath, but her hands still shook. She grasped her reticule in both hands and took one step, then another. She stopped to look in the window of a dry goods store. Bolts of fabric lined the shelves behind the counter. Perhaps she should buy fabric for a new dress instead.

Dr. Bennett's voice rang in her head. *You're just delaying what you know needs to be done.*

Sarah squared her shoulders and continued down the boardwalk.

As she descended the steps to Lower Main Street, the crowd grew larger and rowdier. Uncle James had said the men loitering in town were looking for jobs in the mines, since most of the tracts near last year's successful strikes had already been claimed. Until then, though, they idled in the streets, gambling and drinking, and who knew what else. Sarah walked near the buildings, away from the mudhole that passed for a street, careful to avoid eye contact with anyone. She had been foolhardy to think the camp would be quiet after the dinner hour. Should she turn back and head to the calmer neighborhoods?

Then ahead she saw the largest of the saloons that comprised the Badlands. Girls in bright dresses lined the rail of the balcony above the street, leaning out and calling to the men below them. Sarah's steps faltered. Their laughter was brittle, their words coarse. She steeled herself. Dr. Bennett had said these girls were calling out for help, that they were longing for a savior and that moving to Deadwood was her opportunity to rescue them.

The girl on the end of the balcony spotted her. Sarah turned her eyes away.

"Hey, lady!"

The girl's salutation caught the attention of her friends and several of the men in the street. Sarah's mouth went dry.

The girl leaned over the balcony rail toward her, and Sarah looked up, then away again. Sarah had never seen so much of a person's figure in public.

"Hey, lady! What are you staring at?"

Several of the other girls came to watch.

"Maybe she's here to join in the fun," one of them said.

"Not dressed like that she isn't," said another. "Hey, sweetheart, come on up here. Trixie will help you find a new frock to wear."

The girls all laughed, and the men joined in.

"That's what the Mystic needs, all right," called out a man in the crowd, "some new blood."

Another of the men stepped up onto the boardwalk next to her, mud caking his boots and trousers. Sarah took a step back.

"Look at how shy she is, boys." The man spit onto the boards near her skirt and leaned closer, lifting his hat brim with a dirty thumb. "What do you say, girly? Come on in and I'll buy you a drink."

More of the men stepped onto to the boardwalk next to him, crowding close.

Sarah's stomach plummeted. She could not—she would not—get sick right here in the middle of this crowd. She scanned the ring of laughing faces, looking for someone familiar. Someone friendly. Her hands shook so hard her reticule nearly slipped from her fingers.

Heart pounding, she took a deep breath and looked up and away from the crowd of men circling her to the girls on the balcony. Only one face mirrored her panic. Dovey stood in the background, behind the girls lining the rail. Their eyes met, and then the girl turned and disappeared into the building.

Turning on her heel, Sarah pushed past the men crowding behind her and headed for the wooden stairs leading to Upper Main. She wouldn't cry. She wouldn't faint. She would just go home. Her chin quivered and she walked faster. The men roared with laughter as she went, but footsteps sounded behind her, along with coarse comments from the men who still followed her.

They were dogs, all of them. Worse than dogs. Her chin stilled and a rod of steel formed in her spine. Suddenly she was angry. She turned on her heel, stamping her foot as she faced her pursuers.

"Leave me be."

The three men stopped but swayed. They were as drunk as the proverbial skunk. Smelled like it, too.

"Ho, girly. No need to be so sassy. We're just looking for some fun."

A tall man appeared at her side and she heard a pistol cocked. "You heard the lady. Leave her be."

Sarah bit her lip to keep from crying out in relief. Nate. Swirling gray clouded her vision and she took a deep breath to keep from fainting. Nate was here. She was safe.

"You wait your turn, fella. We saw her first."

Nate moved his hand with a slight motion and planted a bullet at the men's feet. "I said, leave her be. Turn around and go back where you came from."

The men backed away.

"All right, all right. There's plenty more to choose from. You can have her this time." The man pointed toward Sarah. "But if you ever get hankering for the kind of fun a real man can give you, just head on down to the Mystic. I'll be lookin' for you." He grinned and then slipped away with his friends as Nate lifted his pistol again.

Sarah leaned against the closest storefront. Beyond Nate were his horse and Charley's mule, with the children perched on their backs. They had seen everything. Heard the coarse language. Witnessed Nate nearly shooting those men.

She started to slip down the wall, but Nate grabbed her arm and set her upright again.

"What in the world do you think you're doing?"

Nate guided Sarah over to the edge of the walk where the children waited. They watched with wide eyes. Olivia looked as if she might cry, but the only telltale sign was her blotchy cheeks.

At least Sarah didn't resist him. If she lit into him the way he had seen her face down those coyotes, he wasn't sure what he'd do. He patted Lucy's leg as she perched on Scout's back and smiled at Charley and Olivia to reassure them, then turned to Sarah.

"What do you think you were doing back there? You shouldn't be in this part of the camp alone. Ever."

"I thought I'd invite some of the ladies to my school." Her voice faded away as she glanced back down Main Street toward the Mystic.

Nate resisted the urge to try to shake some sense into her. Didn't she know how dangerous going to the Mystic by herself was? But watching her face as she regained her composure, he could tell she did. Or she did now.

"I'll take you home. We're going up that way now." He reached up and pulled Lucy off Scout's saddle. "Charley, you and Olivia take Scout and the mule back to our campsite. Lucy and I will walk with Miss MacFarland."

Charley took Scout's reins and started up Main Street with Olivia hanging on behind him. The mule made her sure-footed way up the slope between Lower and Upper Main, climbing past the mine in the middle of the thoroughfare.

"Will they be all right by themselves?" Sarah's voice shook a little.

"They'll be fine. Upper Main isn't as crowded as it is here, and Loretta will make sure they get home safely." That was one thing he could say for that mule. She always took care of Charley.

Nate shifted Lucy onto his left hip and felt Sarah's slim hand slip into the crook of his elbow as they started up the steps to Upper Main Street. She relaxed as they put distance between them and the Mystic.

"Where have you been today?"

Nate hitched Lucy farther up on his hip. "We've been scouting out land for our homestead."

"Did you find anything?"

"We looked at a few places, but the problem is water. Everywhere there's a creek, miners have made their claims already. But on our way back into town, one man told me about a place near Two-Bit Gulch. The prospectors didn't find any color there last year, so they've abandoned it. We'll head that way next week."

They passed the dry goods store and the newspaper office and then turned up toward the steps leading toward home. Sarah's face was thoughtful as they walked.

"You aren't planning to go back to the Badlands again, are you?"

She looked at him, startled. "Of course not." She chewed on her bottom lip. "But how can I get word to those girls about the school?"

"Give it some time. Sometimes people are a lot like horses. They have to figure out if they can trust you and if you have anything worthwhile to offer before they let you approach."

"And how will they find out?"

"I'll pass the word around, and they'll hear about it. It may take a while, but eventually, if they want to, they'll come find you."

"Meanwhile, I have the academy to think about." She sighed. "But I refuse to be discouraged. Dr. Bennett's ideas are sound. I just don't want to let her down."

"Your Dr. Bennett doesn't know what you're up against here in Deadwood. Has she ever been outside of Boston?"

"I don't think she's ever been to a place like this." She turned toward him. "But it all sounds so logical and reasonable. Wouldn't anyone want to make their lives better?"

Nate's thoughts went to Mattie, to the places he had followed her to. She could have come home at any time. She could have turned to anyone for help. In Denver there had been a mission society that was trying to do just what Sarah had planned. Mattie could have gone to them during the months she was there. But no, she moved on again, just weeks before he made his way to the city.

"I think Dr. Bennett has that part wrong. For some reason, there are some who are happy enough where they are. It isn't logical, and it isn't reasonable."

"Uncle James would say that they've turned their backs on God."

Was that what had happened to Mattie? She turned her back on her family, but did she turn her back on God, also?

When they reached the top of the steps, Charley and Olivia were far ahead of them, just disappearing around the last bend before the MacFarlands' cabin.

"What about you?" Sarah's voice trailed, as if she was asking the question of the air, but she glanced at him, waiting for his answer. "Are you happy where you are?"

Nate let Lucy down as he thought of how to answer her. Lucy took his hand and walked next to him, compliant as always.

"There are things I would change."

"Like what?"

He nodded toward Lucy. "The effect of the last six months. I'd change that if I could."

"Anything else?"

"I'd have the ranch going already. The children need a home again, but it's going to take months just to build up a herd of cattle so we have money coming in. And time to build a house to live in." He slowed his steps so Lucy could keep up. "If I had time, I could catch some mustangs and break them, too. Then I'd have remounts to sell to the army post at Camp Sturgis."

"But you need help."

"I mean to do it on my own, with Charley's help."

"Charley is still a boy. You can't expect him to do a man's work." She bit her lip.

"Go ahead. Finish what you were going to say."

She tightened the hand that lay in his elbow. "I was going to say he needs to be in school, but we've already talked about that." A few more steps took them around the bend, and the MacFarlands' cabin was in front of them. "Bring the children over to the cabin tonight. I can help them with a lesson in reading, and in arithmetic, too. I could spend some time with them each evening, until you're ready to move to your homestead."

Nate stopped and turned toward her. She looked up at him expectantly. The thought of teaching the children had wiped away any traces of the trouble she'd had in the mining camp this afternoon. He had to laugh at her eagerness.

"All right. I don't want to keep the children from learning. And I can see how you do it, so that when we do move out to the homestead, I'll know how to teach them myself."

She bounced a little on her toes, the way Olivia did when she was excited. "Thank you, Nate." Her smile was beautiful. "I know the children will appreciate it, too."

Chapter Six

The next Friday afternoon, Sarah sent the Woodrow children home early. Their mother, Lucretia, had requested the early release, and since they were the only children in school right now, it didn't make a difference.

She gathered books and slates from the benches of her schoolroom. Three children came to the academy. Three, out of the dozens she had seen around town.

She plopped the books on the table she used as a desk and started erasing the chalkboard. The children in this town ran wild, or worked with their families, like Olivia, Charley and Lucy. But even her visits to the homes of those families hadn't convinced them to send the children to her school any more than Nate Colby had been convinced. How could she communicate the importance of education when people were trying to earn enough to feed their children?

Uncle James popped his head in the door. "Are you almost ready to go? Margaret will be glad to see us home early today."

"Nearly. I just need to finish cleaning the chalk-board." Sarah wrung water out of a rag she kept for cleaning and wiped the dusty board. "I heard you talking to someone earlier. Do you think he might come to services on Sunday?"

"He might." James took the broom and started sweeping the floor. "He was certainly a greenhorn, just off the stage and ready to strike it rich. Someone had sold him a bill of goods, though, making him think gold nuggets are lying on the ground waiting to be picked up."

"How did he end up here?"

"Nate Colby sent him."

Sarah turned and stared at her uncle. "Nate? Why?"

"Nate and I have talked about the problem of these young men who are being swindled by thieves back East who call themselves 'outfitters.' I asked him to send them to me when he ran across them. Most of them, like this young man, are naive and easy prey for confidence men."

"What did you tell him?"

"The truth. He said he might stay in town anyway. There are plenty of businesses hiring eager young men who can keep the gold fever at bay."

Sarah rinsed her rag and tackled the dusty board again. She had spent every evening this past week with Olivia and Charley around the small table in the cabin while Nate sat with James and Margaret next to the fireplace. He may have been visiting with them, but she often caught him watching her. There was something about the man that wouldn't get out of her mind. She rubbed at a chalk mark with more force than necessary. She had never been one to be easily swayed by a handsome face. But no, it wasn't only his appearance, it was the gentle way he cared for those children.

Even if he was wrong in how he did it. Olivia and

Charley were so eager to learn. What a difference it would make if she taught them here at the academy instead of an hour around a table at night!

Sarah took the bucket to the door and tossed the dirty water into the gutter. As she did every day, she looked past the crowded streets and crooked roofs of the neighboring buildings to the towering hills beyond. She let the bucket dangle and leaned against the door frame as she gazed at the white rocks at the top of Boot Hill. What would it be like to climb that mountain someday? What dangers lurked up there? She had often heard the scream of a mountain lion at night, and there were rumors of bands of Sioux warriors combing the hills for miners foolish enough to strike out on their own—although Nate still maintained that the danger from the Indians was over.

The clunk of the broom handle against the wall brought her thoughts back to Uncle James.

"The floor is clean," James said, taking the bucket from her hand. "Let's go."

Sarah gathered her books and waited outside the door while Uncle James locked it behind them. He had tried leaving the church unlocked one afternoon, but the next morning he had to evict a man who had taken advantage of the empty building and set up a saloon overnight. Since then, his motto had been, "We will be as harmless as doves but as wise as serpents," and he had been careful to lock the door each night.

Lee Street, where the church was located, was more of an alley than a street. Sarah had learned to step carefully around muddy spots and debris in the thoroughfare and to avoid looking at men. Any man. She didn't want a repeat of last Saturday. That experience was the only thing that kept her from pressing on with her plans for the saloon girls.

She held tightly to Uncle James's arm and kept her gaze on the path in front of her. Somehow, she must find a way to contact the girls who would welcome her help.

At the bottom of the Lee Street steps, Uncle James paused. "I need to have a few words with someone, and I want to pick up a copy of the *Black Hills Gazette*. Will you find your way home all right without me?"

Sarah always felt safer once she was on the steps. "I'll be fine. We'll see you at supper."

When she reached the cabin, Margaret was making sourdough bread, and Lucy sat at the table, her thumb in her mouth, watching.

"Hello, Lucy." Sarah gave the little girl a hug, but as usual, there was no response. She hoped the child would come out of her silence on her own once love and stability returned to her life. Sarah prayed she would, but meanwhile, she felt it was important to treat Lucy as if everything was normal.

"You're getting to be quite the hand with that bread, Aunt Margaret." She sat next to Lucy and the little girl climbed onto her lap.

Margaret pushed a strand of hair out of her face. "I can't believe it, myself. If you had told me a month ago that I'd be able to cook in this kitchen, I'd have thought you were destined for Bedlam."

"Uncle James always says that where God calls us to work, He equips us for that work." Sarah buried her nose in Lucy's curls. She was so sweet it was easy to love her.

No, not love. She'd promised herself long ago that she would never love again, never leave herself open to the aching grief when death or other circumstances took loved ones away. Still, that didn't keep her from giving Lucy another quick hug.

"James certainly had his work cut out for him when it came to convincing me that this was my calling." Margaret kneaded the stiff dough and then patted it into a circle.

"I know you didn't want to come west."

Margaret stopped patting the dough and looked at Sarah. "I'm ashamed of myself. I acted like a spoiled child, when I should have known James knew exactly what he was doing. I don't know what God has planned for our future, but I'm so glad we're here now."

"What has caused you to change your mind?"

Margaret smiled at her and then placed the loaf of bread into the reflector oven standing in front of the fireplace. "It was the sunrise last week. I stepped outside, and the sky was glorious, with the sun still below the tops of the mountains and the sky all shades of pink, orange and purple. It reminded me of the verses from Psalm 139, 'If I take the wings of the morning, and dwell in the uttermost parts of the sea, even there shall Thy hand lead me, and Thy right hand shall hold me.' I knew then that I am where God wants me to be. Here, in Deadwood, at this time." She smiled at Sarah again. "There is nothing that compares with that feeling. I knew the same thing when I married James, and also when he found you in the orphanage and wanted to bring you home." She put her floury hand over Sarah's. "We have been so blessed. I'll always thank God for bringing you to us."

Sarah turned her hand so she could squeeze Margaret's. She remembered that cold November day when a strange man had appeared at the orphanage looking for her. Her! She had given up hope of ever being adopted long before, and by the time Uncle James had come she was seventeen years old and making plans for life outside the orphanage.

Her eyes misted over as she remembered her hopelessness. She had no experience, except her years as a teacher's helper. But there was no money to further her education, no positions open to her except working as a domestic. She knew she only had two choices—spend the rest of her life working in other people's homes or find her own way on the streets. If not for God's grace and His plan to bring Uncle James home at the right time, she could very easily have ended up like one of the girls in the Badlands.

But then Uncle James had come. He knew her name and had been searching for her through all the orphanages in the state. Papa's brother had been called to the mission field as a young man, before Sarah had even been born, and when he returned from China eighteen years later, looking for her became his first priority. Meanwhile, he had married Margaret, and they became a family of three.

The only problem was that no one had asked her if she wanted to live with these strangers. At seventeen, she thought she was an adult and didn't need a family. The memory of those stormy years still haunted her. But somehow they had gotten through that time. James and Margaret were the only people Sarah had made an exception for. She loved them, but only because they had persevered in their love for her. They had shown her what God's love was like.

"How did you end up with Lucy today?"

"I forgot to tell you, Nate found his ranch! He took

Olivia and Charley with him to file the papers at the land office. I convinced him the errand would be too much for Lucy and we'd get along just fine this afternoon." She caressed the little girl's head. "And we've had a wonderful time, haven't we, dear?"

Lucy looked up at Aunt Margaret but didn't say anything.

Margaret filled the teakettle and hung it over the fire. "I thought we could all go out to look at Nate's new homestead. What would you think of an outing tomorrow?"

"That sounds wonderful. We haven't been outside of the mining camp since the stage brought us here." Sarah turned Lucy sideways on her lap so she could look into her face. "What do you think, Lucy? Do you want to have an adventure tomorrow?" Lucy's expression didn't change. Sarah gave her a hug. "We should pack a picnic."

"Oh, yes, that would be fun." Margaret poured cups of tea for the two of them and paused, the teapot in her hand. "Do you think Lucy would like some cambric tea?"

Sarah felt a slight inclination of the little girl's head. "Let's try some."

Margaret got another cup and poured a small amount of tea in it. Then she retrieved the can of milk Uncle James used for his coffee from the cold box he had made outside the back door, and poured it in the cup. "A bit of sugar to sweeten it and we're all set." She placed the cup in front of Lucy, and they both watched her to see what she would do.

Lucy removed her thumb from her mouth and took the cup in both hands. She tasted one swallow and then another. She looked up at Margaret, grinned just as wide as any five-year-old with a treat and took another drink. Sarah exchanged triumphant looks with Margaret.

"It looks like we have a girl who likes cambric tea." Sarah felt like shouting but only took a sip of her own tea. She could celebrate Lucy's smile later.

Sarah and Margaret planned what to fix for the next day's picnic while Aunt Margaret worked on her knitting. As suppertime drew near, Charley came into the cabin.

"Uncle Nate asked me to come get Lucy."

Sarah helped the little girl slide off her lap. "You're home already?"

"We got back a little while ago. Supper is cooking, and the horses are taken care of, too."

Margaret looked up from her knitting. "I thought you might eat supper here tonight."

Charley shook his head. "Uncle Nate said you'd want us to, but we're fine on our own."

"We need to discuss plans for tomorrow." Aunt Margaret laid her knitting in her basket.

Sarah stood and took her shawl from the hook by the door. "I'll go back with the children and tell Nate what we've planned. I'll be home by the time supper is ready."

When she reached the campsite with Charley and Lucy, Nate looked surprised, but happy to see her. The camp was neat and orderly. The pine needles had even been swept away from around the fire ring Nate had built with rocks, and the horses stood under a shelter of pine boughs. Nate had made a home in the wilderness. Was there anything he couldn't do?

"I hear you're an official homesteader now."

He grinned, causing her stomach to flip. It did that too often these days.

"We sure are."

"You should see our ranch, Miss Sarah," Charley said from his seat next to the fire. "Uncle Nate says the horses are going to love it."

"Only the horses?"

Olivia looked up from the biscuits she was placing in their Dutch oven. "I love it, too, and so do you, Charley. I wish you could see it, Miss Sarah."

Sarah turned to Nate. "That's why I walked over here with the children. I wanted to ask you what your plans were for tomorrow."

Nate walked with her partway down the trail.

"I had planned to take the children up to the homestead to start figuring out where to build the house and barn. Why?"

"Margaret and I were hoping we could go along, since it is Saturday and I don't have school. We've planned a picnic lunch, and we can make a day of it."

Nate's eyes were dark under the shadow of the trees. The sun was nearly below the western hills, and the light was soft.

"You would want to go traipsing through the hills with us?" He shifted so his face was in the light. One side of his mouth twitched up.

"Don't you think we'd enjoy the adventure?"

Nate didn't answer but kept looking at her. She shifted her gaze away, to where the children were gathered around Olivia as she sat on a log, opening a book.

"The children look so happy." She hadn't meant to speak, but the scene pulled the words from her. She looked back at Nate.

He watched them, the muscles in his jaw clenching. "Do you think so? Do you think they could ever be happy again?"

Sarah laid her hand on Nate's arm, and he turned to her. "I lost my parents in an accident, much like they did. I learned to be happy again, even though I missed them terribly."

"I'm afraid I'll never be able to make it up to them."

"You don't have to make up anything to them. Just love them and take care of them."

He looked down at the ground, then back to the children. "I think a fun day for them tomorrow would be perfect. A picnic sounds like something they'd enjoy."

"Would you enjoy it, too?"

Nate laid his hand on top of hers, still resting on his arm. "I think I will." The corner of his mouth twitched again. "We'll have to leave at first light, though. Can you and Margaret be ready?"

"You just wait and see." Sarah gave his arm a slight squeeze and then started down the trail toward the cabin.

"Remember," he called after her, "first light."

"We'll be ready." Sarah hugged herself as she hurried to the cabin door, but then stopped with her hand on the latch. What was she doing? God had shown her what her future was, hadn't He? A life of teaching and caring for other people's children. There was no room for a man in that life.

She glanced back at the camp, where firelight danced between the tree trunks. Perhaps there was room for this man.

Sarah and Aunt Margaret had the table set for three when James came home with a visitor.

"You ladies remember Wilson Montgomery, don't you?"

"Of course we do." Margaret went to the door to

greet him with a sweeping walk that reminded Sarah of the society balls they had attended in Boston. "Mr. Montgomery, what a wonderful surprise. You will stay for supper, won't you?"

"If you insist." Mr. Montgomery turned his smile from Aunt Margaret to Sarah. "I don't wish to intrude."

Margaret reminded Sarah of a hen after a beetle. "Oh my, no! It will be a privilege to enjoy your company."

Mr. Montgomery bowed his head slightly. "In that case, I accept."

Sarah set another place at the table as Uncle James and their guest sat in the chairs at the side of the fireplace.

"I wish we had more elegant fare this evening," Margaret said in a whisper, coming to Sarah's side.

"He'll have to be happy with the stew and bread. He knows we're living in a frontier town, not back in Boston."

Margaret sighed, her face worried. "I do hope you're right."

If Wilson Montgomery thought there was anything inappropriate about their meal, his appetite didn't show it. Sarah refilled his bowl twice before he leaned back in his chair.

"That was a fine meal, Mrs. MacFarland."

Margaret blushed. "I hope you'll be able to try Sarah's cooking one day. She's the finest cook in the family."

Sarah rose to clear the table, avoiding their visitor's eye. Surely he hadn't come to endure Aunt Margaret's attempts at matchmaking.

The men rose from the table.

"You wanted to discuss something with me?" Uncle James moved to the chairs near the fire. Sarah set the dishes aside to wash later, and she and Margaret joined the men.

"Yes." Mr. Montgomery glanced at Sarah. "I hope the subject isn't too delicate for the ladies."

"Do go on, Mr. Montgomery." Aunt Margaret picked up her knitting. "Sarah and I are involved in most aspects of Reverend MacFarland's work."

"It's concerning the businesses of ill repute." Mr. Montgomery flicked a bit of lint off his knee. "There is a group of us whose intent is to drive that sort of business out of Deadwood. With the riches coming out of the ground, the miners are poorly equipped to resist the temptations offered to them by these establishments. Our goal is to remove the temptation, thereby making our fledgling town into a center of culture and civilization."

"That has been attempted in other towns, without success."

"In other towns the populace allowed the dens of iniquity take root and grow. We want to nip this problem in the bud, before it becomes too big to handle."

James paused before answering. "I think you're too late. Have you been to Deadwood's Badlands? Have you seen the number of establishments already there?"

Mr. Montgomery brushed at his other knee. "I wouldn't think of setting foot in that part of town. I only know them by reputation, and by the notoriety they are giving our fair city."

Sarah couldn't keep quiet any longer. "But what about the people working in those establishments?"

Wilson Montgomery turned to her with a condescending smile. "Those people are just the sort we don't want to have here. They will move on to other towns and set up their businesses there. They will survive. There are plenty of other places that will welcome them." He turned back to Uncle James. "We hope we have your support. We need the voices of all the decent people in the gulch and surrounding areas."

Sarah leaned forward in her chair. "In my experience, Mr. Montgomery, the best way to rid a community of undesirable activities is to change the people who are involved in them."

He leaned back. "You mean arresting the leaders of the illicit businesses? Publishing the names of the citizens who frequent them in the local papers?"

"Not at all." She scooted her chair toward him slightly. "I mean by reaching the hearts of the people involved. Teaching them new ways to earn a living and to become part of the community. Teach them about the love of Christ."

"Doesn't the Bible tell us not to throw pearls before swine? These people are sinners, Miss MacFarland, not the kind of upstanding citizens we want in a community."

Uncle James shifted in his chair. "I think you both have a point. Sarah—" he looked her direction with an intent gaze that told her she had carried her point a little too far "—is right. We need to work to bring the gospel to such people. And, Mr. Montgomery, you are also right, in that some of the people involved in these activities are hardened to their lives and will never accept the gospel. That doesn't mean we should do nothing to help them, though. I will consider your ideas."

He steered the conversation toward bringing more businesses into the community, and Sarah settled back in her chair to listen. Wilson Montgomery was an intelligent man, and he had some well-thought-out plans to attract various tradesmen and shops to town. As she watched him discuss his ideas with Uncle James, his face lost its bored look and lit up with enthusiasm. His narrow mustache took on a life of its own as he talked, and when he glanced at her, his blue eyes twinkled. She smiled back at him. It seemed that he had enjoyed their earlier discussion, even though they disagreed. But where did his real feelings lie in regard to the men and women who populated the Badlands?

Before very long, though, he rose from his chair.

"I'm afraid I'm keeping you good people from your evening activities, and I have an appointment in town I must keep. Thank you again, Mrs. MacFarland, for the delicious meal." He turned to Sarah. "I hope we can continue our conversation at a future time. Perhaps you would like to join me for dinner some evening?"

Sarah worked to keep her mouth from dropping open. Was he asking to keep company with her?

Margaret stood up, taking Mr. Montgomery's arm as he walked toward the door. "I'm sure Sarah would love to accompany you to dinner, whenever it's convenient for you."

"Well, then," he said, taking his hat from the hook by the door, "I'll be in touch, Miss MacFarland."

With another quick bow, he was off.

Aunt Margaret spun around, her hands clasping together. "Oh, Sarah! What a wonderful opportunity for you! I was certain you had lost your chance with him when you were so outspoken, but it seems he thinks well of you."

Sarah took the kettle from the fire to the kitchen corner and poured it into the waiting dishpan. "But I don't know if I want to have dinner with him. I hardly know him."

"But James knows him and approves." Margaret turned to her husband, who was scanning the titles on his small bookshelf to find the book he had been reading. "Don't you, James?"

Uncle James turned to her. "I suppose so. He comes from a good family and seems a likely chap."

Sarah picked up the bucket next to the sink. "We need more water. I'll go fill the pail from the creek before the children go to bed so I won't disturb them."

Margaret waved her on as she shaved soap flakes into the dishpan. Sarah pulled her shawl around her shoulders and went out. Aunt Margaret was completely wrong. Mr. Montgomery was intelligent enough, and certainly handsome, but she wasn't about to open her heart to anyone.

Nate stood as she approached his camp, Lucy asleep in his arms. Charley and Olivia ran to greet her.

"Did you come to say good-night?" Olivia gave her a tight hug.

"I came to get some water, but I can say good-night, too. Is it your bedtime?"

Charley kicked at the ground. "Uncle Nate says we've had a long day and he's tired."

"And we have an early morning tomorrow." Nate had put Lucy into the wagon and came to join Sarah and the children. "Say good-night, now, and hop into bed." He reached for Sarah's pail and took it to the stream.

"Good night, Olivia." Sarah bent down to give her a hug. "And you, too, Charley." He shied away from her hug, so she tousled his hair.

The children went to the wagon as Nate brought the dripping pail. Sarah reached for it, but he wouldn't let her take it.

"I'll carry it back to the cabin for you."

"The children will be all right?"

The corner of his mouth twitched in the firelight. "It isn't that far."

As Sarah turned to walk back, he fell in beside her. "You had company for supper?"

"How did you know?"

"Like I said, it isn't that far from our camp to your cabin. I could hear someone talking, and it wasn't James."

"Yes, we did. It was Mr. Montgomery from the bank."

"The fancy man with the suit and white hat?"

Sarah smiled at his description. "Fancy man" fit Wilson Montgomery perfectly.

"He's a gentleman from Boston, and Aunt Margaret likes him very much."

They walked up to the doorstep in silence, and Nate handed her the pail. He paused, but his face was shadowed and Sarah couldn't see his expression.

"You said Margaret likes him. What about you?"

"He's nice, and he was good company at supper."

Nate looked off toward the gulch but made no move to leave. "Is he courting you?"

Suddenly, Mr. Montgomery's manners seemed polished and civilized. "I don't know if that's any of your concern."

"I just thought…" Nate took a step back and ran his finger under his neckerchief.

Sarah's face grew hot. "What had you thought?"

"I didn't think he would be the kind of man that would appeal to you."

He took another step backward and Sarah followed him.

"You didn't think a well educated, polite man would

appeal to me?" Did he think she only liked mountain men and miners?

"No, that isn't what I meant." He took another step, shaking his head.

Sarah watched his profile against the evening sky as he stood with his head bowed.

He looked up and moved a step toward her. "I know I'm not the kind of man you're used to keeping company with, but I don't think he is, either. I've seen Montgomery around town, and I don't like him."

Of course Nate wouldn't like Wilson Montgomery. When did country rustic ever get along with cultured and civilized?

"I don't need your approval on every man Uncle James brings home for dinner, Mr. Colby. I don't think you have any right to tell me who I may talk to and who I must avoid."

He sputtered and then stopped, running his finger under his neckerchief again. "You're right. It's no concern of mine." He reached up to tug at his hat brim. "Until the morning, then, Miss MacFarland."

"Until morning."

She watched him fade into the trees lining the trail, her stomach churning as if she had lost a friend.

Chapter Seven

Nate hitched the horses to the wagon as Olivia and Charley washed up from breakfast. The sun had already risen on the prairies behind the hills, lighting the sky with the yellowish pink that came just before dawn. When Charley tied Loretta to the back corner of the wagon, Nate bit back his objection. If the boy wanted to bring the mule, he could.

"Is Miss Sarah coming, too, Uncle Nate?" Olivia helped Lucy into the wagon.

"We're all going, even Miss Sarah." He patted Scout's nose as he moved around the horses.

Charley jumped up to the wagon seat. "Are we moving to the homestead today?"

"Not yet, Charley." Nate straightened Dan's harness. "We need to make plans. Decide where the house will sit and where the best place will be for the corrals."

"And then I can be a real cowboy?" Charley's voice rose an octave in his excitement.

Nate climbed onto the wagon seat next to Charley and reached into the wagon behind him for the boy's hat. "We have to get some cattle before you start being a cowboy." He plopped the hat on Charley's head.

He clucked to the horses, and they started down the trail to the MacFarlands' cabin. His stomach churned at the thought of seeing Sarah again. He could tell he had been rude last night by the hard edge to her voice as she said good-night, but the news of that dandy Montgomery courting her had come like a punch in the stomach. He pushed the memory away. This was a new day and he intended to give the children a good time.

James came out of the cabin with a large basket when they arrived.

"Good morning, James. That's quite a picnic the ladies have packed."

He lowered the back gate and helped lift it into the wagon. Once the basket was settled next to Lucy, James wiped his handkerchief across his forehead.

"I think Margaret and Sarah packed enough food to feed these children twelve times over."

Margaret came out the door, pulling on her gloves. "You know how hungry children get in the fresh air, dear. If we have any left over, we'll just bring it home."

Nate took a deep breath of the enticing aroma coming from the basket. "Do I smell fried chicken?"

"I ran into Peder Swenson yesterday afternoon, and he gave me a brace of prairie chickens." James grinned. "He figured we'd appreciate it, and he was right."

"Dear Peder," Margaret said. "I'm so glad he's attending church. Has he found a job yet?"

"Odd jobs around town, from what he says. He said he found some fellows to go prospecting with, though. They're heading over Bear Mountain next week to have a look at the canyons on the other side. He still hopes to strike it rich." James held Margaret's hand as she climbed into the back of the wagon. Nate had taken the canvas cover off and placed boards across the bed to serve as seats.

He searched the clearing, but Sarah was nowhere in sight. Had she decided not to come with them after their conversation last night? He didn't know he was holding his breath until it whooshed when she came out the door, swinging her shawl around her shoulders. While Margaret's burgundy dress looked as if she was planning to spend the day calling on friends in Boston, Sarah had dressed for a day in the hills, wearing a dark blue cotton dress and boots that were much more practical than the kid shoes she normally wore.

"Are we ready to go?" She climbed into the wagon box and sat next to Margaret. She greeted the children with smiles and returned Olivia's hug.

She had barely looked at him. Maybe she had decided that Montgomery was the right man for her after all.

"We're all set." Nate lifted the wagon gate and shot the bolts home to fasten it closed.

Olivia bounced on her seat. "Uncle Nate said you wouldn't be ready to go, but you were."

Sarah flashed a smile at him, making his knees go weak. "Your uncle was wrong, then, wasn't he? He underestimated our eagerness to see your new home."

It seemed she had forgotten all about Wilson Montgomery this morning. Nate whistled a tune as he walked to the front of the wagon and climbed up next to James and Charley.

Nate had the route to his land memorized. He had never felt satisfaction like that feeling that washed over him when he signed his name on the homesteading papers. He had earned two years' exemption for his time in the army, so he only had to wait three years for the land to be his.

He headed out of the mining camp on Main Street toward the northeast, down the valley that widened out after they passed Chinatown. The banks of Whitewood Creek were filled with men digging in the dirt, shoveling gravel into rockers or standing knee-deep in the cold water, bent over their pans. A few looked up as they passed, but most kept their attention on the specks of gold they were gleaning from the gravel.

Their route climbed out of the valley and up toward the hills, following the freight route that led through Boulder Canyon and on toward Camp Sturgis. When they reached Two-Bit Gulch, Nate turned the team up the narrow trail along the creek bed, then to the right, up a scree of loose rocks and then pulled the horses to a halt.

"This is the edge of the homestead." Even though he had walked through this land several times in the past week, he couldn't wait to see it again.

"Do we have to walk from here?" Sarah had stood up in the wagon box and was looking over Charley's shoulder.

"No. We'll drive on, but from here to those hills you're on Colby land." He grinned at Sarah as Charley let loose with a cowboy yell.

"Can I ride Loretta?" Charley asked.

"Go ahead. Meet us at the pond, in that grove of cottonwoods."

Nate waited while Charley untied Loretta and mounted her. The boy urged the mule to a trot and quickly outpaced the slower team. Then Loretta slowed to a walk and kept Charley within shouting distance. At least, it looked as if Loretta had decided that for herself. He'd never figure mules out.

He drove the team along a natural shelf on the side of the slope and then turned up. As they crested the rise, the sight that greeted him still took his breath away.

Green meadows stretched away in a wide swath at least a half mile across and twice that long, curving around the wooded slopes that crowded close to the open space. An eagle drifted above them against the clear blue sky.

Sarah whispered, "It's perfect."

Nate chirruped to the horses, driving them slowly through the knee-deep grass, heading for the grove of trees at the far edge. In his mind the mountain valley was dotted with horses—brown, black, white, gray— all grazing on the rich green grass that grew in a thick carpet everywhere he looked. Across the meadow, a meandering line of cottonwood trees followed a fold in the grass. That stream cutting through the land was the crowning touch.

He glanced at Sarah, still standing in the wagon bed, holding on to the seat between him and James. Her face was bright in the clear sunshine, the wind pulling loose hair from her bun. Her gaze went up to the tops of the hills surrounding them.

When she looked at him she smiled, and his heart swelled. Everywhere he looked he saw his future, waiting for him to reach out and grasp it. It was as if the past twelve years had never happened and he was just starting out, full of promise.

He ran a finger between his neckerchief and the

scars. Could he hope that this time he could make something out of his life?

"May I get out and walk the rest of the way?" Sarah touched Nate's shoulder as she spoke. Would he understand her need to get down from the wagon? To feel the grass under her feet?

Nate turned with a grin. "I wish I could join you." He pulled the horses to a halt.

"May I take the girls with me?"

"Sure thing. We'll meet you at the cottonwoods."

Sarah grasped Olivia's and Lucy's hands, and they walked through the meadow toward the far side. Her skirt swished through the thick grass, and little yellow wildflowers were everywhere. Olivia soon had a handful of them.

Nate drove the wagon with James and Margaret on through the grass toward the grove of trees on the far side of the meadow. His voice carried across the distance as he talked with Uncle James, and although she couldn't make out the words, their gestures and excited tones told her what they were discussing—Nate's future ranch.

The look on Nate's face when they had reached the edge of the meadow stayed with her. In the time she had known him, she had never seen him so confident and happy. Ever since she had met him a few weeks ago, Nate had seemed driven, anxious and determined to accomplish his goals. But now, in the sunny, open field with the cobalt sky above them, he was a man who was settled. Like a top that suddenly righted itself and spun true, he was at home.

"Oh, Miss Sarah, look at this one!"

Olivia's voice drew her attention back to the girls, kneeling in a spot where the grass gave way to a rock surface. They were captured by the sight of small, bright purple flowers growing out of a fissure in the stony ground. Olivia turned and beckoned to her.

"It's like a shooting star, isn't it?"

Sarah laughed at the joy in Olivia's voice. "You're right. That's exactly what it looks like." She looked closer at the cluster of flowers, each one a yellow star pointing toward the earth with purple petals trailing behind it toward the blue above. "How lovely they are!"

"These are real shooting stars. Somehow they've been caught here in the meadow as they fell from the sky." Olivia's words caught at Sarah's imagination, and her explanation seemed perfectly plausible.

As Olivia reached out to pluck some of the flowers, Lucy grabbed her hand.

"No." The word was raspy but clear. "No."

Olivia stared at her sister. Lucy's face was twisted with the effort of words fighting to get out of her mouth.

Sarah fell to her knees next to the little girl. "Why don't you want Olivia to pick the flowers?"

Lucy looked at her, and Sarah's eyes stung as she struggled. The little girl took a deep breath. "They're too pretty."

Sarah smiled at Lucy. "We won't pick them. Olivia will leave them where they are." She reached out and Lucy leaned into her arms without another word. "You're right. They're too pretty to watch them wilt and die."

Olivia rocked back on her heels. "Do you think we could plant them in a garden, so they can grow by our house?"

Sarah tucked a blond strand of hair behind Olivia's ear. "I don't see why not. Back in Boston, Aunt Margaret's garden club transplanted many wildflowers like this one. When you have the right place for it, we'll dig one up and plant it near your house."

Olivia smiled. "When Uncle Nate builds one for us." She looked at Lucy. "Will that be all right, Luce?"

The little girl nodded, her thumb back in her mouth. She had run out of words for now, but Sarah was confident she would talk again.

By noon they had reached the far edge of the meadow where the small stream widened out into an old beaver pond. The cottonwood trees grew in an awkward circle in the marshy grass and shaded a small rise. Nate and Uncle James had spread a blanket on the soft grass and Aunt Margaret unpacked the fried chicken and corn bread. The children gathered around the blanket, taking seats along the edge, but Nate stood staring at the surrounding hills as if they would disappear.

Finally, just as Margaret lifted the plate of cookies from the basket, he joined them, sitting between Sarah and Charley.

After grace, Sarah took a piece of fried chicken. The walk across the mountain meadow had whetted her appetite. She took two bites from the meaty breast before seeing that Nate was watching her.

"I don't mean to be greedy. It's all so delicious." She wiped her fingers on a napkin.

Nate grinned. "I was just thinking how I'm glad I'm not that chicken." He blushed red and took a piece of corn bread. "This would make a good place for a cabin, wouldn't it?"

Uncle James looked around them. "You're close to the pond here, and there is a nice level spot."

"Plenty of wood around, and a good view of the rest of the place." Nate stared into the distance, the bread forgotten in his hand.

Sarah scanned the meadow in front of them. She could imagine a cabin nestled under the shoulder of the hill. What would it be like to step out on the front porch every morning and be greeted by the sight of the vast meadow with the hills rising up behind it? That would be one sight she would never tire of.

Nate pulled a scrap of paper out of his pocket and smoothed it on the ground. Sarah leaned over to watch as he sketched in the hills, the stream and the meadows.

"I could only claim half of this valley for a homestead. It is at least two sections."

Sarah took a piece of corn bread and broke a small corner off. "But if you're only allowed one section, how could you choose which part to claim?"

"It had to be this one, with the pond, but I hate to give up the rest of the grazing land."

"I wonder if you'd be able to file on the other section as a tree claim," Uncle James said.

Nate took another drumstick. "I'll have to ask. The tree claim program was created for the prairies, though. I'm not sure if they'll allow one up here in the hills."

The children finished their dinners and started a game of tag in the meadow. Even Lucy ran after her brother and sister with all her might. This valley, swept by a clean wind and studded with wildflowers, was a wonderful place for the children to grow up. Such a difference from her childhood in the city.

"This is a perfect spot to raise your horses." Sarah handed Nate a cookie.

Nate nodded, his eyes on the children. As they ran toward the far end of the meadow, a herd of deer bounded away from them, across the valley and into the trees on the other side.

"Look at that," he said, gesturing with the cookie in his hand. "With game like that, we'll never go hungry here."

Sarah watched for the deer to reappear, but when they didn't, she focused on the children. Olivia and Lucy were picking wildflowers while Charley roamed through the grass around them, brushing the long stems with a stick.

"I wanted to tell you something while the children aren't here." She turned to Nate. "Lucy spoke this morning."

"She did? She started talking?"

Sarah shook her head. "Not really talking, but she said a couple words. It's a beginning."

Nate smiled and settled back on his elbows, watching the children again.

She gathered the dishes and placed them back in the basket. Uncle James was lying on his back, his hat over his face. Aunt Margaret leaned against a tree, her knitting in her lap, but her eyes closed.

Suddenly Nate stood and held his hand to her. "Come. Let's go explore a little while James and Margaret rest. We'll celebrate Lucy's progress."

Sarah let him tuck her hand in his elbow, and they walked across the meadow toward the children.

"Six months ago, I thought I had lost everything."

Nate picked the head off a stalk of grass and stuck the stem between his teeth.

"Not everything. You had the children."

He shook his head. "Yes, I had the children, but how could I ever take care of them? I couldn't see our future. Without Andrew and Jenny, and Andrew's dry goods store, how could I provide for them? Besides, Andrew was the storekeeper, not me." Nate halted, looking up into the hills around them. "You said that sometimes God just wants us to change directions." He glanced at her, then back at the hills. "Do you really think there's a God who even cares what we do?"

Sarah bit her lip while she tried to think of a reply. If Nate didn't believe in God, what hope did he have in his life? She thought back to all the times when she had listened to Uncle James in these situations, when he was helping someone understand the difficult questions about God. He always found a way to help the other person reason their way through the problem.

"What makes you think there isn't?"

Nate didn't look at her, but dropped her hand and stepped away, still looking at the hills. "If you had seen what we went through during the war..." He turned toward her, but didn't meet her eyes. "How could any god have allowed that to happen?" His voice dropped. "If He was real, don't you think He would have intervened? Prevented the horror we experienced?"

Sarah's eyes stung. The pain in his voice was too awful to imagine. She hadn't witnessed any battles during the war, but she had seen soldiers who had returned home with lost arms or legs. Broken in body and spirit. But not all of them had turned away from God. Nate had survived the war in one piece, but how many wounds did he carry beneath the surface, where no one could see them? She couldn't imagine the things he had experienced that caused his pain to continue so many years after the fighting was over.

"I don't have an answer for you, Nate." She stepped closer to him. "But I do know that God has not abandoned you." Nate appeared to be listening, even though he still hadn't looked at her. "Everything that happens has a reason, and God works through every circumstance of our lives." When he started to take a step back from her with a shake of his head, she stopped. He wasn't ready to hear more. She silently prayed that he would, and soon.

When he spoke, it was a whisper. "A reason?" He looked up at the surrounding hills again until she thought he had forgotten she was there. And then he turned toward her, running a finger along the kerchief tied around his neck. "I'll think on it." He nodded and lifted one corner of his mouth in a quick grin. "I'll think on it."

The sun still lingered far above the tops of the hills when they returned to Deadwood, but it had been hours since their noon meal. A pleasant exhaustion settled over Nate as he guided the horses back through the mining camp and up to the MacFarlands' cabin. That same happy weariness seemed to have claimed them all. There had been little conversation on the drive.

But part of Nate's own silence came from the closeness of Sarah. She had chosen to sit next to him on the wagon seat so James and Margaret could sit together. The children lay down in the bed of the wagon. At every bump and turn Sarah's skirt brushed against his knee, keeping him constantly aware of her presence.

She must have been as tired as all of them, though. She didn't say a word until they reached the cabin on Williams Street.

"Thank you for the wonderful day, Nate." Her voice was soft, and she smiled as she spoke.

"We sure appreciated your company." He tore his gaze away from those deep blue eyes. They had spent too much time together, walking across his land and making plans.

Plans that she wouldn't have any part in, if he had his way. Life with him—well, he wouldn't ask anyone to share the kind of life he had lived so far. But he couldn't keep from watching her walk into the cabin with James and Margaret, and he gave a nod to her small wave as she closed the door. He sat, staring, until Charley climbed up on the wagon seat in her place.

"What's for supper?"

Supper. Of course the children would be hungry.

"Do we have stew left from last night?" Nate looked at Olivia, the cook of the family.

"We ate it all for breakfast this morning, remember? You had the last bowl."

"That's right. Then it's beans and corn bread."

Nate's announcement brought no response, and he didn't blame them. Last night's stew had been a treat, after finding a squirrel near their camp, but meat was scarce close to town.

"Do you think we can read a story from the reader Miss MacFarland loaned us?" Olivia stood, clinging to the back of the seat.

"You can read one while supper is cooking, while we still have good light." Nate smiled at Olivia's grin.

"Really?" Her eyes shone.

"Sure thing. I want you to practice as much as you can."

As soon as they reached camp, Olivia climbed out of the wagon and went to the pile of supplies Nate had covered with the canvas that morning. She found the book and settled on a stump near the fire circle while she leafed through the pages.

"What are you doing? What about supper?" Charley was all boy, and food was always the first thing on his mind.

Nate reached over and ruffled Charley's hair. "Don't worry about supper. I'm Cookie tonight."

Charley grinned at him. "Cookie? Like cowboys on a trail drive?"

"Mosey up to the fire and we'll get the beans cooking," Nate said in his best dime-novel cowpoke voice. Charley had devoured the one he had found in Chicago, all about "Yellowstone Jack" and his adventures. What more did a boy need?

Lucy settled on an upturned log while Nate stirred up the ashes and brought the morning's fire back to life. A pot of beans had been sitting in the coals, and now Nate lifted it by its bail handle and pulled it to the flat rock they used for a work surface, glad for his leather gloves. Even so, drawing close to the growing fire brought pain, his scars searing in answer to the heat of the flame. Nate ignored the pain and gave the beans a stir. He got a bit of salt pork from the keg in the wagon and cut it into smaller pieces, stirred them into the beans and put the pot next to the fire again.

Olivia took a seat next to Lucy and started reading from her book. "Persev...persev... Uncle Nate? What is this word?"

Nate leaned over to look at the page she showed him. *"Perseverance."*

"What does it mean?"

Nate thought for a minute. "It means to keep trying, no matter what."

"You mean, like we're doing now?"

He looked at his niece. She had endured so much over the past year. He stirred the corn-bread batter, taking his time before he answered. Were they persevering?

"Yes. Like we're doing now. We've had some rough times, but we're persevering. We keep working toward our goals. Making our dreams come true. That's what that word means."

Nate poured the batter into the Dutch oven and set it in the coals at the side of the fire. Charley pitched in, using the small camp shovel to pile coals on top of the oven while they both listened to Olivia read the story about some children trying to fly a kite. One line echoed in his head. *A few disappointments ought not to discourage us.*

Disappointments? They'd had their share, all right. But were they discouraged? Nate looked at the children's faces, listening intently to Olivia's voice as she read. He had to admit it. Some days they were. But as long as he kept working, he'd make it. The children would have a home on the ranch, just as he'd promised.

When the corn bread was done, Olivia put the book away and got out their tin plates. Nate put a piece of corn bread on each one and ladled a scoop of beans on top. He took his spoon and dug in, pausing only to blow on the hot, fragrant beans.

Olivia stared at him.

"What's wrong?"

"At home we used to say grace. And at the MacFarlands' we always say grace. Why don't we say grace now?"

Nate shifted. Charley and Lucy both stared at him, too, waiting for his answer. What could he say? He didn't want his battle with God to become theirs, but he couldn't say thank-you to a God who didn't care about them.

But he had told Sarah he'd think about God. Her peaceful face came to his mind. She would give thanks. She would teach the children to pray before meals, and at bedtime. What would she think if he refused to let the children give thanks for their meal?

"Go ahead." Nate cleared his throat. "Charley, why don't you say the grace?"

He bowed his head while the boy prayed, sounding like Andrew. Of course he would. He had heard his pa pray at every meal since he was born.

During other prayers, the words had run off Nate's head and heart like water off a duck's back. He might as well have been made of wood. But not this time. Charley's clear voice was as confident as if he was talking to someone who was right here in the circle with them. The boy's trust made Nate open his eyes and look to make sure they were alone.

A verse from his childhood came back, echoing behind Charley's words—*For where two or three are gathered together in My name, there am I in the midst of them.*

Was God here? Did He really care what happened to them, as Sarah said?

When the prayer was over, they ate quickly. Even Lucy seemed hungry tonight and looked as if she was enjoying her simple supper.

"Tomorrow is Sunday," Olivia said when she had finished. "Can we go to church with Miss Sarah?"

"I don't know." Nate scraped at the last of the beans in the pot. "We'll see what tomorrow brings."

"I can see their cabin from here." Charley pointed through the trees to the clearing.

"Yeah, you're right." He looked in the direction Charley pointed, to the soft glow of light he knew came from the cabin windows. Every night he had watched that glow until the MacFarlands put out their lamps when they went to bed.

That gentle light drew him like a beacon. Like a lighthouse warning of rocky shoals ahead, pointing out the safe, narrow path he should take. A safe, narrow path with a dark-haired beauty. Why wouldn't he jump at the chance?

Nate stared at the fire as Olivia took his empty plate. That path wasn't for a man like him. That path was for a man like Andrew. A man who could follow through with his commitments. A man who had what it took to make a home for his family.

A man who hadn't watched everything he touched crumble in his hands.

He tossed the last of his coffee, thick with grounds, on the fire and watched the liquid disappear in the coals.

He couldn't ask Sarah, or any woman, to endure going through life with him.

Lucy crawled onto his lap, her thumb in her mouth

and eyes half-closed. Nate pulled her close and rocked a little as the sleepy girl relaxed in the warmth of the fire.

And yet, with all his faults, he had ended up with these children. God sure had a strange way of giving a man what he deserved.

As Sarah entered the cabin behind Uncle James, he took a deep breath. "My, oh, my. That smells like good old New England boiled dinner."

Aunt Margaret blushed. "I thought it would be a good way to use the salt pork you brought home a couple days ago. We had a few potatoes and a can of carrots. It was simple to put the pot in the banked coals while we were gone for the day."

"It smells wonderful." Sarah lifted the Dutch oven out of the coals and removed the lid, then she ladled the meat and vegetables into a serving bowl that Aunt Margaret put on the table. "And it looks delicious, too."

"Thank you, dear." Aunt Margaret stood back to admire the table. "It isn't quite as elegant as our Boston dining room, but the food will fill us up."

After saying grace, Uncle James shook out his napkin. "I forgot to tell you, I had a conversation with an interesting man yesterday afternoon, before I ran into Wilson Montgomery."

"Who was that, dear?" Aunt Margaret spooned some vegetables and broth onto Uncle James's plate.

"There's a new merchant in Chinatown. He's recently come to Deadwood and has opened a grocery."

Margaret passed the bread. "Why did he want to talk to you?"

Sarah handed her plate to Aunt Margaret. When Uncle James had left her at the bottom of the steps, she had wondered where he had gone. With his experiences in China as a missionary, he enjoyed his visits to the Chinese section of Deadwood.

"He heard that I had spent time in Ningbo and thought I might know Charles Williams. It turns out that Charles is the man who taught Hung Cho the Bible. He's a Christian."

"I thought all those people in Chinatown were heathens." Aunt Margaret sniffed. "With their opium dens and such."

"You've been talking to Mrs. Brewster again." Uncle James pointed his fork at her. "You know that woman is a gossip." He cut a potato in two. "It is true. Most of the Chinese are Buddhists, and some of them do run opium dens and other unsavory businesses, but there are more who provide good services for the town, and even a few Christians."

"Will they be coming to our church?" Sarah broke a bite off her bread.

Uncle James shook his head. "Hung Cho speaks English fairly well, but a lot of them, especially the women, only speak Mandarin. He wants to start a Christian church in Chinatown and asked if I'd be willing to preach on occasion."

"You haven't spoken Mandarin for years." Aunt Margaret spooned some more vegetables onto his plate. "Will you be able to speak well enough to preach a sermon?"

"I am a bit rusty, but it will come back with practice."

Aunt Margaret turned to Sarah. "I wonder if some of the Chinese families would send their children to the academy."

Sarah pushed a potato with her fork. "I can try calling on the families, but I can't seem to get any of the children in town to come. They are needed at home, or working in their parents' business. Some are even working claims. The only time they are willing to come to town is on Sunday."

Uncle James pushed his plate away. He gave Aunt Margaret a smile of thanks as she poured a cup of coffee for him, and then he looked at Sarah. "Perhaps you should adjust to the people's needs. If the children are in town on Sunday, maybe that's when you should have your classes."

Sarah shook her head. "What kind of learning can they get on only one day a week?"

"More than they're getting now." Uncle James sipped his coffee.

"It could be a Sabbath school." Aunt Margaret poured two more cups and then hung the coffeepot at the side of the fireplace to keep warm. "You could keep teaching the students you have now during the week, but on Sunday have Bible classes for the children."

Sarah toyed with the idea. "Bible classes would be just the thing. The Woodrow children could come, and perhaps some of the others from the community and the outlying camps." Perhaps even Nate's children, if he was willing to let them. After all, Sabbath school wasn't the same as her academy.

"I couldn't believe my eyes last Sunday." Sarah finished her supper and took a sip of her coffee. "All the businesses in town were open, as if it was a Saturday. Doesn't anyone here go to church or honor the Sabbath?"

"That was one thing I found hard to get used to." Uncle James took another slice of bread. "But the miners are scattered all over the area. Most of them have to walk five or six miles or more to come into town, and they work every chance they get. Most don't work on Sunday, so that becomes the day to buy supplies or visit with their neighbors." He dunked the bread in his coffee. "I think you've probably noticed there aren't many who attend church."

"But you think the ones with families would bring their children to school?"

Uncle James dunked his bread again before he answered. "I think it's worth a try. The folks around here don't have anything against education or church, but it isn't as important to them as their work. Most of them came here with nothing, and if they don't work as hard as they can, they'll have nothing when they leave. Or, worse yet, they'll have spent all their resources and end up destitute. They come to Deadwood thinking the gold is here for the taking, but nothing can be further from the truth."

"Surely some have struck it rich, haven't they?" Aunt Margaret put her cup down. "It isn't all some kind of lie to lure people here, is it?"

"Some have struck it rich. There is gold here—in the streams, in the mountains—and there is a lot of it, if the estimates are correct. But like most gold rushes, a few people will get very rich, and some won't make enough to pay their expenses. Most will only pull enough gold out of their claims to pay their way back home."

Sarah drained her coffee cup as she rose to start washing the dishes. It seemed Nate Colby had chosen a wise course when he decided to raise cattle and horses rather than search for gold. Stacking the plates and cups, she wondered how Nate and the children were doing tonight. Were they warm enough? Who cooked their meals? Did Nate remember to tuck the children into their beds?

She set the dishes down on the table. "I'll be right back." Her aunt and uncle were intent on their conversation and didn't notice as she slipped out the door. Dusk had turned to darkness.

Standing at the edge of the rimrock across from the cabin door, raucous singing, gunshots, drums, a trumpet and all kinds of sounds drifted up to her from the town below. The nightly revelries reminded her of the great hopes she had to save the young women down there from their sordid life. But she hadn't made any progress toward contacting them since that disastrous trip to the Badlands. Dr. Bennett had convinced her that the women would flock to her for help, but they ignored her and went on suffering from the unfortunate consequences of their choices. How could she help women who had no interest in making their lives better?

She turned to her left, where she could see the glow of Nate's campfire filtering through the young pine trees. She tried to tell herself that the children were the ones who were the focus of her concern, but it was no good. In her mind, she could see Nate sitting by the side of the fire. Was he finishing a last cup of coffee while the children settled in their beds for the night?

Sarah leaned against the rough, dusky bark of a ponderosa pine. Sometimes the man could be cheerful and friendly, but other times as rough and unyielding as this tree. Would she ever figure him out?

Chapter Eight

Sunday morning. Nate lay still on his bedroll near the fire, listening to the snorts of the horses as they woke and the light snores coming from Charley's bedroll on the other side of the fire. The birds' morning noises nearly drowned all other sounds as they sang in the treetops. Under it all was the faint roar of the wind in the tops of the pines.

Something was different this morning. Nate cast his mind back, over the picnic the day before, settling the children in when they returned, the usual chores around the campsite. He stretched and sat up before he remembered. There had been no nightmare.

He took a deep breath and whooshed it out. No fighting in the dark, no fires licking at his dreams, no panic. Only a restful night's sleep. He ran one hand through his hair. This was what it would feel like if he were free.

Sounds from the other side of the stand of pines told him the MacFarlands were up and starting their day. A smile interrupted his yawn as he thought about Sarah. What would she be up to today? Maybe they could take a walk up Boot Hill. The white rocks at the top beckoned him every time he looked up there. They could take the children and…

Hold on. It was Sunday. Sarah would be busy with church this morning, and he'd have no opportunity to see her.

Nate rubbed at his whiskers. Unless he went to church, too.

He glanced at Charley, sound asleep under his blanket. No sounds came from the wagon. The girls were still sleeping, too.

Could he show up at church just to see Sarah? Wouldn't she think he was there to listen to the preaching?

He threw his blanket aside and stood up. It was time to start the morning chores, Sunday or not. As he built up the fire, he considered what going to church meant. Once he went, the children would want to continue going, and he'd have to take them. He couldn't bear the disappointment in their faces if he didn't.

But he wouldn't be able to bear listening to some holier-than-thou so-and-so preach to him about God.

Nate shook his head at his own thoughts as he poured a measure of grain into each of the horse's nose bags. James MacFarland wasn't like the preacher back at the church in Michigan, or even the soldier-preachers he had heard during the war. James would be the same in the pulpit as he was sitting on the bench in front of his cabin. He had never met a man with more compassion for his fellow human beings or who spoke of God as if He was an intimate friend.

He slipped the nose bag over Scout's ears and patted the horse's neck as he munched on the grain. "What do you think? Would it do me some good to go to church?"

He moved on to Ginger, who reached eagerly for the bag in his hands. "So, you think I should go, too, do you?"

Pete and Dan were next, and then Nate eyed the mule. Its ears turned backward at his approach. "We're not going to have a fight about this, are we? You like your grain."

Loretta bobbed her head down and then up and pulled her lips back, looking as if she was grinning at him.

"See, Uncle Nate?" Charley was sitting up on his bedroll. "She's learning to like you."

Nate growled, "That'll be the day." But he couldn't keep a frown on his face. The mule stuck her head into the feed bag and he slipped it over her long ears. She didn't even try to nip at him.

Nate peeked over the side of the wagon. Olivia was still sleeping, but Lucy's eyes were open. She smiled when she saw him. He smiled back at her. "How are you this morning, little bluebird?"

Lucy climbed out of her bed and wrapped her arms around his neck, holding tight. Nate's eyes grew moist as he hugged her back. She was getting better. She was coming out of her shell. Sarah had told him that Lucy had spoken yesterday, though she hadn't said another word after that. But it was a beginning.

He lifted her up and over the side of the wagon so she could go behind some trees where he had dug a latrine for them to use. He'd do anything to help her make more progress. Anything. Even… Nate looked up at the bright blue sky between the tall pines. Even pray? The trees grew blurry as his eyes filled. Yes, even pray.

Wiping at his eyes with the corner of his neckerchief,

he reached over the side of the wagon and shook Olivia's foot. "Hey there, sleepyhead. It's time to get up, unless you want me to be Cookie again this morning."

Olivia kicked at his hand and sat up, pushing her hair back from her face and yawning. "No, I'm getting up."

"Hurry up, Olivia," Charley said from his seat by the campfire. "We don't want to eat Uncle Nate's cooking again!"

Nate turned toward Charley, his hands held out from his sides in a pretend gunfighter's stance, straight out of Charley's dime novel. "You try saying that to my face, cowboy."

He snarled, but Charley charged straight at him, knocking him to the ground. As they wrestled in the pine needles, Nate couldn't help laughing right along with Charley.

Sarah smiled at Peder as he dashed through the swinging doors of the former saloon. He grinned and snatched the hat off his head.

"Good morning, Miss MacFarland. I hope I'm not late."

"You're not late at all, Peder. Aunt Margaret is just getting ready to start the prelude." She watched the lanky young man make his way to the third bench from the front, his usual seat. The Woodrows with their five children and twin baby boys took up the fourth bench, and Wilson Montgomery and a couple other businessmen sat on the second but the rest of the benches were empty. A few more stragglers might show up before Uncle James started the sermon, but few people came to church in this town that was so crowded. Even this early in the morning, shouts, brass bands and gunfire were all she could hear from the street.

"Go ahead and take your seat, Sarah." Uncle James joined her at the door. "We'll be starting the service in a couple minutes."

Sarah walked to the front of the room and slipped into her seat on the front bench. She could hardly bring herself to call the old saloon a church yet, when the cracked mirror still hung on the wall behind the bar. But Uncle James was making progress. The piano had been repaired and tuned, and he had built a pulpit and some benches to serve as pews. She glanced up at the soot-stained ceiling. It didn't matter. As Uncle James always said, the church was the people, not the building.

As Margaret started playing a quiet hymn for the prelude, Sarah heard footsteps at the door and whispered voices as Uncle James greeted the newcomers. She resisted the urge to turn around as the footsteps came closer to the front bench but had to look up as Olivia took the seat next to her. Nate gave her a sheepish smile as he and Charley filed past her and took their seats.

They had only just sat down when Uncle James took his place at the pulpit and asked the congregation to rise as he read the call to worship. Sarah was too dazed to hear which verse he had selected. Nate brought the children to church?

Through the service, Sarah tried to keep her mind on the hymns they sang, and the scripture, but by the time Uncle James started his sermon, she was ready to give up. Even with Olivia on one side of her and Aunt Margaret on the other, she wasn't aware of anyone except Nate sitting on the other side of Charley with Lucy in his lap. The first time she'd stolen a glance in his direction, he'd met her eyes and turned bright red before focusing his attention on Uncle James. The last time she'd looked down the bench, he hadn't noticed. He was listening to the sermon, watching Uncle James intently. Was he having second thoughts about his refusal to believe in God?

A smile forced the corners of her mouth up, in spite of her trying to keep it under control. She had prayed for God to bring Nate and the children to church but hadn't expected it to happen so soon.

After the service, the children gathered around Sarah. "I'm so glad to see you all here today." She gave Olivia and Lucy each a hug and laid her hand on Charley's shoulder. She could hug him in private, but he certainly wouldn't appreciate it here with the Woodrow children looking on. She glanced up at Nate. "Good morning. What brought you to church today?"

Could his face have turned more scarlet? Before he could answer, Lucretia Woodrow was at her elbow.

"Oh, Sarah, I can't tell you how much I appreciate your willingness to teach our children. And now I hear you're starting a Sabbath school? Tell me all about it."

Lucretia hooked her elbow in Sarah's and led her off to the side of the room, leaving Nate to shake hands with Lucretia's husband, Albert. Bernie Woodrow was looking Charley up and down while his sister, Laura, smiled shyly at Olivia and Lucy. Knowing Nate and his family were in good hands, Sarah launched into a description of what she and Aunt Margaret hoped to achieve with the Sabbath school. She was facing Nate as she talked, and she couldn't help glancing at him occasionally. Uncle James joined in the conversation with Albert Woodrow.

Wilson Montgomery, on the other hand, had waited to speak to her until it became clear that Lucretia would continue to dominate her time. Then, with a nod to her when she happened to look his way, he took his leave. Sarah turned her full attention to Lucretia then, thankful she had avoided talking to him. He hadn't made good on his promise to invite her out to dinner yet, and she didn't want to have that discussion with him when Nate was nearby.

Lucretia finally followed her family out the door, with the assurance that her three older children would attend the Sabbath school when Sarah started it in a few weeks. Then Sarah turned to greet the others who had come that morning, but other than Peder, who joined them for dinner each Sunday, only Nate and the children remained.

"Are we ready to go home, then?" Uncle James asked as he and Peder picked up the hymnals from the benches and stacked them neatly on the end of the bar.

Nate cleared his throat. "I haven't had a chance to ask, but I was hoping Sarah would like to come on an outing with me and the children. I thought we'd pack a picnic and go for a walk in the hills."

Uncle James glanced at her. "It's up to you. We don't have any plans this afternoon except to enjoy the delicious meal Margaret has prepared, right, Peder?"

Peder grinned in response. "If Miss MacFarland isn't there, we'll just have to eat her share."

Sarah laughed. "I'm sure you will, Peder. I've never seen anyone who can eat more food than you."

Charley grasped her hand. "Then you'll come? Please say you will."

"Yes, I'll come. As long as you let me stop by the cabin and change into a more appropriate outfit."

Nate leaned close to her as they followed the children out the door. "I can't believe any other outfit would be more appropriate than the one you're wearing. You're beautiful."

Sarah stumbled on the threshold and Nate caught her elbow, sending tingles down her arm. Beautiful? He thought she was beautiful? She looked up at his face, certain she'd see his grin that would tell her he was making a joke, but only saw his warm smile. She smiled back. This afternoon promised to be a wonderful one.

Nate followed Charley up Boot Hill, following the faint trail to the formation of white rocks at the top. In front of him, Sarah walked next to Olivia with Lucy between them, holding both of their hands.

He could kick himself. He shifted the cloth bag holding their lunch higher on his shoulder. Why had he told Sarah she was beautiful?

He hadn't meant to. He had meant to say her dress was beautiful, but whenever he looked into those violet eyes, he lost all sense. At least no one else had heard what he said. He was thankful for that. Watching her now, as she and the girls climbed the last steep slope up to the rocky crown at the top, he thought he might be losing his senses again. All he could think of was how perfect it felt to have her here. Since last fall, when Andrew and Jenny had died, he had tried to make a life for the children. To make a family with them. But it was like eating bread made without salt. Their lives—his life—was tasteless and flat. But when she was here, everything was right.

He couldn't tell her, though. How could he ever ask her to become part of his life when all he touched went wrong?

As they reached the bottom of the rocky towers, Charley and Olivia ran on ahead, and Sarah helped Lucy up the steep slope.

They had today, though. He could enjoy her company today.

He pushed himself to catch up with the others, and they reached the grassy top of the hill together. All around them the white rocks towered above, as if they were standing on a head crowned with white quartz. Charley hoisted himself up on the side of the nearest rock, clinging to cracks in the stone.

"Don't climb up there, Charley."

"Why not?"

"Look how far you'd go if you fell."

Charley looked over the side of the hill. The trail they had climbed was steep enough, but on this side there was a sheer drop to the mining camp below.

Sarah looked and then stepped away from the edge, Lucy's hand firmly in hers. "I think we'll do just fine looking at the view." She turned to the east, where Bear Butte rose above the distant prairie. "Oh, it's so beautiful."

Nate couldn't look beyond her profile. Yes, she was right. It was beautiful.

He cleared his throat. "We should find a spot to have our picnic. It's a bit breezy up here."

Sarah turned to him with a smile, the wind whipping her hair around her face. Her cheeks glowed in the bright sun. "We passed a grassy spot a little way down, and it was out of the wind. Let's go down there."

The simple meal of bread and cheese was finished quickly. Lucy lay down with her head pillowed on Sarah's lap, while Charley and Olivia explored the area around their picnic site.

Sarah stifled a yawn. "If I'm not careful, I'll fall asleep like Lucy." She smoothed the curls out of the little girl's face. "You'll start building your cabin tomorrow?"

Nate leaned back against a tree. "I'd like to, but a corral needs to come first. We can continue living in the wagon, but the horses need space."

She sat in silence for a moment. "Then that means you'll be leaving your campsite soon."

He picked up a twig and broke it in half. That had been the plan all along, but then why did he feel as regretful as her voice sounded?

"We might wait a few days before we move out there. I want to make sure the stream is going to be a good water supply." Nate let his voice trail off.

She leaned back on her hands, careful not to disturb Lucy. "It's going to be a beautiful homestead, the way you described it yesterday."

"Yeah, maybe."

"You don't think so?"

Nate threw the twig away. "I've made plans before, but they don't work out. Try and fail. That seems to be how I do things. I'll be happy to be able to keep the children fed and clothed." He shook his head. "Sorry. I just don't have good results when it comes to being a success."

"It depends on what you mean by success. I think the only successful life is following God's will. Whether you're successful in the eyes of man or not makes no difference."

"What do you mean?"

"Well, look at Uncle James. You'll have to ask him to tell you about his years in China. While he was there, he had to move from one city to another several times because the mandarins didn't want him teaching about Jesus. The other missionaries avoided him because he believed as Hudson Taylor did, that he should immerse himself in the Chinese society in order to reach the people. And then when his first wife died, he thought God had abandoned him."

Nate's throat tightened. He hadn't had any idea James had endured such hardships. "It looks like he was right, doesn't it? How could he think he was successful in those circumstances?"

Sarah was silent for a minute. Charley and Olivia's voices floated to them from farther down the trail where they were playing.

"I asked him that same question once. He said he spent many hours on his knees, asking God to show him what His purpose was in taking him to China."

"And the answer?"

She looked at him, her eyes moist. "He had gone to China because he thought he would win lost souls for Christ. But what he learned was that God only wanted his obedient spirit and willing heart. Once he learned that, he said his preaching changed. He was no longer trying to do God's work, but allowed God to work through him. He built a church, taught the Bible and trained men to be pastors. His students—all Chinese— started a dozen more churches, in places he would never have been able to reach on his own. By the time he came home, he knew his success wasn't in what he did, but who he followed."

Nate picked up another twig, methodically breaking it into one-inch pieces. How did he fit into Sarah's story? He didn't. His plan wasn't to save souls, it was to keep his family together. He threw the pieces of twig into the grass. And a fine job he had done of that so far. Ma, Pa, Mattie, Andrew, Jenny. He had lost them all. Ashes to ashes, dust to dust.

He dug his fingers into the long grass. "I still think the only way to measure success is if you do the job you set out to do, and my job right now is to get a roof over our heads before winter comes again."

That was success as far as he was concerned. Survival.

Tuesday afternoon, Sarah shooed Alan and Bernie Woodrow out the door to follow their sister home and closed the door. She leaned against it, glad for an opportunity to rest for a minute. Teaching was both energizing and exhausting. Sarah pushed a stray curl back into place with her forearm. As eager as she was to start each school day, she welcomed the quiet at the end of the afternoon, as well. Sometimes teaching the three siblings was more work than a classroom full of students. A sigh escaped as she picked up a book from the nearest bench and added it to the pile on her desk.

She hadn't seen Nate at all yesterday. He had taken the children out to the homestead early in the morning, before Sarah had left for school, and they hadn't come back to their camp until after dark. She had waited to see if he would come to tell her about his day, but as she sat on the bench outside the cabin, the campsite on the other side of the trees had grown silent.

Why was she looking for him, anyway? It wasn't as if he owed her an explanation of his activities.

Sarah took the rag and wiped the chalkboard clean and then straightened the benches. No, Nate would move to his homestead, and there would be no more picnics at White Rocks or long days spent with the children. She took the broom and attacked the ever-present dust in the corners. She wouldn't have the opportunity to see Nate again, unless he continued coming to church. But she couldn't count on that.

Opening the door, she swept the pile of dirt out into the alley.

"Miss Sarah!"

Charley was racing toward her from the street at the alley's head, followed by Olivia. Behind them came Nate and Lucy. He returned her smile before she turned her attention to the children.

"How are you?" She leaned the broom against the wall just inside the door as they all came into the classroom. "Tell me what you've been doing today."

"We've been out to our ranch." Charley had to pause to catch his breath. His face was ruddy from the sun and all three children were windblown and hot.

Sarah shot a look at Nate. His smile made him look like the proverbial cat that had swallowed a canary. "So you'll be moving out there soon."

"We already started." Olivia grasped Sarah's hand. "We took the wagon out today and set up camp. Uncle Nate started a corral, and he's going to build us a cabin."

Sarah sank onto the nearest bench. "Already?" She

put one arm around Olivia. "We weren't neighbors for long, but I'm going to miss you being next door."

She pressed her lips together to keep them from trembling. Lucy came over and Sarah lifted the little girl into her lap.

"You'll have to come visit us." Charley hopped on one foot as he spoke. "We're going to build fences and more corrals and a lean-to for the horses and a big cabin."

"You're going to be very busy. You won't have time for visitors."

Olivia leaned closer to her. "We'll always have time for you to visit. Won't we, Uncle Nate?"

Sarah looked up at him. They were leaving. Nate would be too busy with the homestead to come into town, and she had the school… When would she see him again? This was exactly why she refused to open her heart, so she wouldn't feel the blow when she had to say goodbye, but somehow, it was breaking anyway.

Nate turned his hat in his hands, his eyes meeting hers. "Don't forget, Olivia, we're going to be away for a while."

Away?

Charley stopped hopping. "We're going to Wyoming to buy some cattle. I'm going to be a real cowboy."

Lucy snuggled closer to her and Sarah felt that steel rod of stubbornness that warned her she was going to interfere. Of all the ideas a man could come up with, this had to be one of the worst she had ever heard of.

"You're taking three children on a cattle drive?"

Nate twisted the hat brim. "Of course I am. They did fine on the trail when we came here from Michigan. Why wouldn't they come with me now?"

"On the trail with a crew of freighters is one thing. You were in a group and had plenty of protection in case of trouble. But this?" She stood, lifting Lucy in her arms. "This is ridiculous. Who is going to drive your wagon? Olivia? And what if the cattle run off, or one of you gets hurt or if the Indians…" A hiccup interrupted her. She couldn't go on.

She met his blazing eyes. He shoved his hat onto his head. "We'll be fine. I'll take care of the children, and I'll hire men to help drive the cattle home."

He didn't lower his gaze, and neither did she. Couldn't he see how pigheaded he was being? But what other choice did he have?

"Leave the children with me. I'll take care of them while you're gone."

"No."

"You know they'll be safer here, and you know I'll take good care of them."

"They're my responsibility, and they're coming with me."

Sarah pressed her lips together. Lucy wiggled in her arms and she lowered her to the floor. She glanced at Olivia and Charley, who were staring wide-eyed at her and their uncle.

The steel rod melted, leaving her trembling. She was just as pigheaded as Nate. "You're right. They're your responsibility. But please, think about what's best for the children."

She sat back down on the bench and looked at the floor, waiting for his decision. He paced from one side of the schoolroom to the other. He stopped in front of her and turned his hat in his hands again. He ran one hand through his hair and sighed.

"I can't help but feel that what's best for the children is to be with someone they love and trust. And that should be me."

Sarah's heart fell.

Nate paced the room again, his boot heels echoing with each step. He stopped in front of her, started to speak and then strode to the window.

After staring out at the sunny alley, he came back and squatted down in front of her with another sigh. One side of his mouth tugged up. "But I don't see any way around it. You're right. A cattle drive is no place for children." His words were soft, only for her. He paused, glancing at the two older children. They still watched him, waiting for him to decide their fate. "If you're willing to care for them while I'm gone, I'm beholden to you. I know I'll leave them in good hands."

"But, Uncle Nate," Charley said, "I was going to be a cowboy."

Nate stood up and faced the boy. "You will be a cowboy, but you need to learn how. I can't teach you and drive cattle at the same time." He laid one hand on Charley's shoulder. "Besides, the trip could be too dangerous for your sisters."

Charley nodded, and Olivia caught Sarah's eye, bouncing a little on her toes.

Sarah's mouth trembled. "And school? Can they attend school while you're gone?"

He shrugged. "I guess they'll have to, won't they?" He looked at the children again and then back at her, his eyebrows knitted together in a frown. "I trust you to do what is best for them while I'm gone."

Sarah nodded. "You don't need to worry. We'll get along fine."

Nate took Lucy's hand and ushered the children toward the door, but then hung back after they went out into the alley.

"I don't want you to think I'd put the children in danger, but I just assumed they'd come with me. They're my responsibility, and I don't take that lightly. It goes against my better judgment to leave them with someone else."

Nate rubbed his chin as he watched the children play. He was having second thoughts.

Sarah touched his arm. Just one touch, but it brought his gaze to hers. "Don't worry about them while you're gone. We'll take good care of them."

He rested his hand on hers, and the warmth of his fingers burned on her skin. "I'll leave at first light tomorrow and bring the children to the cabin on my way out of town, but I'll be back as soon as I can."

She longed to tighten her grasp on his arm, to hold him back, but she couldn't keep him from going. He needed to buy the cattle for his ranch. She put a smile on her face, hoping it looked genuine.

"Take care of yourself, and we'll be looking forward to your return."

Chapter Nine

Nate shifted in his saddle, studying the cattle Barker's cowboys had sorted out for him. Most were young longhorns, thin and restless after a winter on the range. In the mix a few cows with spring calves cropped at the rich grass. Brown, white, piebald and spotted, they spread out over the prairie east of Camp Sturgis, in the shadow of Bear Butte. The rest of the steers, sleek and healthy, bawled as the cowhands drove them into the army's waiting pens.

"What do you think?" Justice Cooper pulled his hat off and wiped the sweat from his forehead with a practiced gesture.

"I think I'm happy we're at the end of this drive." Nate shifted in his saddle, weary and sore. "And this herd will be a good start for my ranch. I owe Mr. Barker my thanks for letting me put them in with the cattle he was sending to Camp Sturgis."

Coop rode as if he lived on his horse. Nate had the passing thought that maybe the young man had never learned to walk, but started riding as a baby. Coop had become a good friend on the drive, nearly as close as a brother. He hadn't left Nate to himself the way the other Barker Ranch cowhands had, but had sought him out. The cowboy taught Nate the finer points of herding cattle, teaching him to anticipate each animal's next move.

But by the time the Barker herd had reached Camp Sturgis from Wyoming, Nate was dead tired. Driving cattle was a tough job, no matter how you looked at it. Between keeping them moving when they wanted to graze and stopping the young steers from heading up every dry draw they came to, the days were long in the saddle.

The nights were no better. Three times they had to fight off small bands of raiders. Indians or cattle rustlers, it didn't seem to matter. The raiders would edge up to the outskirts of the herd in the dark and drive off as many head as they could. By the time the night guard reached the spot, they'd be gone. They lost a few head of cattle in each incident.

And then one of Nate's cows had died along the way, just as they got into the Black Hills. She lay down while they watered the cattle at the Belle Fourche River near the Devil's Tower and didn't get up again. Cookie had let her calf ride in the chuck wagon, but it was touch and go with the little bull for a while. Nate hoped he'd be able to make the fifteen-mile trip up to the homestead from the military camp.

When the army's steers had been sorted out from the herd and bunched in a corral, the trail boss, Jed Slaughter, rode up to Nate and Coop. Jed's sun-browned face was hard and wary.

"Got bad news for you, Colby. The commissary officer doesn't care if we ran into rustlers, he still wants the full count of cattle he paid for. I offered him a refund, but he wouldn't take it when I had cattle standing in front of the man."

Nate watched a couple hands cut a bunch of his steers out of his group and move them toward the corral. He didn't have the practice to count them on the hoof the way Jed or Coop could, but he could tell he was left with far less than the hundred he had paid for.

"How many did I end up with?" He kept his voice low, his jaw tight.

"There are around seventy-five left."

"Am I going to have to take the losses on my own? I paid for a hundred."

Jed shifted in his saddle. "I know that. I'll give you a refund for some of them, but you have to expect a few losses on a drive like this."

"But not the army. Shouldn't they expect some losses, too?"

Coop leveled his gaze at Jed, who shifted in his saddle again.

"I'll refund the money for ten of your cattle. That's all I can do."

"That won't cut it, Jed." Coop edged his horse closer to Nate, still staring at Jed.

"Aw, come on, Coop. I have to answer to Barker."

"But you're asking Nate to take a bigger loss than Barker. You know that isn't right."

Jed leaned forward. "Colby here knew his cattle weren't all going to make it. I think his percentage is fair." He turned toward Nate. "Take it or leave it."

"And if I leave it?"

The trail boss shrugged. "The army will be happy to buy another seventy-five head, and I'll be able to give Barker the full amount he expects." He turned his horse toward the army camp. "Let me know what you decide by morning."

Coop watched Jed ride away. "I'll tell him what I decide. Barker's a fair man to work for, but I'm not going to hang around as long as Jed is the boss. He'd shave his own ma to make a profit." He leaned down to pat his buckskin's neck. "Maybe I'll see what's happening up Deadwood way." He tilted his head toward Nate. "Know any outfits that need a cowhand?"

Nate and Coop both turned their horses toward his herd of cattle. "I'd hire you in a minute, if I had any way of paying you."

Coop plucked a head of grass as they rode and stuck it between his teeth. "Maybe we could work something out. Didn't you say there was another claim next to yours?"

The rest of the mountain meadow, up for grabs to whoever claimed it. "Yes, but I've taken on as big a section as I'm allowed."

"What if I filed on it?"

Nate reined in his horse. "You'd want to settle down? Have the responsibility of a homestead claim?"

Coop shrugged and pulled his horse up facing Nate. He leaned on the horn of his saddle and looked beyond Nate to the foothills surrounding Boulder Canyon and the mountains beyond. "When I look at those hills yonder and think of the country we've been driving the cattle through the last couple weeks, I feel an urge to be part of it." He looked at Nate. "Did you ever feel that way? You take a look and know that you've found the place where you belong?"

The muscles around Nate's heart constricted. Yes,

he knew. From the first moment he had seen his land, he knew.

Coop didn't wait for Nate to answer. "That's how I feel when I look at those hills. Not as high or wild as the mountains farther west, but a man can put down roots in them. Build something to last. That ranch you have in mind, raising horses and cattle, that's something that I can do." Then he looked at Nate and grinned. "And if I decide settling down isn't for me, I'll sell my claim to you after I prove up on it. Until then, we can be partners."

Nate followed Coop's gaze up into the foothills. Could he partner with Coop? Did his friend even know what he was getting into, offering such a thing? Taking up a yoke with him might not be a smart idea for the cowhand. While some people turned everything they touched to gold, for Nate everything turned to ashes.

But all along the trail, as Nate had watched Coop and the other cowhands handle the cattle, he had discovered just how complex a job he had taken on. Herding wild longhorns in this Western land was nothing like taking care of cows in the East. This bunch of his was more like a herd of deer or mountain goats than cattle. How would he ever learn to keep them alive without some experienced help?

Coop was offering more than a chance at gaining the other section of land as part of his homestead. He was offering his knowledge, his experience and his life. At least for the next five years.

Without Coop's help, would he even be able to prove up on his homestead? Without Coop's help, would he ever have a home for the children? A home to offer to

Sarah... He wouldn't let his thoughts go any further down that path.

During the long hours inside his own thoughts on the drive, he had been forced to face the truth. Every time he thought of the future, the homestead and his family, Sarah was always part of the picture. But Miss Sarah MacFarland deserved better than what he could offer her.

He had to admit, though, that he needed the help. He glanced at the cowhand next to him. He not only needed his help, he needed his friendship and the partnership he offered.

With Coop's help, the future he envisioned might become a reality.

Nate stuck out his hand. "Partners."

"Miss Sarah," Olivia called from the church half of the building, "do you want me to clean the windows, too?"

Sarah straightened the last bench in the row and went into the front room where the children had been sweeping. "No, we don't need to wash the windows today, but you can dust the windowsills."

Looking around the large room, Sarah smiled. What had once been a run-down saloon was now a clean and comfortable place of worship. The building had been transformed since she had first seen it, and even Margaret hummed as she polished the walnut veneer on the piano. The poor thing still sounded tinny, but no one complained. Margaret's playing was a blessing.

Margaret gave the piano a final rub with her cloth. "Are you ready for our first Sabbath school, Sarah?"

"I think so. I've chosen the creation story to start with. I just hope we have students."

"We'll have at least three." Margaret tilted her head toward Olivia and Charley as they raced each other to finish dusting the windows. Lucy sat on a bench, holding her rag doll while she watched them.

"And the Woodrow children are planning to come." Sarah ran her dust cloth down the slats of the swinging door and then stopped with a sudden thought. "Uncle James put notices in the newspapers, didn't he? And flyers in the stores? Star and Bullock's store and Furman and Brown's?"

"Yes. Of course, many folks won't see the advertisements until later in the day, but the families who come to church will know about it."

Olivia finished the windows and brought her rag to Sarah. "They're all done. What else do we need to do?"

Sarah glanced at Charley, making a second round of the windowsills with his rag. "We're all finished. Everything is ready for tomorrow, so we'll head home for dinner." Lucy slipped off her seat on the bench and took Sarah's hand. Sarah crouched down to the little girl's level. "Are you hungry, Lucy?"

She waited. Charley's running steps echoed in the big room while Olivia and Margaret chatted about what to make for their meal. Lucy lifted her eyes up and Sarah held her breath. Even though the smiles were progress, Sarah still longed to hear Lucy speak again. But the little girl gave only a nod. Sarah smiled, hiding her disappointment, and gave her a quick hug before standing and following the others out the door.

Nate had been away for three weeks while the children stayed behind. At first, Sarah was afraid Lucy would retreat further into herself again when Nate left, but she seemed to understand his absence was temporary and made herself at home with the MacFarlands.

Sarah both dreaded and welcomed the day Nate would return. She looked down at the little girl next to her as they walked. Somehow, these children had wormed their way further into her heart than she had thought possible. Giving the children back to their uncle would be difficult, but she couldn't keep her affection for them from growing stronger with each day. The longer Nate stayed away, the more she let herself love and enjoy the children as if they would always be together.

But at the same time, she missed Nate. She missed watching him with the children, missed his wry grin when he teased her with pointed barbs and she missed the way his hand felt when he laid it on hers.

At that thought, Sarah's face heated even though they walked under the awning of the Custer House. She swung Lucy's hand a little. Lucy glanced up at her and swung Sarah's hand harder. When Sarah exaggerated the swing even farther, Lucy giggled.

Lucy giggled! Sarah looked to see if the others had heard, but they were walking several feet ahead, and the street was crowded and noisy.

Sarah laughed and repeated the high swing, almost pulling Lucy onto her toes. She was rewarded with another giggle, and she picked the little girl up in her arms and twirled her around.

"I love to hear you laugh, Lucy! You have the prettiest voice."

A hand grasped her elbow and she turned to meet Wilson Montgomery's frown. He propelled her across the walk and against the hotel's wall.

"Miss MacFarland, you're making a spectacle of yourself." He glanced around them, released her elbow and dusted off his suit.

Lucy's smile was gone, her face blank. She threw her arms around Sarah's neck and turned her face away from Wilson.

No one had noticed Wilson or Sarah, and the crowd around them continued their regular business.

"I don't think playing with a child attracted undue attention, Mr. Montgomery."

"You don't know what people were thinking. I saw several men looking your way just now. Calling attention to yourself is inappropriate for someone of your position."

Sarah bit her lip and counted to ten. Slowly. The one dinner she had shared with Wilson Montgomery last week had convinced her there was no future in their friendship, but he continued to assume a relationship that was nonexistent. For Uncle James's sake, and for Aunt Margaret's, she would be civil to him.

"I will take your opinion under consideration."

Wilson pressed closer to her as a young woman, dressed in bright pink flounces, passed by on the boardwalk followed by several admirers. The woman blew a kiss in Wilson's direction as she passed and then put on a pretend pout when he didn't acknowledge her.

When he spoke again, his voice was low. "I would urge you to control yourself in public. You don't want to be compared with the likes of that woman."

He nodded in the direction of the girl in pink, who had turned around and was teasing the men following her in a bright, ringing voice. Everyone around had stopped to watch her, but she kept glancing toward Sarah—or was she trying to get Wilson's attention?

Wilson took her elbow again and guided her past the crowd, moving so quickly that Sarah was almost running as she clutched Lucy in her arms. He didn't stop until they caught up with Margaret and the other children at the bottom of the Lee Street steps.

Margaret smiled and blushed. "Why, Mr. Montgomery, what a surprise to meet you again."

Wilson released Sarah's elbow and removed his hat, bowing slightly toward Aunt Margaret. "Mrs. MacFarland, it is always a pleasure."

"It is so kind of you to escort Sarah through these crowded streets."

Olivia and Charley stood on either side of Aunt Margaret, but Wilson hadn't acknowledged them.

"May I escort you ladies home? I have business at the bank, but nothing that can't wait for ten minutes."

Sarah saw Margaret's smile start and jumped in with her refusal before her aunt could gush her acceptance.

"We don't want to take any more of your time, Mr. Montgomery. We will have no trouble getting home on our own from here."

"As you wish, Miss MacFarland." His smile didn't go any farther than his thin lips as he bowed toward her and then toward Aunt Margaret. He took his leave, still not glancing at the staring children.

Sarah set the quiet Lucy on her feet and took the girl's hand. Olivia joined them, a slight frown on her face.

"Miss Sarah, is that man courting you?"

"Isn't it wonderful?" Aunt Margaret swept over to Sarah. "Wilson Montgomery is going to be an influential man in Deadwood very soon, and he is honoring you with his interest. Has he asked you to dinner again?"

Sarah flexed her left elbow, still sore from Wilson's attention. "No, Aunt Margaret, he hasn't." She held up her hand to stop Margaret's protest. "And I don't want him to. He may become an important man someday, but I have no desire to let our friendship go any further." If it even was a friendship.

Olivia let Margaret and Charley go up the steps ahead of them.

"I'm glad," she said, taking Lucy's other hand. "Because I want Uncle Nate to court you."

Sarah felt her face heat. "Your uncle Nate hasn't said a word about courting." She stopped, and Olivia looked at her. "And I don't want you to mention it to him. If Nate Colby wants to come courting, it has to be his own idea, not yours or mine."

Olivia grinned. "Then you do like him. I knew it!"

Sarah started up the path again. "Of course I like him. He's a kind man and takes good care of you children." She glanced at Olivia's triumphant face. "But that doesn't mean I want to marry him."

She laughed as Olivia's face fell. "But don't worry, whatever happens or doesn't happen between your uncle and me, we'll still be friends."

Olivia grinned again. "Forever?"

She stopped, giving both girls a hug. "Forever." She kissed the top of Lucy's head and then Olivia's cheek. "No matter what happens, we'll always be friends."

Sunday morning's service started out like every service of the past month, with a scattering of families filling the rows of benches here and there and Peder Swenson in his usual place in the third row. Sarah smiled at the children she knew and introduced herself when a new family paused in the doorway.

"Good morning," she said, extending her hand to the wife. Her face was drawn, her eyes hollow. "You're welcome to come in and join our worship service."

The wife glanced at her husband and then shook Sarah's proffered hand. "We didn't know there was a church here. We live up in Galena and haven't been to town since last fall."

Her husband stepped closer to the door, peering in as Margaret started playing a hymn for the prelude. "I think we have time, Katherine." He glanced at Sarah, looking her up and down and then at his wife. "But we ain't dressed for church. We'll have to come another week."

"Nonsense." Uncle James met them at the door and ushered them into the building. "You're dressed just fine. Please, take a seat and join us."

Sarah turned to Katherine, smiling at the two boys hiding behind her skirt. "We have a Sabbath school this afternoon for the children. Perhaps your sons would like to attend while you and your husband do your shopping."

Katherine's tired face brightened. "We'd like that. We'd like that fine. I hate to see the boys growing up without Bible learning."

Sarah watched them take their seats on one of the benches, and then turned back to the door. A grizzled miner was standing there, and he snatched his hat off when Sarah greeted him. "Never mind me, ma'am. I'll just find a place. I heard you have good hymn singing here."

By the time Margaret had finished the prelude and Sarah had taken her seat on the front bench with Charley, Olivia and Lucy, three more miners had followed the first. Sarah turned her attention to Uncle James as he read the call to worship from the book of Psalms, silently thanking God for bringing new people to their small church.

After the second hymn, Margaret left the piano and sat next to Sarah. She leaned over and whispered in Sarah's ear, "There's one of those girls from the Badlands outside the door. She's going to drive good people away from the church, don't you think?"

Sarah didn't answer. Aunt Margaret had never understood her need to help these poor women. She had never confided her fears to Aunt Margaret. She knew how fine a line lay between the naive orphan she had been before Uncle James found her and the girls who worked in the saloons. Between the scripture reading and the sermon, while Uncle James was arranging his notes, she glanced back at the door. She could see the top of a girl's head above the swinging saloon doors and her bright red skirt underneath.

She leaned close to Margaret. "I'll be right back."

As the first words of the sermon started, Sarah slipped out the door, startling the girl in red. It was Dovey. She was much younger than Sarah had thought at first, and she jumped like a spooked deer. She clutched a flimsy purple lace shawl around her bare shoulders.

"Don't go." Sarah reached out a hand to stop her as the girl edged away.

She looked down at her dusty slippers. "You don't want someone like me here. I'm sorry I intruded."

She glanced at the open doorway of the church and bit her lower lip.

"You're not intruding." Sarah stepped closer to the girl. "You're the one they call Dovey, aren't you? Is that your real name?"

The girl looked at her then and smiled shyly. Face powder barely covered an old bruise on her cheek. "My name is Maude, but Tom—Mr. Harris—said it wasn't a good name, so he gave me the new one."

"I'm Sarah. My uncle is the pastor here. You're welcome to come in and sit down."

Maude blushed and backed away. "Oh, no, ma'am. I know my place. I just stopped to listen to the singing and then the Word. That's a powerful Word he read, isn't it?"

Sarah's eyes pricked when she remembered the passage of scripture Uncle James had chosen for his sermon that morning, the story of the woman caught in adultery. "You heard Uncle James read the scripture?"

"Yes'm." Her face broke into a smile. "When I heard that Jesus kept the people from stoning that woman…" She blushed again and looked down. "I didn't know the preacher could tell a story about someone like me in church."

"It isn't only a story. It's true. Jesus kept the people from stoning the woman and then told her to go and sin no more. Did you hear that part?"

Maude nodded, her face suddenly sad and hard. "That's how I know it can't be true. Once you're like me, you can never change."

She pressed her lips together, and Sarah waited for her to say more. Uncle James's voice drifted through the door, preaching the grace of God's forgiveness, but Maude took a step back.

"I shouldn't have come. It's too late for me." She pulled her shawl tight around her shoulders and slipped behind a passing wagon.

Sarah nearly went after her, but she had disappeared into the mass of people filling the streets on this Sunday morning. Between the bands playing in the Badlands, trying to attract miners to their shows and the street preachers shouting in the intersection, the morning was anything but peaceful. She prayed that in all that chaos, God would protect that young woman.

Nate eased out of the saddle, stiff and tired after days on the trail. But now he was home.

He led Scout to the small stream meandering through the meadow and let him drink while Nate tilted his head up to take in the hills surrounding his land spread out in front of him. The cattle were already settling down to grazing on the lush grass. Even the little orphan bull calf pulled at the green carpet.

His land.

He flipped his hat off and wiped the sweat from his forehead with one arm. This was what he had been working toward for years. His own place.

Coop rode up next to him. "They look like they're going to like it here."

Nate grinned at him as he dismounted. "They better like it here, because I'm not taking them one step farther."

"It's a good range with plenty of good water." Coop squatted down upstream from the horses and scooped some of the clear water into his mouth. "Yep. This is perfect." He stood and looked up into the surrounding hills. "Your claim would start just left of that rock out-

cropping—" Nate pointed across the valley "—and include the far end of the meadow and up into the hills."

Coop shoved his hat back onto his head. "I like what
I see. If you agree, we'll start the partnership right now."

Nate shook his partner's hand, waiting for the churn
of regret in his stomach, but there was only the buoy-
ancy of anticipation. "Let's get into town. I've got children to collect, and you have a claim to file on."

They walked their horses toward town, making their
way to Two-Bit Gulch and then to the trail along Whitewood Creek. Now that the cattle were settled on the
claim, it was time to bring the children out here for good.
How had they been during the weeks he was away?

He should have worried about them more, shouldn't
he? But every time his mind flew back to Deadwood
and the children, he knew they were all right. He could
trust James and Margaret to take good care of them.

And Sarah. He urged Scout into a faster walk. Had
she thought about him while he was gone? He longed to
look into those violet eyes of hers, and perhaps she would
even let him hold her hand for more than a brief minute, if he could presume on their friendship that much.

As they rode past the mining claims along the creek,
Nate counted only a few men scattered here and there, all
of them sitting idle by their claims. One of them reached
for his rifle as they rode past, but didn't say a word.

Coop came alongside Nate when the narrow trail
widened. "Where are all the miners?"

"It's Sunday. Most of the miners take Sunday off and
go into town for supplies and to break loose a little."

Or go to church. Did James still have his small flock
attending each Sunday? And Sarah had said something
about a school for the children on Sunday afternoon.

Olivia would like that. Maybe he should let them continue after they moved out to the claim. He urged Scout into a trot as they reached the edge of the mining camp nestled in the gulch. It would give him an excuse to see Sarah every week, too.

When they reached the trail leading to the MacFarlands' cabin, Nate turned to Coop. "This is where I turn off. The claim office is up Main Street there, about four blocks."

"All right. I'll meet you back at the ranch."

Coop headed off, and Nate couldn't help grinning after him. Ranch? The cowboy was right. With cattle grazing on the green grass, he certainly couldn't call it a claim anymore.

The cabin was empty when he reached it. The MacFarlands must still be at church. He rode back to his old camp, where he had left the horses in James's care. They stood in the small corral, their ears pricked. As Nate dismounted, Scout reached over the fence rails toward the other three horses.

Nate patted each nose in turn. "Hey there, Pete old boy, how are you doing?" He scratched ears and greeted each horse until he reached the long black face with the gray nose waiting for him at the end of the row. Loretta greeted him with bared teeth. He ignored the mule and unsaddled Scout. He turned him into the corral with the others and gave each of them a measure of grain in preparation for the short trip to the homestead. Nate caught himself with a laugh. The ranch.

By the time he had finished caring for the horses, he heard voices on the trail from the mining camp. He left his chore and went to the MacFarlands' cabin to watch the children walk toward him. Lucy and Olivia were both wearing new dresses, and Charley was wearing a tie. Sarah had decked them all out for church. She shouldn't have made new clothes for them.

He looked beyond the children to Sarah and his irritation rose. There was that Montgomery fellow behind her, escorting her up Williams Street as if she belonged to him. The afternoon sun glinted off the watch chain spanning the banker's brocade vest, and his jacket was spotless. The five of them made a right cozy family.

Nate rubbed at his whiskers, weeks old. Suddenly his trail-worn clothes weren't comfortable anymore. He wanted to retreat back to the waiting horses, but Charley spotted him.

"It's Uncle Nate!" His yell made everyone look at Nate, and he was too late to escape their notice.

Instead he put a welcoming smile on his face and waited for the children to reach him. He didn't have time to think about Montgomery anymore as he was grabbed by Charley and Olivia.

"Uncle Nate!" Olivia's voice squealed. "How long have you been here?"

"Only long enough to take Scout's saddle off."

As Sarah reached the group, she stumbled and Nate shot his hand out to steady her, but he was too late. Montgomery was already there with a hand at her elbow. Nate felt his face turn stone cold at the smile Sarah gave the man.

He gripped Charley's and Olivia's shoulders. "You two go get your things together." He spoke without looking at them. He couldn't take his eyes off Sarah as she exchanged a few words with Montgomery. "We need to get out to the ranch so we can get settled in before dark."

Charley was off to the cabin with a yippee, but Olivia didn't move. He tore his eyes from staring at Montgomery's hand resting lightly in the center of Sarah's back and looked down at his niece.

"Didn't you hear me? We need to get going."

Olivia chewed her bottom lip as she looked from him to Sarah, whose violet eyes were finally turned to him. He could lose himself in her smile, if Montgomery wasn't hovering behind her.

"I'm so glad you made it home safely, Nate." She turned to Lucy, who had not left Sarah's side. "Don't you want to say hello to your uncle?"

Lucy stared at him, stuck her thumb in her mouth and stepped sideways to hide behind Sarah's skirt. His stomach constricted. What had happened to his Lucy while he had been gone?

Sarah turned back to him, her eyes shining. "She's made such great progress while you've been away." She stepped forward and put her arm around Olivia's shoulders. "We've all had a wonderful time, haven't we, Olivia?"

Montgomery stepped next to Sarah, nearly touching her, and held out his hand. "We're happy to see you back safe and sound, Colby."

Nate ignored Montgomery. The *we* in his comment made the situation all too evident.

"Olivia, Lucy, we need to pack up and get to the ranch. Go get your things, right now."

Olivia's eyes brimmed with tears. "But, Uncle Nate, Miss Sarah and I were going to…"

Sarah leaned down with a quiet voice. "We can continue our plans another time, Olivia. Now is the time to obey your uncle."

"Yes, ma'am."

Olivia didn't look at him again, but took Lucy's hand and went into the cabin.

Nate's face burned under caked dust. "Thank you for taking care of the children while I was away."

Sarah's eyes met his, and he felt a smile start. She was more beautiful than he had remembered.

"It was my pleasure. I hope you'll let them come and stay with me often. I enjoy their company so."

Montgomery stepped forward, cupping Sarah's elbow in his hand once more. Was it only his imagination that a look of irritation passed over Sarah's face?

"I'm sure that won't be necessary, dear. Colby is going to be busy, and he'll need the children to help him. I'm sure we won't be seeing much of him from now on." He turned his calm, cool smile on Nate. "Will we?"

The cold rock that had been turning in Nate's stomach turned once more and then dropped. Nothing sounded better than getting out to the ranch with the children and never coming into town again. He turned toward the cabin and stepped forward to take a bundle from Charley.

"We need to get the horses hitched up. Are your sisters coming?"

"Yup. Lucy's crying, though."

The rock turned again.

"Nate," Sarah said. She pulled her arm out of Montgomery's grasp. "You can at least stay for supper, can't you?"

He turned toward the trees screening the old camp. "I want to get out to the ranch before dark."

He heard footsteps behind him and turned when she laid her hand on his shoulder. Her eyes were wide, ques-

tioning. Nate let himself swim in them for a second…
two…

"Montgomery's waiting for you. You can have supper with him."

He left her standing there and followed the boy. They harnessed the horses in silence, and Charley tied the mule to the back of the wagon. His nephew must have figured out that he was in no mood to talk, and that was good. The way that rock was seething red-hot in his gut told him he wouldn't be civil to anyone. Even Charley.

Finally they were ready. He drove the wagon to the front of the MacFarlands' cabin, where the girls were waiting for him. Lucy clung to Sarah's skirt, and even Olivia was crying as she stood with her arms wrapped around Sarah's waist.

When he reached for the children's bundles to load onto the wagon, Sarah took Olivia's hands in her own. She leaned down to talk to both girls. "You know we'll see each other again."

"But it won't be the same." Olivia hiccupped.

Sarah smiled, but Nate could see the tears in her eyes. "I'll see you at church next week. Won't I?" She looked at Nate, but he couldn't answer.

Sarah gave both girls a hug and a kiss and helped them into the wagon. "Remember what we talked about? We need to trust God for the future and not worry." Nate twisted the reins in his hands but couldn't watch the last goodbyes. His mouth was as dry as ashes. He shook the reins and the horses started down the trail. He didn't look back. Sarah had made her choice.

Chapter Ten

Sarah listened until the creak and rumble of the wagon wheels disappeared in the general noise from the mining camp. Suddenly, the clearing was very large and very quiet.

She let the tears fall as she went into the cabin. She had been looking forward to Nate's return, but he was so distant. So quiet. So…angry. Had something gone wrong on his trip? Why hadn't she asked him?

Kicking a chair away from the table, she took a left-over biscuit from under the towel that covered them and sat down. She knew why she hadn't asked. That overbearing Wilson Montgomery. He had insisted on escorting her home. He had even presumed to speak for her when all she wanted to do was welcome Nate home.

But she had had no words when Nate's manner had been so grim. Even though he was dirty, sweaty and trail worn, she had wanted to greet him with more enthusiasm than was proper. Even with the children present, she had almost made a fool of herself. He certainly wouldn't appreciate her being so forward as to give him a welcoming hug. But between his stony face and Wilson's presence, she had resisted the urge.

Could Wilson have been the cause of Nate's mood?

She broke off the edge of her biscuit and popped it into her mouth.

The only reason for that would be if Nate resented the banker for some reason. And the only reason she could think of for him to dislike Wilson was that he was jealous.

The biscuit was dry powder in her mouth.

Jealous because he cared for her?

She rubbed at the tense spot between her eyes. Could it be that Nate cared for her? He couldn't. They weren't more than friends, were they?

Nate Colby was just a friend. That was all.

She swallowed the dry biscuit.

But if he was only a friend, then why did it feel so right when he laid his hand on hers?

She spread her hand on the table, feeling the wood grain beneath her fingers. When she was a young girl, she had decided that she would never love anyone. The pain when her parents died in the boating accident was too much to bear, and she didn't ever want to go through that grief again. But then James and Margaret had amended her decision with their persistent love, and she had made an exception.

Still, to love opened her heart to pain, and she knew that pain so well. It was part of her, like a Gordian knot filling her with its intractable complexity. No one could loosen it. No one could set her free of its bonds.

But somehow, the children had tugged at the cords until she had to admit she loved them, in spite of her resolve. She had no choice but to let them into her heart.

Nate, though, was another matter. If she loved him, the pain would be unbearable when he left. She wouldn't let that happen. She couldn't.

Leaving the table, she went to the dry sink, where a pail of water stood. She lifted the towel covering it and lifted the dipper for a drink. The cool water cleared her throat and her mind.

She had sent Wilson away as soon as Nate had followed Charley to their campsite. Once they were alone, she had turned on him. She rarely needed to be so blunt with a person, but Wilson seemed to ignore her suggestions and hints. She had told him to leave and hadn't let him protest or even apologize. She regretted she hadn't helped him down the trail with a nudge from her foot.

Sarah finished the biscuit and wandered out to the bench in front of the cabin. She and Olivia had planned to look for the next reader among the books Sarah had brought with her from Boston and then climb up the hill behind the house to a grassy spot they had found. All three children had enjoyed the time they spent up there during the warm summer evenings, Olivia and Charley taking turns reading aloud or lying on their backs to watch the sky as the day passed into twilight and it was time to return to the cabin.

And so quickly they were gone. Not only the children, but Nate, too. If he didn't bring them into town to school, or to church, would she ever see him…them…again?

A low-down, thoughtless skunk. That was what he was. He had no right to be angry at Sarah. She could keep company with whoever she chose.

Nate turned the horses off the road up the trail toward his ranch, the noise of the jangling harness finally drowning out the sniffles from the wagon behind him. They'd get over whatever was bothering them. He gripped the reins between his fingers, urging the horses through the rough grass. It was only right that they'd miss Sarah.

He drove along the creek until he reached the cattle, still bunched from when he and Coop had left them earlier in the afternoon.

"There they are." Nate nudged Charley with his elbow. The boy hadn't said anything on the drive out from Deadwood. "Seventy-five head of the prettiest cattle this side of the Missouri."

The rough ground made Charley jostle on the seat next to him. "Those are the ugliest cows I've ever seen."

"They're longhorns. You've seen longhorns before."

Charley sighed. "Yeah. I guess."

"It's our ranch, Charley." Nate shifted a glance sideways toward his nephew. "Aren't you the one who couldn't wait to be a cowboy?"

"But why did we have to leave Miss Sarah? Why can't she come out here with us?"

Nate's gut wrenched. If things were different, then maybe. "Miss Sarah has her own home with her aunt and uncle, and her school. And her friends."

"But we're her friends, aren't we?"

As they reached the small knoll by the old beaver dam, Nate pulled the horses to a halt. He couldn't think of an answer to Charley's question.

"Let's get the horses unhitched." The pole corral he had put together before leaving for Wyoming was still in place, and the ring of rocks where they had built their fire still encircled the gray ashes. It was as if he had never been away, except for Montgomery's possessive hand on Sarah's elbow.

"Come on, Olivia. You and Lucy come on out of the wagon, and we'll get supper started. I'll get a fire going after we take care of the horses."

Olivia climbed out of the wagon and paused, looking back the way they had come. "Someone's coming, Uncle Nate."

Nate followed her gaze. "It's Coop. I hope he has good news for us." He unharnessed Ginger. Charley led her to the corral as Nate turned to Scout.

"Who is Coop?" Olivia was still watching the horseman riding across the grass, skirting the cattle.

"He's a friend I made on the trail. He's going to be part of the ranch."

Charley took Scout's lead rope but didn't move. He stared as the cowboy rode up to them.

Coop nodded toward Nate, then removed his hat and dismounted in one smooth motion in front of Olivia and Lucy. "Now, who are these two lovely ladies?"

"This is Olivia and Lucy. And over here is Charley. Say hello to Justice Cooper."

Charley's mouth hung open until Nate laid his hand on the boy's shoulder. He laughed at Charley's expression but couldn't blame him for staring. Coop looked as if he had just ridden right out of the pages of Charley's dime novel.

"Nate, when you told me you were going to fetch some children, I never suspected they'd be such fine young folks." He grinned at the girls and shook Olivia's hand. "Pleased to make your acquaintance, ladies." He turned to Charley as he replaced his hat. In the two weeks he had known Coop, Nate hadn't seen his head bare for more than a couple minutes at a time. "And you're the cowboy, right?"

Charley stuck out his hand. "Yes, sir. That is, I want to be."

"Your uncle and I will make a cowhand out of you in no time flat."

"How did things go at the claim office?"

The cowboy's grin widened. "I'm a homesteader, thanks to you. Now all we need to do is keep those cattle growing fat and sassy."

Coop's arrival lightened everyone's mood. Before the fire had settled into coals, Nate's and Charley's bedrolls were laid out under the wagon and Olivia had mixed up a batch of corn bread. While it baked, the sky turned to dusky blue. Orange-streaked clouds floated above the hills to the west.

"What's the first thing we need to do to get this ranch going?" Nate asked Coop as they ate the corn bread and canned beans.

"We need to mark those cattle before very much time goes by. Have you decided on a brand?"

Nate nodded. "I've been thinking on it, and I have a design in mind. I'll draw it out for you tomorrow and you can let me know what you think." He sopped up the last of his beans with the edge of his corn bread and stuck the mess into his mouth. "Are all the cows bred, do you think?"

Olivia looked up from her supper. "Miss Sarah said not to talk with your mouth full."

He swallowed and then stared at her. Across the fire, he saw Coop's grin before the cowboy ducked his head. "Did Miss Sarah also say that children should respect their elders?"

"Yes. But that part about not talking with your mouth full is important."

When did she get so grown-up? "You're right. I should

mind my manners. Thank you for reminding me." He reached over and squeezed her shoulder. "Now you'll mind your manners and let Coop and I talk. Right?"

"Right. Except..." Olivia pushed her beans around on her tin plate.

"Except what?"

"What about school?" She looked up at him, her eyes wide. "I really want to go to school, and if we're branding cows and all the other stuff, we won't be able to go."

Nate looked from Olivia to Charley. The boy was watching him, waiting for his answer.

Lucy pulled on his sleeve. "I want to go to school, too. I want to see Miss Sarah."

"Lucy! What did you say?"

"I want to go to school."

Not just a word or two. A complete sentence. Nate looked from Lucy to Olivia, and then to Charley. "How long has she been talking?"

Olivia shook her head. "She hasn't been. It just happened."

Nate's empty plate fell to the ground as he grabbed Lucy in a big hug. "You can go to school. Anything you want." Sarah had thought Lucy might start talking all at once like this, but he had given up on ever hearing her again.

Lucy pushed back from him and rubbed at his whiskers. "Can we go tomorrow? Miss Sarah said I could draw a picture tomorrow."

He couldn't contain his grin. "Of course you can go tomorrow." He glanced across the fire at Coop. "I'll take you into Deadwood and order the branding irons while I'm there."

And he'd see Sarah. Could he bear seeing her, after watching her with Montgomery today?

He smoothed Lucy's hair and gathered her in as she settled in his lap. He needed to thank her for helping with Lucy, for whatever she had done, even if she didn't want to see him again.

By the next day, Sarah had convinced herself she wouldn't see the Colby children at school. Even if Nate did agree to bring them, they were still in the process of setting up their home on the ranch.

As she followed Uncle James down the steps to the mining camp, she let her mind drift to Nate's homestead. The one day she had spent there seemed like a dream. Removed from the smells of the town and the noise of stamping mills, the mountain meadow had been a quiet, windswept retreat. More than once during the past few weeks she had let her mind drift to the ranch, but no more. She shook herself and hurried to catch up to Uncle James. That dream was out of reach this morning.

The Woodrow children waited for her at the doorway to the school.

Bernie Woodrow ran to meet her. "Where is Charley?"

"The children's uncle returned yesterday afternoon, and they moved to their homestead."

Laura held Sarah's books as she unlocked the door. "Are they coming to school?"

Sarah forced herself to smile at the girl. "I don't know. Mr. Colby and I didn't have an opportunity to discuss it yesterday." They hadn't had time to discuss anything. She opened the door and took her books from Laura. "Why don't you three water our plants while I get things organized for the morning?" She nodded toward the tomato seedlings the children had planted a few weeks ago. The south-facing window gave them plenty of light, and being in the schoolroom protected them from the crowded streets outside.

Bernie and Alan took the pail from its hook and went out to the horse trough on Main Street while Laura turned the plants to give each one the benefit of the best light. Sarah wrote the date on the chalkboard and below it wrote the Bible verse for the day.

Just as she finished, Bernie came into the schoolroom with Charley. When Olivia and Lucy followed behind them with Alan, Sarah's throat grew tight. It seemed silly that she had missed them so when they had only been gone one night. She hugged the girls, and Lucy clung to her.

"I missed you so much, Miss Sarah."

The little girl whispered the words in her ear so softly, Sarah almost didn't hear them. But they were there. Lucy had spoken!

"I missed you, too, Lucy. I'm so glad you came to school today." Sarah drew back, holding Lucy's hand in her own, and knelt so she was on the child's level. Tears threatened to blur her vision, and she wiped them away with her handkerchief.

Lucy grinned, her dark eyes shining. "Are we going to draw today?"

As if speaking was the most normal thing in the world!

"Of course we are. I brought everything we need, and we'll get out the art supplies after we finish our reading and arithmetic."

A shadow covered the doorway, and Sarah looked up into Nate's eyes, so much like Lucy's. He leaned against the doorframe with his hat in his hands, a half smile on his face as he looked down at the two of them.

"Lucy, why don't you help water the plants while I speak with your uncle?"

Lucy wrapped her arms around Sarah's neck, nearly knocking her over. "I love you, Miss Sarah."

Sarah hugged the girl tight and then released her as Lucy ran off to the window. Sarah had no choice but to stand and face Nate. She walked toward the door, and he stepped back into the alley so they could talk out of the children's hearing.

"When did Lucy start speaking?"

He avoided her eyes. "She joined in our conversation last night at supper as if she had been talking all along. I thought maybe she had started while I was away, but Olivia said she hadn't."

"She was as quiet as ever while you were away. Maybe she's happy that you're home."

Nate curled the hat brim but didn't answer.

"Thank you for bringing the children to school this morning. I'm sure you didn't have time to make the trip in from your homestead."

Nate turned his hat in his hands. "I needed to come to town anyway, and, well…they wanted to come." He took a step closer. "I wanted to thank you." She watched his hands twist and roll the hat brim. "When Lucy spoke to me last night…" He looked at her then flicked his eyes down to his hat again. "Well, I about fell over. You said she had made progress, but I had no idea."

"I didn't, either."

"I had tried everything I could think of to help her." The hat brim twisted again. "But nothing I could do or say made her better. She just seemed to fold into herself. Some days she wouldn't even look at me, or Olivia or Charley. I was afraid there was something broken deep inside her that I couldn't fix." He shifted his gaze to her face, and her knees wiggled like jelly. "But you reached her, somehow. You reached that broken place and fixed it. What did you do?"

Sarah shook her head. "I really didn't do anything. I just…" She cast about in her mind. What had she done? Only waited and prayed.

"You just loved her." Nate rubbed at his chin with one hand. "You loved her, and she felt safe. I can't let her lose that safe feeling, so if it's all right with you, I'd like to keep bringing the children to school."

"That would be just fine." Her mouth was dry. He stood as if there was a wall between them. "I enjoy them in the classroom, and they've become good friends with the Woodrow children. We're having an art lesson today, and Lucy's looking forward to…"

She let the words drift to a halt. He didn't want to listen to her ramble on. She wanted to retreat to the schoolroom, where the unsupervised children would be more peaceful than the beating of her heart.

Nate turned to leave, but she stopped him with a touch on his sleeve.

"Is everything all right?"

He shoved his hat on his head. "Of course. Everything is just fine. I'll be back this afternoon to pick up the children."

"I know Aunt Margaret and Uncle James will want to see you. Won't you and the children come for supper?"

"I need to get back to the ranch." He took a step away and her hand fell back to her side. "And I'm sure you'd much rather spend your time with someone else." He turned to leave.

"Nate…" He didn't turn but walked down the alley and around the corner onto Lee Street.

Sarah slipped into the noisy classroom and closed the door. Tears pricked at her eyes. Yesterday afternoon, and now this morning. Maybe she had been right about him being jealous of Wilson, but he had no reason to be. None at all.

"Miss Sarah." Olivia tugged at her skirt. "The boys are chasing flies again."

If she didn't bring order to the classroom, the day would be lost. Sarah turned and clapped her hands. The sharp claps broke through the children's shouts, and as they turned toward her, she sat behind her desk. "We need to get our school day started. Please take your seats."

Six sweaty and disheveled children sat on their benches, grinning at her. She lifted her Bible from its place to begin the day with scripture, but the looks on the children's faces stopped her.

"What is it?"

Laura giggled into her hand. Her brother Bernie looked at the floor, his feet scuffing the wood planks. So he was the guilty one.

"Bernie, I want you to tell me what you are all laughing at."

Her back itched. One time the boys had placed a hairy spider on the back of her chair and had watched it crawl up her arm and into her hair before she had noticed the creeping tickle. Bernie and Charley exchanged looks and she jumped from her chair. No spider.

"I'll tell you, Miss Sarah." Olivia stood as if ready for recitation.

"Yes, Olivia?"

"They said you have a beau." At this Olivia collapsed on her bench with her hand over her mouth, giggling as hard as Laura.

"A beau?" They couldn't mean Wilson Montgomery, could they? The children would have noticed his unwavering attention yesterday.

"It's Uncle Nate." Lucy wiggled in her seat.

Olivia finished for her. "Uncle Nate is your beau, Miss Sarah. When are you going to get married?"

Sarah grasped the side of her desk as her face grew hot. How had they ever come to that conclusion?

She cleared her throat and waited for the giggles to subside. "You are all mistaken. I do not have a beau." She took her seat and lifted her Bible again, turning to the Psalms. Olivia's frantic waving called for her attention.

"Yes, Olivia?"

"If Uncle Nate isn't your beau, then why are you always so happy when you see him?"

Sarah put on her best schoolteacher face. "That is none of your concern." She looked from face to face. "It isn't a concern for any of you." Clearing her throat, she leafed through her Bible until she found the right page. "Children, this morning we're reading from Psalm 91."

As she read, Sarah's mind wandered to Nate. She had never been so confused in her life. Why did she care about this new distance between them? If she didn't know better, she would think he was worming his way into her heart the way the children had.

She reached the ninth and tenth verses in her reading. "Because thou hast made the LORD, which is my refuge, even the most High, thy habitation, there shall no evil befall thee, neither shall any plague come nigh thy dwelling."

Her voice faltered. The Lord was her habitation. The Lord was her only refuge, not any man.

Chapter Eleven

Nate waited until the corner of the church was between him and the door of the school and then leaned with one hand against the wall. A fool. He was a fool. He had no right, no place in her life. No call to be putting himself forward when she needed a man who could care for her the way she deserved. A man who could provide for her and one she could count on to protect her when danger threatened.

And that man wasn't him.

A footstep thumped on the wooden porch. "Good morning, Colby." Montgomery's voice was ice cold. "What are you doing here?"

Nate straightened, running his eyes up and down the banker. Montgomery held a pair of white kid gloves in one hand and hit them against his palm with a restless motion.

"I brought my children to school." He took a step closer. "And what are you doing here?"

Montgomery sniffed and laid a finger under his nostrils as if some scent had offended him. "I'm here to talk business with Reverend MacFarland. It's none of your concern." He waved his gloves toward Nate. "You can go on your way."

Nate bristled at the other man's dismissive attitude, but he couldn't think of a reason to stand outside the church any longer. He watched Montgomery go into the former saloon and headed toward Main Street. He may not be the right man for Sarah, but that narrow-faced, slicked-up weasel sure wasn't, either. He reached the corner and glanced back toward the church. He'd do anything to protect her from a man like that one.

He rolled his shoulders. The hot sun beating on his back made his scars itch. Was he judging Montgomery too harshly? The man went to church and seemed to be an upstanding citizen, but something about the banker rubbed him the wrong way.

Crossing the street, he passed a familiar figure leaning against the wall of the hotel. Nate turned the face over in his mind as he walked down Main, past the printing office, a bath house and the dry goods store. Nate reached the end of the block before he could place the man leaning against the hotel. It was Tom Harris. The man whom he had nearly fought with over that girl Dovey. Was it only a coincidence that he had seen both Harris and Montgomery in the same few feet?

His imagination was running rampant. The two couldn't be connected. Montgomery was too worried about his reputation to risk associating with someone like Harris.

He passed through the Badlands on his way to the forge where he had left the horses and wagon. As he went by the Mystic Theater, he ignored the scantily dressed women on the balcony calling to him. One on the street, at the corner of the building, drew his attention, though. It was Dovey. Her red dress advertised her profession, but she lacked the brassy demeanor of the girls leaning over the railing above. She stared at him as he walked by, then he heard footsteps behind him and a hand plucked at his sleeve.

When he turned, Dovey pulled at him, toward the alley next to the Mystic.

He pulled his sleeve out of her grasp. "I'm not interested in what you're selling, miss."

"I only want to ask you a question." She peered down the alley to the back of the building and then toward the street. Her pinched face was pale.

"What is it?" Nate was leery of talking to this girl, even if she did remind him of Mattie. Men had been ambushed in alleys like this.

"You know the girl at the church? The one with the dark hair?" She wouldn't look into his eyes, but twisted a worn flounce on her dress between her fingers.

She must mean Sarah. "Yes, I do. But what does she have to do with you?"

Her face reddened. "Shh. Don't talk so loud." She glanced down the alley again. "You just saw her, didn't you? You take your children to the school."

"Yes, she's teaching today."

"She spoke to me once. I stood outside the church and heard the preacher. I can't get the Word out of my head. It won't let me be."

She met his eyes, challenging him. She must have been to the church on a Sunday, and Sarah had spoken to her. "What do you want?"

"She'll speak to me again, won't she? She can tell me what it means."

Nate nodded. If anyone could explain what a Bible passage meant to this girl, it was Sarah.

"Can you tell her? I mean, that I want to see her?"

He had told Sarah that if she wanted to help these girls, she'd have to wait for them to come to her, but he really hadn't thought one of them would seek her out. "I'll give her the message."

She stiffened as the sound of measured footsteps on the boardwalk drifted down the alley, and then pushed him away.

"If you don't want any fun," she said, her voice loud and petulant, "then go away and make room for someone who does."

She ran down the alley as Nate turned and looked into the face of Tom Harris. He held the man's gaze as he brushed past him and then continued on his way toward the blacksmith.

This idea of Sarah's could be more dangerous than she thought.

Sarah tilted the watch pinned to her shirtwaist to read the time. Nearly four o'clock. Her scholars leaned over sheets of newsprint she had begged from the printer, faces serious as they attempted to draw their chosen model. What Lucretia Woodrow would think of three novice artists' portraits of their teacher, she had no idea. What Nate would think? She skirted her mind away from the thought.

The students concentrated as they used her treasured oil pastels. She had instructed them on the proper use and admonished them to take care. As far as they were from civilization, and as expensive as freight was, the pastels may as well be irreplaceable.

At a knock on the door, she glanced over to see Nate waiting outside. She looked at her watch again and beckoned to him.

"All right, children, it's time to go home. If you aren't finished with your drawing, you may place them here on my desk to finish tomorrow."

Olivia lifted her drawing to admire it. "May I take mine home, Miss Sarah?"

"Yes, if you're finished, you may take it home. Let me show you how to roll it to protect it from the wind as you carry it."

As Sarah rolled up Olivia's paper, and then Charley's and Bernie's, Nate opened the door. He stood aside as the Woodrow children burst out of the classroom.

"You three can go out with your friends for a minute. I want to speak to Miss Sarah."

Olivia turned her back to Nate and mouthed the word *beau* to Sarah. Sarah felt her face flush as she gave Lucy a hug goodbye.

"I'll see you all tomorrow."

After they followed their friends out the door, Nate took a step closer to her.

"I have a message for you, from that saloon girl Dovey."

Sarah looked at him, all thoughts of the children's teasing forgotten. "Dovey?" She had included the girl in her prayers but had no idea if she'd ever see her again.

"She said she was here at the church one Sunday and that she hoped you'd explain the Bible passage for her."

"What did you tell her? When can I see her?"

"Now, hold on."

His frown fell on her like a bucket of cold water. He wouldn't try to stand in the way of this girl learning about God, would he? But even as she faced his stormy expression, her mind flitted from one possibility to another. Where could she meet Maude to talk? What questions did the girl have? What other Bible passages could they discuss?

"You don't really think that girl wants to know anything about the Bible, do you?"

"What do you mean? Of course she does. I could see it in her face the morning she was here—she's hungry to hear about Jesus and to see some light of hope in her life."

"Those girls just want to use people. That's all they do."

Sarah felt her chin lift. "You met her. She has a name. Not Dovey, but Maude. Didn't you see she's different from the others?"

Nate shifted his feet, and his face softened as he considered her words. "You may be right. There was something different about her. But you live in a separate world from her. You can't just have her come to the church like…"

"Like anyone else? We're talking about a young woman, Nate, not some kind of leper."

He took a step toward her. "I know, Sarah, better than anyone. But there is a difference." His soft voice penetrated her defenses. "She has chosen a path that puts her in a place in society you aren't part of. Men look at her differently than they do you. She is welcome places you aren't, and she can't think of going places you take for granted."

"Like church?"

Nate nodded. "Like church. And that's not all. You enjoy a certain safety, even in Deadwood, because of the kind of woman you are. Even the most hardened ruffian respects a gentlewoman, and you can walk down most streets without fear of being accosted. She can't go anywhere without meeting someone who would use her without a thought. She isn't safe from that anywhere."

Sarah turned away from him. She had never imagined what kind of life a girl like Maude led—no one had ever told her the details beyond the obvious sinful activities connected with her line of work. Her mind flitted back to the orphanage, not long before Uncle James had come to claim her. She had overheard a comment from one of the patrons of the orphanage about her future. The only words of the conversation she had heard were spoken in a tone that told her of the possible shame and degradation that awaited her, an orphan with no means to support herself and no prospects.

"Hire her out to a good family," the woman had said, addressing Mrs. Blair, the matron. "You don't want her to end up on the streets, the poor victim of some man's schemes."

Sarah had hurried away from the open door, mortified that she had been eavesdropping.

How close had she come to living a life like Maude's, or Nate's sister's? Alone and forced to support herself? She shuddered at the thought.

"Maude is someone's daughter. She was a child once, like Lucy or Olivia. Maybe she didn't have someone to love her, like they do. Maybe she didn't have a choice when she…" Sarah shook her head, banishing the thought of what Maude may have gone through to arrive at the place where she was now. What had Nate's sister gone through? No wonder he had spent so many years searching for her.

"If she's asking for help, I can't turn my back on her. I have to try."

Nate stepped up behind her. She felt his hands brush her sleeves, but he didn't touch her.

"No, you can't, can you? You wouldn't even be able to turn your back on a starving kitten."

Sarah's eyes stung. He understood the situation even more than she did.

"I'll help you, Sarah. I don't know what we can do, but you only need to ask, and I'll be there."

She turned around, but his hands didn't move. She froze, his strong chest inches away, her forehead nearly brushing his chin. He closed his hands, grasping her arms, and pulled her close. She couldn't look up into his face, but she couldn't back away, either. Taking a deep breath to steady her nerves, she inhaled the scent that clung to him—leather, horses, woodsmoke. His hands held her gently, his strength restrained. This was Nate, not the man who had kept her at arm's length this morning. She felt his lips brush her forehead, lingering as he breathed in. She wanted to raise her face to his, to let him give her the kiss hovering between them, but he dropped his hands and backed away.

"Just let me know what I can do." His eyes avoided hers. "I'll bring the children to school in the morning." He shoved his hat on and slipped out the door.

Sarah sank down on the closest bench. After all her resolve, she would have melted into his embrace if he had kissed her. She chafed her arms, trying to feel something other than the burning brand of his hands. She couldn't love him. She wouldn't. She shook herself and rose to clean the chalkboard, putting thoughts of Nate out of her mind. She paused her vigorous wiping.

It was no use. She would never forget the way she felt in his arms. He held her as if she was something precious.

But she couldn't let her imagination run away with her. Nate Colby didn't have any special feelings for her. He couldn't. She wouldn't let him, not when he could change his feelings at any time. She wouldn't risk his refusal.

She forced her thoughts to another problem. What to do about Maude? She must see the girl somehow, and it wasn't likely to be here at the school or the church. If it was any other girl, any of her friends in Boston, she would call on her one afternoon. She would walk to her house, present her card to the maid and they would spend an hour or so chatting while they occupied their hands with needlework. How many afternoons had she spent visiting with her friends that way?

Sarah gathered the papers scattered on her desk into a neat pile.

Aunt Margaret carried out such visits with the ladies of Deadwood, the few that braved the mining camp to settle here with their husbands. Sarah hadn't been able to accompany her, since her responsibilities at the school occupied her time.

She could call on Maude. Sarah stacked her schoolbooks. She chewed on her bottom lip as she wiped her pen and corked the inkwell. Maude worked at the Mystic, and lived there, too. But she couldn't risk going there again.

The memory of Nate's frowning face loomed before her. Of course he wouldn't approve of her seeking out Maude. Neither would Uncle James or Aunt Margaret. But would God approve? What did He want her to do?

As she picked up her books to take home, she resolved to pray about it. Prayer had never failed to help her reach the right answer.

* * *

A week later, Sarah ate her Monday morning breakfast with only half her thoughts on the sourdough pancakes Margaret had prepared. The rest of her mind was preoccupied with Maude.

Sarah had hoped Maude would come to the church again, but she hadn't. Yesterday's heavy rain had kept most of the families away, at least the ones who lived outside of Deadwood gulch. Nate hadn't brought the children, but she could hardly expect them to make the journey in the storm.

Maude only had a short walk down the block, though. She might have stayed away because she thought she would feel uncomfortable in church. Sarah pushed at a pancake with her fork. What if Mr. Harris was preventing her from coming? She had to talk to Maude.

Every time she thought of approaching the Mystic Theater again, her stomach went into convulsions. She didn't want a repeat of that Saturday afternoon, but how else could she contact the girl?

"It's going to be a beautiful day after yesterday's rain," said Uncle James. He sopped up the last of the sugar syrup with the final bite of his pancakes. "What do you have planned today, dear?"

Aunt Margaret refilled all three of their coffee cups and set the pot back on its hanger by the fire. "I thought I'd do some visiting this afternoon. Mrs. Brewster has a new knitted lace pattern she wants to show me, and I'm going to take her some of that green thread I have left."

"Could you take a few minutes to stop by Star and Bullock's? I need more pipe tobacco."

"Oh, my, no. No respectable woman goes shopping on Mondays. You remember that, surely."

Margaret's tone brought Sarah's attention fully on the

conversation. Her Monday afternoons had been spent in the classroom, but she had never noticed anything different about that one day of the week. "Why not? What happens on Mondays?"

Her aunt sniffed, then took a sip of her coffee. "That's when the saloon girls do their shopping." Her eyes shifted to Sarah's. "Remember that. Never go shopping on Monday afternoon."

"I'll keep that in mind."

Sarah let the rest of the conversation continue around her as an idea formed in her mind. This may be her only opportunity to see Maude without going to the Mystic to seek her out. She finished her coffee and started up the ladder to gather her schoolbooks from her bedroom.

"I must be going if I want to get to school on time." She hesitated. "And, Aunt Margaret, I have a few things to take care of after the children leave, so I may be later coming home."

Aunt Margaret started clearing the breakfast dishes. "That's fine, Sarah. I'll see you this evening."

In the loft, she took her second-best dress from the peg on the wall. It was clean and would fit Maude perfectly. She folded it carefully and wrapped it in a bundle. Then she picked up her books and slipped down the ladder and out the door. Now all she had to worry about was if Maude went shopping with the rest of the girls and if she could find her in the busy streets.

That school day dragged. The children behaved well enough, even though Uncle James wasn't in the next room. He spent the day visiting families who lived outside Deadwood.

One disappointment was that the Colby children came into town alone, all three riding on Charley's mule. She hadn't realized how much she was looking forward to the quick hello from Nate to start her morning on the right foot, even though he remained as distant as ever. As if those few moments in the classroom the previous week had never happened. Finally, four o'clock rolled around and she sent the children on their way. Closing and locking the door, a twinge of guilt made her look back through the window to the sunny room. She had never left a classroom without cleaning it first, but today she couldn't take the time. She pocketed the key, took her pile of books in one hand and the bundle in the other and started off for Main Street.

Yesterday's rain had made a miry mess of the streets. Horses walked in mud nearly up to their knees, while the drivers of the wagons shouted curses to keep their teams from stopping before they got to firmer ground.

Sarah crossed Lee Street on the wooden crosswalk and paused on the corner, looking up and down Main. Aunt Margaret had been right. The saloon girls crowded the boardwalks in front of the stores, their bright silk dresses and fancy plumed hats lining the street like a show of exotic tropical flowers. Not one "respectable" woman was in sight.

Finally, she caught sight of Maude's red dress and purple shawl in a cluster of girls outside a peanut vendor's next to The Big Horn Grocery on Upper Main. She hurried across the street on the wooden walk, soaking her kid shoes in the slime as the boards sank into the mud beneath the weight of the crowd doing the same. Thankfully, she climbed the stairs between Lower and Upper Main, out of the mud for a change.

When she approached the group of girls outside the peanut vendor, Maude recognized her right away.

The girl hurried to meet her. "Sarah, what are you doing here?" She glanced at the girls behind her.

"I came to see you. I have something for you." Sarah held the bundle out to the girl, who took it with hesitant hands. "It's a dress. Something you can wear when you want to come to church, or visiting, or anything."

Maude pulled the corner of the wrapping back to reveal the green calico. "It's lovely." She looked at the girls behind them again. "I'll have to keep it secret. Tom, I mean Mr. Harris, wouldn't want me to have it."

"Surely he isn't concerned about what you wear when you aren't working, is he?"

Maude looked at her with a mixture of pity and envy in her eyes. "You wouldn't understand. He says I owe him money for my trip here, and my room and board, and until I pay him back I have to do what he says."

Sarah took a step closer to the other girl. "You mean you can't even leave if you want to?"

Maude shook her head. "Not until I pay him back."

"How are you going to do that?"

"He keeps my earnings and pays for my room and board at the Mystic, and then the rest goes to him."

"How long has it been?"

The other girl bit her lip and glanced behind her again. "It's only been six months."

Six months of slavery. Sarah bit her lip, too, but only to keep back the words she longed to say.

"I'll help you leave this life, if you want to."

"You can do that?"

Maude's face held such hope that Sarah longed to take her hand and run home with her. But over the girl's shoulder she could see that the other girls had noticed them talking, and coming down the boardwalk behind them was Tom Harris with a couple other men. They wouldn't get farther than the top of the stairs leading to Lower Main before they would be stopped.

"We can't talk now, but I will help you. If you can, meet me in the afternoons at the Wall Street steps. School lets out at four o'clock, and I'll pass by there on my way home when I can. Even if we can't talk, at least I'll know you're all right."

"Yes, oh, yes."

"What do we have here?" Tom Harris stepped up beside Maude and draped a possessive arm around her shoulders.

Sarah straightened herself to her full height. She would not be intimidated by this bully on Main Street in the middle of the afternoon. Hours of listening to Dr. Bennett's lectures on the evils of men who took advantage of young women came back to her, and she raised her chin.

"We were just visiting. Women quite often enjoy visiting on a fine afternoon like this."

Harris narrowed his gaze. "You're that preacher's niece, aren't you? The schoolteacher?"

Sarah nodded. "Yes, I am."

He moved Maude behind him and stepped closer. Sarah took a step backward.

"If you know what's good for you, you'll leave my girls alone. Nothing good can come from them talking with you."

Sarah looked from Harris, to the two thugs who flanked him, to Maude, who cowered behind Harris. She had accomplished all she could this afternoon.

"I'll be on my way, if you'll excuse me."

She turned and made her way to Lee Street and the route home. To safety. But would Maude ever find her way home?

Chapter Twelve

⌒

The next several days were busy ones for Nate as he and Coop worked to get each cow and calf branded with the new C Bar C brand they had designed.

Coop had protested using both of their initials in the brand. "I don't know how long I'll be around. What if you find a new partner whose name doesn't begin with *C*?"

Nate had straightened up after releasing the first branded calf and brushed the dust off his chaps. "No matter. *C* stands for Colby as well as Cooper, and someday, if Charley is running this ranch on his own, his initials will fit right into it." He had grinned at Coop. "Besides, I have a feeling these hills are in your blood. You'll find a nice girl, build your house under that rocky outcropping, and you won't be going anywhere."

Coop had shoved his hat back on his head and gazed at the hills surrounding them. "Yep. Maybe you're right. I can't imagine leaving this place."

After the branding was finished, he and Coop started felling trees for the cabins they needed to build before winter set in. As busy as they were, Nate couldn't justify taking the time to escort the children to school when they were able to make the two-mile ride on their own.

Even if Sarah would rather spend her time with Montgomery, he had looked forward to a glimpse of her. By the next Sunday morning, though, he knew he couldn't stay away any longer. He had to see her, even if it pained him.

The morning dawned bright and hot. Just as Nate started hitching Pete and Dan up for the ride into town for church, Coop took over for him on Pete's harness, fastening the traces.

Nate whistled at the other man's shaved face and polished boots. "What are you all slicked up for?"

"It's Sunday, isn't it? You're going into town for church, and I'm going along with you." He grinned at Nate. "Every time we need something from town, you hightail it off the ranch like you were off to see someone special, and I want to know who it is."

Nate felt the back of his neck heat up. "There's no one special. I'm just taking the children to church."

"And I'm coming with you."

By the time Nate had helped the children climb into the wagon, Coop had his buckskin saddled.

"You're coming with us, Coop?" Charley almost fell out of the wagon in his excitement.

"Sure am, cowboy. It's Sunday morning, isn't it?"

Lucy bounced on her seat. "Will you sit by me at church, Coop?"

Coop leaned over and patted Lucy's curls. "I can't pass up an invitation like that."

Nate chirruped to the horses and the wagon started down the trail through the meadow. It was almost a road already. Coop rode ahead of them, checking on the cattle. When they reached the road to Deadwood, he fell back to ride with the wagon.

"The cattle are looking good. These days on that rich grass is putting some weight on them, and the calves are doing well. That little orphan bull calf is doing just fine, too."

"You were right when you said this was a good herd to start with."

"Tell me about your church. The preaching is good?"

"I've only been there once, but I think you'll like Reverend MacFarland. He won't put you to sleep."

Coop grinned at him. "Good preaching rarely puts me to sleep."

Nate shifted the reins through his fingers. "I never figured you for a churchgoing man, Coop."

"How can you look at all this beauty around you and not know in your heart of hearts that there is a God who set all these things in place? I just figure He deserves my praise every day and my worship with other believers whenever I can."

Nate watched the other man as they rode along. Coop's eyes were turned up to the crests of the surrounding mountains, ignoring the scarred and torn creek side they rode past. From the stories he told around the campfires along the trail, Coop hadn't had an easy life. Nate thought about what Sarah had told him about her uncle's experiences in China. These men had both seen hardships, even tragedy, yet they insisted on worshiping God as if they didn't hold Him responsible for what had happened to them.

No, not that they didn't hold Him responsible. It was almost as if they thanked God for the difficulties He had put them through.

Would he ever think of thanking God for what he had experienced in the war? For the fire that took Andrew and Jenny? Nate shook the reins to keep the horses moving past a particularly green patch of grass. He couldn't imagine being thankful for that.

They reached the outskirts of town and Coop dropped behind the wagon. Pete and Dan picked their way through the crowded streets. As they passed the Mystic, Nate glanced at the balcony, where a few girls lounged on the rail, but he didn't see Dovey's red dress. He hadn't seen Sarah since he had promised to help her meet the girl. She wouldn't be so foolish as to try to seek out the girl on her own, would she?

He turned the horses down Lee Street and pulled up in front of the church. Several families crowded the boardwalk, greeting each other as they went into the former saloon. He didn't remember that many people attending the last time he had attended the services.

Sarah met them just inside the door, giving Nate a smile before turning her attention to the children.

Charley reached for Coop's hand. "This is Coop, Miss Sarah. He's a real cowboy."

Coop took off his hat and nodded to Sarah. "Justice Cooper, miss."

"It's good to meet you, Mr. Cooper. You're a friend of Nate's?"

Nate cleared his throat, turning her smile back to him. "Coop and I are partners. He's taken the claim adjoining mine. He knew I could use his expert help."

James walked up to the group just as Nate finished. "Did I hear you say the two of you are ranching together?" He shook Coop's hand. "That sounds like a fine idea. Are you from the West, Mr. Cooper?"

He and Coop walked away, leaving Nate to watch Sarah greet the children as if she hadn't seen them in weeks. She bent her dark head toward Lucy's curls. They could be mother and daughter, the way they looked alike and with the love they had for each other. Nate took a step back. It was almost as if they were the family and he was the outsider.

Margaret sat at the piano and the first measures of a hymn flowed into the room.

"It's time to sit down, children." Sarah turned them toward the benches then faced Nate. "Will they be staying for the Sabbath school this afternoon? We start an hour after the service."

He lost himself in those blue eyes. "Yes, of course. They would enjoy that."

Sarah rewarded him with a smile, and then her gaze strayed past him to the door. "Oh, she came!"

Nate turned to see who Sarah meant. Dovey stood just inside the door, as if she wasn't sure if she was in the right place. Her red dress was gone, and in its place was a green dress he had seen Sarah wear often.

Sarah took the girl's hand and brought her over to him. "Nate Colby, I think you've met Maude Brown. This is her first Sunday with us, so I'm going to sit with her. Would you and the children like to join us?"

Nate looked into Dovey's—Maude's—face. She wouldn't meet his eyes. He knew that feeling. She was afraid someone would recognize her—that someone would know who she was and what she was. How many times had he felt that condemning gaze when people knew his cowardice had killed his brother? But here, in Deadwood, he had left the past behind. He glanced at Sarah's face. She held her bottom lip between her teeth, waiting for his reaction. As if he thought this girl was any less deserving of a fresh start than he was. Had anyone ever given Mattie this same chance?

He smiled at the girl and gave her a nod. "I'm pleased to meet you, Miss Brown."

Her face reddened. "You don't recognize me?" Her voice was low, quivering. She glanced at the other people in the room, all finding seats on the benches.

"Of course I do. I'm happy to meet you under different circumstances this time."

Her eyes met his, wet with unshed tears. "Thank you, Mr. Colby," she whispered.

Sarah pressed her hand on his in thanks and then led the other girl to a seat on one of the back benches. Of course she wouldn't sit in front. That would make Miss Brown uncomfortable.

The children filed into the row after Sarah, and then Coop took his seat next to Lucy. Nate sat on the end of the bench. When he spotted Wilson Montgomery two rows up, he felt a warmth of satisfaction. At least the man wasn't sitting with Sarah in church. Yet.

As the service ended, the families of the congregation drifted out of the warm church onto the covered boardwalk in front to enjoy visiting in the breezy shade. Sarah stood with Maude near the end of the building. She refused to think of the girl by her professional name.

"Would you like to have dinner with us? I'm afraid it will be quite hurried, since the children will be coming for Sabbath school before long."

The girl shook her head. "No, I can't. I have to get back before they miss me." Maude grasped Sarah's hand. "I just want to thank you. I never heard what your uncle was saying before today…that everyone is a sinner. I thought…" She bit her lip. When she spoke again, her voice was a whisper. "I thought it was just me."

Sarah leaned her head close to Maude's. "No one is immune to the sin that affects us all. The difference is in what God did to redeem His people. When we understand that, then we know how marvelous God's grace is."

"Do you really think I could be saved?"

"Of course. It isn't a question of whether God is able to do that. You have already felt Him working in you. That's why you came here—why you are looking for Him. And once He draws you to Himself, He will never let you go."

Maude's eyes filled. "But how can He do that when I'm living like I am? He can never forgive me, can He?"

Sarah squeezed the girl's hand. "Of course He can. And He can help you live differently. We'll both ask Him, all right?"

But Sarah could tell Maude had stopped listening. Her eyes were fixed on something…someone…behind Sarah, and her face had blanched. "I have to go." She turned, gathering her skirts. "I'm sorry. I shouldn't have come."

Maude disappeared into the crowded street. Sarah turned around to see what might have driven her away, but she only saw the people from the congregation, gathered in groups as they talked together. Wilson Montgomery stood off to one side, watching her. When he caught her eye, he lifted the brim of his hat in acknowledgment.

She fixed a friendly smile on her face as Wilson came near. She hadn't seen him since the Sunday afternoon when she had to ask him to leave the cabin. The expression on his face as he walked between the churchgoers who were making their way to their wagons and buggies told her he harbored no ill feelings for her blunt treatment of him.

"Hello, Sarah." His voice was smooth. Cultured. Familiar.

"Hello. How are you this fine day?"

"Excellent." He stroked his clipped mustache. "Do you have plans for dinner? I would be honored to have you dine with me at the Grand Central Hotel."

"You must have forgotten. I'm teaching the children's Sabbath school in a short while. I'm afraid I don't have time for a leisurely dinner." Sarah's stomach twisted at the thought of another meal in this man's company. He was friendly enough, but she certainly didn't want to encourage him.

"I wanted to ask you who that young woman was."

"What young woman?" Why would he be interested in Maude?

"You were just talking to her. She is quite young and pretty. Where does she come from?"

His eyes were daggers, looking past her heated face to the truth behind it. She had the passing thought that he knew exactly who Maude was.

"I think she's new in town." Would he see past her attempts to hide Maude's occupation? "Today was her first Sunday attending church."

He smiled, and she was reminded of a snake. "We'll have to make her feel welcome if she comes back, then, won't we?"

"Yes. Yes, of course."

Wilson touched the brim of his hat. "I hope you have a good time with your students, Sarah."

"Thank you." She watched him step off the boardwalk and melt into the crowded intersection of Lee and

Main, just as Maude had done. She rubbed her hands up and down her arms, suddenly chilled.

"Miss MacFarland." She turned to Justice Cooper, standing next to her with his felt hat in his hand. The cowboy inclined his head in the direction Wilson had disappeared. "Is that man a friend of yours?"

"He's an acquaintance, and a friend of my uncle's. Why? Do you know him?"

"No, ma'am. It's just that I saw him watching you talk to that girl, and then he came over to you as soon as she left. I thought perhaps he was bothering you."

Mr. Cooper's voice was gentle, his manner courtly. He smiled as he spoke, his eyes sharp and surrounded by fine lines, as if he spent his days gazing across the prairie in the bright sunlight.

"Thank you for your concern, but Mr. Montgomery was just..." She paused. Why had Wilson been so curious about Maude?

Nate joined them. He and Coop both towered over her. She had never felt so protected.

"Your aunt asked me to tell you she has your dinner ready."

Sarah glanced at her watch. "Oh my, it is getting late, isn't it?" She smiled up at both men. "Will you and the children be able to join us? I'm afraid we have nothing fancy to offer, just a cold lunch."

Nate backed away. "I have errands to run while we're in town. I'm sure the children will be happy to eat with you, though."

With a tilt of his hat, he was gone, with Coop threading through the crowded street after him.

Nate leaned against the wall of the freight office on Upper Main Street, Coop next to him. He hadn't exactly lied to Sarah. They had browsed through Star and Bullock's store while they waited for the children's Sabbath school to finish, but he could have accepted her invitation to join them for lunch. The sight of her talking to Wilson Montgomery ate at him, so he had left.

Coop shook his head as they watched the crowds surge and flow through the streets of the mining camp. "I never thought I'd see so much humanity in one spot. Where do they all come from?"

"Nebraska, Kansas, Illinois, Minnesota, Montana, Wyoming, Colorado, California, you name it. Once someone let out that there was gold to be found, every man and his uncle showed up for their share."

Coop looked at him. "But not you."

"Nope. Not me. The more I see these poor beggars digging in the dirt for scraps of dust, the more I'm happy to be banking on a sure thing."

"I wouldn't call cattle a sure thing." Coop pushed his hat back on his head.

Nate grinned at him. "Maybe not. But we're not standing knee-deep in icy water or breaking our backs hauling gravel to a sluice to do it, either."

A brass band marched down the street. The banner in front advertised a show at the Mystic that evening.

"Things never stop around here, do they?" Coop nodded down the street toward the Badlands, where a fistfight between two miners had held up the progress of the band. The upstairs girls hung over the balcony rail, calling to their favorites in the fight and egging them on.

"Nope, they never do." He watched Tom Harris push his way through the crowd toward Lee Street. Where was he going?

"That schoolmarm." Coop's voice was nonchalant, but Nate was on the alert. He hadn't missed the way

Coop had looked at Sarah. "She's the one, isn't she? The reason you come into town so often."

"Maybe." Harris reached the Custer Hotel on the corner and leaned against the wall.

"If she isn't, you're missing out on something."

Nate turned his attention to his friend. "What do you mean?"

"I tried to get her attention, but when you showed up I may as well have been a bump on a log for all she cared."

"I thought she was pretty interested in you." Hadn't she kept her eyes on Coop the whole time they had been talking? Harris moved away from the corner of the hotel as families with children appeared from the direction of the church. "It looks like the children are done for the day. Are you ready to go home?"

"Yup."

Nate led the way through the crowd toward Lee Street. He had lost sight of Harris. Once they reached the alley next to the church, they left the crowds behind. Their horses stood in the shade of the building, hips cocked as they rested.

As they approached the door, a man's voice drifted out to them.

"Just leave her be. She's no concern of yours. She works for me, and you have no right to use up her time."

Nate opened the door, coming face-to-face with Harris. Behind the thug, Sarah stood straight, tall and trembling. She had Charley by the arm, while the girls hid behind her skirt.

Stepping aside to let Coop into the room, Nate looked from Harris to Sarah. "Are you and the children all right?"

"Yes, Nate. Thank you." Her voice was quiet. She took a step back, pulling Charley with her.

Nate looked back at Harris. "What's going on here?"

Harris grinned through scraggly whiskers. "The lady and I were just having a talk about a mutual friend. There's no harm done."

"A bully like you intimidating a lady? I'd say there's been plenty of harm done."

"I'm just telling her to mind her own business. What kind of lady keeps company with a girl from the Mystic, anyhow? I'd say she's no lady."

"It's time for you to leave, Harris."

"I'll say when it's time." As Harris spoke, he grabbed a pistol from his belt and pointed it at Nate.

But Coop's gun was faster and Harris's hand wavered. "I suspicioned you might try something like that." Coop reached over and pulled the pistol out of the other man's hand. He threw it out the door into the dusty alley.

"I think you had better go now."

Harris spat at Nate's feet. "You haven't seen the last of me. You don't know who you've tangled with." He pushed past Coop and out the door.

Sarah let go of Charley and threw herself into Nate's arms. "I'm so glad you came when you did."

Nate clasped her close and then held her away so he could see her face. "Did he hurt you? Did he hurt the children?"

She shook her head, tears threatening now that Harris was gone. Lucy clung to her skirts while Coop stood watching them, his arms around Olivia's and Charley's shoulders. "No. No, he didn't come in until all the children had left, except…" She sniffed, and Nate untied the bandanna from around his neck and handed it to her. She blew her nose. "…except yours. And he just came right in the door."

"Who was he talking about?"

Her eyes met his. "Maude. He threatened to hurt her if I didn't leave her alone." She blew her nose again and leaned into his chest. "The poor girl." Her voice was muffled. "How can I help her?"

Nate looked past her to where Olivia stood, staring at them with wide eyes. Even Charley looked shaken. Nate caught Coop's eye.

"Why don't you take the children back to the ranch, Coop? I'll see Miss Sarah home, and then I'll be out to the ranch later."

Charley shrugged off Coop's arm and stepped toward him. "Are you going to find that man, Uncle Nate?

Nate laid his hand on Charley's shoulder. "A man doesn't have to go looking for trouble. You and Coop need to take care of your sisters and I need to make sure Miss Sarah gets home safely."

"What about that man? Won't he come back again?"

Nate glanced at Sarah. She was pale and shaken. "He might, and if he does we'll deal with him then." He tousled the boy's hair. "Now you get on home with Coop."

As Charley led his sisters out to the alley, Coop stepped in close. "You watch yourself, Nate. I wouldn't put it past Harris to try to bushwhack you between here and the ranch."

"I'll watch my back trail."

The schoolroom was silent as Coop and the children drove past the window and out of the alley. Sarah turned and started cleaning the chalkboard. Nate straightened a row of benches before he heard a sniff.

He moved to the next row of benches, the one closest to the chalkboard. Another sniff.

"You aren't going to let that tough worry you, are you?"

Sarah took one last swipe at the board. "I'm not

worried about myself. It's Maude." She turned to him. "What will he do to her when he gets back to the Mystic? Or what has he already done? Maude said he can get violent."

"Was all this because she came to church this morning?"

Sarah nodded. "I asked her to come. I thought that since it was Sunday morning, Mr. Harris wouldn't begrudge her a little time." Her nose was pink from holding back tears. "But she said Mr. Harris watches her every minute. He gets angry every time she…" Her face reddened and she looked at the floor. "Every time a gentleman comes calling. But if she doesn't…entertain them…he threatens to dope her up with laudanum so she won't care."

Her hands were shaking. Nate grasped one and led her to the bench, where he took a seat next to her. As her tears started to fall, he moved closer so she could lay her head on his shoulder, and let her cry.

When her tears subsided, he moved away while she sat up. "I told you that you and this girl were from different worlds."

She nodded and sniffed. "You were right. I had no idea."

He pushed the burning anger down. "I wanted to protect you from this."

"Protect me from knowing about the sufferings of my fellow human beings?"

He wanted to smile at how quickly he had gotten her dander up. "No, you wouldn't put up with that." He looked into her deep blue eyes. "I would protect you from knowing the bare truth of that kind of life. A girl like Maude, well, isn't it too late for her? Maybe you should concentrate on the girls you can help before they fall too far. One of your students would never become a saloon girl."

Sarah shook her head. "No. No, it isn't too late for anyone. Maude came to me. She asked for my help. I can't turn my back on her."

"But will she be able to turn her back on the life she's leading?" Nate studied the boards beneath his feet. "If Harris has been giving her laudanum, that means she could be addicted to it. Just like someone can be addicted to whiskey. It's an awful thing. A snare you can never be free of. How could she turn her back on that?"

"With God's help, she can."

God again. If Sarah had ever seen a person in the last stages of drug addiction, she might not be so quick to assume God would be able to intervene. But he had talked to Maude. Her eyes were clear, her hands steady. Maybe she hadn't gotten caught in its clutches yet.

Sarah laid one hand over his. "I have to try to help her, Nate. I have to."

He took her hand in his and looked into her face. The tears were gone and her mouth was set in steely determination. He would kiss that mouth if she was his.

"Don't do it alone. Don't visit her on your own, don't try to contact her. I don't want Harris coming after you again. If you need to get a message to her, I'll take it. You need to stay away from the Mystic."

Her firm lips trembled up at the corners. "You'd do that for Maude?"

He squeezed her hand. He'd do it for her, and for Mattie.

Chapter Thirteen

"I won't be able to say my piece, Miss Sarah. I know I won't."

Sarah looked over her shoulder at Olivia. With pins held tight between her lips and the bunting threatening to end up in a heap on the floor instead of festooned across the front of the schoolroom, Sarah was at a loss. She held the bunting in place with one hand and took the pins out of her mouth with the other.

"You've said it perfectly every day this week, Olivia. You'll do fine tomorrow night." She pinned the bunting in place and slid a step to the left on the bench. Another pin and another swoop of bunting.

"But that was only in front of you. When everyone is here, I know I'll forget. Can you hear me say it again?"

Sarah counted the remaining flounces. "Three more pins, and then I can." She slid another step along the bench. "Are the boys done washing the windows yet?"

"Yes. They went out front to wash the church windows."

A six-week school term was short, but it had been a good start. It was the end of June, and with the weather turning hot, the children were looking forward to a summer break before classes started again in September. Sarah pushed another pin into the soft wood. Not only the children. With no school schedule to keep, she hoped to be able to spend more time with Maude. Despite her best intentions, it was Thursday already, and she hadn't seen the girl since Sunday morning. When she had gone to the appointed meeting place after school, Maude hadn't been there. Had Harris hurt her as he had threatened? She had no way of knowing.

She pinned the last flounce to the wall. Mr. Woodrow had loaned the bunting to decorate the academy for the final exercises of the term. Not only would the children's parents be attending the program, but other townspeople would, too. Perhaps they would help spread the word and more children would attend school in the fall.

"Now, Miss Sarah?"

Sarah climbed down from the bench and sat facing Olivia.

"All right, Olivia. Go ahead."

Olivia stood straight, her hands clasped behind her and eyes focused on a spot behind Sarah's head. "'Tis a lesson you should heed, try, try again."

Sarah held up her hand. "Slower, dear. You aren't running a horse race. If you speak too fast, your listeners won't be able to understand what you're saying."

"All right." The girl took a deep breath. "'Tis a lesson you should heed…"

Olivia's voice went on, reciting the poem from the McGuffey's Fourth Reader perfectly. Sarah let her eyes drift to the table against the wall, where Lucy and Laura put the finishing touches on their art projects. The children all knew their recitation pieces. After saying the poems from their readers, the four older students would take turns relating the events of United States history. The younger ones, Lucy and Alan, would demonstrate doing sums for the audience, and then the evening would finish with a spelling bee. Sarah smiled. It had been Aunt Margaret's idea to have all of the attendees participate in the bee, and it promised to be a lot of fun.

"Did I do good, Miss Sarah?"

"You mean, did I do well?"

"Yes, ma'am. Did I do well?"

"You recited your poem perfectly, Olivia." Sarah checked her watch. Nearly four o'clock. "It's time to gather our things. Will you call the boys in please, Laura?"

Sarah tried to quell the flutter in her stomach. Since the run-in with Mr. Harris, Nate had been bringing the children to school and taking them home again every day. And each day, at nine o'clock and at four o'clock, that flutter told her she would be seeing him soon. But they had little time to exchange more than a short greeting before he had to be off again. He still kept that invisible wall between them.

She smoothed her skirt and turned to the gathered children. "Remember, children. Tomorrow is the last day of the term. You must finish your homework tonight and return it to me in the morning." A step on the porch outside the door drew her attention. Nate removed his hat as he ducked inside the open door and her stomach did a flip. "Tomorrow we will go through your recitations one more time and finish decorating the classroom for our program in the evening." She smiled at the children. "Class dismissed."

"Uncle Nate," Charley said when he saw his uncle, "Bernie and Alan want to show me their new puppy. Can I—" He stopped short and glanced at Sarah. "May I go see it before we go home?"

Nate grinned at Charley. "A new puppy? Do you think Lucy and Olivia would like to see it, too?" He turned to Bernie. "Do you think it would be all right if all of them stopped at your house for a little while this afternoon? I need to talk with Miss Sarah."

"Sure thing."

The children were gone to the Woodrows' house in Ingleside before Sarah could say a word. Her stomach threatened to revolt when Nate looked at her. Why, after all this time of knowing him, were her nerves on edge at the thought of talking to him now?

He ran his finger between his bandanna and his neck. The afternoon had grown warm, and sweat beaded on his forehead.

He pointed to one of the benches with a flick of the hat in his hands. "Can we sit and talk for a minute?"

"Yes, of course."

When she was seated he sat next to her. "I saw Dovey—I mean Maude—today."

All thoughts of her nervous stomach disappeared. "You did? Where? How? Is she all right?"

He didn't look at her, but sighed and set his hat on the bench next to him. "Yes, she's all right. I'm not sure I did the right thing, but I hadn't seen her all week, even though I pass the Mystic morning and afternoon." He turned his gaze toward her. "But today I talked to her, and she's doing as well as you can expect."

"But how did you manage it?"

"I saw Harris leave town, heading toward Crook

City, so I knew he'd be gone long enough for me to try to see her."

"What did she say? Does she still want me to help her?"

"She's desperate to leave. She said Harris is watching her day and night. He won't let her out of the building unless he or one of his men escorts her."

"How can we help her?" Sarah's mind went to the Mystic, with the barred windows facing the cliff wall below Williams Street, and the constant presence of armed guards. The guards... "How did you get past the guards to see her?"

His face reddened as he shifted the toe of his boot on the floorboard. "I had to pay to see her. I didn't dare try it when Harris was there, but I knew the others wouldn't recognize me."

Sarah felt her own face blush as she considered the implications of what he had done. She laid her hand on his resting on the bench between them. "You did what you had to. It was providential that Mr. Harris was gone so that you could see her."

"It wasn't providential, it was just good timing, and I don't know when we'll get another chance like that again. But when we do, we have to be ready."

Sarah moved her hand away from his. Couldn't he admit to God's hand in all of this? "Do you have a plan?"

"Not yet. But I'll come up with something."

"I'll be praying."

He leveled his gaze at her, one corner of his mouth turned up. "You really believe prayer will make a difference in the outcome."

"Certainly it will. It's much better than relying on timing."

Nate stood and she rose along with him. "Maybe you're right." He smiled at her. "I have to admit, something sent Harris on an errand just when I was in town and able to see Maude."

"Do you mean that you might be willing to concede to the existence of God?"

"I had to admit to that weeks ago. Your uncle is a pretty convincing preacher." He paused, searching her face with his eyes. "You're pretty convincing, too."

"Why? What have I said?"

He gave a slight shake of his head. "It isn't what you've said, it's what you've done. I've never known anyone who cares about other people as much as you do. That has to be one of those gifts from God James talked about."

He stopped, as if he was lost in thought. Sarah watched him as his eyes focused on the bunting at the front of the room. With a start, she realized that his scars had faded. The angry scarlet burns had turned to dusky red over the weeks she had known him. He had changed.

Had she changed as much?

His gaze turned to her. "Maude will be ready when the time comes. I want it to be soon, before Harris gets suspicious. I'm afraid for you, though."

"For me? He wouldn't know I'm involved in Maude's escape, would he?"

"Maybe not. But I can't help it." He stood up, ready to leave. "I can't help feeling you're in danger, and I don't know what to do about it."

She smiled as she stood, choosing to remember Dr.

Bennett's words. "Don't worry about me. Dr. Bennett always said that those who do right are protected by God."

He reached out and stroked her sleeve with a light touch. "But be careful. Dr. Bennett could be wrong, you know."

Sarah stepped closer to him. The wall that had been between them wavered like a desert mirage. "I know she is wrong, so you be careful, too. And I don't care what you think about it, I'm going to be praying for you."

"Then go ahead and pray." He grinned as he turned and walked toward the door. "We both need all the help we can get."

Nate ignored the children's chatter on the way home. Olivia and Charley couldn't stop talking about the Woodrows' pup, but Lucy leaned against him and slept. He let Loretta pick her path up the trail leading to the ranch ahead of him, the older children both on her bare back. He and Lucy followed on Scout.

His mind drifted from his visit with Maude to Sarah, and back again.

It had been a shameful thing to pay for time with the saloon girl. The knowing wink from the madam had been bad enough, but the leer from the guard patrolling the hall started his blood to boil. The guards were present to keep the peace, they claimed. To prevent jealous customers from doing harm to each other or to the girls. But they were really there to intimidate the girls, Maude had said.

All the girl wanted was to go home to her brother's family in Omaha, but Harris kept her working on the pretext that she owed him money for her stagecoach passage the previous fall. Nate shook his head. It was hard to believe that so many men had fought and died to preserve the Union and to abolish slavery just a dozen years ago, and yet this scheme of Harris's was just as much slavery as that had been.

And Sarah. Nate shifted Lucy on the saddle in front of him as Scout climbed the last slope up to the rolling grassland of the ranch. The half-finished log house rose out of the meadow at the base of the hill, with the tree-covered slope rising behind it. It was more than a house. It was the fulfillment of his dream of giving the children a home. Being with Sarah gave him a glimpse of what his life could be. A wife, children, a home. He hoped that he could rid himself of this cowardice that seemed to poison everything he touched, but until then he had to forget about a wife. Forget about a future with Sarah.

But before he could think of a future, he had to get Maude out of the Mystic. If he couldn't save Mattie, at least he could help another girl in her position. And he had promised Sarah. He would follow through on that promise no matter what.

Coop had supper ready when they reached the camp. All through the meal and while he helped the children settle for the night, Nate ran possibilities of Maude's rescue through his mind. Having been inside the Mystic—seeing the layout of the place, the number of guards and how they were armed—helped him form a plan.

Darkness covered the eastern sky by the time he poured himself a final cup of coffee. The western horizon still glowed soft yellow above the hills, and pale clouds floated on a northern breeze.

Coop filled his tin cup and settled next to Nate, his

eyes on the slowly changing sky. "You've been quiet all night."

"Hmm." Nate took a sip of the coffee. Coop sure knew how to brew a good pot.

"That schoolmarm giving you fits?"

Nate grinned at the smirk on his friend's face. "As a matter of fact, no. But a friend of hers is."

"Maude."

"Yup."

"You're going to try to get her out of Harris's clutches?"

"And as far away from Deadwood as she can get." Nate took a sip of his coffee.

Coop lifted his cup to his mouth in tandem.

"It's either going to take a couple stealthy men or an army, the way I see it." Coop leaned back against a rock.

"I've got a plan. I went to the Mystic today, and I think I know a way I can do it."

"You mean we."

"I'm not dragging you into this."

"You aren't dragging me, I'm volunteering."

Nate took another sip and then turned the cup in his hands as he swallowed the hot coffee. "I need someone to take care of the children and the ranch."

"How long do you aim for this to take?"

Nate set his cup on his knee. "I saw how the guards at the Mystic are armed. I know Harris won't let her go easy." He turned to Coop, keeping his voice low in case one of the children was awake. "This is a dangerous business. I need someone I can trust to take care of the children and the ranch in case something happens. The land will be Charley's when he's old enough, and

I know I can trust you to keep it for him and teach him to work it right."

Coop gazed at the western horizon, where darkness had overtaken the pale light. The moon hadn't risen yet.

"Are you doing this for Maude or for Sarah?"

Mattie's face swam before Nate's eyes, the way she looked when they were children, with her impish grin and her nose peppered with freckles.

"It's something I have to do."

"I hate for you to go in there alone." Coop shifted against his rock.

"If things go right, no one will even know she's gone until it's too late."

"You need God's blessing." Coop sat up and threw the dregs of his coffee in the fire. "And you need to be surrounded with prayer."

"This has to remain quiet. No one can know."

"Then you know I'll be praying, and I'm sure Sarah will. You just be careful, you hear?"

Nate grinned into his cup. "Yes sir." He downed the last swallow.

"When are you going to do it?"

"Tomorrow night, after the school program. I need to act as soon as possible, and Friday night is chaos in the Badlands. I'm hoping the guards may be looking the other way."

Coop rose and dusted off his pants. "Then you know what I'll be praying for."

As his friend went off to find his bedroll, Nate put another log on the fire. Before going to bed, he sat, watching the flames lick the edges of the new wood. He could pray for the success of this venture. Did God even hear prayers of men like him?

* * *

Sarah ignored the trickle of perspiration in the small of her back. Even though the evening air had cooled as the sun lowered toward the tops of the hills, the crowded schoolroom was hot and stuffy. But the program had gone well, and the spelling bee was down to its last two contestants.

Uncle James stood at the front of the room, his eyes on the toes of his boots, as his opponent, Hiram Turner, spelled his word. These two men had spelled down the entire room full of students and guests, and they were head-to-head with every word Sarah put before them. In exasperation, she turned to the very back of the spelling book.

"Uncle James, your word is *mucilaginous.*"

Mr. Turner rose up on his toes and down again while Uncle James smoothed his mustache with his fingers. He cleared his throat. *"Mucilaginous. M-u-c-i-l-a-g-e-n-o-u-s."*

"I'm sorry, that's wrong."

The crowd behind her erupted in hoots of delight— from Mr. Turner's team—or groans from the team on the other side of the room.

Sarah faced Mr. Turner. "If you spell this word correctly, your team has won the bee. *Mucilaginous.*"

Hiram Turner rose up and down on his toes, waved to his teammates and twirled the end of his mustache between his fingers. Finally he said, *"M-u-c-i-l-a-g-i-n-o-u-s. Mucilaginous."*

"That is correct."

As soon as Sarah spoke, the room rang with shouts and whistles. Mr. Turner's team surged forward to congratulate him and watched as the two final contestants shook hands.

Aunt Margaret caught her elbow. "Oh, Sarah, this was so much fun. Let me help you with the refreshments."

As they made their way to a table set up at the back of the room, Lucretia Woodrow joined them, holding one of her two-month-old twins. Aunt Margaret stirred the lemonade while Lucretia removed the napkins covering plates of cookies and slices of cake.

"Sarah," Lucretia said, "this evening has been a wonderful success. You have shown this mining camp the kind of civilized entertainment a school can bring to a community. You are to be commended."

"Your children worked hard, and they deserve the recognition. I'm glad so many people attended."

"I'd like you to meet Mrs. Broadmoor, our neighbor."

As she turned to greet Lucretia's distinguished-looking friend, she caught sight of Wilson Montgomery watching her. He stepped forward as Lucretia and Mrs. Broadmoor turned their attention to the refreshments.

He smiled as he caught her hand in his and brought it to his lips for a kiss. "You've become quite a success with your little school, my dear."

Sarah worked to keep smiling as she pulled her hand back. "The children have made it a pleasure, Mr. Montgomery. They have applied themselves to their studies, as I'm sure you could see tonight."

He gave her a mock frown. "How many times must I insist you call me Wilson?"

"Yes… Wilson." She turned to indicate the refreshment table. "Would you like some lemonade and a cookie?"

"I'm afraid I can't stay. I have a meeting this evening, and I'm sorry business has to pull me from your side." He glanced at the crowd pressing around them. "Would you walk with me to the door? I have something I'd like to say to you in private."

Sarah let him take her elbow and guide her through the crowd. She nodded thanks to those who spoke to her, but all the time looked for Nate. Finally she spotted him with Mr. Cooper, standing in a line for refreshments with the children. He held Lucy in his arms, and just as she reached the door, he looked across the room and caught her eye. A frown appeared on his face as Wilson led her outside.

She faced him as he let go of her arm. "What did you want to say?"

It may have only been the glare of the lamplight through the schoolroom window, but it seemed his face changed from affable to cruel for an instant. Then when he looked at her, his usual faint smile was on his lips.

"I have a concern I want to discuss with you. It has to do with some of your activities."

Sarah crossed her arms, suddenly chilled in the fresh air. "What do you mean?"

"You've been seen frequenting—ah, no, visiting—a certain part of town." His smile broadened but his eyes were ice crystals. "A part of town far too crude for your delicate sensibilities."

How could Wilson know of her arrangements to meet Maude in the alley between the back of the Mystic and the Wall Street steps? "I was visiting a friend."

His mouth hardened in a thin line, but his voice remained pleasant. "I don't think it's a good idea for you to venture into the Badlands. And as far as your friend is concerned…"

"Why are you discussing this with me? What concern is it of yours?"

"We can't have the wife of the richest banker in town carrying on in this way, can we? If you want to do charitable work, there are other ways to go about it that won't endanger your reputation."

Sarah's stomach churned. "I'm afraid you presume too much, Mr. Montgomery."

"Wilson, please." He reached for her hand, but she pulled it away.

"I don't intend to marry you, Mr. Montgomery. I wish you would forget the idea right now, before this goes any further."

He stepped forward and grasped her wrist in one quick motion. "I want you to understand. I always get what I want, and I want you for my wife." His voice had lost its soft tone. He twisted her arm, bringing her closer to him. The odor of shaving soap and stale cigars was overpowering. "You will obey me, and you will behave. I won't see you in the Badlands again, will I? And you will forget that girl you call your friend. Do you understand me?"

Sarah gritted her teeth. "I understand you perfectly."

He released his hold, and the smile was back on his face as if nothing untoward had happened. "I must be off. My business awaits." He put his hat on with a smooth motion. "Good night, my dear. Remember what I said."

Sarah rubbed her wrist as she watched him round the corner of the building, heading toward Main Street.

She took a deep breath. A step in the doorway behind her made her jump.

"This is where you are."

She turned to Nate, trying to control the quivering corners of her mouth. He had a glass of lemonade in each hand. She twisted her fingers together, wanting nothing more than to throw herself into his arms.

He set the glasses on the windowsill and stepped closer to her, peering at her face in the dim light. His face was set and grim.

"What is it? What has happened?"

She shook her head. Nate and Wilson were already wary of each other. If she told Nate what the banker had said, what might he do?

"N-nothing. Nothing is wrong."

"It isn't nothing. You're upset. Did Montgomery say something?"

"No." Sarah grasped at the first thought that came to her mind. "He only asked me if I'd... We found we have a difference of opinion about something." Nate looked past her toward the street where Wilson had disappeared. "You don't need to be so concerned. Wilson is a pillar of the community. What could he say that would upset me?" She gave a little laugh, hoping he'd forget she had been on the verge of tears a moment ago.

He eyed her, his face pensive. She hadn't convinced him yet.

"Did you bring lemonade for me?" She indicated the forgotten glasses on the windowsill.

"Yes." He handed her one of the glasses and took a sip of his own. "The program went well. Were you satisfied with it?"

"The children were wonderful, weren't they? And the spelling bee was so much fun."

Nate took a long drink of his lemonade and then paused, turning the delicate cup in his hands. "Tonight is the night, Sarah."

"For Maude?"

He nodded. "There's a stage heading to Cheyenne in the morning. I can get Maude out of the Mystic around midnight, and then I'll need to hide her until she can get on the stagecoach. That will be the crucial part."

"But how will we—"

Aunt Margaret appeared in the open doorway. "Sarah, the ladies are asking for you. Why have you disappeared out here?"

"I needed some fresh air. I'll be right in." Sarah waited until Aunt Margaret had gone back to the circle of ladies just inside the door. "I want to know what your plans are. You know you need me to help you."

Nate sighed, taking her empty cup. "I'll ask Coop to take the children home, and then I'll come up to your cabin later this evening. We'll discuss it then. But you're not going to help me tonight. I don't want you anywhere near the Mystic."

Not anywhere near? Who else would be better able to help Maude get out of Harris's clutches?

"But—"

Nate stopped her protest with a raised finger. "We'll do this my way or not at all. Understood?"

Sarah pressed her lips together to keep from firing back a retort that would ruin any possibility of him including her. No matter what he said, she was going to be part of rescuing Maude.

Chapter Fourteen

Nate swung Lucy onto the front of Coop's saddle.

"You'll all be asleep before I get home tonight. Behave yourselves for Coop."

He went to help Olivia onto the mule's bare back behind Charley.

"Where are you going, Uncle Nate?" Her voice was sleepy already.

"I need to talk to Miss Sarah and then take care of some business."

Charley patted Loretta's neck. "Are we going to go scout out those wild mustangs tomorrow, like you said?"

Nate couldn't lie to the boy, and he wouldn't make any promises he couldn't keep. "We will if we can, Charley. We'll see what tomorrow brings."

He patted his nephew's knee and then stepped closer to Coop. "I'll be back when I can. If…"

"I know." Coop interrupted him with a nod toward the children to remind him of their listening ears. "You've said all you need to." Coop shook his hand. "My prayers are with you."

Why the sudden catch in his throat? He nodded in

answer. Coop's prayers meant something. A Bible verse his mother used to quote came to his mind, swift and sure—*The effectual fervent prayer of a righteous man availeth much.*

Nate turned back to the school, where Sarah, along with her aunt and uncle, were cleaning up after the evening program.

Finally, after they left the schoolroom and made their way to the MacFarlands' cabin, Nate and Sarah were alone. They sat together on the bench by the front door, the quiet of the evening marred by disjointed music and raucous voices drifting up the hill from the mining camp. James and Margaret had gone inside, but not before James had shaken Nate's hand with a nod of approval. Nate's scars itched in the unaccustomed humidity of the evening, and the thought that James assumed he was courting Sarah set his nerves further on edge. But he couldn't tell James the truth of his business here tonight. Not yet.

Sarah gave a tired sigh and sat up straight, rolling her shoulders.

"You're exhausted from the program tonight. You should go in and get some rest."

She leaned back again. "Not until you tell me your plans."

He leaned forward, his arms on his knees. "I don't want you anywhere near the Badlands tonight."

Sarah stood, pulling him up with her. "Let's walk a bit. I don't want Uncle James and Aunt Margaret to overhear."

They walked to the edge of the gulch. Below them, Lower Main Street was brightly lit. The Mystic was ablaze with lanterns in every window and torches along the edge of the wide porch. But behind the building, close under the cliff face below Williams Street, was dark shadow. All the noise and activity was focused in the front of the building. Nate pressed his lips together in a grim smile. It was the perfect setup for his plans.

"Why won't you let me help you?"

"For one thing, my plan is for one man, and one man only. Any more than that will attract too much attention. For another thing, it's much too dangerous for you to be involved."

"But you're involved."

He turned toward her just enough to catch her profile in his vision. Her chin tilted up and her mouth was set in a determined line. Stubborn was only one of the names he could call her. Stubborn and beautiful. He had no guarantees he would succeed in this scheme to get Maude away from the Mystic. In fact, he could almost guarantee it wouldn't work. He had to try, but he didn't want Sarah there to witness his failure.

"I'm a man."

Her head whipped around. "What does that have to do with anything?"

"My job is to protect you, and I can't if you show up at the Mystic on a Friday night. That place draws a rough crowd."

Her gaze drifted back to the camp below them. "I hate the thought of Maude down there when she wants to leave so desperately." She gripped his elbow. "Tell me how you plan to do it."

"Promise me you won't do anything foolish."

She shifted her feet. "All right. I won't do anything foolish."

"My plan is to pay for time with Maude, like I did yesterday."

"What if Harris is there? He knows you. Won't he be suspicious?"

"I hope he'll be too busy to notice who the customers are. There's a different person who takes care of that type of business."

"All right. You pay for your time with her." Sarah paused. "I hate to think about what that means and what it will do to your reputation."

"Never mind that. Once I'm in her room, we'll go out the window and make our way to a hiding place until morning." Nate fingered the pouch of gold dust in his pocket, Coop's contribution to the effort. It should buy enough time that they wouldn't have to worry about anyone disturbing them for a while.

"But aren't those windows too small for you to fit through?"

The windows along the back of the building were tiny and at least ten feet from the ground. They were covered with bars and oiled paper that let no air through and only the faintest light on a bright afternoon. Maude was so slight that she should have no problem going through once he got the bars off, but would he fit? It didn't matter, as long as Maude was safe.

"If I can't get through, I'll have to slip out the other way."

"Someone will see you."

"No one is worried about me. They're only concerned with the girls."

Sarah shifted her feet again. Her profile against the glow of the lights from the mining camp drew him close. He wanted to hold her, promise her everything would turn out fine, but he couldn't make that promise. He pushed away the insistent voice saying that he was no good, that everything he touched turned to ashes. That he would fail tonight, too. He wouldn't be able to face her afterward, to see the look of pity and disappointment in her eyes.

Instead, he scuffed his own foot in the thin layer of dirt. The sounds from the camp intensified. The hour was growing late.

"Where do you plan to hide until the stage comes?"

"Above Williams Street along City Creek. There's a thicket by the creek, and it isn't far from the stage station. We'll wait there until dawn, and then I'll go down to the stage office and buy her ticket."

She turned toward him. "I'd like to say goodbye to Maude. What time does the stage leave?"

"At six o'clock."

"I'll be there then." She looked toward the Mystic again. The tilt of her chin unsettled him.

"I don't want you there." He grabbed her arms, turning her toward him. "Do you understand? It's too dangerous. I don't want you anywhere near the Mystic or the stage office."

"You might need my help."

Of course she would think that. There was every possibility that he would die tonight, and then Maude would be worse off than if he had done nothing. His gut churned. But if he didn't carry out this plan, Sarah would do it on her own. Not even a coward would let a woman be part of this business.

"I won't need your help. And if anything happened to you, James and that Wilson Montgomery would both be after my hide."

Her face stiffened. "Wilson has nothing to do with this."

Nate dropped his hands from her arms and turned to go. "Montgomery has everything to do with this."

* * *

As soon as Nate disappeared down the trail, Sarah went up to her loft. How could he expect her to sleep peacefully in her bed while he rescued Maude?

She changed her dress from the lilac one she had worn to the school program to the dark blue calico she had worn the first day they had visited Nate's ranch. Reaching the rear of the Mystic would be hard enough without being seen. Wearing dark clothes would help.

Letting her hair down, she brushed it, then gathered it in a simple bun. She reached for her reticule but stopped and sank onto the edge of her bed. She had promised Nate she wouldn't do anything foolish, and that was exactly what he would think her plans were. But it was even more foolish for him to think he could manage Maude's rescue on his own. She had to help him.

Sarah waited, listening until her aunt and uncle's murmured conversation turned to snoring. She counted to one hundred. Uncle James had to be sound asleep before she tried descending the ladder.

Finally the time came. She let herself out of the cabin, pulling the heavy door closed with a quiet thump. Hurrying down Williams Street, she stopped at the top of the Wall Street steps. Below her, at their foot, was the center of the Badlands. The brightly lit edge of the night's revelries nearly blinded her. She crept down the steps. To her left was the shadowy alley that lay between the backs of the saloons and the cliff below Williams Street. If it hadn't been for the reflected light from Main Street, she wouldn't have been able to see anything.

Behind the first building were three little houses, only large enough for one small room. She had seen them many times, but tonight one door was open, the interior lit by a kerosene lamp. Sarah glanced into the doorway as she went by. A girl, dressed in a gauzy pink gown and with her dark hair tumbled about, lay asleep, or passed out, on a couch. Dark lashes brushed her pale cheeks. An upended freight box next to her held the lamp and a hypodermic needle. Sarah shuddered and hurried on.

Pausing to get her bearings, Sarah stepped into the shadow of the wall. The second story rose above her and raucous laughter spilled out of the windows. Sarah turned her mind from the activities and noises that pressed in from all around.

She had reached the Mystic, but which window was Maude's? Stepping around piles of garbage and a mound of split firewood, Sarah reached the far corner of the building. An alley divided the structure from its neighbor. Sarah drew back into the shadows against the building when a large man stepped to the corner. He glanced along the narrow rear yard and then turned back. His measured paces faded as he walked toward Main Street. Sarah started breathing again.

She stepped back from the building and scanned the row of windows above her. One, the third from the left, was missing its oiled paper cover. Nate's head appeared as he worked to remove the last bar. Then his head and shoulder disappeared into the room, there was a pause and a rope snaked down the wall. Next came Maude's feet through the small opening. Sarah reached to help her down.

Nate poked his head out the window once Maude was through and saw Sarah. "What are you doing here?" he demanded in a loud whisper.

"You need help."

"I told you I don't want your help."

She put her hands on her hips. "You need me. Just admit it."

Nate was silent. His lips pressed together. His hands clenched into iron-hard fists. "You are the most stubborn—"

Sudden pounding on the door behind him interrupted whatever he was going to say.

"Dovey! Dovey, who's in there with you?" The shouts were garbled, slurred. More pounding. "You get out here, Dovey. Now."

Maude clutched at Sarah's arm. "It's Harris, and he's been drinking."

Nate gripped the window frame and tried to force his shoulders through.

"Nate, hurry! Hurry!" Sarah glanced toward the edge of the building. The guard could turn the corner again at any moment.

He pulled at the window frame. A few splinters came off in his hands, but it didn't budge. He backed off and threw his shoulder against the wall, but it didn't give at all. The pounding on the door came again, louder, along with Harris's shouts.

Maude pulled at Sarah's arm. "We have to go." Her whispers were hoarse. Tears streamed down her face. "He'll kill me. He will. I've never heard him this bad."

Nate tried once more to fit his head and one shoulder through the narrow window, but he couldn't do it. "You two get out of here. Now."

Maude fled down the alley toward the steps. Sarah couldn't follow her. Not yet.

"I'm not going to leave you here."

"Yes, you are." Nate looked toward the alley with

a wild glance. "Someone is coming. Go. I'll catch up with you. It's Maude they want, not me."

He disappeared back into the room. Sarah couldn't make her feet move. A gunshot rang out from inside Maude's room, loud even against the rest of the night noises. She couldn't follow Maude now. She had to see what had happened. As she backed away, hoping to get a better look through the window, strong hands pulled her back.

"Hold on there, miss. What do you think you're doing?"

The guard. She struggled, but his hands held her in a vise. He pulled her back to the brightly lit alley, then pinned her against the wall at the foot of an outside staircase. She couldn't hear anything above the noise from Main Street. What had happened to Nate?

"Where did you come from? You aren't one of Harris's girls."

She struggled again, but he was too strong.

"Maybe you were looking for a job?" He pinned her against the wall with one hand. His face was shadowed by his hat brim. Sarah closed her eyes as he held her with one hand and lifted the other to stroke her cheek.

"Here, you. Leave that young woman alone."

Sarah's eyes flashed open. She knew that voice.

Wilson Montgomery tapped the guard on the shoulder with his cane. "Let her go. Don't you know who this is?"

The guard backed away. "She wouldn't give me her name, Mr. Montgomery."

Wilson's nostrils flared. "Sarah, what are you doing here?"

Sarah moved away from the wall, toward the back of the building. "I could ask you the same thing."

He glanced up the stairway to the door above. "You don't need to be concerned with my business." His eyes narrowed as he took a step closer to her. "I told you I didn't want you to come here. This is no place for you." He motioned for the guard. "I want you to escort Miss MacFarland home."

Sarah took a step away from both of them. Would Wilson commit her to the keeping of this thug?

"Sure thing, Mr. Montgomery."

She turned and ran, around the corner of the Mystic into the darkness of the back alley. Past the little houses and up the Wall Street steps. When she reached the top, she paused for breath, listening for sounds of her pursuers. She saw them below her, looking between stacks of firewood and behind privies. When they reached the foot of the stairs, she melted into the shadows of the trees.

Both men swore, making her ears burn.

"She's gone." Wilson turned on the guard. "If you see her again, you let me know immediately, do you hear? And no one is to touch her."

"Yes, sir, Mr. Montgomery. Whatever you say."

As they made their way back to the Mystic, Sarah sank down onto a tree stump. Wilson Montgomery was doing business with Tom Harris? The pieces fell into place, one by one. His interest in her friendship with Maude. His mysterious business meetings. And he had to have been the one who told Harris that Maude had come to church. Even his efforts to close down the businesses in the Badlands must have been only an attempt to cut down the Mystic's competition.

Wilson's eagerness to maintain a spotless reputation was only a mask that hid his true nature. He had fooled Uncle James and Aunt Margaret, and he had nearly fooled her, too. But Nate hadn't been taken in by the man's polished manners. He had never trusted him.

A brass band struck up a rowdy tune on Main Street, drowning out all other noises, but the alley behind the Mystic was dark and quiet. Nate knew the plan. He would follow Maude…if he could. The echo of the gunshot rang through her head. If he could…

Sarah hiccupped. She wouldn't cry, not now. Not when Maude's future rested with her.

She stood, peering toward the Mystic through the underbrush on the hill next to the steps. No sound. No movement. Feeling the way with her feet, she backed up the steps, her arms wrapped around her middle. She let herself love him when she knew better. She should have kept to her rule. That was her mistake.

Nate pulled back into the tiny room as the pounding continued. He could try shoving the bed against the door, but what would that do?

Buy the girls time to get away.

The pounding at the door increased. "Dovey, open this door!"

Nate shoved the bed toward the door. Other voices joined Harris in the hall. Voices trying to talk some sense into the bully, from the sounds of it. Wedging the other end of the bed against the door, he leaned on the wall and checked the rounds in his pistol. He could use it if he had to, but these were close quarters for bringing a gun to the party.

"Why isn't the girl answering?" Harris again.

"The man paid for the entire night. Ten dollars in gold," the madam's voice whined.

Nate pressed his lips together at the woman's lie. He had given her at least twenty-five.

A slap. A heavy body hit the wall. Harris growled. "I told you she was mine tonight."

"I thought you'd want the money. You could take another girl." Her voice snarled. Uneven steps stumbled away.

"Who's in there with her? Did anyone see him?"

Silence.

"Get that door open."

A gunshot rang in Nate's ears as a hole the size of his fist appeared where the doorknob used to be. The bed gave way as two thugs pushed it and the door into the room. When they saw Nate, they both trained their pistols on him.

Harris appeared between them. His eyes narrowed. "You. You're the last one I thought I'd find here." He reached over and grabbed Nate's pistol from his hand, sticking it into his waistband. He glanced around the room, crowded with the four men. "Where's Dovey?" He tossed the folding screen aside and then lifted Maude's red dress, discarded on the floor. He glanced at the open window and walked over to look down into the yard behind the building. Swinging his bull head around, he jabbed his finger into Nate's chest. "You don't think she's going to get away from me, do you?" He leaned in close, reeking of whiskey. "No one." He poked again. "No one takes what's mine."

He motioned to the two thugs. "Make him think twice about coming back. When you're finished, take him out back with the rest of the garbage. I'm going after the girl." He pushed his way out the door.

Nate gathered himself. Two against one? He had survived worse odds. But these two were both taller and heavier than he was, and there was no way to maneuver in the close quarters. His only hope was to get out the door before they could do any damage. He leaned his shoulder forward and thrust it toward the man in the blue shirt, hoping to throw him off balance. The thug took the blow and returned it with a fist to Nate's belly.

Nate doubled over, but he drew his fist back for a punch into the guy's midsection. Before he could deliver, the second thug grabbed Nate's arms behind him.

He was held in the bulldog grip of one tough while the other one pulled back his fist for a punch to his ribs. Another one to his kidney. A dim thought that they were sparing his face drifted by. Another blow to his ribs. He felt searing pain as one cracked. They didn't want to risk knocking him out. They wanted him to feel every punch.

Finally thug number two lifted and dragged him out to the hall, Blue Shirt clearing a path by tossing the bed aside and shoving the broken door out of the way. They pulled him through the outside door and down the wooden steps to the alley.

Nate's vision swam as he fought to remain conscious. He had to follow Sarah. He had to protect her. A figure stood at the bottom of the steps, watching the proceedings. The face was familiar, smiling as the thugs dragged him to the refuse heap behind the saloon.

Wilson Montgomery. His presence here was too much of a coincidence.

The thugs dropped him on the pile of garbage, but Nate kept his eye on Montgomery as the banker slipped down the alley. He disappeared into the crowd on Lower Main just as thug two's fist collided with Nate's jaw.

Chapter Fifteen

Sarah took one step down. She had to find Nate. That gunshot still rang in her ears with all the horrible possibilities it could mean. But if Wilson caught her near the Mystic again… His callous disregard for her safety sent a shudder through her.

She took another step down. Nate or Maude? Which one needed her now?

"Please, God, show me the way."

Even before the breathless words left her lips, she saw the guard on his rounds behind the Mystic. Instead of glancing down the alley behind the saloon, he let his gaze wander up and down, probing every shadow.

With silent steps, she moved back to the top of the stairs. But she couldn't abandon Nate to whatever fate Harris had in mind.

She had to find someone to help. Uncle James.

With that thought, she ran down Williams Street to the cabin. Breathless, she opened the cabin door.

"Uncle James?"

She lit the lamp on the table and called again with a low voice, "Uncle James?"

"What is it, Sarah?"

Oh no, she had awakened Aunt Margaret, too.

"I need Uncle James's help. Nate is in trouble."

That brought both of them out of their curtained-off bedroom, Aunt Margaret tying the belt of her wrapper.

Uncle James ran a hand over his face. "What are you talking about?"

Sarah explained everything as quickly as she could, ignoring Aunt Margaret's gasps.

"I know Nate is in trouble, but I can't help him. He's in the Mystic, possibly hurt—" a sob escaped with a shudder "—or worse. And poor Maude is waiting for me. She thought I was coming right behind her."

Uncle James disappeared behind the curtain to get dressed.

Aunt Margaret pulled off her nightcap and started coiling her long braid into a bun. "I know there's something I can do to help, too."

"You're not going to stop me from finding Maude."

Margaret raised her eyebrows. "Of course not. I'm going to find Peder and have him take me out to the ranch. James will need Mr. Cooper's help, and I'll stay with the children." She gathered Sarah into her arms. "Don't worry. The men will find Nate, and you'll get Maude on that stagecoach out of town in the morning. And we'll all be praying for God's protection."

Sarah returned her aunt's hug. "Thank you, Aunt Margaret."

"You go on now. After the stage leaves, you come back here. By then, the men would have found Nate, and we'll all have a celebration breakfast out at the ranch."

"The stage. Maude will need money for a ticket." Sarah ran up the ladder to her loft and threw open her trunk. She felt in the corner of the tray for the only money she had—a twenty-dollar gold piece wrapped in a scrap of velvet. She slipped it into her pocket.

She left the cabin and hurried toward the opposite end of Williams Street as fast as she could. She found Maude waiting at the edge of the thicket along City Creek.

"I thought you were behind me, but when you didn't come, I didn't know what to do."

"It's all right." Sarah pulled the younger girl into her arms. "We both got away. Now all we have to do is wait for morning."

They found a downed tree near the back of the thicket where Forest Hill rose steeply behind them. Sarah huddled next to Maude, suddenly chilled. She shut away thoughts of Nate. She couldn't help him now.

Maude rubbed at her nose. "That girl, did you see her? The girl on the bed in the little house?"

Sarah couldn't forget the pale pink gown and the ugly needle. "Do you know her?"

A sniff. "Yes. She's new. Her name is Josie."

"She looks so young. How did she end up here?"

"Tom Harris promised her a job as a maid in his hotel, just like he did me."

"But it was a lie."

"Yes." Maude's voice was hollow. "I wish I could have warned her, but it's too late. She was so ashamed of what happened, of what she did when the men gave her whiskey to drink. She had never had it before." Maude sniffed again. "She said she couldn't live with the shame."

Sarah closed her eyes, the sight of the perfect dark lashes along the pale cheek rising before her. So many girls could tell the same story.

"Do you think she took laudanum tonight?"

Maude squeezed Sarah's arm. "For some girls, it's the only way they can see. Either to stay doped up on laudanum or use a derringer," Maude whispered. "It could have been me."

Sarah took a deep breath. Such a horror, only a few short blocks from the church and school. What could she do to help those poor girls? "But it wasn't you. And it won't be you."

"How, Sarah? How can I just forget the last year?"

"You'll start over. When you get to Omaha, you'll start a new life."

Maude shivered and Sarah scooted closer to her. Thunder rumbled behind the hill.

"But if I run out of money, or if someone recognizes me from here, or…" She wiped at her face with one hand. "How can I keep from going back to my old life?"

"Shh." Sarah put her arm around Maude's shoulder. "When you belong to God, He gives you His Holy Spirit. The Spirit lives in us, helping us turn our back on sin. All you need to do is ask, and He'll give you the strength you need."

Maude was quiet. The thunder rumbled again.

"Do you think I belong to God?"

"I think He's working in your heart to bring you to Himself. You've wanted to learn about Him, and you've taken the right step in wanting to leave your old life. Have you prayed to Him? Have you asked Him to forgive you for your sins?"

"Yes." She could hardly hear Maude's whisper.

The breeze grew stronger, making the trees above them sound like the waves in Boston Harbor.

"Then you can be sure that God has covered you

with Christ's righteousness. When He looks at you, He no longer sees your sin, but only the righteousness of His Son."

Maude sniffed again. "That's a wonderful thing, isn't it?"

Sarah's eyes burned with tears. "Yes, it's a wonderful thing."

"I hate to ask, since you've done so much for me already, but would you help Josie? Help her leave this life before it's too late? Before she does something worse to herself than take laudanum?"

"I will. I promise." She would help Josie, and any of the other girls who needed a way out.

They sat in silence. Sarah's back was stiff and tired. The storm clouds let loose a few large raindrops and then moved on to the east. Perhaps it was raining at Nate's ranch.

Nate. The wall between them was back, as thick and high as any fortress. His face had been hard, his features chiseled as if from marble as he told her his plan for rescuing Maude. And then when he saw her in the alley... Could he hate her that much? She should never have gone against his wishes. But if she hadn't, what would have happened to him? At least now Uncle James and Coop knew where to look for him. With the passing of the storm cloud, the sky cleared. The moon, a bright partial disk just a few days after the full moon, shone in the sky, descending toward the west. Nearly morning. She shifted and helped Maude lie on the log, her head in Sarah's lap.

Sarah blinked to stay awake. The wind following the storm was cool and fresh, but her feet felt like ice.

The sky in the east was lightening. She dozed, sitting on the tree trunk.

When the sun was fully up, she woke Maude. Six o'clock wasn't far off, and Nate still hadn't arrived.

"Let's go to the stagecoach office and buy your ticket. The coach will be leaving soon."

The six-horse hitch at the front of the stage stamped their feet, eager to be off in the cool morning air.

Sarah and Maude bought her ticket to Cheyenne, where she would catch the train to Omaha. Maude climbed aboard and took her seat. She leaned out the window. "I wish Nate had come. Do you think he's all right?"

Sarah forced herself to smile. It wouldn't do any good for Maude to worry about Nate all the way to Omaha. "I'm sure he just got held up somewhere."

A movement from the other side of the street caught her attention. Between the horses she watched a man's figure move from storefront to storefront, trying the doors. He peered in the glass-plate window of the Shoo Fly Café, just opening for business, and then turned toward the stagecoach. It was Harris. Sarah's cold feet froze.

"Sarah? What's wrong?"

Sarah couldn't move her eyes away. She didn't want to lose track of him. "It's Harris. He's across the street and looking this way."

The driver came out of the stage office, pulling on his fringed gloves.

"We need to get going." The lanky man climbed onto the driver's box, followed by the guard.

Two more passengers climbed onto the stage while Maude's hand clung to hers.

"Thank you." Maude's words were a whisper, but

they echoed in Sarah's heart. "If it weren't for you and Nate…"

Sarah squeezed her hand. "Write to me. Let me know how you're doing."

"I will."

With a "Gee-up" to the horses and a crack of his whip, the driver started the team on their way, south toward Cheyenne. And for Maude, toward the train and home.

As the dust settled in the coach's tracks, swirling in the early sunshine, Harris appeared out of the cloud. Sarah's insides quivered as she turned away from him and started toward Wall Street and the path for home. She hurried faster as she heard his heavy tread behind her on the boardwalk. She stifled a scream as his beefy hand caught her elbow and spun her around.

"Mr. Harris, what do you think you're doing?"

"Who did you put on that stage?"

She looked the man in the eye. "I was saying good-bye to a friend, but I don't see where it's any concern of yours." She pulled her elbow out of his grasp and took a step away from him.

"Dovey has disappeared, and that Nate Colby was involved."

Sarah stopped. Harris had been there when the gun went off.

Harris stepped closer. "I think you helped them. I think you just put her on that stage."

Sarah turned to face him again. "What have you done to Nate?"

"I told my boys to teach him a lesson." A slow grin pulled his face into a distorted mask. "He wouldn't listen to reason any more than you would." She turned away but he grabbed her elbow and spun her toward him again. "But I think you're going to be very useful. You're my ticket to getting even with Colby."

She pulled away from him, running blindly down the street. As she stumbled down the flight of stairs leading to Lower Main, she risked looking behind her. Harris followed, clumping down the wooden steps.

Her chest heaving, she looked all around. The streets were empty of people. Even the shopkeepers weren't around at this early hour on a Saturday.

When she reached the bottom of the Wall Street steps, Harris caught up with her. He clamped a filthy hand over her mouth and seized her around the waist. She struggled against him as he dragged her into the alley behind the buildings of the Badlands, to the three little houses with their doors all closed.

He wrenched open the door of the third house and threw her in. She landed on the cot, and before she could regain her feet he thrust a filthy cloth into her mouth to gag her.

Sarah struggled for breath as he bound her hands and tied them to the metal frame. She gathered her strength and kicked at him with her feet, but he grabbed them and tied them together.

"You wait here and be quiet. Mr. Montgomery will know what to do with you."

Sarah struggled against the ropes but only succeeded in pulling the knots tighter.

Harris chuckled as he watched her until she gave up, and then walked out the door and locked it with a snick of a padlock. His footsteps faded away.

Sarah adjusted herself to a more comfortable position. Someone was sobbing in the little house next to hers. She tried to remember—which one had Josie been in? She turned on the bed, slipping to her knees on the floor as well as she could with her wrists tied to the bed frame, and started praying. Only God could bring her out of this pit.

"Nate." The voice came nearer. "Nate."

Nate jerked awake, pain radiating through his body. He lifted a hand to his forehead, opening his eyes as he reached up. Only one eye opened. His hand came away bloody.

He tested his other arm. His legs. Nothing broken there, that he could tell, but from the feel of things, at least one rib was cracked. He hadn't been beaten this badly since the time he had stumbled on a Confederate patrol in Tennessee during the war. They had left him for dead. It felt like those two thugs had done the same thing.

"Nate?"

A man shifted near him in the semidarkness.

"James, is that you?"

"How are you feeling?"

Nate lay back against the foul-smelling heap. "Like I fell off a cliff and bounced on the way down." He tried to laugh at his own joke, but ended up coughing in searing bursts of pain.

"Take it easy, there."

Nate steadied himself with shallow breaths. "Where is Sarah?"

"She told me you were in trouble, so I came to find you. Sarah went to make sure Maude gets on the stagecoach, and Margaret and Peder went out to the ranch to tell Coop what happened."

The raucous noise from the street in front of the Mystic made Nate's head ache. Here he was, helpless. The whole plan hinged on him, and he couldn't even stand up and make sure a girl got on the stagecoach. Sarah was in danger because of him. And James was sitting on a garbage heap in the back of a saloon. This was no place for a preacher.

He fought to stay awake. "You shouldn't be here. I can wait for Coop alone."

"I won't leave you, Nate."

Nate barely heard James's words as he drifted away. He had heard those words before, hadn't he? James's voice became Ma's voice, reading from the family Bible. *He will not leave thee, nor forsake thee.*

When Nate woke again, the sky was lighter and the noise from the Mystic had lessened. Coop and James stood near his feet, discussing him. He caught snatches of words but gave up trying to decipher them.

From the look of the gray sky, the time must be near six o'clock. If he could walk, he could find Sarah, send her home where it was safe and take Maude to the stagecoach office. But when he tried to sit up, his ribs burned in answer.

"Whoa, there. Don't try to be going anywhere."

Coop knelt by his side and helped him ease back down onto his questionable bed.

Nate licked his cracked lips. "The children?"

"Margaret and Peder are with them."

James motioned to Coop. "Let's get him to the cabin while he's awake. It's quiet enough around here this morning that we don't have to worry about anyone from the Mystic bothering us."

With the two men supporting him on either side, Nate found himself standing upright. He swayed, gray lights swirling in his vision, but strong arms kept him from falling. Somehow, he stayed awake as they made their way past the three little cribs behind the saloon, to the base of the stairs and, gritting his teeth at every step, up to the cabin. James and Coop laid him down on the bed and he eased into the warm, soft mattress.

"I'll go get Doc Henderson," James said.

Nate drifted into a half-awake state where Sarah walked at the edge of his vision. Every time he tried to focus on her, she faded away. Coop made him drink some water. Later he smelled coffee brewing. And then pain again as he was brought to a sitting position and his ribs were wrapped tight. The pain eased and he was laid back down once more.

"That should do it." The doctor snapped his bag closed and peered at Nate. "You got banged up pretty hard, but you've seen worse. Those scars of yours tell quite a story." The older man eased a black felt hat onto his head. "Keep quiet for a day or two, and you'll be good as new." He nodded to James and Nate, and left.

Nate propped himself on one elbow. James and Coop were at the table with coffee cups in front of them. He put his feet on the floor and pushed himself to a sitting position. The pain was tolerable.

He grabbed his shirt from the end of the bed and pulled it on, easing his arms into the sleeves. Next were his boots. Shoving his feet in took effort, but he finally got them on. As he pushed the heel of the second boot down on the floor, Coop noticed what he was doing.

"Hold on there. Where do you think you're going?"

"Have you noticed how late it's getting? It's almost eight o'clock. Sarah should be here by now, but she isn't. Something is wrong and I'm going to find out what it is."

Coop and James looked at each other, and then Coop

stood and grabbed his hat from the hook by the door. "If you're going to wander around town in that condition, I'm going with you."

"Why should you? I'm the one who made this mess, and I'll be the one who cleans it up."

"Wait a minute," James said, coming to the bed to help Nate stand up. "Why do you think Sarah being late is your fault?"

Nate's head pounded. "I'm the one who came up with this crazy idea, so it's my fault Sarah is involved at all."

"Do you really think you could have stopped her from helping Maude?"

Nate couldn't meet the older man's level gaze. "She can be pretty stubborn when she sets her mind to something, can't she?"

"Whatever happens, or doesn't happen, it isn't your fault, Nate."

Nate started to protest, but James went on. "God is in control of this and every situation. Trust Him to take care of Sarah and trust Him to show you what you need to do. Go find her, help her if she needs help, but don't try to take the blame for something that's out of your control. That's the worst kind of pride."

Nate met his eyes then. "Pride?"

"You think you are more powerful than God? You think you can do anything to change His plans?"

James's point slid into place like a key fitting into its lock. God was the general and he was a private. All he had to do was stay on his mount and follow orders.

He took his hat from the chair at the foot of the bed. "Let's go do what we need to do."

Chapter Sixteen

Sarah's knees ached when she woke up. She rolled onto the little cot from her kneeling position on the floor.

Breathing slowly to keep herself calm, she looked around the little room. In the growing daylight, it looked the same as the one where she had seen Josie the night before, except there was no needle on the table next to the lamp.

The gag tasted foul and drew all the moisture from her mouth. Her wrists burned where the rope binding them had chafed, and her feet were numb. Harris had not been gentle when he tied the knots.

What would Dr. Bennett think of her now? Tears trickled down her cheeks at the thought. She had been so naive back in Boston, sitting in Dr. Bennett's parlor on those Sunday afternoons, soaking up every word that had dropped from the fiery woman's lips.

Had Dr. Bennett been wrong?

Not completely. Sarah had to believe that education was the way for adults and children alike to improve their situation in life. But Dr. Bennett's high ideas of people—that they would naturally embrace the opportunities presented to them—were so misguided. The woman had lived her life in the privileged areas of Boston and London. Life was different than she had led Sarah to believe.

Aunt Margaret had always maintained that the fault with Dr. Bennett's ideas was that she left God out of the picture. Without God, there was no hope.

Sarah had to admit Aunt Margaret was right.

She twisted her hands, trying to loosen the rope, but it only brought more pain.

A noise made her stop. She held her breath to listen. Voices. Harris was back, talking to someone, and close by.

Then she heard a key in the padlock and the door swung open, blinding her as the sudden morning light streamed in. Two figures stood in the opening, looking at her. Harris and… She tried to flip her hair out of her eyes. It was Wilson Montgomery.

"I put her in here. What else was I going to do?" Harris's voice whined.

"You fool. This isn't some girl out of the saloon. She has family and connections. Connections I wanted to stay on good terms with. What were you thinking?"

"I want Dovey back. I thought Colby would bring her back if I had the teacher."

"You thought?" Wilson smashed his fist on the doorframe and Harris cringed. "You thought?"

A cold shiver ran through Sarah. Wilson leaned over Harris, every word, every motion, out of control. He was an animal.

Wilson turned from Harris to her, running his hand through his hair as he stared at her. He strained to gain control, and with a little shake, he did. He smiled, but the ice blue of his eyes sent panic running through her. She strained at the bonds holding her wrists.

"Thanks to you, Harris, I have to leave Deadwood." His voice was as pleasant and controlled as if he was sitting in a fine parlor. "My lovely wife and I will have to start over in another town." He took a step closer to Sarah. If she didn't know better, she would think he was looking at her with the kindest regard.

His smile grew broader and he stroked her calf. Sarah flinched and his smile froze. He held her in a pinching grasp that shot pain up her leg. "Don't ever resist me, Sarah."

He released his hold and turned to Harris. "I'm calling in your loan. Payable at ten o'clock this morning. You have two hours."

Harris fell against the door. "Calling in my loan? But how am I supposed to raise that kind of money? I'd have to sell the Mystic."

Wilson turned toward the door. "Sell the Mystic, get a loan from another bank. I don't care how you do it. Just have my money ready by ten o'clock." He stepped into the alley and then swept his gaze to Sarah again. "And keep my wife here. I'll come for her soon."

Harris followed him out. Sarah tried to pull her hands free again. She would never leave town with Wilson. Never. She had been afraid of him after the school program last night, but this morning he terrified her.

Her wrists were slippery with blood, but she made no progress. She had an idea. She scooted up on the cot until she could reach her fingers with her mouth and worked the gag loose. By the time she had it out, she was exhausted with the effort. She laid her head on the frame of the cot next to her bound wrists, breathing freely for the first time since Harris had captured her.

Once she had rested, she worked at the rope with her teeth. Only minutes had passed since the men had left her, but the room had grown hot in the morning sun. She finally loosened her wrists, untied the bonds around her ankles with stiff fingers and then stood, trying to work some feeling into her swollen feet.

But she was free. She grabbed the doorknob. It didn't budge. Harris had fastened the padlock again as he had left. Her throat burned from thirst. She slid to the floor, leaning against the unyielding door. There was no way out until that door was opened when Wilson came to claim her.

She curled on the floor and tried to pray. Someone had to find her first. They had to.

Nate leaned a hand against the wall next to the ticket-office window. According to the board, the stage for Cheyenne had left on time. He turned slowly to survey the street as Coop drilled the ticket agent. Saturday-morning crowds gathered in the usual places—in front of the assayer's office, the three banks, the claims office. All the usual business of the mining camp.

But in that entire crowd, he didn't see Sarah anywhere. Maybe he and Coop had missed her, and she was back in the cabin, where James was waiting for her, safe and sound. The churning in his gut told him otherwise.

Coop turned from the window with a sigh. "I don't like this."

Nate straightened, grimacing as pain told him he had moved too quickly. "What is it?"

"The agent said that the girls were here. And he said Maude got on the stage."

Maude got on the stage. His plan worked. She was safe. He rubbed a finger across his forehead, trying to ease the pain. He hadn't failed. He whooshed out a breath.

But where was Sarah?

"There's something you aren't telling me."

"He said Sarah was being followed by a man when she headed down toward Lower Main, and from his description, it could have been Harris."

The familiar lead dropped in his gut. Was James right? Could God be in control, even now?

Nate took a deep breath. "So let's go."

"Where?"

"We follow them. We head toward the Mystic."

Coop's long legs brought him up beside Nate. "You think he caught up with her? Somehow got her to go with him to the Mystic? Isn't that too public?"

"Do you have a better idea?"

"Somewhere away from the saloon, where they wouldn't be noticed."

Nate stopped at the top of the stairway leading to Lower Main. "She's too well-known in town. He'd have to hide her." An accusing voice rang in his head. This was all his fault. He had put Sarah in this danger. He pushed it down.

"We need to think this through, Nate. If we go into the Mystic half-cocked and accusing Harris of kidnapping her, we'd be walking right onto his own turf."

Nate looked down the crowded boardwalk at the foot of the stairs. A familiar figure caught his attention. Wilson Montgomery emerged from the narrow alley between the newspaper office and the Wall Street steps. He straightened his string tie, adjusted his vest and crossed the street toward his bank. And suddenly Nate was sure the banker was involved in whatever Harris was doing. The two fit together like a pack of coyotes.

But where had he come from? There was nothing back there, except...

"I know one place Harris could hide someone. Behind the Mystic are some cribs. He could have locked her in one of those, and no one would ever know."

Coop's gaze narrowed. "Do you think he would do that to Sarah?"

"The man was out of his mind with jealousy last night, and crazy drunk, to boot. He could have been capable of anything. And I think Montgomery is involved, too."

"The banker?"

Nate nodded, sending throbs of pain through his head. "Montgomery was at the Mystic last night. He and Harris are thicker than thieves. And I just saw Montgomery come out of that alley next to the steps."

Coop looked toward the spot, and they both watched as Harris left the same alley and headed down the street toward the front door of the Mystic.

The cowboy nodded. "All right. Let's go see what they've been up to."

They threaded their way through the crowds and turned down the alley next to the newspaper office. The way between the corner building and the hill was narrow, but it widened out when they reached the Mystic. The privies, the refuse heap, even the open window with no bars that had been Maude's room, all seemed unreal to Nate. Last night's events were of no account next to finding Sarah. Once they were together again, he would never let her go.

The three little houses squatted under the hill, opposite the back wall of the saloon. Nate looked from one to the other. The last one in the row was padlocked.

He pointed it out to Coop, and they walked toward it, keeping one eye out for a guard. Nate tried the padlock and then called in a low voice, "Sarah."

"Nate?"

It was her. Relief flooded through him. He pulled at the padlock again, but it was new and well made.

"You hold on. We're going to get you out of there. Are you all right?"

"Yes. Just hurry."

Coop pointed to the hinges on the outside of the door. Crude and easy to dismantle. Coop took his knife and pried the pins out, wincing as each one screeched in protest, but no one took notice.

Finally, they wrenched the door forward, and Nate slid past it into the hot room. Sarah huddled on the floor. He knelt next to her and pulled her into his arms. It was over, and he hadn't failed. Confident and sure, he held her close.

"I'm here, Sarah. I'm here."

Sarah clung to Nate.

"You're safe. I thought they might have killed you."

Nate stroked her hair. "They tried to, but I don't kill easy."

"We have to get out of here." She pushed away from him. "Harris and Wilson are coming back. Wilson said something about Harris paying him the money he owes him, and then he's leaving town." Her eyes grew blurry.

"I'm so glad you found me. Wilson is insane. He thinks I'm his wife." She couldn't control the trembling.

"We'll get you home." Nate grimaced as he stood and pulled her up from the floor to stand next to him.

"You're hurt?"

Nate put an arm around her waist and guided her to the door. "Don't worry about it. The important thing is to make sure you're safe."

As they stepped out the door, Coop put out a hand to stop them.

Wilson Montgomery faced them, his usual kind expression belying his purpose. "Colby, I think you have your hands on something of mine." He smiled and held his hand out to Sarah.

"Move away from me, Sarah." Nate's voice was low, close to her ear. "Get behind the bed."

Sarah slipped back into the room and crouched next to the cot.

"We're just on our way home, Montgomery." Nate put his hands on his hips. For the first time since she had met him, Nate had no gun. "And I don't see that I have anything that belongs to you."

Wilson shifted his stance, rolling back on his heels. Sarah's gaze was captured as if he was a deadly snake, ready to coil and strike.

"You might be glad to know I'm leaving town this morning." Wilson nodded at Coop. "And your friend here can relax. There's no call for him to be fingering his pistol like that. I've just come to collect Sarah, and then we'll be off."

"You're not taking her anywhere." Nate took a step closer to Coop, away from the doorway, and drew Wilson's gaze away from Sarah.

Wilson's smile grew broad. "Of course I am, Colby. She's mine, isn't she?" He smiled at Sarah and she turned away, her stomach roiling. He sounded so calm and sure of himself. Would he convince Nate and Coop that she wanted to go with him? "I thought while we were waiting for my business with Harris to be concluded, we'd stop over at Furman and Brown's and buy a new dress for you. You'd like a new dress for the trip, wouldn't you?"

Nate took a step closer to Wilson. "I told you, she's not going anywhere with you."

Wilson reached into his coat and drew out a pistol. His smile didn't change. "Yes, she is."

He pointed his pistol at Nate, but as Coop drew his gun, Wilson flicked his hand toward the cowboy and fired. Sarah screamed as Coop fell to the ground.

Nate launched himself toward Wilson and threw him to the ground. Wilson's gun went flying, and Nate punched the banker in the jaw.

Sarah ran to Coop as Wilson pushed Nate off and scrambled to his hands and knees. Coop was on his back, bleeding from his right shoulder. He reached toward his gun with his left hand. Sarah picked it up from the ground where it had fallen and handed it to him.

As Wilson scrambled for his pistol, ten feet away, Coop stood up, his gun steady, and aimed at the other man.

"Don't even try, Montgomery. I can shoot just as well with my left hand as with my right."

The snake wasn't done. In spite of Coop's warning, he lifted his pistol with a quick motion and pointed it at Nate. He fired at the same time as Coop. As soon as Wilson fell back, a red bloom seeping through the shoulder of his immaculate vest, Sarah ran to Nate.

He was lying on the ground, groaning, with blood staining his left sleeve.

Sarah knelt next to him and took his hand. "Nate, he shot you."

"It's just a scratch. I'm all right."

Coop checked Wilson and then walked over to Nate. "You're not all right. You're going to kill yourself trying to wrestle snakes with your broken ribs." He handed his pistol to Nate. "If you can keep Montgomery from doing anything foolish when he wakes up, I'll go find Sheriff Bullock."

Nate stood up slowly, keeping an eye on Wilson, but the other man didn't move. Nate reached out for Sarah, and she moved close to him, clinging to him in the dust and dirt of the alley.

"I never want to go through the last twelve hours again. When I didn't know where you were, I about went crazy." Nate held her close to his left side. "I don't know what I would have done if I had lost you."

Sarah smoothed the front of his shirt. "I felt the same way. When I heard that gunshot last night, I was afraid you were gone."

"I never want to risk losing you again, Sarah." He leaned close to her, his cheek brushing hers, and she felt a gentle sigh. She turned and he caught her lips in his for a sweet kiss. When he finished, he didn't pull away, but touched his forehead to hers. She looked deep into his eyes. She shouldn't let him do this. She should pull away from him, refuse to let him kiss her. But she was helpless. Nate's kiss was the blade that destroyed her last defense. The Gordian knot of her fear was gone, vanquished by his gentle touch.

Love for him flooded her heart. It felt so perfect, as if her world had been turned right side up.

"Sarah," he whispered, "I love you. I can't help it."

"Oh, Nate, I love you, too."

She circled her arms around his neck, and with one hand behind her waist he pulled her closer, enclosing her in his strong arms. She rested her head against his chest. She had never known love could feel like this.

"Be mine."

She lifted her eyes to his. "What?"

"Marry me. Be mine. Let me take care of you. Let me love you for the rest of my life."

"Oh, Nate." She threw her arms around his neck. "Yes, yes."

He pulled her close, and she lost herself in his kiss.

Epilogue

The last Saturday in April, Sarah put the loaves of bread into the oven and then straightened, rubbing her swollen stomach. Not long now, and she would meet her own little baby. She glanced at Lucy and Olivia playing with their dolls in a corner of the spacious room.

"Girls, it's almost time for your uncle Nate and Charley to come home. What would you think if we walk out to meet them?"

Olivia looked at her with a frown. "Are you sure you feel like walking that far?"

Leave it to Olivia to guess that she was expecting a baby. At least she hadn't passed the secret on to Lucy or Charley.

"I feel fine. Be sure to put on your coats. There's a cold wind out there today."

The three of them set off across the meadow. Scout watched them from the top of a rise where he could survey the entire ranch and keep an eye on his wives. All twelve of them. Nate kept Ginger and her foal in the corral near the barn, but Scout was in charge of the mustang mares.

They walked as far as the gate before Sarah saw Loretta's ears, and then her head, coming up the trail. Nate followed, driving the wagon. Sarah waved when she saw Uncle James and Aunt Margaret in the wagon with him, and the girls slipped through the gate and ran to meet them.

Tears filled Sarah's eyes. She had been crying more than ever since she knew the baby was coming. Every little thing that filled her heart with thanksgiving brought tears. Every calf born, every mare found to be in foal, every time she stood on her front porch and looked over the land that their grandchildren would call home.

And every time she saw Nate.

The tears were often mingled with laughter when Nate was the reason. Why had she ever been afraid to love him?

Nate pulled the wagon to a stop when they reached her.

"It's so nice to see you!" Sarah climbed into the wagon and gave Margaret a hug. "I'm so glad you came out. Can you stay for dinner?"

"We brought it with us." Aunt Margaret lifted a basket. "And we have enough time for a good, long visit."

"I brought the mail. You got a letter from Maude." Nate's eyes never left hers as he handed her the letter.

Nate drove the wagon up to the house while Aunt Margaret told her the news from town.

"Lucretia Woodrow has a new baby. It's a girl this time, and Laura is so happy after six brothers!"

Olivia caught Sarah's eye and smiled her secret smile.

"And Peder is getting married!"

"He's just a boy, isn't he?"

"Only nineteen years old, but he's doing very well. He sold his claim and is building a little house in Ingleside. He recently took a job writing for the *Black Hills Gazette*."

"Who is he marrying?"

"You know her. Mary Connealy. Her father is the attorney who moved here last September."

Sarah felt the tears starting again. Every little thing. Every little wonderful thing.

Once they were in the cabin, Sarah opened the letter from Maude and scanned it.

"Oh, listen to this," she said. "Maude says there are now six girls in the home." Maude's church in Omaha had established the home, a place for girls to start over once they left the saloon life. Josie and Maude were the house mothers. "She says the new girl we sent to her, Nancy, is doing quite well and is learning to be a very talented seamstress."

"That's wonderful. Do they have room for more young women?"

"She says they have two more beds and possibly another one by summer. The girl who we sent the same time as Josie is getting married."

A yeasty scent reminded Sarah to take the bread from the oven. The loaves were a beautiful brown. She put them on the table and covered them with a towel to cool.

By the time the men came in from the barn, including Coop, Margaret had heated up the soup she'd brought, and they all sat down at the table to a hot dinner.

Once grace had been said and they had all been served, Nate cleared his throat. "There is something

Sarah and I have been hoping would happen for a long time."

Both Aunt Margaret and Olivia gave Sarah a knowing glance, but she only smiled back at them. She knew why Nate had gone into town this morning.

"Olivia, Charley and Lucy..." Nate waited until he had the attention of all three children. "I went to see Judge Lessman today, and he has drawn up all the necessary paperwork, so now we only need your approval." He paused and glanced at Sarah. "We want to officially adopt you. Instead of being your aunt and uncle, we would like to be your parents."

Nate paused again, waiting for the children's reactions.

Charley was first. "You mean we can call you Pa?"

"And we can call you Mama?" Olivia asked, turning to Sarah.

Lucy slid down from her seat and came to Sarah. She climbed into her lap, just as she used to, and wrapped her arms around Sarah's neck. "You'll be my very own mama."

Aunt Margaret wiped her eyes, but Coop summed it up.

"I think you've got yourself a family, Nate."

* * * * *

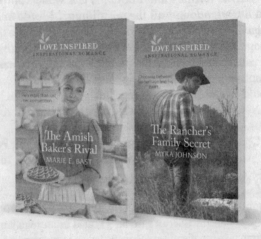

*After a traumatic brain injury, military vet
Behr Delgado refuses the one thing that could help
him—a service dog. But charity head Ellery Watson
knows the dog she selected will improve his quality of
life and vows to work with him one-on-one. When their
personal lives entwine with their professional lives, can
they trust each other long enough to both heal?*

Read on for a sneak peek at
The Veteran's Vow *by Jill Lynn!*

Ellery approached and held out Margo's leash for him. She was so
excited he was doing better. The thought of disappointing her cut
Behr like a combat knife.

Margo stood by Ellery's side, her chocolate face toggling back
and forth between them, questioning what she was supposed to do
next. Waiting for his lead.

Behr reached out and took the leash. If Ellery noticed his
shaking hand, she didn't say anything.

"I want to teach her to stand by your left side. That's it. She's
just going to be there. We're going to take it slow." Ellery moved
to Behr's left, leaving enough room for Margo to stand between
them.

A tremble echoed through him, and Behr tensed his muscles in
an effort to curb it.

Margo, on the other hand, would be the first image if someone
searched the internet for the definition of the word *calm*.

"Heel." When he gave Margo the command and she obeyed,
taking that spot, Behr's heart just about ricocheted out of his chest.

This effort was worth it. Was it, though? He could get through life off-kilter, running into things, tripping, leaving items on the floor when they fell, willing his poor coordination to work instead of using Margo to create balance for him or grasp or retrieve things for him, couldn't he?

Ellery didn't say anything about his audible inhales or exhales, but she had to know what he was up to. The weakness that plagued Behr rose up to ridicule him. It was hard to reveal this side of himself to Ellery, not that she hadn't seen it already. Hard to know that he couldn't just snap his fingers and make his body right again. Hard to remember that he needed this dog and that was why his mom and sisters had signed him up for one.

"You're doing great." Ellery's focus was on Behr, but Margo's tail wagged as if the compliment had been directed at her.

They both laughed, and the tension dissipated like a deployment care package.

"You, too, girl." Ellery offered Margo a treat. "Do you want me to put the balance harness on her so you can feel what it's like?" she asked Behr.

He gave one determined nod.

Ellery strode over to the storage cabinets that lined the back wall. She returned with the harness and knelt to slide it on Margo and adjust it. Behr should probably be watching how to do the same, but right now he was concentrating on standing next to Margo and not having his knees liquefy.

Ellery stood. "See what you think."

Behr gripped the handle, his knuckles turning white. The handle was the right height, and it did make him feel sturdy. Supported.

Like the woman beaming at him from the other side of the dog.

Don't miss
The Veteran's Vow *by Jill Lynn,*
available March 2022 wherever
Love Inspired books and ebooks are sold.

LoveInspired.com

LIEXP0122

LOVE INSPIRED

Stories to uplift and inspire

Fall in love with Love Inspired—
inspirational and uplifting stories of faith
and hope. Find strength and comfort in
the bonds of friendship and community.
Revel in the warmth of possibility and the
promise of new beginnings.

Sign up for the Love Inspired newsletter
at **LoveInspired.com** to be the first
to find out about upcoming titles,
special promotions and exclusive content.

CONNECT WITH US AT:

f Facebook.com/LoveInspiredBooks

🐦 Twitter.com/LoveInspiredBks